WEIGHT OF EVERYTHING

A MEADOW STREET BROTHERS NOVEL

ANNA WINEHEART

CONTENTS

1. The Most Humiliating Wardrobe Malfunction — 1
2. Gage is Intrigued — 6
3. Ulric Forgets His Phone — 10
4. Gage is in Trouble — 22
5. Tensions—And Other Things—Rise — 29
6. Ulric Doubles Down On Losing Weight — 34
7. Gage Moves In — 40
8. Why Does Gage Have To Make The Perfect Breakfast, Too? — 47
9. There Is Only One Couch — 54
10. Insecurities — 68
11. The Better-Than-Sex Cook-off — 76
12. The Other Side of Ulric — 83
13. The Better-Than-Sex Cook-off, Part 2 — 94
14. Gage Doesn't Realize It, But — 105
15. Burn — 119
16. Burn Part 2 — 128
17. New Arrangements — 138
18. You're Dating An Alpha? — 155
19. The Surprise — 162
20. So You Want A Baby? — 168
21. The Box At The Back Of The Fridge — 179
22. Ulric Has A New Secret — 184
23. Gage Is Suspicious — 194
24. Gage Finds Out — 207
25. The Wrong Gamble — 213
26. Gage Gets Grilled — 219
27. Trouble Befalls Ulric — 223
28. Gage Makes Amends — 230
29. Gage Convinces Ulric That He's Beautiful — 238

30. A Family...?	254
31. Making Babies	260
32. Pregnancy	278
33. Childbirth	290
Epilogue	300
34. Bonus Chapter	305
Also by Anna	323
About the Author	325

Copyright Anna Wineheart 2020

This is a work of fiction. Names, characters, businesses, places, events and incidents are either the products of the author's imagination or used in a fictitious manner. Any resemblance to actual persons, living or dead, or actual events is purely coincidental.

All rights reserved. No part of this book may be reproduced or transmitted in any form or by any means whatsoever without express written permission from the author, except in the case of brief quotations embodied in critical articles and reviews

This novel contains graphic sexual content between two men. Intended for mature readers only.

Warnings: Past emotional abuse, Present emotional abuse from an abuser, Past bullying, Past child neglect, Some consensual dubcon-play, Some violence and gore

Welcome back to Meadowfall!
You are beautiful.
You are worthy.
You are loved.

1

THE MOST HUMILIATING WARDROBE MALFUNCTION

ULRIC STEPPED self-consciously into the gym, trying not to attract any attention to himself. *Eyes on the floor. Don't take your time. Look like you know what you're doing.*

No one here knew him, after all. He'd moved away from New York a week ago, traveling all the way across the country to the quiet town of Meadowfall. The warm southern California weather was such a change—it put a spring in his step and some cheer on his face... all the way until he'd arrived at the gym.

The last time Ulric had stepped into a gym, he'd been in high school, the stares of other alphas heavy on his skin. Physical Ed classes were his least favorite. Nothing like being scoffed at, or being picked last to join a team. And then having everyone on the team act like you didn't exist. All because you had some extra weight you couldn't get rid of.

At least, making friends wasn't a requirement for this gym.

Ulric hurried to the alphas' locker room, picking out an inconspicuous locker. He shoved his duffel bag in halfway, took out his towel and his phone, and then paused when he realized that the locker didn't come with a lock.

What did the membership fee pay for, then?

He turned and glimpsed a bit too much skin—a couple of men had stripped down in front of their lockers, all bulging biceps and trim abs.

Yeah, that. That was what he was paying for.

Ulric tore his gaze away, hurrying past them. He felt like a bit of a whale next to these guys. Maybe he should've brought a bath towel to wrap himself in.

He stepped out of the locker room and made for the far end of the gym, where no one was. There were some treadmills there, and some cycling machines. He could start with that. Better yet, the treadmills faced a window overlooking a forested area. Ulric could pretend that he was in a world of his own.

Except the funny thing was, he'd come to the gym because he was tired of being alone.

His last boyfriend—friend with benefit? College roommate-turned-on-and-off-partner?—had straight-up said that Ulric wasn't his type anymore. Mick had found an omega, a slender pale wisp of a man, and he'd told Ulric that he was tired of all of Ulric's extra flab. Not to mention that Ulric was an alpha.

Ulric had kind of been in love with him. And it had hurt, a lot.

He pushed the heartache aside, powering on a treadmill. The control panel had way too many complicated buttons. Which Ulric should be able to figure out, since he'd majored in statistics and all. It was just... He wasn't really here to get healthy. He just wanted some weight gone, he wanted to look good enough to land a boyfriend, and...

He wanted to be normal. He wanted to be an alpha who liked omegas, but he wasn't. He wanted to look like the alphas on magazine covers, he wanted... someone to gaze at him, and not be repulsed.

He pushed a button to start the treadmill. It was kind of slow. He found the button to speed it up. Then he sped it up even more. His shoes pounded against the treadmill belt, his heart thumping with the strain. Sweat beaded on his skin. Some discomfort was supposed to be good for you, right?

Ulric grasped the support arms on the treadmill, leaning on them a little. Maybe he should slow the machine down. The belt rolled by too quickly, and he was starting to struggle to keep up.

He tried to find the speed toggle button. But between the jogging and his glasses bouncing around on his nose, he couldn't see enough to stop the machine.

Ulric tripped; his stomach dropped and his entire weight lurched forward.

He hit the moving rubber with a jolt of pain, his legs sliding out from under him. Ulric saved himself by gripping the support arms—just so he could keep his face from smashing into the belt.

But pressed intimately against the treadmill, Ulric hadn't accounted for the belt's friction. It dug into his exercise shorts and dragged it downward: down his waist, down his hips.

If Ulric didn't stop it soon, the machine would strip him naked.

He lifted his hand to reach for the controls, at the same time his waistband slid down his cock, to his thighs. The treadmill belt ground rough and uncomfortably against Ulric's sensitive head, trying to pull it further down—as though this had turned into some really weird sex scene.

It felt like he was being dragged across a rough surface, except his cock bore the brunt of that friction, every inch of it plastered against moving rubber—without lube.

And his fat ass was bare. Everyone could see it.

Ulric reached for the control panel, his tip kissing the rubber belt, his fingers just inches away from the console, desperately seeking the word Stop.

Just as he was about to hit it, someone stepped up to the machine, powering it down. The belt slowed. It stopped trying to pull his cock into a fourth dimension.

Ulric looked up to thank the person. His voice stuck in his throat.

Of course, who else had to witness his humiliation but the most handsome alpha in the gym?

It was one thing to embarrass yourself in front of an omega. But alphas were a different breed entirely. As an alpha, you wanted to be better than the next alpha. You wanted to be *more*, you wanted *them* to respect *you*.

And this was one hell of an alpha, with his pine scent and broad shoulders, his pecs bulging behind his tank top, his biceps thick and lovely. He had styled black hair and stunning green eyes, he had kissable full lips and a strong jaw.

Everything that this alpha was, Ulric wasn't.

He was ready to bet a million bucks that Mr. Handsome had dates lined up every night until next year. Or maybe he already had a boyfriend. Or he was married. And somewhere out there, Mr. Handsome had an internet mailing list for "Notify me when this man becomes available."

He yanked his exercise shorts up his thighs, stuffing

his cock out of sight. Bad enough that Mr. Handsome had seen his ass. He didn't need to know that a chubby alpha like Ulric had gotten hard for *him*.

Except when he looked again, he found Mr. Handsome's gaze raking back up to his eyes. There was an odd expression on his face. Did he think... that Ulric had done this on purpose? Did he think Ulric was a flasher or some sort of pervert?

"Are you okay?" Mr. Handsome asked, holding a hand out to Ulric.

Ulric straightened his shoulders. He was an alpha. And he wasn't about to show any weakness in front of anyone. "I'm fine. Thanks."

He ignored Mr. Handsome's hand and picked himself up. Then he took his phone and towel, making his way back to the locker room. Several people stared at him along the way. Ulric's skin prickled all over—he could feel them judging. He wished he'd worn black instead of gray—black was a slimming color, right? Maybe it would make him feel less out-of-place.

It would be a month, maybe three, before he returned again. Probably at midnight so no one would recognize him.

Not for the first time, Ulric felt all the pounds he'd put on when he'd let himself go after the breakup. At the back of his mind, he heard the constant whispers from school, telling him he was fat and ugly and everything undesirable.

It was okay to be fat. Ulric just wished... that he believed it, himself.

2

GAGE IS INTRIGUED

"I'll be right back," Gage told his client. Which was the first time he'd ever done that in the middle of a training session.

Thing was, he couldn't just let this go. The look on that alpha's face when Gage had powered down the treadmill... He knew that look of abject humiliation.

Gage hadn't meant for him to feel that way. Deep down, he understood what it felt like to be so embarrassed that he wished the ground would swallow him up.

If it had been one of the regulars at the gym, Gage would've just brushed off the incident—they would recover from it easily enough. But something about that alpha... Maybe it was the way he'd looked so helpless, for a split second. Maybe it was because he didn't have Gage's looks. Maybe Gage pitied him.

Gage had seen some overweight guests come and go from the gym. Some stuck around and lost weight. Others gave up before they could gain much headway.

The way this guy had sprawled across the treadmill—Hell, even Gage would've left and never looked back.

He stepped into the alphas' locker room, thinking maybe he would offer an apology or something. Anything to be a good gym employee.

Besides, he couldn't afford to lose his job right now. The eviction notice from this morning still lingered fresh in his mind. Actually, maybe he should've just stuck with his client. Gage had never been known for his good sense.

"Hey," he said to the man on the far end of the lockers.

The alpha looked over. Then he recognized Gage and tensed, his shoulders straightening, his entire body pulling tight in a show of aggression.

"It's fine," Gage said. "I just thought I'd check up on you."

"Why, because you thought I'd break some bones with all this fat?" the man snapped.

Rude. Gage reined in his temper. He was part of the staff. Whatever that man said to him, he couldn't answer in kind. "It's part of protocol to make sure our guests don't get hurt," Gage said. He was kind of fibbing. But the man wouldn't know that. "Liabilities and all."

The man glowered, shoving his towel into his duffel bag. "I'm perfectly fine."

"That's great to hear." Gage tried to keep the sarcasm out of his voice. He knew the sort of power he could wield, if he wanted. He had the looks. He had the strength. Someone like Chubby had nothing on Gage when Gage wanted to play suave.

But Gage didn't want to be a bully. He'd seen others like him become abusers. His own sister had fallen prey to some looker of an alpha who had beaten her up and swindled her of her hard-earned savings. By the time Gage had gotten to him and punched out his daylights, all that money had been long spent.

So he kept silent, watching as the man yanked his duffel out of the locker. The alpha strode over to where Gage stood in the locker room doorway, his eyes narrowed, his mouth a thin line.

He wasn't a looker; he was plain in the way that Gage sometimes wondered about.

Gage never had trouble landing a hookup or a favor, or any item he could possibly want. All he had to do was smile. But his looks were a double-edged sword—he'd never had a relationship that lasted. People flocked to him demanding things—always hungry for what he could give them: If not sex, then his connections, or money. Because good-looking alphas were always rich, right?

So when Chubby spurned Gage's offer to pick him up, Gage had been... offended. And also intrigued. What did it feel like to be someone invisible? To have people befriend you not for your looks, or what you could offer them?

He couldn't help studying that face—hazel eyes, brown hair that looked soft. Chubby smelled like honey oak, and his chest wasn't so defined. Neither were his arms.

But if Gage knew anything, it was that Chubby very definitely had some muscles beneath those curves. If he were to punch Gage, it would hurt. A lot.

"The fuck are you looking at?" Chubby muttered.

Gage glanced up, only to catch the alpha glancing at *his* chest. Chubby's gaze swept down, heavy on Gage's body, all the way to his hips. Gage's skin prickled.

Alphas at the gym sized Gage up all the time. But

none of them had gotten hard because of him, not like this man had.

He'd glimpsed that length hanging between this alpha's thighs, and it had been clear that it wasn't only Chubby's arms that were thick. Then Chubby had looked up, he'd seen Gage, and his hard-on had been... flattering. It was the sort of cock that would make an omega throw his head back and beg for more.

Gage shouldn't be curious about the feel of it against his palm. He shouldn't want to know if he could make this alpha come.

He was in enough trouble with that eviction notice. He couldn't afford to play around with his job, checking on someone who didn't need the attention.

All the same, Gage couldn't help seeing the thick line behind Chubby's shorts, and he couldn't help remembering the heavy balls that hung beneath.

Chubby narrowed his eyes, curling his fingers in to flip Gage off.

Gage's instincts roared, *Pin him. Subdue him. Let him take your cock.*

He barely bit down his response. Because he could see it now—this man beneath him, snarling, Gage's cock opening him all the way up.

Gage growled, his own length shoving against his pants.

"Fuck you," Chubby muttered, shouldering past Gage as he stalked off.

From the way Gage throbbed, he was sure Chubby wouldn't be the one ending up on top.

3

ULRIC FORGETS HIS PHONE

Ulric had gotten all the way home, unpacked his duffel, eaten three juicy beef burgers topped with sautéed onions and mushrooms, when he thought about checking his phone. His mom probably wanted to know if he'd found an omega.

He'd said multiple times over the past years, that he wasn't into omegas.

She'd told him not to come home until he had one.

Maybe he didn't need his phone, after all.

But it didn't sit well with him, knowing that it was somewhere out there. Ulric double-checked his house, before turning his car inside-out. He checked the duffel again. And he arrived at the stomach-sinking conclusion that he must've left his phone at the gym.

That bastard was probably still there, secretly laughing at the fat ass who'd fucked up and was a mess enough to drop his phone. Ulric sighed and scrubbed his face. This wasn't the fresh start he'd envisioned.

He pulled on some better clothes—a baggy button-down shirt that hid his belly some, and dark pants. At least he knew he looked better this way, than with a clingy T-shirt showing off all the curves he didn't want to see. He imagined Mr. Handsome's reaction when he stepped in.

I shouldn't care what he thinks. Ulric ignored the thrum of his pulse, the heat creeping up his neck. Why the hell would he fixate on the most handsome alpha around? That was a sure path to heartbreak. Or embarrassment. Or humiliation. Or all of the above.

He clenched his jaw and made his way back to the gym, praying that Mr. Handsome had gone home for the day. He didn't breathe until he'd scanned his membership card and stepped in.

There was one lady behind the receptionist's desk. Relief filled Ulric's chest; he hurried over, keeping his head down.

"Hi!" She smiled. "How may I help you?"

"I lost my—"

"Hey, Nan. Do you happen to have—"

Ulric knew that rumbling voice. His heart sank as he looked up, meeting the eyes of the last person he wanted to see.

Mr. Handsome raked his gaze down Ulric's front—head, shoulders, chest—sending tingles through Ulric's skin. And he straightened, standing taller. Like *he* needed to.

Ulric gritted his teeth. He didn't care that he would lose in every kind of competition to that guy. He wasn't going to show any damn weakness in front of Mr. Handsome.

"You first," Handsome said.

Ulric narrowed his eyes. "No, you first."

"Ah, but you're a guest." Handsome waved Ulric toward the receptionist. "Go ahead and help him, Nan."

And let him discover Ulric's fuck-up? "No, it's fine. I'll be back later."

He turned, striding for the exit. Ulric was about to open the door when someone grabbed his arm. A warm, firm touch.

Ulric almost swung a punch at him.

"If you want a fight, I'll give you a fight," Handsome growled, his voice raking all the way down Ulric's spine. "Give me a time and place."

Up close, they weren't so different in height. About the same, although Handsome was maybe a few years older than Ulric's twenty-seven. And Ulric smelled fresh sweat on him, along with pine and a trace of musk. Had he jerked off during work? What did his cock look like?

Ulric shoved that thought out of his mind. He didn't need to know. "Fuck off."

"I saw the way you looked at me," Handsome murmured, his voice sliding into Ulric's ears like silk. "Fight me. In bed."

Ulric's hole squeezed. Fuck, fuck. He would lose to this man. And it would be glorious. And humiliating. And maybe Ulric wanted to know what that would feel like.

Handsome huffed triumphantly. "Your place."

Desire and wariness twisted through Ulric's veins. If he let Mr. Handsome anywhere close to his body... he would get laughed out of his own bed. "No."

Not just that—maybe this was just a huge joke. Like the time in high school when a pretty alpha had asked Ulric to close his eyes, and instead of kissing him, the boy had slipped away. And Ulric had sat there for a good ten minutes, just waiting.

He should just retrieve his phone and get the hell out

of here. He'd drop this gym crap and find some other way to lose weight.

Ulric shook off Handsome's grip and stalked to the reception desk. "I lost my phone earlier. Do you know if it's here?"

"Yeah, someone reported a lost phone," Handsome drawled behind him.

Ulric bit down his snarl. He didn't need to be strung along again, and told he wasn't someone else's type. "Fuck off," he hissed.

Nan looked curiously between them, before focusing on Ulric. "I'll need to see your driver's license," she said.

Ulric handed it over, feeling the weight of Handsome's stare. Then, before Nan could take the card away, Handsome leaned closer and rumbled, "You're from New York. Ulric, huh?"

The way he said Ulric's name—no one had growled it all low and seductive before. Ulric's heart skipped several beats.

He really needed to leave this place. Before he went and developed a crush on that bastard, and Handsome shattered Ulric's heart.

Handsome met his eyes. He was standing so close that Ulric felt the heat rolling off his skin. For a moment, Ulric dreamed about a relationship where he could be happy. Where someone accepted him for who he was.

"I'll need you to describe your phone, Mr. O'Neil," Nan said, breaking that perfect image.

Ulric sighed and told her. "I'll even tell you the passcode and everything."

Nan looked thoughtful, but she took Ulric's phone out of a drawer. Ulric's anxiety eased a little. "We don't usually require you to unlock the phone as proof," Nan said.

"That's fine. I'll tell you anyway." Ulric recited the passcode, waiting for Nan to tap it in. The phone unlocked to display his home screen—with about twenty bright yellow cartoon ducks filling up the background.

"Oh, those are cute," Handsome said.

Ulric didn't know if he should feel offended; his face heated up anyway. "They're just ducks," he muttered.

"Better than dicks." Handsome grinned. "That would be awkward."

Ulric dragged his eyes away from that man. He needed to leave this place and never return. But if he wasn't going to return... maybe he could fuck up a bit more. "I don't even know your name."

Surprise flickered through Handsome's gaze. Then a slow grin spread across his lips. "Gage Frost," he said, extending his hand. "I'm a personal trainer here. Feel free to schedule an appointment with me. We'll sort out *all* your physical needs."

Fuck. Ulric's blood swooped south. He shoved his phone into his pocket, staring at Gage's hand. He shouldn't touch it. The less he felt of this alpha, the sooner he'd forget him.

But Gage's hand looked strong. Sturdy. And Ulric had been wishing he'd taken Gage's proffered hand earlier this morning. Just for a bit of touch to tide him through to his next lay.

What the hell, he told himself. *It's just a handshake.*

He took Gage's hand. Gage gripped him firmly, his fingers calloused, his warmth soaking into Ulric's skin. Ulric tingled all over. What would Gage's touch feel like, further down?

Ulric suppressed all his thoughts, snatching his hand away. "Thanks," he muttered. "I'll keep that in mind."

He left the gym feeling like a coward. Gage hadn't

laughed at him, but... maybe he was doing it in secret. The handsome ones always did.

Ulric sighed, climbing back into his car. When he got home, he was going to start work—data analysis felt like such a safe place, away from all the tricky social interactions. Ulric sucked with relationships.

And so he was certainly never returning to that gym, even though he'd paid for a full year's membership there.

A MONTH LATER, he went back.

It had been a moment of weakness. Ulric had been flipping through the dating apps on his phone, and after much consideration, he'd put up new photos as his profile picture. No one had contacted him—across three different apps. The alphas he'd sent messages to—they didn't answer him, either.

Why would they, when there were better-looking alphas around? When people like Gage-fucking-Frost could smile, and half the world would drop their pants?

Ulric was starting to get stir-crazy. It had been months since he'd slept with anyone. And even then, sex with Mick hadn't been all that great—Mick often came first, and he'd left Ulric alone to finish off.

At least in porn movies, people finished at the same time. Or at least, their partners hung around until they did.

Feeling awfully lonely, Ulric pulled on his gym clothes —black this time—and packed his duffel.

He wasn't exactly sure what he'd do at the gym. Maybe he'd get on one of those bike machine things and pedal until... something happened. And then he would go home.

He drove to the gym, grabbed his bag, and scanned his card. This time, he made sure to search out the bike machines discreetly. Then he dumped his bag in a locker, grabbed his towel and water bottle, and wove between all the machines, avoiding as many people as he could.

He found a machine that was furthest from everyone else. Then he sat on the cushioned seat and... stared at yet another complex control panel. Ulric sighed. Why was it so difficult to exercise?

Before he could spy on his neighbors in an attempt to figure this out, someone stopped next to him. He smelled familiar pine even as the alpha rumbled, "Haven't seen you here in a while."

Ulric's stomach flipped. He was half-glad for Gage's presence, and half-annoyed. Did he think Ulric couldn't figure this out on his own? He turned with a glower. "It shouldn't matter to you."

Gage had his hands in his pockets, his biceps beautiful as ever, his green eyes locked onto Ulric. Years back, Ulric would've given anything for an alpha to look at him, smiling like that.

Now... he figured it was just part of Gage's job. It felt like he was paying for Gage's attention. And yet, Ulric still basked in that smile.

He was so distracted that it took him a moment to notice the shadows under Gage's eyes. Ulric stared harder. "What's wrong with you?"

Gage's smile tightened. "Aside from the bumps I'm facing, trying to help our new guest?"

It really wasn't any of Ulric's business. Why would someone like Gage confide in him, anyway? So he shrugged, looking back at the bike machine console. "I'm fine."

Gage paused. In a lower tone, he said, "Tell you a

secret. Use the fancier bike. That one gives you some scenery to ride along to."

A fancy machine also meant more buttons to fuck up with. Ulric looked back at his own machine—hell, he didn't even know how to start this thing.

"I'll help," Gage murmured. He wriggled his fingers discreetly, beckoning Ulric over.

For a second, Ulric was torn. Then he figured that (1) Gage was a gym employee. It wasn't as likely for him to make a fool of Ulric in public, and (2) Ulric had the option to go home.

He heaved himself off the machine and followed Gage to another bike—also set away from the other guests. This one had an extra screen mounted to the top of the control panel. Gage was already pressing buttons even before Ulric sat down—the screen turned on to display a road winding through a beautiful mountainside.

"Typically, people set goals for a session," Gage explained quietly. "This button lets you adjust your session duration. There are various resistance levels on this machine—the more resistance you cycle against, the more calories you'll burn. There are different workout presets, too."

Ulric stared. That was... a lot to decide.

"What are your session goals for today?"

His insides tightened. "Uh." It seemed like it'd be a bad idea to say *I don't know. I just came here to get out of the house.* So Ulric kept his mouth shut.

"Here, why don't we try something easy," Gage said. "This workout lasts for fifteen minutes. Give it a go. If, by the end of this, you want to do it again, hit this button."

He looked at Ulric. Even though it wasn't a

challenge, Ulric sure felt the need to... what, prove Gage wrong? Prove that he could do more than the beginner workout?

"I'll get on it," Ulric said, his neck burning. Bad enough that Gage had to give him the beginner's talk. "Thanks."

He waited until Gage walked away. Then he started the machine, pedaling slowly. Ulric had learned his lesson—no speeding things up until they went out of hand. The video showed him cycling up an incline—at the same time the resistance against his feet increased.

Ulric stared at the pedals, amazed. He'd tried exercise bikes in the past, but none of them had done this. It felt as though he was actually cycling on a hill. So he looked back at the mountain road video, gaining a new appreciation for it.

He was sweating slightly by the end of fifteen minutes—but not enough to give up yet. A quick glance around showed that Gage was helping someone else. While he was distracted, Ulric poked around with the buttons, half-expecting one of them to sound an alarm and tell everyone he was fucking up.

But the machine didn't do that. He found the list of preset exercise routes; the next easiest route gave him a preview of a mountain road in autumn, full of fire-red leaves. Ulric started the exercise. The pedals had more resistance to them now—nothing Ulric couldn't handle. He lost himself in the red leaves.

In fact, he liked the autumn leaves route so much that he started it again, even though he'd told himself to try a more difficult routine next.

He did the autumn leaves route a third time. Then a fourth time.

Ulric was starting to wish it were autumn right now,

maybe every day of the year, when Gage stopped by next to him. Ulric stiffened.

"Still here?" Gage gave an easy smile. Ulric thought Gage might scoff. Then Gage said, "You're doing great."

Oh. Ulric knew it was a thing Gage said to everyone at the gym, but that didn't stop his heart from missing a beat. "I just like the leaves," he muttered.

"Yeah, they sure make it real lifelike." Gage nodded at the screen. "Have you seen the beachfront one? They have some winterscapes, too."

Ulric thought about Gage using this same machine, his ass planted on this very same spot. He tried not to fixate on it. "You have a favorite?" he blurted.

"The one where it takes you through the scenic streets of Europe." Gage gave a crooked smile. "I've never been."

Ulric had, on a family trip some time back. It had been beautiful. "Maybe one day."

Gage's smile turned rueful. "Maybe."

His answer didn't sit right with Ulric. Could Gage not afford to go? Ulric had grown up wealthy, but in recent years, he'd seen more of the world, and he'd learned about people who didn't have the fortune he did.

Briefly, Ulric wondered how Gage would react if Ulric paid for his trip overseas. Maybe a couple weeks. And then Ulric gave himself a mental smack. *What am I thinking? He won't fall in love with me just because of that. For all I know, he already has a boyfriend.*

Would Ulric pay for Gage and *his boyfriend* to go traveling? No, probably not.

There was something very wrong with Ulric, if he was already thinking about shit like that. Furious with himself, he hit the Stop button. "I need to leave."

He glanced down to check that he'd grabbed

everything, and found the seat damp with his sweat. Ulric grimaced; Gage pointed him to the sanitizing towel dispenser nearby.

When he got back to the bicycle machine, Gage was still there. Ulric's stomach flipped. His nerves tingled. He wasn't anyone special. Why would Gage hang around with him?

Surprisingly, Gage walked with Ulric to the locker room. His heat brushed into Ulric's arm, and Ulric fought with his instincts. He wanted more of Gage's warmth. He wanted to know what it'd feel like when Gage pressed up against him.

But the more he wanted Gage, the more it would hurt when Gage inevitably rejected him. And Ulric knew his own self-control was shit.

"You aren't sleeping well," Ulric said. Something personal so Gage would get offended and put some distance between them.

Gage's expression flickered—he almost scowled. And that was something real, something that wasn't supposed to slip through the friendly-employee facade.

Ulric's heart kicked. Yeah, that was something he could get behind: burrowing under Gage's skin, forcing him to lose his cool.

Fight me, Gage had said a month ago. Ulric had been jerking off, wondering how that would turn out.

He had no hope of Gage ever liking him. But he sure as hell could get Gage to hate him. And that would land him in Gage's thoughts more often than not. Ulric's breath snagged.

He went for the throat. "So, you can't afford to travel, huh?"

Gage stiffened, shock flashing through his eyes.

"Must be really sad for someone like you," Ulric

continued. "Do you depend on handouts when you go begging?"

He didn't know what the fuck he was doing. This wasn't what he'd say even to people he hated. But... he knew his heart, and he knew he was going to fall for Gage Frost, sooner than later.

Ulric didn't want his heart broken again. "You think you're so great, all handsome like that," he growled. "But you'll be left with nothing when your looks go away."

Anger flashed in those green eyes. It gave Ulric a kick, at the same time a sick feeling twisted through his stomach.

He was very definitely never returning to the gym. Ulric grabbed his duffel and strode out of the locker room, his heart pounding in his ears.

I'm fucking up. I'm really fucking up. He didn't know how he was going to get himself out of this mess.

But the one thing he knew, was that he'd just saved himself from the heartbreak of the century.

4

GAGE IS IN TROUBLE

What the fuck, had been Gage's first thought. Then he'd thought that for the rest of the evening, until he'd gotten off his shift.

He showered and pulled on some casual clothes—stuff that he'd wear at home, usually. Then he left the gym, squeezed into his car, and tried to ignore the piles of clothes and things piled up in the backseat.

Screw traveling. Gage didn't even know when he'd have an actual home again.

Two weeks ago, he'd moved out, cramming everything he could possibly fit into his car. The rest of his stuff, he'd parked at a self-storage place. Sure, he was earning wages. But he was also paying for his sister's cancer treatment, and he'd told her not to worry about it. He could manage—she'd had to stop school to undergo chemo. Their parents were already worried about the bills. Their brother, Wilkie, was also helping. The least Gage could do was contribute as much as he could.

So he'd kind of forgotten about paying rent these past few months. And so he'd been evicted.

He reclined the seat as much as he could, stuck some flimsy car shades on his windows for some scant privacy, and tried to close his eyes. He thought about the bills. Then he thought about Ulric O'Neil, and a wave of hot anger rose up through his chest.

You can't afford to travel, huh?

Seriously, what the fuck? Gage had been nothing but nice to him. Sure, he'd flirted with that alpha. Sure, he'd been a bit of a busybody. He'd thought that bastard was actually interested.

For the first time in a long while, Gage had taken a chance. Something about that man made his instincts prickle. And his gamble had backfired right in his face.

Served him right for trying to trust someone. He should've learned his lesson years back.

Gage scrubbed his face, biting down all the rude profanities he wanted to spew. If that man never returned to the gym, it would still be too soon.

He yanked his pillow over from the backseat, thinking maybe he should take up some booty calls, make some extra money on the side. He hadn't. He didn't think Debbie would want him to pay her bills that way, and, well. He didn't want to tarnish his love of sex. Being paid meant having to yield to his clients' demands.

He could probably screen his clients, but... what if someone like Ulric hired him? Someone who had seemed so vulnerable suddenly kicking him where it hurt?

Gage scowled. He didn't have much left. Just his car and some random things. So no, he wasn't selling his body, despite whatever the bastard thought about him.

And then his stomach started to growl. Gage sighed. He'd stashed some food in the gym's staff pantry, but he was running low. Maybe he'd go back later tonight to microwave his frozen dinner leftovers—no full kitchen there. At least he still had a bit of protein powder left.

Gods, if Ulric were to see him like this... he would scoff, wouldn't he? Gage fumed. *Stop thinking about him.*

His phone buzzed. It was a message from his cousin, Jesse. *Gonna be a barbecue party at the lake tomorrow afternoon, the station guys are inviting family. You in?*

Gage's stomach growled louder. Well. He wouldn't say no to food. *I'm bringing my appetite,* he texted back.

Jesse's answer was a *LOL*, but that was good. Gage could stuff his face a bit at the party. It'd tide him over for a while.

He grabbed his blanket from the backseat, pulled it over himself, and tried to sleep. It eluded him like it had been doing lately.

THE LAST PERSON Gage expected to see at the barbecue party was, of course, That Bastard.

Chubby was from New York. How the hell did he know any of the Meadowfall firefighters? Gage stopped at the edge of the pavilion, staring at that figure as though it would go away. Did he really need this crap?

He blinked again, but O'Neil was still there. All heavy curves and plain appearance, but it was definitely him. Just that he was in a different shirt from before.

Gage was about to turn away, but O'Neil must've felt his stare. He glanced up—straight at Gage—and tensed. He looked surprised. Wary.

Well, good. Gage was glad he wasn't the only one.

"What's wrong?" an omega asked O'Neil. "Ulric?" He glanced between Gage and Chubby, and touched that alpha cautiously—not an intimate partner.

Before Gage could hear his answer, Jesse bumped into his side. "Gage!" They bumped fists. "Thought you were gonna get here sooner," Jesse said. "Have you grabbed a drink?"

Jesse Sinclair was one of the cousins Gage had grown up with, until Jesse had disappeared one year. He'd returned a decade later, silvery scars on every inch of his body. Then he'd gotten married to a fellow alpha from the fire station, and they had a kid together. Gage thought it was weird, Jesse falling in love with an alpha. Things like that actually happened?

Actually, Jesse seemed to have a beer belly now. That was fast.

"You been drinking?" Gage could've sworn that Jesse looked perfectly trim some months back. How did he maintain his toned biceps while still having that belly? It went against all of Gage's knowledge as a physical trainer.

Jesse laughed, glancing at his husband, Dom. "I'll tell you in a couple months."

Dom sauntered over and slipped his arm around Jesse's waist, kissing his lips. Gage didn't know how to feel about that. Two alphas kissing. It didn't seem right.

Then they shared a look that was tooth-rottingly happy. Gage almost wanted to gag, except... He'd never felt anything like that before. He'd had relationships, he'd had multiple girlfriends and boyfriends, but... in the end, they'd let him down, or he'd let them down, or it was a combination of both.

Dom was older, and Jesse was scarred. Maybe that was the key to a relationship. When you weren't so handsome that people fell over each other trying to get into your pants. When you didn't have so many options that you were forced to make a relationship work. Maybe

Chubby O'Neil had better luck with relationships because his looks weren't everything.

Was that why he'd scoffed at Gage?

Gage found himself looking back at Chubby. Who was also staring at Jesse and his husband.

For a moment, something flickered in his eyes—the same vulnerability that had snared Gage's attention in the first place. O'Neil looked... lonely. Like he wanted a person to be with.

Gage's instincts murmured, *Protect.*

Right after, Gage shook that thought off. *What the fuck?* He didn't need to protect another alpha. Chubby could hold his own perfectly fine. He wasn't the least bit vulnerable.

Gage was fuming at himself when Jesse showed up back at his side. "Something wrong?"

Gage scowled. "No."

"You keep looking at him." And now Jesse seemed smug, or maybe too knowing.

"Fuck off."

"Nope. Want a drink?" Jesse made for the drinks table; Gage followed him. "Beer?"

"Nah. I won't be staying long." Gage watched as Jesse poured himself a soda. "Not drinking, yourself?"

Jesse smiled a secret smile, one that got on Gage's nerves. He punched Jesse's arm; Jesse grabbed him in a headlock, and they wrestled for a moment. Then Gage swung his fist at Jesse's beer belly, and Jesse blocked that blow so fast, Gage almost didn't see him move.

"Ow, fuck." Gage hissed, his arm pinned behind his back.

"Not in the belly," Jesse growled.

Why was he so damn protective over some fat? Gage tapped out. Jesse released him, scowling a little.

Dom returned and kissed Jesse hard on the lips, growling something. Gage decided he'd had enough of their sap.

He stalked over to the grill, assembled a sandwich with the leftover ingredients, and scarfed it down. There was a variety of party food to the side—hash brown patties, pizzas, fries, finger sandwiches... Nothing particularly healthy, but after a whole night of hunger pangs, Gage wasn't about to be picky.

He found some wings slathered in BBQ sauce. Then some salad. He took some, added ranch dressing for the calories, and emptied his plate.

When he turned back, he found Chubby watching him. Chubby snatched his gaze away, his neck turning red. Served him right. Why was he looking at Gage, anyway, if Gage was a poor rat compared to him?

At least Chubby didn't seem vulnerable anymore. Gage *didn't* need to feel sorry for him.

"Why's he here?" Gage asked Jesse.

Jesse shrugged. "Shouldn't he be? I think he knows Flores—that's Gareth's omega. Not sure how they met, though."

And it wasn't Gage's business. Gage hung around for a few more minutes, he said hi to Jesse's three-year-old, Owen. A couple of kids ran around with streamers in the air—snakes? They were kind of cute, but most of these guys weren't Gage's own family. He didn't want to intrude.

He headed back toward the parking lot. Someone's presence trailed behind him, not quite friendly. Definitely O'Neil. All of Gage's instincts growled—he wanted to spin around, he wanted to knock that alpha to the ground and make him submit.

Gage made it all the way to his car before he turned,

itching for another fight. He wanted to win this time. Wanted to pin that man down.

Chubby stopped a few paces away, looking wary. As he should well be.

Then he frowned at Gage's car—there was so much crap piled into it that he couldn't possibly come to any other conclusion. Gage's skin prickled with embarrassment.

He knew the moment O'Neil understood the full extent of his circumstances: O'Neil's mouth fell open. Then he looked... regretful? Pitying?

Gage didn't need his pity. Not from someone like him. "What the fuck do you want?"

O'Neil stiffened, his chest heaving.

And Gage wanted to punch the hell out of him. Just so he had the upper hand again. "You have a minute," Gage muttered, "before I sink my fist into your face."

5

TENSIONS—AND OTHER THINGS—
RISE

Shit, shit. Ulric froze, his thoughts crashing into one another. He'd fucked up big time.

Dark shadows filled Gage's car—multiple hangers full of clothes, pillows and blankets piled high in the backseat. Random things were piled precariously to the ceiling, and more stuff had been tucked around them.

There was moving house carload by carload, and then there was being homeless. Ulric hadn't known that Gage was in such dire straits.

And he'd gone and rubbed Gage's financial difficulties in his face. *If he didn't hate me before, he definitely hates me now.* Ulric's stomach twisted.

Gage stalked forward, his fists clenched. He looked angry, he looked like his punches would hurt, and it was all because of Ulric.

Vaguely, Ulric remembered being pummeled into a corner at school, in the first days after he'd presented as alpha. He'd thought being alpha would stop the other kids from beating him up, but it had only become worse.

They'd made fun of him not only for being fat, but also for being a fat alpha. They'd rained their fists on him, and when he'd hit another boy back, he'd left a bruise. The boy had run crying to the teacher, who'd sided with him. Life just wasn't very fair. And fights were certainly not Ulric's thing.

They were definitely Gage's, though.

Somehow, or maybe because of Ulric's trepidation, he recognized the danger in Gage's tense shoulders, the full lips pressed into a thin line. Gage was the sort of alpha you'd drool over in movies, the sort that was in control of everything, even when he was at rock-bottom.

Envy coiled through Ulric's chest. But far more potent was the quiet admiration and the curiosity: what would it feel like to have Gage's body on his? Gage pinning him, so close that Ulric could breathe the scent off his skin?

His nerves tingled. His heart thumped. If he could fend off Gage's blows, maybe Gage would fight harder. And he'd come closer.

Maybe... their cocks would rub together.

Heat swooped between Ulric's legs. And he knew he couldn't get hit, he knew he had to catch Gage's punches before they landed.

Gage swung his fist; Ulric barely caught it, jerking his head sideways. Gage snarled and yanked his fist back, striking again. His fist connected this time; pain throbbed through Ulric's head, robbing him of his breath. Before Gage could hit him again, Ulric grabbed Gage's hands and heaved him back against another car. Then he pushed their bodies together—his belly against Gage's solid abs, his chest against Gage's broad pecs. Gage's eyes flashed; he was warm and strong—a decadent presence.

Ulric's cock thickened, jutting up so much that, for a moment, it tented his pants and brushed Gage's fly. He wondered if Gage could feel that.

But Gage only narrowed his eyes. He shoved his entire body back, snapping his hips, a hard pressure that went straight through Ulric's pants and into his tip. Pleasure shot up his spine. Ulric gasped.

Gage used that distraction to slam Ulric back against his car. The impact shook through Ulric's bones; the part of him that was alpha *roared*.

His entire body grew hot, ready to tackle Gage, ready to shove every inch of bare skin against him. He would let Gage feel his cock, he'd push it up against Gage and come all over him, marking Gage with his own scent.

Ulric shoved Gage back against someone else's car, he snapped his hips, and this time, their cocks pressed together in a sweet, slow grind. Gage's eyes flashed.

"You won't get the better of me," Ulric snarled, pushing their intimate parts together, pushing into Gage's space, rubbing his cock all over Gage's just because he could.

It seemed like a damn good idea to threaten Gage with that.

Gage heaved him off; Ulric's lower back hit his car. "Fuck off," Gage hissed. Then he shoved their hips together in another delicious slide, and Ulric *throbbed*.

Musk billowed between them.

Gage paused, his nostrils flaring, his eyes narrowing. He'd recognized the scent of arousal. And it was so terribly obvious that it wasn't from him. Ulric stiffened, torn between pinning Gage down, and covering up.

"What the fuck," Gage whispered, glancing between them.

Despite his trepidation, Ulric let him look. His bulge betrayed him, a thick bluntness straining against his pants. All the proof in the world that he wanted Gage Frost.

It was supposed to be a secret.

Gage stared at Ulric's cock—Ulric felt the weight of his gaze through his pants. He grew so hard, it hurt. Then Gage looked up, aghast.

Ulric knew he should back off. He knew he should listen to the part of him that said, *Gage will find this repulsive*, except something about Gage's touch made him reckless. It made him want to snarl, it made him want to prove that he could be just as good of an alpha.

Ulric shoved Gage back, a new sort of confidence thumping in his veins. "Yeah, 'what the fuck,'" Ulric growled.

And maybe he wanted to prove that he could get into shape, he wanted prove that he could be desirable.

Maybe... he could become so desirable that Gage would want him.

Gage released him, eyes narrowed. Ulric turned away. He should leave. He owed Gage nothing—maybe an apology. And an offer.

Over his shoulder, Ulric said, "There's space in my house if you need a room. You won't have to pay rent."

That was enough of an apology. He didn't want to say the actual words, not so obviously that Gage would know he felt bad about the insults.

Gage scowled. "I'm not desperate enough for that."

That stung. Ulric breathed it out—he'd brought this on himself. No point lingering on it.

He strode off and got into his car, driving away. After those insults, he'd thought he wouldn't see Gage again.

But Gage knew about Ulric's tendencies now. He would probably scoff even more.

So Ulric decided that he was heading back to the gym. Was it possible to change so much that he could impress even Gage?

It wasn't the best of ideas. But Ulric had his membership, and he had time. What could go wrong?

6

ULRIC DOUBLES DOWN ON LOSING WEIGHT

OVER THE NEXT COUPLE WEEKS, Ulric changed his habits. He did his research on diets. He threw out the cakes and cookies and ice creams that he loved so much. He emptied his bottles of soda down the sink. He bought meat and veggies and made lettuce burgers, and he tried to eat less food.

That killed him some. Several times a day, he ached for a fizzy mouthful of sweet soda, he ached for fluffy icing and moist chocolate cake on his tongue. He badly wanted to dive into a pile of freshly-baked bread and stuff himself senseless.

It felt like he'd broken up with his favorite food. That probably hurt just as much as when Mick had dumped him.

In the daytime, Ulric worked at his data analysis job. At night, when he was certain that Gage's shift had ended, he went to the gym and did some hours of cycling. He built himself up to the levels with the highest resistance, the ones that had him leaning forward, panting as he pedaled against wheels that felt like they'd grown ten times as heavy.

Ulric finished with his cycling, wiping off his sweat. He was exhausted. But... he'd promised himself a tiny slice of cake—tiramisu from a bakery—if he tried something new tonight.

He could already taste the coffee in every bite of cloud-soft cake, he could imagine licking sweet whipped cream off his fork.

Maybe he could do a bench press for just five minutes.

He headed cautiously to the weights section, avoiding the couple of people already there. He wasn't going to make a fool of himself again. From the corner of his eye, he watched as one of the guys added weights to his barbell.

Ulric added a couple of small weights to his own. Then he added a couple more, because starting out with the smallest weight seemed... kind of pathetic.

He knew he shouldn't, he knew he should do the minimum just to get used to it. But Gage wasn't here. It was okay if Ulric fucked up, right?

He tested the barbell—it wasn't too heavy. So he lay back on the bench, made sure his grip was comfortable, and lifted the barbell off its support.

It was a little heavier from this angle, he realized. His muscles strained. Ulric did a rep, then another. He felt embarrassed, counting them out one by one instead of sets of five like the gym rats seemed to do. He lowered the barbell a third time, then a fourth, his arms starting to ache.

After he returned the barbell to the rack, he gave himself a few minutes to rest. He gulped down some water. Then he lay back, grasped the barbell, and tried to lift it.

The emergency exit door opened some paces away. Someone stepped in, dressed in a T-shirt and shorts. He was muscled. He had tanned skin, a shock of dark hair, and—Ulric had been dreaming about those perfect lips.

His heart sank. Why did Gage have to show up now? He hadn't seen Gage in weeks. He'd missed that guy. He'd missed the initial kindness Gage had shown him, he'd missed how flirty Gage had been with him at first.

He'd gone and forfeited all of that, though.

Ulric clenched his jaw, lifting the barbell to try and blend in with the other gym rats. With luck, Gage wouldn't have noticed him. Ulric's black T-shirt and shorts was camouflage enough... right?

He held his breath and lowered the barbell, his arms trembling with the strain. *Don't look over. Please don't.*

Gage paused mid-step. Then he turned, he looked right at Ulric, and Ulric's stomach dropped.

Gage narrowed his eyes and strode over. Ulric felt like the greatest embarrassment in the world.

"You should get a spotter if you're new with this," Gage muttered.

Ulric scowled. "I'm perfectly fine."

He did another rep, his arms trembling a little. If he managed to hit ten... maybe he could have two slices of cake?

Gage set something on the floor. Then he crowded close, leaned in a bit, and now his pecs were all Ulric could see, his thighs spread open around Ulric's head.

It felt like something out of a weird porn game—when did you ever get an alpha like that leaning over you, strong muscles barely hidden by his clothes?

Gage curled his hands around the barbell, looking as

though he might take it right out of Ulric's grasp. Except he just waited there. "Keep going."

All Ulric could smell now was pine, all he could focus on was Gage's thick thighs, and the way his shorts clung to his skin. If he were to tilt his head back... he would see Gage's cock, wouldn't he? It was just inches from his face.

Ulric gulped, his heart pounding. He lowered the barbell as far down as he could, before raising it back up. He did three more, his muscles straining, his teeth gritted. He wanted that cake. And he wanted to prove that he could do this.

He wanted to—in his own way—somehow impress Gage.

He was on his ninth rep when his arms gave out. He struggled. Except the barbell grew lighter—Gage pulled it up and helped him fit it on the rack. Ulric's arms felt like someone had plucked out their bones.

"Go home," Gage said.

It sounded... a lot kinder than Ulric expected. He struggled to sit up, watching as Gage collected a water bottle from the floor. Gage began to step away, completely ignoring him.

Ulric's chest tightened. He grabbed some sanitizing towels and wiped down the bench real quick. Pulled the weights off the barbells. Then he hurried after Gage to a staff-only area. It was a pantry, he realized. And he didn't belong here.

Gage turned, his eyes narrowed. "What do you want?"

"You didn't have to spot for me," Ulric blurted. His heart thumped so fast, it felt like it would escape his chest.

Gage shrugged. "I'm a personal trainer. It's my job."

"But you're off-duty."

"Still a trainer."

Ulric stood awkwardly, covered in sweat, just as heavy as he was before. The diet had shaved some pounds off his body. But after the initial bout of weight loss, it had slowed down. To Gage, Ulric probably didn't look much different from before. Hell, Ulric barely looked different to himself.

Gage turned, filling his water bottle. He looked... kind of uncomfortable, actually. Was that because of how hard Ulric had gotten for him?

Why was Ulric still here, anyway? He had nothing going for him. Just a heart that still quietly longed for Gage—he was such a fool.

"I... should go." Ulric turned. Gage probably didn't even like alphas to begin with. Ulric should just stop kidding himself.

He was almost out of the pantry when Gage said, "Hey."

Ulric paused, glancing back.

"About before." Gage looked like it pained him to say this. "You still looking for a roommate?"

That took Ulric a second. Then his heart skipped. "Yeah. I am."

"I'll split the rent with you," Gage said. "Fifty-fifty."

Ulric tried to squash his burgeoning hope. "I told you. You could live with me for free."

Gage scowled. "No. I'll split it evenly."

Part of Ulric wanted to point out that the rent might still be too much for him, even when split. The other part just wanted to tell Gage it was some small amount, just so Gage didn't have to hole up in his car anymore.

As an alpha, he knew other alphas didn't take kindly to being belittled, or thought of as incapable. So Ulric lied, "I got the place for cheap. It'd be $800 a month, your share."

To be honest, it should be more than twice that, but that was a secret Gage didn't have to find out.

"Fine." Gage narrowed his eyes, holding his hand out.

Ulric shook his hand—Gage's palm was warm, solid, and it sent tingles racing all over his skin.

Gage was coming to live with him.

It sounded like a dream and a nightmare rolled into one.

Ulric looked for a scrap of paper. But there was no pen in the pantry. So he pulled out his phone. "Tell me your number. I'll text you the address. You can move in anytime."

His hands shook—he tried to bite down his smile, he tried to tell his heart to stop pounding. *It's not real until he moves in,* he tried to tell himself.

With a wary glance, Gage told Ulric his number. Ulric saved it and typed his address into a text message. Then he hit Send, and something else buzzed in the room.

"I work from home, so I'll be there most of the time," Ulric said. "Feel free to move in tomorrow or something."

"I'll think about it."

Ulric didn't linger—no chance of fucking up if he disappeared. He hurried out of the gym, grabbed his duffel, and it was only when he'd shut his car door, hiding his face against the steering wheel, that the most glorious smile burst across his face.

Gage Frost was coming to live with him. It didn't mean anything. But Ulric would get to see him and smell him, and... that had to be enough.

7

GAGE MOVES IN

Gage read the text from O'Neil about five times. Meadow Street, was what O'Neil had sent. Eight hundred bucks a month.

This place didn't cost $1600 to rent. Nowhere even close. Gage had frowned when he'd entered this neighborhood—it was all nice houses with sprawling front yards, houses with large French windows for their living rooms and double doors—*double doors*—as entrances.

Some of them had exquisite landscaping. Others had fancy rustic-farmhouse facades. Hell, Gage had seen someone riding a horse a couple blocks down.

What sort of people could afford *horses?* In expensive southern California?

He pulled up just outside the house O'Neil supposedly lived in, feeling like he'd been played. Eight hundred bucks? O'Neil clearly didn't think Gage could afford much more.

Truth be told, he would be right. Were Gage in any

other circumstance, he would've driven off and ignored every message O'Neil sent.

Except Gage's supervisor at the gym had said, *We can't have you camping in the parking lot. Your car gives our clients a really bad impression.*

Gage had protested that he'd been parking behind the building. His boss had pointed out that the back was for overflow parking. Now that the weather was starting to warm up, they were getting more guests at the gym. Which meant that Gage couldn't park anywhere in that area.

Besides, he was getting really, really tired of sleeping in his car seat all night—it fucked with his back. He missed sleeping in an actual bed, he missed poaching eggs and frying steaks and just... having his own kitchen.

And this house promised a large kitchen, space he could really work with. He could install his own exercise machines instead of using the ones at the gym. He wouldn't get gym regulars recognizing him, and asking him to spot for them when all he wanted was to get some water and go back to bed.

The only drawback was that he'd have O'Neil as his roommate.

O'Neil, who had been struggling with the barbell last night. O'Neil, who had fought with Gage at the park, and that fight had somehow aroused him. O'Neil, who, despite those awful insults that day, had not offended Gage any more.

Gage didn't understand that man. But O'Neil got on his nerves for a reason he couldn't explain. He'd been wondering why the hell O'Neil had been doing bench presses with more weights than he could handle. He'd wondered if O'Neil had still been working on the bike machines. He seemed to have lost a bit of weight since Gage last saw him.

We'll give it a try, Gage told himself. A week. He could get a bed moved in, he could get out just as quickly if he needed.

He left his car and crossed the wide driveway, pressing the doorbell.

It took so long for O'Neil to answer that Gage almost thought he'd fallen asleep.

"Hi?" O'Neil opened the front door, looking flustered. He was barefoot, dressed in a worn T-shirt and shorts. "Sorry, I didn't think you'd show up."

Gage shrugged. He didn't have much choice. "Mind if I move in today?"

O'Neil's eyes widened. He stepped back, waving Gage into the house. "Sure. Go ahead. Here, I'll show you your room."

Gage followed him upstairs. There were about three regular-sized bedrooms on that level, not including the master bedroom. That particular room had its door ajar, and it smelled like honey oak in there. Next to it was the study. Two empty rooms sat on the other side of the hallway.

"Pick one. Or both." O'Neil shrugged. "Do you need help moving your stuff?"

Gage shook his head. "I've got it. Thanks."

O'Neil shoved his hands into his pockets, glancing at the empty bedrooms. Then he looked at Gage for a second, before tearing his gaze away. Was it Gage, or had O'Neil's entire face turned pink?

This didn't have anything to do with his getting hard... did it?

"I'm heading out to make you a set of keys," O'Neil

said, turning away. "Text me if you need anything. You know my number."

"Thanks."

O'Neil hurried into his bedroom. Then he shut his door, and Gage breathed in the honey oak scent lingering throughout the house. He made his way downstairs, glancing around the spacious living room—just one couch in front of a big TV—and then the kitchen. That was fully-equipped; Gage didn't even need to unpack his cooking appliances, maybe.

O'Neil hurried out of his room a few minutes later. Except he wasn't dressed in the way Gage expected. O'Neil had brushed his hair and styled it, he'd put on a button-down shirt that fitted him pretty well, and... It felt like he'd dressed up for a semi-formal event.

He cleaned up well, actually. He looked different.

Gage had a bit of trouble tearing his eyes away. "I thought you were going to make some keys."

"Uh. Yeah. I've got a couple more places to go." O'Neil straightened his shirt collar, looking uncomfortable. Then he strode out of the house and drove off.

Gage unloaded his car, picking the room across from O'Neil's study. He put away what little he had, took a quick shower, and then checked the fridge to see how much space he'd have for his own groceries.

An hour later, O'Neil returned with bags of stuff. He set them down in the kitchen and handed Gage a set of keys. "That's for the front and back doors. I also got some food—I hope you're okay with steaks and spinach."

Gage blinked. Those steaks were expensive. Did O'Neil expect Gage to pay him back for them? "No, I'm fine. I can get my own food."

O'Neil winced. "Are you a vegetarian?"

Gage didn't want to say *I can't afford to eat entire steaks every day,* but he wasn't sure how he could put it across in a way that wasn't awkward. "I prefer chicken."

"Oh." O'Neil looked sheepish. "I'll get some chicken—"

"No, it's fine. I can do it myself."

A frown creased O'Neil's forehead. "I can—"

"I don't need you to wait on me," Gage growled.

O'Neil stiffened, his face turning red. "Oh. Yeah. Okay. I'll just—just put this away. You're welcome to it, if you want."

He fumbled a little, shoving the food haphazardly into the fridge. Then he took the last box with him—it was a clear package with what looked to be two slices of cake, along with a Ben's Buns logo. O'Neil grabbed a fork and hurried out of the kitchen, retreating upstairs.

Guilt crept into Gage's chest. He hadn't meant to make O'Neil feel guilty. The guy was being nice. Why the hell had he dressed up, though? If he was just coming back home to eat some cake?

A thought struck Gage, one he'd briefly entertained but shoved aside: Maybe Ulric O'Neil... liked him.

It explained the erections. It explained the red faces. And the offer to let Gage be his roommate.

He insulted you. He could pull that crap again. You can't trust him. Except Gage couldn't help trusting that flusteredness, a little bit. You didn't get flustered around people you didn't like.

Gage left the house, heading to his self-storage place to pick up his mattress. He tied the mattress to his car, grabbed a few more things, and made it back to Meadow Street.

Halfway through maneuvering the mattress through

the front door, O'Neil came down the stairs, frowning when he saw Gage. "You need help?"

"Actually, yeah." Especially when it was something bulky like this.

They brought the mattress upstairs into Gage's room. O'Neil's biceps flexed. Gage had bigger muscles, but... O'Neil didn't look too shabby. Even if he'd struggled with beginner-level weights.

He was trying. Gage liked that about him.

"Do you need help with anything else?" O'Neil asked.

Gage shook his head. So O'Neil turned to leave, except Gage stopped him. "How was the cake?"

O'Neil's ears turned pink. "It was fine."

"Just 'fine'?"

O'Neil frowned. "What am I supposed to say?"

"Ben's cakes are some of the best around."

The alpha stared. "You sound like you know him."

Gage shrugged. "It's a small town. You'd be missing out if you haven't had his buns."

For a second, O'Neil looked as though he'd been punched. Then Gage remembered—maybe O'Neil liked him. And this talk about Ben made him jealous. Even though Gage was talking about Ben's confectioneries, instead of his bottom.

It made Gage wonder, though—how riled-up could he make O'Neil?

"He's a pretty sweet omega," Gage said mildly, his instincts rumbling. "Did you meet him when you went? He's kinda pretty."

O'Neil tensed, his lips pressing into a thin line. "Maybe? I don't know."

Gage put a bit of fondness into his voice. "You'll recognize him. He's about this tall, blond—"

The alpha scowled and turned, heading for the door. Yeah, he was jealous, all right.

Gage wasn't sure how to feel about that. He wasn't into alphas. He'd never dated them, never slept with them. But this felt like a challenge somehow.

He followed O'Neil into the hallway, his pulse thumping in his ears. "You like me."

O'Neil spun around so fast, he surprised Gage. But the look in his eyes—that stopped Gage in his tracks.

Gage expected many things of other people. But he hadn't expected Ulric O'Neil to look so brittle in that moment, scared and vulnerable and defensive.

"No, I fucking don't," O'Neil snarled.

Then he stalked away and slammed the door to his own room, and for the longest moment, Gage couldn't move.

8

WHY DOES GAGE HAVE TO MAKE THE PERFECT BREAKFAST, TOO?

"Let's be friends," Gage said, surprising Ulric the next morning.

Ulric almost dropped his spatula. "What?"

All he'd intended was to fry up some bacon, scramble eggs for his breakfast, and retreat upstairs. He'd thought Gage had left for work. He should've put on some decent clothes. And styled his hair. And shaved.

Gage stepped into the kitchen wearing his gym trainer clothes, a towel slung across his shoulders. His hair dripped from a recent shower, and... well. He looked as handsome as always. Ulric wanted to taste the water droplets trickling down his neck.

"Friends," Gage said. "You know, we become bros. We watch TV and have game nights and everything."

Ulric stared suspiciously at him. Surely Gage had discovered Ulric's feelings after yesterday's outburst. Why wasn't he scrambling the hell away? "You already have friends."

Gage shrugged. "I can make more friends, right?"

"With me?"

"Why not?" Gage glanced at the coffee machine on the counter. "Mind if I grab some coffee?"

"Sure. There's plenty of mugs."

Gage peeked into the cabinets, his gaze locking onto the mug that stood out against all the rest—the one with rows of little cartoon ducks all the way around it. Ulric's favorite.

For a moment, Gage looked as though he might grab that mug. Ulric stopped breathing and just stared, wondering if he wanted Gage to use it. Wondering if he wanted Gage's lips on where Ulric had put his mouth.

Gage glanced over his shoulder, meeting Ulric's eyes with a smile. "Nah, I won't give you a heart attack."

He took the next mug instead, but Ulric's heart had stuck on that quick *thump-thump-thump*. He watched as Gage poured himself coffee—black, no sugar. Gage gulped some down, his eyebrows lifting. "This is good stuff."

Ulric shrugged. "It's freshly-ground beans."

"No, like. It's expensive stuff." He took another sip, his throat working. "I've had this once before. At a fancy restaurant. It cost twenty bucks a cup."

Ulric looked back at his bacon. Gage was right, actually. It was one of the priciest coffees you could get your hands on—it had a rich, dark flavor, earthy and smooth, slightly bitter. Ulric had figured he'd need something special to get through today. "Well, don't waste it, then."

"I won't." Gage grinned and wandered over. Ulric tried not to breathe in that pine scent. He tried not to fixate on Gage's smile.

He didn't know what had possessed him to invite Gage here, but this still felt like a dream. Gage in his house, drinking his coffee, smiling at Ulric and asking to be his friend. Gage smelled like soap and pine, and his skin looked soft. His lips, too.

He's going to hurt me. Ulric flipped the bacon and turned on the burner for the other pan. "I'm making scrambled eggs. You want some?"

"I'll cook them. Can't let you do all the work."

Ulric frowned. But Gage only winked, in that suave way that weakened Ulric's resolve.

"I make a mean plate of scrambled eggs." Gage pulled the egg carton from the fridge. Then the cream and butter. "We could do a cook-off, but maybe another day. I have to get to work."

"Maybe." Ulric wouldn't say no to Gage making him food. "Pot roast?"

"Ribs." Gage grinned. "Juicy, pluck-the-bones-out ribs that are so tender, it's better than sex."

"You can make food better than sex?" Sex with Gage would already be incredible. "I doubt it."

Gage bumped his arm, looking smug. "Yeah, tell me that after you've eaten my food," Gage growled. "I'll bet you fifty bucks you'll groan like you're about to come."

"I'll bet you a hundred."

Gage's smile grew, a confident slash of pink that just about dropped Ulric's pants.

Ulric made himself focus on the bacon. Next to him, Gage melted some butter in the pan. He cracked eggs into a bowl and beat them up, adding generous pours of heavy cream.

It was going to be a decadent meal—Ulric could already tell. "That's what you make for your morning-after breakfasts, isn't it?" he muttered.

"How'd you guess?" Gage poured the eggs into the pan. "I haven't had a single person complain about it."

Ulric didn't want to think about Gage's one-night stands, either. He pulled his cartoon duck mug from the cabinet, poured himself coffee, and added cream. Then he allowed himself a bit of sugar. It was All Hell Breaks Loose week. If he imploded over the next few days, at least he would've had some decent coffee before he met his end.

In between stirring his eggs, Gage turned, surveying Ulric. His gaze swept over Ulric's face, then his mug, warm like a lover's touch. Ulric almost blushed. And Gage looked thoughtful. "You know, you look kind of cute like that."

Ulric sprayed coffee all over the stove. "What the fuck?"

"No?" Gage squinted and tilted his head, scrutinizing Ulric. "You're wearing your glasses, which is a plus."

"These are just glasses."

"But they make you look smart."

Ulric stared. Had Gage hit his head sometime during the night? It didn't seem as though he was joking. In fact, Gage looked completely serious. So why...? "I'm fat," Ulric said eventually. It wasn't something he wanted to mention, but Gage had to know this.

Gage's attention coasted down Ulric's chest, to his belly. Ulric held his breath and poked at the bacon. He didn't want to hear Gage talking about all his extra pounds. Bad enough that they were so difficult to shed.

Gage shrugged. "Yeah, well."

Didn't it matter to him? "You're a physical trainer."

"It just means I see people with all kinds of body types."

Was he... pitying Ulric? Was this why he was being nice? "You haven't dated anyone fat before," Ulric said.

Gage almost looked guilty as he folded in the scrambled egg. "I guess not."

Ulric breathed out the crushing *I knew it* in his chest. "Anyway, you said we're going to be friends."

Not boyfriends. At least Ulric didn't have to get his hopes up that high.

"Yeah. Movie night tonight?" Gage smiled. "You pick something."

That... almost sounded like a date. "Sure. I like horror movies."

"Those make me scream like a baby." Gage laughed. "Are you sure?"

Someone like Gage, screaming? "No way."

"Yes way."

"We'll watch the Bloody Hollows movie that just released, then," Ulric said. "I've been wanting to see it."

Gage scowled. "I'm not watching that."

"Chicken."

That slipped out of Ulric's mouth before he really thought about it—a remnant from his past. But instead of getting offended, Gage straightened his shoulders, looking obstinate. "Fine. I'll watch it."

"I'll get some popcorn," Ulric said.

"I'll make it. It's fantastic when you top it with powdered parmesan. Mm." Gage grunted, looking so satisfied that Ulric couldn't help staring. "Here. Egg's almost done."

He dished breakfast. Ulric added bacon strips to the plates. Then they moved to the dining table and sat across from each other. That was slightly awkward.

Ulric stared at his morning-after omelette, cooked to perfection—it glistened in the sunlight, golden yellow and creamy, dusted with pepper. "It'll go perfectly with toast," he blurted.

Gage made to stand. "I'll pop some in the oven."

"No, you don't have to."

"Why not?"

Ulric flushed. "I'm on a diet."

Gage thought about it, still halfway out of his chair. "Sliced tomatoes?"

"This is fine." Ulric popped a bite of omelette into his mouth. It fell apart on his tongue, warm and buttery and a touch salty, and it tasted so good that he might've groaned.

He scooped another chunk into his mouth, then another. Egg was delicious. Especially cooked this way. Especially because Gage had made this for him. It wasn't until he'd emptied half his plate that he looked up, to find Gage sitting down hard, watching him.

"Good, huh?" Gage murmured.

Ulric froze. That wasn't what he'd planned. He hadn't meant to stuff his face in front of Mr. Perfect. Nor had he meant to groan and make weird sounds while eating Gage's food.

Gage smiled. "Are you set to do the cook-off this weekend? I'll bet you two hundred bucks that my ribs will beat the best sex you've ever had."

Fuck. Ulric knew Gage would win, hands-down. It wasn't like Ulric had experienced mind-blowing sex before. "Sure."

"I can't wait until you taste my meat," Gage said, his smile slow and confident. "And I'll taste yours."

Ulric's face burned. Gage had to know what that sounded like.

"I should get back to work," Ulric mumbled, hurrying back into the kitchen before his body betrayed him further. He did the dishes, put away the leftover bacon, and refilled his coffee mug. Then he hurried upstairs, away from Gage's too-shrewd gaze.

Maybe he shouldn't have agreed to movie night. Maybe he shouldn't let himself be so vulnerable, but he couldn't help it.

Ulric locked himself in his study, hoping Gage would have the good sense to stay away.

9

THERE IS ONLY ONE COUCH

Of all the people in the world... Gage hadn't expected O'Neil to moan over his food.

He'd made omelettes for others. Girlfriends, boyfriends, one-night-stands... None of them had ever reacted the way O'Neil had. At best, he'd received a sweet thank you, or maybe a blowjob in return.

Then along came Ulric O'Neil, who had taken one bite and groaned, his head thrown back, his jaw working slowly like he was savoring the most decadent thing he'd ever tasted. He'd scooped up mouthful after mouthful, every bite drawing a new sound from his throat.

At his reaction, something primal had stirred in Gage's gut. He'd never heard an alpha groan before, not like that. Never when they were eating his omelettes.

He'd started wondering if O'Neil would groan, eating his ribs. Or his steaks. Then he'd wondered if O'Neil would groan if he tasted Gage's cock.

And Gage had hardened, thinking about pushing his tip into O'Neil's mouth, O'Neil with that look of bliss on his face.

He would love it, wouldn't he?

Suddenly, Gage had known what O'Neil would sound like, if Gage ever sucked his cock. He'd known, too, the thickness of O'Neil's tip in his mouth, the weight of it on his tongue, the salt of his precome as he yanked on Gage's hair, panting.

It had been... kind of hot.

Gage had grown hard that morning—for an alpha, of all things. He wasn't sure why. He wasn't sure what to do about it.

But O'Neil was also his landlord. And Gage very definitely owed him more than $800 for this month's rent.

He could... owe that alpha favors. He could even suck O'Neil's cock. Just to see what it'd be like. Just to taste him, and—gods, just to see him come apart.

Gage swallowed, pulling up outside the house. It was getting late. He'd had dinner out, just so he wouldn't try and cook for O'Neil and end up springing another erection. Especially if they were going to watch a movie together.

When he stepped through the front door, he found the living room lights dimmed, O'Neil already on one side of the couch, his body faintly lit by the TV's blue glow.

"I have a bowl for the popcorn," O'Neil said, nudging the huge mixing bowl sitting in the middle of the couch.

Yeah, good idea to leave some space between them. Gage shut the door, kicking his shoes off. "I'll get the popcorn started. Have you eaten?"

O'Neil nodded. "Have you?"

"Yeah." Gage thought about lingering, maybe chatting with O'Neil about his day. He headed into the kitchen, stuck a bag of popcorn into the microwave, and wandered back out. "We're really watching your horror movie, huh?"

O'Neil looked curious. "You don't want to?"

Gage tried not to wince. "It's not my thing."

"What movies do you like to watch, then?"

"What I tell everyone? The superhero action movies."

O'Neil studied him. "What *don't* you tell everyone? The movies that are your guilty pleasure."

That was a secret that only Gage and his siblings knew. He pursed his lips. "Why should I tell you?"

But O'Neil just grinned. "I guessed it! You have secret kinks you don't tell anyone."

"It's not a kink! Just my taste in movies!"

"What kind of taste is it?" O'Neil raised his eyebrows.

Gage flopped down on the other end of the couch; the bowl bounced between them. "Not telling. You'll laugh."

O'Neil sobered. "I don't laugh at people."

"Of course you do."

"No."

He sounded so serious that Gage stared. "Why not?"

O'Neil examined the floor, silent for a long time. "I was laughed at my whole life. For being fat."

Shit. Gage stopped breathing. He should've known, but... Part of him wanted to hold back and brush it off, treat it like it wasn't a big deal so this wouldn't become an involved friendship.

But deep down, he remembered being humiliated, too. He remembered the shame, he remembered feeling so awkward that he wanted to crawl under the floorboards and hide somewhere. He remembered wanting everyone to forget he existed.

Had O'Neil felt that way his whole life?

Gage felt bad for him, suddenly. He knew that feeling

of being alone. And he didn't want O'Neil to keep on feeling it.

"There was once, a long time ago." Gage tried to find the words for a memory so terribly repressed. Maybe O'Neil would laugh at him anyway. "During high school prom. I had a schoolmate who was damn jealous of my looks."

O'Neil looked up, his forehead furrowed. He didn't say anything, so Gage continued, "Actually, I should start from the beginning. Ramsey used to be my best friend. We went to elementary school together, we sat with each other in middle school. I used to think, if one of us presented as alpha, and the other as omega, we'd get married and... whatever."

That sickened him to think about now. "Thing was, we both presented as alpha. We were still best friends and all that. Did projects together, pooled our money together and bought games. Except when we got to high school, he fell in love with an omega. And that omega fell in love with me."

O'Neil winced. "What happened next?"

Gage remembered the fights, he remembered Ramsey spitting poisonous words at him. And the arguments—so many of them. "We had a huge falling out. I didn't want the omega. He said I should hook him up with her. I tried pushing her toward Ramsey, but she wasn't interested. Ramsey thought I was telling her shit about him, so he started trying to backstab me.

"He spread rumors about me in school. He told the teachers I cheated on tests. He told our friends I slept with every fucking omega in our class."

O'Neil looked horrified. "Did you do anything about it?"

"Yeah. I pulled rank and told him to fuck off." Gage

huffed mirthlessly. "These looks get me some power, you know. I got most of them to believe me. 'Course, Ramsey was furious. Every lie he told, I tried to fix. The teachers loved me. Then he stopped being a twit, and I thought maybe we could be friends again."

Probably the stupidest thing Gage had done.

O'Neil looked wary, sympathetic, like he wanted to reach out and hold Gage's hand. "Except prom night happened."

"Yeah." Gage blew out a deep breath. "That."

Gage had worked a couple of part time jobs, trying to save some money so he could rent a nice suit for prom. Everyone had told him he'd be picked as Prom Alpha, and Gage didn't doubt them. He'd been close to the stage, Ramsey with him, when they'd called him up to receive his crown.

"Anyway, I got Ramsey to hold my drink. Then I went up on stage, and the next thing I knew, Ramsey yelled. And he climbed up onto the stage and threw my drink in my face. In front of the entire school."

O'Neil looked horrified.

"That wasn't even the worst part," Gage said, his heart heavy. "He'd pulled on a mask. And he'd pulled a jar of stuff out from somewhere—I didn't even know what it was. Until he emptied it all over my head and I realized it was piss. And it was still warm."

"That's awful." O'Neil grimaced.

Gage didn't look at him. He wasn't proud of that moment in his life. "He'd gotten some other friends of his to come up on stage. And they broke my nose and beat me up. In front of the whole school. I tried to fight back, but honestly, there were too many of them."

Those guys had punched Gage in the gut, they'd choked him and pulled off his pants and poured more piss on him, and at the end of it, Gage had been winded, beaten down into a crumpled heap.

"I couldn't even put my pants back on, they were so torn up." Gage forced a smile. "So I tried to make a joke out of it. Black eyes and all. The entire hall was so silent, you could hear a pin drop. And no one came forward to stop them."

Gage remembered the betrayal he'd felt. The bewilderment. The sinking realization that he wasn't strong enough to shove off all those guys. Then he'd felt the humiliation, he'd heard Ramsey's laughter even before he left the stage.

"Weren't they caught?" O'Neil asked, looking defeated.

Gage shook his head. "They had their scents suppressed. I should've realized something was up. No one tried to catch them."

The emcees had told him to go and wash the piss and blood off. After Gage had left the stage, they'd given the Prom Alpha crown to someone else. The stares and jeers he'd received in the following weeks almost made Gage stop going entirely.

He brushed off the memories, exhaling. O'Neil looked shaken. So Gage reached out, squeezing his arm. "I'm fine. It happened a long time ago."

For a moment there, he thought maybe O'Neil might've lost some respect for him, or maybe he'd lose interest in Gage entirely. But O'Neil just stared quietly at Gage for a long time. "I didn't know people hated you."

Gage shrugged. "Comes with the territory."

That only seemed to upset O'Neil more. He set the popcorn bowl aside. Then he scooted across the couch and pulled Gage into a tight hug.

"I'm glad it's over," O'Neil murmured, his glasses

bumping into Gage's ear, his body warm and soft against Gage's side. Despite his appearance, O'Neil's embrace was tight, strong, and... there was no judgment in him at all. Just a quiet comfort.

Gage couldn't remember the last time someone had given him a hug, just so they could comfort *him*. And a tension in his body—that he hadn't been aware of—uncoiled, taking his anxiety away. Gage relaxed. "I'm fine, really."

"Are you sure?" O'Neil's breath was warm on his ear. "It's okay to be upset."

"It's in the past," Gage said. As comfortable as this was, he wasn't sure if he wanted to return the hug. He thought... maybe he should. But he didn't have it in him to reach out, to trust someone enough that they could hurt him again.

O'Neil released him some time later, pausing with his face right in front of Gage, as though... what, he wanted to kiss Gage on the nose?

Gage wasn't sure how he felt about that. But O'Neil shook himself and pulled away, leaving cool air on Gage's skin. Gage missed the heat and pressure of his touch.

"I should get the popcorn," O'Neil said. "It's probably already cold."

"Nah, I'll get it. I told you I'd make popcorn."

O'Neil scowled. "No, you sit."

Gage rolled his eyes. "Not gonna."

O'Neil lunged off the couch, heading for the kitchen. Gage chased him and smacked him lightly on the ass. O'Neil yelped.

"What was that about?" He grabbed his asscheeks incredulously, as though he was trying to protect them from Gage.

"That was punishment," Gage said. "I'm making the popcorn."

O'Neil gaped. Then he turned and reached for the microwave, and Gage smacked his ass again. O'Neil grabbed the popcorn bag.

Gage alternated light smacks between his cheeks. O'Neil's was soft. It jiggled with every impact. And maybe Gage wanted to pat him there again. Just to see the way his body reacted to his every touch.

"You know, I never thought an ass could be this bouncy," Gage said.

O'Neil's ears turned pink. "I'm going to get the popcorn bowl. Apparently neither of us remembered it."

"No, I'm getting it," Gage said.

O'Neil hurried out of the kitchen like this was some kind of a race and the bowl was his prize. So Gage followed him out and smacked his ass again. He tapped one cheek, then the other, and then he tapped between them. O'Neil spun around with the bowl pressed against his hips, his cheeks red. "What're you doing?" he panted.

Right, Gage had gone too far. He held his hands up. "I figured it was just some bro fun. I'll stop."

O'Neil's shoulders sagged a little. Did he... want Gage to continue? Gage stole the bowl out of O'Neil's hands, and O'Neil squawked.

He hurried to the kitchen. He dumped the popcorn into the bowl, reheated it, and then sprinkled some powdered parmesan all over the popcorn. When he brought it back to the couch, O'Neil was back in his seat, a cushion tucked over his crossed legs.

There was a hint of musk in the air, but Gage couldn't be sure if it was his own arousal, or O'Neil's. "What're we watching?"

"You pick."

Gage scowled. Was this because of his prom memory? "I'm not picking a movie just because you pity me."

A grin crossed O'Neil's face. "How about we watch Bloody Hollows, then?"

Ugh. "Do we have to?"

"What about Teddy Comes Alive?" O'Neil scrolled to the poster of that movie.

"Hell, no. That's fucking creepy."

"The Birth of Dinosaurs?"

Gage frowned. "This is movie night, not documentary night."

O'Neil flipped through the movie reel, purposefully skipping over all the superhero movies. "What do you want to watch, then? What about this one about a rockstar—"

"I don't know. Something interesting." Because like hell Gage was going to admit what had caught his eye.

"What about..." O'Neil flipped back through the movie posters. "This one. The children's movie about meatballs."

Damn it. Gage's ears prickled. He wasn't going to ask for it. Animated movies were something he watched by himself, or when he was with his siblings.

O'Neil's smile grew. "That's it. We're watching this one."

Before Gage could stop him, he hit the Buy button.

"Hey," Gage protested.

"You like cartoons." O'Neil looked delighted. "You just can't admit it."

"They aren't cartoons," Gage muttered. "It's 3D animation. I did an animation class once when I was in school. It's pretty neat."

"Why do you get so embarrassed about it, then?" O'Neil watched him, but there was no judgment in his eyes. Just fondness. "Are you afraid it's not alpha enough?"

Yeah, basically that.

"Ramsey laughed at me when I talked about watching one of those," Gage admitted.

"Fuck him," O'Neil said. Then he paused, looking worriedly at Gage. "But not that way."

That made Gage laugh. "No, I wouldn't."

O'Neil grinned, leaning in. His gaze dropped to Gage's mouth, and for a second, he looked... like he wanted to kiss Gage. Except he yanked his gaze away and started the movie.

Gage wasn't sure what to think of that. He'd had some alphas hit on him before, but O'Neil... he seemed trustworthy. And kind. And vulnerable. And maybe... Gage could relax around him a little. Enough to share the popcorn, at least.

"Here." He took O'Neil's cushion away. For a second, O'Neil panicked—until Gage put the popcorn bowl in his lap. "That's for you."

O'Neil stared at the bowl, his eyes round. "All of it?"

"I'll steal some." Gage grabbed a handful. But O'Neil relaxed and smiled, turning his focus toward the movie.

About five minutes in, O'Neil leaned in, their arms brushing, his honey oak scent wafting into Gage's nose. The close contact felt good. It felt like something casual, like they could relax without committing to anything serious. Gage slung his arm across the back of the couch; O'Neil scooted closer so his bicep brushed Gage's side.

The characters in the movie threw around some bad food puns. Gage smiled; O'Neil snorted. Gage had thought maybe O'Neil might lose interest, but he was smiling both times Gage sneaked a glance at him.

Finally relaxing, Gage grabbed more popcorn, savoring the evening's peace.

It was sometime toward the middle of the movie, when the characters were trying to escape from a leaking boat, that Gage reached for more popcorn. This time, his hand encountered no puffy, airy snacks.

Gage curled his fingers around something soft—where was the popcorn? Why did it feel like fabric? And what was that firm thing underneath that fabric?

It felt like a cylinder. A firm bread stick? He squeezed it, thinking maybe he'd be up for some bread.

Funnily enough, it grew thicker. It was quite a handful, actually. Was it... hard? He could've sworn it was just firm a moment ago. Gage tried tugging the cloth away in his search for the mysterious bread stick. He couldn't get the cloth to peel off.

On the screen, the characters were leaping onto chocolate logs that had suddenly turned into crocodiles. One of them almost got bitten. The graphics were fantastic.

And the bread stick had... gotten as hard as a rock. Gage squeezed it again. What kind of bread was that?

He finally tore his eyes away from the movie, looking down. He found some gray fabric in his hand. It had wrapped around his bread stick, and there was a line across its tip that... was very definitely not bread-like.

In fact, that looked like a cock. It was heavy, like a cock. But it was far bigger than any other cock Gage had touched, save for his own.

Gage came to the sinking conclusion that he was, in fact, holding O'Neil's cock.

O'Neil was an alpha. Gage had grabbed him like popcorn.

As he stared, O'Neil jerked against his palm, a dark spot spreading across the fabric. Gage released him like he'd been burnt. "Fuck, I'm sorry. I didn't mean to."

O'Neil wheezed, his face red, his chest looking like it might burst. He grabbed a cushion off the floor and shoved it down onto his lap, his eyes locked on the TV. "It's fine," he rasped. "Watch the movie."

But Gage smelled the musk in the air now. He knew how it felt, having his own cock swell like that. He knew the tingle of arousal, he knew the feeling of his blood swooping between his legs.

His own body grew hot.

It shouldn't. He'd never been turned on by other alphas. O'Neil was the exception. Gage stared blankly at the screen, his focus shifting. Next to him, O'Neil swallowed, squirming uncomfortably.

For a while, nothing happened. Then the far corner of the cushion lifted, and Gage thought he saw O'Neil's hand slipping under the cushion. Then came the slow back-and-forth rhythm, the one Gage *definitely* knew.

He heard the hitch of O'Neil's breath, he saw when O'Neil parted his lips in pleasure, his musk rolling between them. Was he stroking himself through his shorts? Or had he pushed his hand inside, and it was skin on skin?

Gage shouldn't be curious. But he also remembered O'Neil moaning over his eggs. O'Neil looking so godsdamned pleasured.

He wanted to know if he could make O'Neil moan with his mouth. Besides, he had a favor to repay, right?

"I can help," Gage said.

O'Neil froze. "What?"

Gage nodded toward the cushion. Then he slid off the couch, kneeling in front of O'Neil. And he grasped the cushion, tugging at it.

O'Neil swore; his breath rushed out of him. For an instant, something flashed in his eyes. Something primal. Something ferocious.

He looked like he might roar and slam Gage into the floorboards, he looked like he wanted to cram his entire cock into Gage's mouth. Gage's instincts wanted to meet that challenge head-on, he wanted to prove that he would win that fight.

"Fight me," Gage rasped, yanking that cushion away.

O'Neil's cock shoved up between them, straining so hard against his shorts that Gage thought it would rip a hole straight through the fabric.

It was big. Ravenous. It felt like a threat and a challenge, and Gage's entire body tightened, preparing for a fight.

But O'Neil shoved his cock down, his eyes flashing. "I'm just going to bed."

His voice had turned husky, dangerous. Sexy.

Gage never thought he'd describe this man as *sexy*.

Then O'Neil stood, and Gage got a faceful of his musk. Held down, O'Neil's cock came within inches of his mouth. And for a second, O'Neil hesitated, his cock looking like it wanted to sate its hunger. Inside Gage.

What would that feel like?

"Good night," O'Neil growled.

Then he turned sharply and made for the stairs, his shorts clinging to his ass with every step.

What would that ass look like, spread open? Impaled on Gage's cock? Was his hole just as pink as an omega's? Just as tight?

Gage licked his lips, shoving down his suddenly-hard length.

He watched until O'Neil disappeared. Then he pumped his cock, feeling distinctly disappointed.

Why? Because he didn't get a chance to feel O'Neil come apart beneath him?

10

INSECURITIES

For the rest of the week, Ulric couldn't bring himself to face Gage.

Every morning, he listened for the sounds of Gage leaving the house. It was only when he was certain that Gage had driven off, that Ulric emerged from his study to make himself breakfast.

In the evenings, Ulric's alarm clock would ring. He'd jump and drop his reports, and change into his gym clothes. Ulric would wait for Gage to shut himself in his room, before sneaking out of his own house, getting into his car, and driving off.

He'd begun spending hours at the gym, just waiting for Gage to go to sleep. He'd start one of the relaxing bike rides through the autumn leaves, cycling as the minutes ticked by. Then, when he'd moved through all the difficulty levels, he'd head over to the bench press, doing a few reps. Then a few more.

Sometimes, he wished Gage would step into the gym like he had that one night. He wished that Gage would spot for him on the bench press again, he wished he

WEIGHT OF EVERYTHING

would get to see Gage up close, his pecs beautiful, his legs open around Ulric's head.

Ulric had noticed some new things in the other bedroom. Not the one with Gage's bed, but the empty one. Somehow, Gage had gotten a bench press in there, along with an exercise bike and a few other pieces of equipment. Most of which Ulric didn't even understand.

Gage had even stuck a note on the door. *Feel free to use these,* he'd written.

Ulric appreciated his generosity. The thing was, he did not want to attempt to use one of Gage's things—and somehow fall flat on his face. He wasn't even going to take a chance. Gage probably knew that, too.

This evening, Ulric slipped out through his front door, listening for Gage. The house was silent. So he hurried to his car, pausing when one of his neighbors jogged by with a dog.

"Hey." The man smiled, slowing down. He was an older alpha—Ulric had glimpsed him a couple times before. In fact, he almost looked familiar. "You moved in recently, didn't you? I'm Phil. My friends call me King."

King seemed friendly. Ulric hadn't been sure how well he'd fit into a street like this. If it was money they were concerned about, at least he had that. "Ulric O'Neil. I moved here from New York. And, uh. I've got a friend living with me. His name is Gage."

King shook his hand. "What a coincidence—I moved here from New York, too. Great to meet you guys. Hey, Crumbs. Don't get your paws all over him."

Crumbs seemed to be a mutt of some sort. He'd sniffed at Ulric, and then he'd all but pawed up Ulric's thigh, wagging his tail.

Warily, Ulric held still. He wasn't sure he liked dogs. He'd heard stories about dogs biting people, and he'd spent his life holding his breath whenever he passed them, thinking they might bite him, too. But if he was being logical, all the dogs he'd met had only ever wanted to sniff at him.

King tugged his dog back with a laugh. "Sorry. He can be a bit enthusiastic."

"That's fine," Ulric said.

King gave a friendly smile. "You haven't met the rest yet, have you? The rest of us on this street."

Actually, Ulric hadn't. He was a bit of a homebody. And he hadn't had great experiences with his neighbors in the past.

"Tell you what, we're having a small get-together tomorrow. Why don't you and Gage join us? Over at Phinny's place. 4PM. That one."

King nodded at the house at the end of the street. A tall iron fence surrounded that entire property—kind of foreboding.

"Sure," Ulric made himself agree. This was a new beginning. He figured he should get to know his neighbors, since he wasn't planning on returning to New York. "I'll see if Gage is free."

King gave him a thumbs-up. "Great. See you then."

King jogged off with Crumbs, leaving Ulric standing awkwardly in his driveway. Slowly, Ulric trudged over to his car, half-wishing he hadn't accepted the invitation. It meant he had to talk to Gage about it. Now. Because the get-together was tomorrow.

Ulric sighed. As much as he wanted to avoid Gage, he shouldn't just send Gage a text. He had to return to the house, look for Gage, and—maybe Gage might be half-naked, shower water dripping down his chest.

Okay, maybe Ulric wanted to go talk to him.

He swore at his traitorous body, trying not to feel

WEIGHT OF EVERYTHING

awkward. He hadn't met Gage face-to-face since Monday night. And it was now Friday evening.

How likely was it that Gage would've forgotten that disastrous night? Not likely at all.

Wishing he were more of an alpha, and less attracted to other alphas, Ulric stepped back into the house. The downstairs lights were still dimmed—was Gage upstairs? One of the bedroom lights was on. The one for Gage's home gym.

Ulric paused at the door, knocking before he peeked into the room. Then he froze.

Gage was lying flat on his bench press, lifting what looked to be a couple hundred pounds of weights.

He was shirtless. He was wearing a pair of shorts. And only that. Ulric wanted to taste every inch of his exposed skin.

Gage glanced at Ulric. He did a couple more pumps before saying, "Hey. Mind spotting for me?"

Ulric's throat went dry. "Um. Sure. I don't know how, though."

Gage heaved the barbell back onto its rack, nodding behind himself. "Stand here. You've seen me spot for you. Here, I'll demonstrate."

He sat up, his chest a glorious expanse of muscle, his abs so defined—he belonged on the front page of a magazine. Or on a billboard, or something.

Gage stood behind the bench press, showing Ulric the right posture for spotting. Then he demonstrated the hand holds, the motions, and got Ulric to do the same. When he was satisfied, he lay back down on the bench, stretching out like an exquisite spread of half-naked alpha. "I'm thinking of doing another thirty reps. You ready?"

"Yeah." Ulric held himself over Gage, his hands curled

under the barbell, ready to catch it in case it fell. Gage had a lot of control, though. He pumped the barbell in reps of five, his biceps flexing, his chest rising as he breathed in. Ulric focused on the barbell. For Gage's safety.

In fact, he was so focused on counting the reps, on trying not to look at Gage's bare chest, that it took him by surprise when Gage completed his thirtieth rep and leaned over, kissing Ulric's knee.

It was a soft, damp touch, there and gone.

Ulric spluttered. His entire face burned. Gage had kissed him. On the knee, of all places. "What was that for?"

"For spotting for me." Gage smiled, toweling off his sweat. "What did you come back to tell me?"

"Uh." Ulric struggled to remember. While he pawed through his memories, Gage lay back, his gaze roving over Ulric's chest. And Ulric felt far too heavy next to Gage's defined muscles and gorgeous thighs. "Lemme put some clothes on."

"You're fine like that."

"No, I'm not." Ulric turned, needing to grab a few shirts. Maybe a pair of pants. Just so he wouldn't look so... lacking.

"Hey, O'Neil." Gage grabbed his hand.

Ulric froze. He felt like some kind of virgin, blushing over every single thing. Just because he liked Gage, just because Gage had kissed him. And Gage was now holding his hand.

Sometimes, Ulric wished he wasn't such a sap.

"You look fine," Gage said softly.

That tore through Ulric's defenses faster than he could think.

"I'm fucking not." He whirled around, anger swelling

through his chest. "I'm fat, Gage. You know that. I know that. Nothing you say is going to change it."

Gage stood. "No, I meant it. You're fine."

Ulric stared. "What part of this is fine?" He glanced down at his belly, he tore off his T-shirt just to show Gage the flab on himself. "You fucking see this crap." Ulric jabbed a finger at himself, hating that he had to point this out to the most handsome alpha on the planet. "I can't lose it. I'm trying. I just want to look like everyone else, for fuck's sake, and I can't. Every time someone looks at me, this is what they see."

He panted, his adrenaline spiking, his heart thumping, trying to shore up his defenses because he didn't know how he'd get through this if Gage agreed that he was ugly.

Gage fell silent, his gaze dragging heavy down Ulric's body. Then he looked back up, and Ulric expected to see his revulsion.

But all Gage did was step forward, pulling Ulric flush against himself. Ulric's belly bumped against Gage's sweaty abs, their chests met when Gage leaned in—it felt like some sort of parody of Gage hugging a pregnant omega, except Ulric was just... fat.

Gage wrapped his arms tightly around Ulric. "You're fine as you are," Gage murmured.

"I'm fucking not—"

"Ulric." Gage shoved his fingers into Ulric's hair, pulling back to look into his eyes. "You're really fine."

That just sounded wrong. "How can you say that when you're the most—the most damn perfect alpha around?"

Ulric fought against the tightness in his chest, he fought against the burning in his eyes. All the years of being laughed at, all the years of trying to fade into the background—they didn't explain why Gage Frost was being nice to him.

"Ulric." Gage cupped his face, their gazes locking together. "Listen. I don't care about my looks, okay? And I don't care what you look like. We can be friends."

Ulric stared. Gage's words sank in. Gage had said 'friends'. And that felt like a different sort of gut-punch.

He breathed in deep, thankful that he hadn't fallen in love with Gage. That would hurt so much more. "Okay. Okay."

Ulric stepped away, but Gage hauled him in. Then he kissed Ulric on the cheek, a gentle, lingering touch that made Ulric's heart skip.

"This is us being friends, right?" Gage whispered, kissing Ulric's cheek again. "We're good?"

Ulric's head scorched. He wanted more of Gage's cheek kisses. And more of his hugs. He didn't even care that it made him seem desperate. "Yeah. Sure."

Gage smiled, releasing him. "Are you gonna work out, or shall we continue that movie?"

Ulric tried to focus on Gage's question. "Movie?"

"From Monday. Remember?"

The one Ulric had stopped watching when Gage had put his hand on Ulric's cock. Gage had squeezed it and tried to tug on Ulric's shorts, and Ulric had grown so hard, he'd thought Gage would be repulsed. Instead, Gage had volunteered to suck him off, he'd stared at Ulric's barely-hidden erection, his gaze roving heavy along it. That memory alone stole Ulric's breath. "Oh. Yeah, that."

Gage could never find out how many times Ulric had jerked off to him since that night. It had only been five days, and Ulric's cock was already sore.

Gage looked oddly at him. "Did you ever finish watching that movie?"

Ulric shook his head. "Did you?"

Gage shook his head, too, his smile rueful. "I was waiting for you so we could finish watching it together."

Ulric's heart tumbled. "No more popcorn."

Gage laughed. "Or I could hold the bowl. If you grab me, that'll be fair play."

Ulric gulped. That was too dangerous. He didn't only want to grab Gage—he wanted to lick him and taste him and milk him for every last drop of his come. And whatever Ulric looked like when he did that... he wasn't sure he wanted Gage to witness it. "I'll pass."

"Fine." Gage smiled, looking perfect. Ulric melted a little inside. "I'll shower, and then we'll continue our movie night."

"Fine." Ulric wrapped his discarded shirt around himself, still feeling self-conscious. Movie night sure sounded a lot better than spending hours alone at the gym. And maybe... Ulric might get to cuddle up with Gage, just a little.

That alone was enough to cheer him up.

11

THE BETTER-THAN-SEX COOK-OFF

"Ready?" Gage asked, cracking his knuckles.

"If you are." O'Neil—Ulric—didn't look too certain.

They'd discussed this last night. Early this morning, they had gone to the grocery store to get ingredients for their cook-off. They'd just gotten home, and there were still some hours to go before the visit to Phinny's.

So, it was time for the showdown.

Except O'Neil—*Ulric*—looked as though he regretted agreeing to this.

Gage sidled over, nudging him gently. "What're you worried about? The way I see it, I should be more worried about forking over the $200."

Ulric sighed. "You'll probably do this a lot better."

Well, Gage had grown up learning his mom's ribs recipe. And it was hands-down the best thing ever. He wouldn't have suggested the bet if he wasn't confident about winning. "We haven't started the cook-off yet," he said to make Ulric feel better. "For all you know, I'll take one bite of your meat and jizz all over."

Ulric froze, his eyes growing wide.

"Uh. I didn't mean it that way." Really, Gage hadn't. "Although I did bet that this was going to be better than the best sex you've ever had."

"You did." Ulric cracked a smile. "Promise?"

"Promise." Gage nudged him harder. "But c'mon, I'm sure your ribs are good, too. Make them good. Make me come."

Ulric flushed a vibrant red, but he growled, "Fine."

That thrilled Gage in a way he couldn't explain. He knew Ulric wanted him on some level. He felt the lingering electricity between them. He wasn't sure he wanted to reciprocate; it was dangerous.

But this friendship between them—it was nice. Last night, they'd sat together on the couch, and Ulric had cozied up against Gage's side.

They could still be friends, right? If Gage did him a few small favors here and there? Maybe sucked his cock a few times?

As long as he stopped Ulric from doing crazy things like fall in love?

He set his ribs in a pot, added some garlic, onion, and bay leaves, and covered the ribs with water. While he brought that to a boil, Gage toasted some peppers, before soaking them in some water so their skins would peel off more easily.

Then, since the ribs had to simmer for a while, Gage stole across the kitchen to spy on Ulric's prep. He found Ulric at the kitchen island, tenting some foil over his ribs.

"That's basically it," Ulric said. "Steak seasoning, and then I throw BBQ sauce on at the end."

Gage rumbled, imagining that taste. "Sounds good to me."

Ulric cheered up. He stuck the pan into the oven,

before peeking at the rest of the ingredients Gage had laid out. "Yours looks complex."

"Sometimes you need extra work for something to taste damn fucking good." Gage winked.

"Sage advice for basically everything in the world," Ulric said.

"Exactly."

There wasn't much else to do but wait while the meat cooked, so Gage opened the fridge, looking for a snack.

"Celery?" Ulric made a face when Gage pulled out the celery bundle—he hadn't touched the vegetable at all since Gage brought it home from the store.

"It's pretty good." Gage broke off a couple of stalks, rinsed them, and sliced them into sticks. "Want one?"

Ulric looked at the celery like it had grown tentacles. "It's awful."

"It's good for you." Gage took a bite. "Have you tried it recently?"

"No. I just remember being forced to eat them when I was a kid."

"Try it." Gage waved the celery sticks at him.

"That's too much." Ulric looked positively ill.

"Half?" Gage bit off part of a stick. Ulric seemed to waver, so Gage bit off more, and held it out. "One bite?"

Ulric reached for it, looking as though the celery might grow teeth and bite him. But their fingers brushed, and a jolt of *something* whispered up Gage's spine. Ulric sucked in a quick breath. Had he felt it, too?

"Eat it," Gage murmured.

Ulric rolled his eyes. "You sound like you're trying to tempt me into sin."

Gage laughed, rolling his hips. "Yeah, baby. Eat my celery stick. Imagine if someone said that in bed."

"Ugh." Ulric stared at the bite of celery for a long time, looking torn. He studied it along with Gage's mouth, and finally, carefully, pushed the celery bite past his lips.

"Tolerable?" Gage asked.

Ulric looked at the floor, his mouth working. Was he... feeling it up with his tongue? A blush rose up Ulric's neck. Then he chewed and swallowed. "It's... okay, I guess."

"Here, try another one. You might acquire a taste for it." Gage waved a full stick at him.

"Still too much." But Ulric looked slightly more convinced now. So Gage bit off half the stick, and handed it over.

Ulric still made a face as he ate it, but he was eating the thing. That was an improvement. Gage bit into his remaining stick, blinking when Ulric reached for that, too. Ulric hadn't even finished his previous stick. "Here, I'll get you more."

Ulric seemed agreeable to that, all the way until Gage sliced them into bite-sized pieces. Ulric made a face, turning away. "No, I've had enough."

"But these are tiny." Gage was confused. "No commitment at all."

"Nope. Enough." Ulric bit into the sticks Gage had handed him—he ate them from the sliced ends first, crunching through them all the way to where Gage had left teeth marks in the celery. There, he paused. Their eyes met.

"Why're you watching me?" Ulric asked.

Gage shrugged. "Just... making sure that you're eating your veggies."

Ulric scowled. "I'm eating them. You don't have to watch."

Then he stepped out of the kitchen, and it was odd that he was being defensive now.

Gage crept after Ulric, peeking around him. He found Ulric with that half-eaten celery, except he was touching the end with Gage's teethmarks, a tiny smile on his face.

Gage froze. *Oh.* "You're not falling for me, right?" he blurted.

The celery shot out of Ulric's mouth. "What?"

"This... This thing." Gage wriggled his finger between them both. "We're friends. That's it."

"Yeah." Ulric darted after the celery on the floor, his ears turning pink. "I just, uh."

"It'll pass," Gage said. He'd had friends and girlfriends who'd had crushes on him, and he knew how things would inevitably play out. Gage always ended things before they could get too serious.

Ulric had a crush on Gage—Gage knew that. And he also felt like he was maybe taking advantage of Ulric's generosity and feelings and everything, except... he couldn't bring himself to step away. It wasn't so often that Gage found someone his gut wanted to trust.

Ulric's blushing smiles looked really good on him. He was so quietly eager to be around Gage, and Gage... hadn't had a best friend in a long time.

That was probably why he was being this affectionate around Ulric. It wouldn't last, though. *Maybe we can pretend to be really good friends. I just need to remember that it'll end at some point.*

"Hey, let's do something together," Gage said.

Ulric gave him an odd look as he headed back into the kitchen. "What?"

"I don't know. There's still a while to go before the ribs are done." Gage watched as Ulric rinsed off his fallen bite of celery. This time, Ulric crunched up the celery and swallowed it, and he ate the other stick he'd taken from Gage.

It would be a really odd game, getting Ulric to eat his veggies. It seemed that all Gage had to do was take a bite out of anything, and give the rest to him. But Gage wasn't in the mood for more snacks right now.

"I know," he said. He waited until Ulric had swallowed the last of his celery. Then he *pounced*, shoving Ulric bodily against the island counter.

Ulric tensed; Gage dug his fingers hard into Ulric's ribs and *tickled*. Ulric froze up even more; he looked like he was struggling real hard not to react, he looked like he was on the verge of breaking out into squeals.

So Gage cheated and kissed his cheek. Ulric snorted and broke, and Gage felt the tremble of his body, he felt Ulric dissolving into helpless laughter, even as he smacked Gage's hands away, hard. That hurt a little. But it wasn't enough to stop Gage from returning, tickling him again.

Ulric doubled over, his face crashing against Gage's chest, his arms going up to try and defend himself. So Gage tried harder. The worst of his tickles.

"Quit it," Ulric gasped between his laughter, his eyes flashing, his teeth bared in a snarl. Then he reared up and shoved back at Gage, and Gage's back hit the opposite counter.

Ulric lunged, digging *his* fingers into Gage's ribs, hard enough to bruise. Gage wasn't ticklish. But because he wasn't distracted, he saw the sudden ferocity in Ulric's eyes. The dangerous gleam, the part of him that was alpha, through and through.

Gage's instincts lit up that threat. He planted his hands on Ulric's chest and heaved him off, and then he followed Ulric, punching him lightly in the jaw. Enough just to offend, not enough to hurt.

Ulric snarled, swinging his fist. Gage barely blocked it—there was power behind that strike. It would've hurt pretty bad. Except that only raised the stakes.

Gage gave a sharp smile. "Try harder, Ulric."

12

THE OTHER SIDE OF ULRIC

Gage yanked Ulric closer and caught him in a headlock; Ulric *moved*. Gage felt his balance slip; he tumbled forward, falling flat onto his back. The shock jarred his entire body. But the surprise and approval he felt—that was something Gage didn't come across so often.

He hadn't known that Ulric O'Neil could throw him onto his back *that* easily.

"No more tickles," Ulric growled, his eyes narrowed.

Gone was the easygoing shyness. Gone was the part of Ulric that blushed and yielded. Gage had glimpsed this side of him a few times before, but it was out in the open now, a creature that Gage wanted to tame. He wanted this side of Ulric to yield to him. Because.

"I can't promise no tickles." Gage rolled onto his feet, rounding the island counter. "You'll have to fight me for it." He stepped out of the kitchen, crooking his finger at Ulric.

Ulric followed him, ferociousness rippling off his skin, all alpha threat. Gage knew there were omegas out there who would drop their pants, if they saw Ulric like this.

How much hotter could Ulric get? Could this alpha... burn off *Gage's* pants?

Gage hadn't gotten far when Ulric lunged. Gage barely managed to twist around; Ulric slammed him into the wall, knocking the breath out of his lungs. Gage's instincts roared at him to get the upper hand.

"Playing rough, huh?" Gage growled.

"I'm gonna win this," Ulric hissed, shoving their abdomens together, his breath falling hot on Gage's lips.

"Prove it."

Beneath the softness of Ulric's body, he was warm, strong. Gage grabbed Ulric's arm and flipped them around, crushing Ulric against the wall. Ulric's breath rushed out of him; his eyes darkened.

He raised his fist to punch Gage; Gage blocked it and punched him back. Ulric snarled, shoving Gage backward. Gage stumbled; Ulric shoved him again so he lost his balance and fell. He hit the floor, pain jolting through his bones. Gage barely had time to roll over—he needed to get his feet under him.

Except Ulric barreled into his back and slammed him flat against the floor, and he sat down hard on Gage's ass, one hand pinning Gage's shoulders down, the other locking Gage's arm behind his back.

"I win," Ulric whispered.

And, with his weight firmly planted on Gage's ass, Ulric rolled his hips—a slow, heavy slide of fabric on fabric. But not only that. There was something distinctly hard between them, something thick and long, that pushed an indent into Gage's asscheek.

Gage knew what it was. He knew what it smelled like.

WEIGHT OF EVERYTHING

And he knew Ulric wanted to thrust it inside him. Probably every single inch of it.

"Fuck," Ulric hissed, sitting back so his cock no longer rubbed up against Gage. "Sorry. Didn't mean to do that."

But his voice was husky; Gage could smell the musk rolling off him now.

Gage owed him a favor. And this... he wouldn't mind it.

Ulric made to leave—Gage caught his wrist. Ulric paused, his stare burning.

"Whatever you want to do, do it," Gage murmured.

Ulric didn't answer for a long moment. "What?"

"I'm open to trying it," Gage said, meeting Ulric's gaze over his shoulder. "As long as you keep it outside my clothes. I don't care if you use me to get off. Jizz all over me. You won."

Ulric swallowed loudly, his chest heaving. For the longest moment, he couldn't tear his eyes away from Gage. He glanced down at his own spread legs, and the thick bulge that strained behind his pants. His neck flushed.

"I can't," Ulric choked.

"Yes, you can." Gage rolled his own hips—just slightly, since it wasn't easy with Ulric's weight on him. "Put your cock on me."

Ulric went so still, Gage didn't think he even breathed. "What's in this for you?"

"I'm helping you out."

"I don't need help," Ulric growled.

"Think of it as a prize."

"You'd let me—" Ulric bit his words off. "As a *prize?*"

He was retreating behind his politeness and his mild

manners, and as adorable as it was, Gage wanted to see that *other* side of him again.

He pushed himself up, arching his spine as far as it would go. "Look, this is the only chance you'll get," Gage offered. "To rut against me. Wherever you want. You can even take my pants off. Leave my boxers on."

Ulric's breath rushed out of him. "You can't be serious."

"Get off me. I'll show you."

Slowly, disbelievingly, Ulric leaned his weight to the side, freeing Gage. Gage unbuckled his belt. Shoved down his pants. They caught on his boxers, dragging them partway down his ass. Ulric gulped.

Gage let him look. Ulric's admiration felt nice, actually. Gage pulled his pants down further; this tugged his boxers completely off his ass. Ulric's stare scorched.

It was a good ass, Gage knew. He'd been working on his glutes lately. He gave Ulric another couple seconds. Then he pulled his boxers back over his asscheeks, and lay down on the floor. "There."

Ulric bit off his groan. "You can't be ser—"

Gage pushed his ass up into the air, and Ulric snarled. He was upon Gage in a heartbeat, grasping Gage, slamming their hips together, his cock a prominent line against Gage's ass.

Gage's instincts told him he was on the wrong end, they told him he needed to turn around, to put *his* cock inside Ulric's ass. But he'd promised Ulric. And Ulric panted above him, rocking their hips together, his bulge pushing between Gage's cheeks.

It was a lot thicker than Gage remembered. A lot more dangerous. It wouldn't fit inside him.

"Take it out," Gage murmured.

"I'll fucking blow if I take it out," Ulric hissed.

"Then blow," Gage snarled. "Do you want this ass, or not?"

"Fuck." Ulric pushed harder, and Gage felt his cheeks open up. Ulric's expression changed. His gaze turned dark, hungry, demanding, a sort of depravity that struck a chord with Gage's own instincts.

"Turn away," Ulric whispered. "I don't want you to look."

"Why not?"

"Just fucking *do it*."

How many people ever saw this side of Ulric? Gage didn't know. But he turned to stare at the floor, his entire attention locked onto this man.

Ulric's breath shook out of him as he rubbed his bulge between Gage's cheeks. He stroked Gage's ass through his boxers, his touch reverent.

For a long while, that was all he did—slide his covered cock against Gage, back and forth, not enough pressure for anything. Then he grasped Gage's ass through his boxers, he pressed his thumbs against Gage's cheeks, trying to open him there.

Gage stopped breathing. There was a layer of fabric between them. But he still felt vulnerable like that—thin cotton was no match against an alpha, especially one as hungry as Ulric looked.

Ulric's thumb slipped lower. For a second, Gage thought Ulric might reach his hole, and Ulric might touch him there. But Ulric pulled away.

"You're really okay with this," Ulric rasped.

"Yes," Gage growled.

He wasn't sure when his own voice had changed. But he sure as hell heard when Ulric unbuckled his belt. Then came the pop of his jeans button, and the rasp of the zipper.

Ulric was taking his cock out. It was bare, hard for Gage. Gage knew what it looked like, growing fuller now that it wasn't being constrained. Growing redder.

He smelled musk. A lot of it. And he also smelled Ulric's honey oak scent mixed in with his own.

Was he horny, himself? He didn't know. His pulse was pounding everywhere, and Gage figured it was adrenaline.

Then came a soft pressure, one that rested against his crack. Gage felt the shift of Ulric's body, he felt that heavy length rubbing against him, muffled through the cotton.

He'd never touched another alpha's hard-on before Ulric's. It felt a lot bigger than he would expect.

"Fuck," Ulric whispered.

The pressure grew heavier; Ulric pushed his cock more firmly against Gage. Heat soaked through Gage's boxers and into his ass. Then Ulric ground deeper, easing Gage's cheeks apart with his cock.

Gage stopped breathing. He'd done this with omegas before. He'd let them feel his cock, he'd teased them with what he would thrust inside. And here was Ulric doing the exact same thing, except now Gage was on the receiving end.

And holy fuck, Ulric was big.

Ulric snarled, suddenly. He leaned in, anchoring his arm across Gage's chest. Then he drove his cock hard between Gage's cheeks, like how he'd thrust inside, and he forced Gage's asscheeks completely open. His cock ground against one spot in particular—that had to be Gage's hole, because it tingled with every thrust against it. Then Ulric snapped his hips, his breath growing ragged as he rutted against where he wanted Gage to stretch for him.

Ulric groaned, a feral, throaty sound that went between Gage's legs.

There was one layer of cotton between them. Thin enough that Ulric could probably tear through it with his cock. What would happen if he broke that barrier? If his head shoved against Gage's hole, and it pushed inside?

Gage's cock grew so thick, it hurt. He didn't know why. Or how. "Damn it, O'Neil," he snarled.

Ulric swore and pinned Gage down, and his thrusts turned desperate, his cock sliding against Gage's hole, back and forth, back and forth.

Like how he'd fuck Gage, given the chance.

"You don't own me," Gage growled.

"Fuck yes, I do," Ulric hissed. And he *thrust,* Gage's boxers so thin that it may as well not be there at all, because he felt the heat and hardness of Ulric's cock, he felt its hunger and need, he felt the tap-tap-tap of Ulric's balls against his taint.

Gage ached. It was only when he reached down to rub the pain away, that he realized he was so hard he could burst.

Because an alpha was rubbing up against his ass, because Ulric was so close to ripping through Gage's boxers, and fucking inside him.

With each stroke, Ulric shoved Gage's cock against the floorboards. Pleasure twisted up his spine.

Gage didn't want to jerk himself off. It didn't seem right. But Ulric held him down and rutted against his ass, his breathing going ragged, his precome soaking through Gage's boxers, smearing wet against his skin.

"Mine," Ulric hissed. His breathing stuttered. He pushed his tip hard against Gage's hole, demanding to be let inside. Gage almost yielded. He almost asked Ulric to stretch him out.

He almost wished… that Ulric would rip through that fabric.

Ulric swore, his fingers grasping Gage bruisingly-tight. Then he fucked a final time against Gage, and wetness spurted through Gage's boxers onto his hole, at the same time Ulric roared, grinding the entire length of his cock against Gage, smearing his come all over Gage's ass, as though he was trying to push his come *inside*.

Something broke within Gage. He didn't know if it was because of Ulric's pleasure, or his need, or the unexpected mind-blowing hotness of Ulric's come between his asscheeks. Ulric fucked against him, and pleasure ripped through Gage's body, all the way down to his cock, electricity jolting up his spine.

Gage came and came, waves of bliss rolling down his nerves. He could only ride it, his entire body tense, until the crescendo faded and he could breathe again.

Ulric leaned away, the sudden loss of his heat a shock against Gage's skin. Gage turned, searching him out. "Where'd you go?" he mumbled. He couldn't get up from the floor.

Ulric flushed. "Cleaning up."

He was shoving his cock back into his pants, his knot already starting to swell. Gage eyed the redness of it—he'd been right about how it looked. And it looked good.

Before Ulric, Gage had never thought that about an alpha's cock before. He wasn't sure what this turn of events meant.

"I'll get you a washcloth." Ulric wobbled to the kitchen. He returned with a folded-up dishtowel, handing it to Gage.

The towel was warm. It was exceedingly comfortable, actually. Gage pulled down the back of his boxers; Ulric flushed, yanking his gaze away.

"Nothing you haven't seen," Gage said.

He scrubbed off the come from between his cheeks, trying not to remember how hot that had been. He probably needed a shower. Then he pushed himself upright, and winced at the white streaks on the floorboards. Funny how that had worked. His boxers did a poor job of keeping come from going anywhere.

Ulric froze. "Wait."

Gage wiped off the come, but he couldn't hide the length straining behind his own clothes. "I couldn't tell you how that happened," Gage admitted. "I've never slept with an alpha in my entire life."

"Oh." Ulric's face turned pink. Still adorable.

When had Gage started thinking he was adorable, anyway?

"I'll grab a shower," Gage said. "I stink."

"Same here." Ulric looked away, and Gage pulled up his pants, climbing the stairs awkwardly so he could get to the bathroom.

Fifteen minutes later, Gage returned to the kitchen. The house was starting to smell like delicious cooking meat. Ulric was nowhere to be found.

Gage prepped the sauce from his mom's recipe, just waiting for him. He gave Ulric another half-hour. When Ulric still didn't show up, Gage went back upstairs, knocking on the master bedroom door. "Ulric?"

"Yeah?" Ulric sounded hesitant. He'd retreated back into his shell again.

"Can I come in?"

A pause. "Sure, I guess."

Ulric's bedroom was lit by a large window above his headboard. It smelled like a mix of honey oak and old musk, and bookshelves lined one wall. A fancy laptop stand perched over his bed, surrounded by clothes strewn haphazardly across the sheets.

Ulric saw Gage looking and tensed, snatching the clothes off. But not before Gage recognized one of *his* shirts in that pile. It was a robot movie T-shirt his sister had given him one Christmas. "Hey. Do we have the exact same shirt, or is that mine?"

Ulric flushed a bright red. "It's, um. I found it when I was doing my laundry."

He was lying. Gage had thought it odd that he'd smelled honey oak in his room the other day. Come to think of it, he didn't remember putting that shirt in the wash. "You took it from my laundry hamper?"

"I-I was just curious." Ulric shoved the shirt at Gage. "I was going to return it to you."

He looked so embarrassed that Gage's heart melted. "Naw, it's fine. You can borrow it."

"No, here." Ulric folded the shirt and handed it over.

Gage took it, studying the closed-off look on Ulric's face. Was Ulric planning to steal another shirt from Gage's dirty laundry, just to replace this one?

He pressed it to his nose, drawing a deep breath. And he found an odd mix of smells on it—his own pine, Ulric's honey oak, and a trace of old sweat. And musk.

It smelled good, if Gage was being honest.

There was a splotch of something crusty on one corner of the shirt. Gage picked at it, puzzled. He didn't remember leaving a stain.

"Shit, shit. No," Ulric blurted, his face turning the brightest red Gage had seen on him so far. He snatched the shirt out of Gage's hands. "Lemme wash that before you wear it again."

Gage studied him, tickled by this alpha who got so much more embarrassed than any omega he'd dated.

"Naw, it's fine. I can throw it in with the rest of my load. Any idea what that crusty stuff is?"

Ulric choked on his spit. "Um. I, uh. I spilled something on it."

Ah. Gage bit down his smile. "You were getting really worked up, huh?"

"I—" Ulric looked like he might burst. "Yeah."

Before this, if anyone had told Gage that an alpha would jerk off onto his shirt, he would've been really weirded-out. But now that he'd gotten used to the idea of giving Ulric sexual favors, now that he'd come just from Ulric grinding against his ass... He rather liked the thought of Ulric being intimate with his shirts.

It was a bro thing, right? Giving your best friend a shirt to help him work off some steam?

Gage decided that he could contribute to Ulric's cause. "Here, I'll give you this one in exchange."

He stripped off the new, clean shirt he'd just pulled on after his shower. It smelled like pork and spices. Better than old sweat.

Ulric groaned. "No, put that back on."

"Why?" Gage scrunched it up, sniffing at it. "Doesn't smell as bad as that old one."

"You need to wear a shirt." Ulric looked around the room, as though he was trying his best not to stare at Gage.

So he liked how Gage's chest looked, too? Gage fought down his smile, deciding to go easy on him. They still had to decide on the results of the cook-off, after all. And after that, the house visit that Ulric didn't sound so certain about.

Gage had found that strange. Ulric seemed to come from a wealthy family. Why would visiting some neighbors make him uneasy?

13

THE BETTER-THAN-SEX COOK-OFF, PART 2

Ulric waited until Gage had stepped outside and shut the bedroom door. Then he pulled a pillow over his face, groaning into it. *I went and rutted against him. I came all over his ass.*

That had been one of the most glorious moments of his life. Having the freedom to do whatever he wanted to Gage. Ulric had barely stopped himself from burying his face in Gage's ass, he'd told himself he wouldn't kiss Gage there, because it was far too intimate.

But he'd humped Gage's crack, he'd pushed his cock against Gage's hole, and even now, the memory still gave him a giddy rush.

How many alphas got to say, *I let Gage Frost feel my cock?*

Except Gage also knew just how twisted Ulric was now. Ulric tried not to think about that. He tried not to remember his mom snapping, *It's just a phase. You'll grow out of it.*

Maybe Gage would just assume that Ulric hadn't had

an omega in too long. Maybe he wouldn't think Ulric was a freak.

Ulric rubbed his face, his heart pattering nervously. *Just pretend nothing's wrong. Fake it 'til you make it.*

Suddenly filled with the urge to eat something just to escape his anxiety, Ulric bit his lip. He didn't want Gage to see him stuffing his face. But he also didn't want to feel this uncomfortable in his own skin.

Ulric pulled on a dress shirt to hide his body better. He styled his hair, too. And shaved. In fact, he made sure he looked good enough to attend a formal event. And now, at least, he appeared to be in control.

Then he crept down the stairs, trying to listen out for Gage.

How was he supposed to act around Gage now? When Gage knew that Ulric had been using his shirt to jerk off? His face burning, Ulric stepped into the silent kitchen.

Gage was tucked into the corner, the one spot Ulric couldn't see from the doorway. Ulric froze. Gage glanced up from his phone—his gaze coasted appreciatively down Ulric's body. Ulric's heart felt like it might burst.

Gage smiled. "Hey. Ready for the taste test?"

Ulric fumbled for a reply. Why did Gage have to be so damn beautiful all the time? He composed himself, checking his own ribs. "I guess. Mine won't be ready for another couple hours, though."

"That's okay. We'll taste yours when it's done."

"But that isn't fair, is it? If we don't do a side-by-side comparison?"

Gage winked. "You'll get extra points for that."

Judging by the way Gage's ribs smelled, Ulric would need every extra point he could get. He watched as Gage brought his skillet to the island counter.

In addition to being simmered in broth, Gage's ribs looked like they'd been further stewed in a thick red sauce. When Gage began slicing them up, the meat yielded easily beneath his steak knife, falling off the bone. Ulric's mouth watered. "That looks amazing."

Gage grinned. "Doesn't it?"

He laid the ribs carefully on a pair of white plates. Then he slid one across the counter to Ulric. And he waited.

Ulric frowned. "Aren't you going to taste it?"

"I already know what it's like." Gage looked expectant. "Try it and tell me what you think."

Ulric picked up a rib—it was piping hot. He couldn't resist sinking his teeth into the tender meat. Flavors exploded across his tongue. Beneath the notes of oregano and thyme, he tasted peppers and a hint of garlic.

None of the spices overpowered each other—instead, they'd melded together like an orchestra in his mouth, and the juicy pork fell apart between his teeth in the very best of ways.

Where had Gage—Gage and his *ribs*—been all his life?

Ulric groaned, his eyes rolling back. He inhaled the rest of the meat and went on to attack the next rib. He licked his fingers and sucked lightly on the ends of the bones, chasing every drop of that glorious, meaty flavor.

Then he looked at Gage's plate, feeling guilty for wanting that, too.

Gage smiled, nudging it over. Ulric stared. "But that's yours."

Gage nodded at the skillet. "Still plenty left."

Ulric bit off his moan, carefully picking up a third piece. He knew he should stop. But the moment he sank his teeth into that perfectly-cooked meat, Ulric knew he'd only leave the kitchen when Gage took the ribs away.

He didn't want Gage to taste the ribs that were still going in the oven—these had to be award-winning. They'd put Ulric's attempts to shame. Ulric made himself set down his third bone, licking his fingers clean.

"There's one left." Gage nodded at the fourth rib.

"That's yours," Ulric muttered. But gods, did he want it, too.

Gage laughed. Then he picked up the last serving, and Ulric's heart sank. Yeah, that was fine. He should share his food.

Gage stepped over, wrapping his arm around Ulric's shoulders.

"Are you seriously going to eat that in front of me?" Ulric blurted.

Gage huffed. "Do you think that poorly of me?" And he leaned in, rubbing the juicy fourth rib against Ulric's lips.

Heat blazed through Ulric's face. "What—"

"C'mon." Gage smiled. "I want to hear you eat it."

"There's nothing to hear!"

Gage pushed the end of the rib into Ulric's mouth. Ulric's thoughts ground to a halt. Gage had done that. He'd actually pushed his meaty bone into Ulric.

Ulric tried not to think about what else Gage could push into him. This was just food. Nothing sexual.

He wrapped his lips around the pork, biting off whatever he could. Its decadent flavor burst through his mouth, Ulric moaned and sucked that meat off its bone, working to get every last scrap off.

"Fuck," Gage growled. "Do you suck on meat like that all the time?"

"Just yours," Ulric said around the clean end of the

bone. Then he realized what he'd blurted, and he wanted the floor to swallow him. "I mean. Just your meat. Your ribs. Fuck."

He shoved Gage off, so pissed with himself that he wanted to storm out of the kitchen. No more ribs.

"Hey," Gage said, stopping him in his tracks. "Just one question before you go."

Ulric turned, wishing he could stop humiliating himself in front of Gage. "What?"

"The real question, the one that we were betting on. You haven't answered it. Were these ribs better than the best sex you've ever had?"

Ulric froze. They were. Gage was watching him carefully, and Ulric didn't know if Gage could read it from his face, just like that.

He glanced out the kitchen doorway, wanting to say that, yes, all the sex he'd ever had was pretty mediocre. Except he glimpsed the dining room, the spot on the floor where he'd ridden Gage to orgasm.

That was the exception. And it had been even better than Gage's ribs. Better than Gage pushing his meaty bone into Ulric's mouth.

"The short answer is yes," Ulric muttered, his ears prickling.

"The long answer?" Gage smiled; Ulric's resolve weakened.

He shouldn't tell Gage how much he'd enjoyed that romp. Ulric pulled out his wallet, lobbing it over. "There. Take your two hundred bucks. Leave me alone."

Gage caught his wallet. Ulric stalked out of the kitchen, flopping onto the living room couch. He would've gone back to his work, except he couldn't stop thinking about how much he'd fucked up in one single day. So much for dressing up.

A couple minutes later, Gage emerged from the kitchen, scrutinizing something. "Were you eighteen when you had this pic taken? You were a pretty cute kid."

Ulric's heart sank. Of all things, Gage had to dig out his driver's license with that horrible photo? "Why're you looking at that?"

Ulric regretted ever having that photo taken. That was before he'd had his braces done—he'd smiled too wide, and his crooked teeth had been immortalized in that photo. Back then, he'd also been fat—not so different from how he was now.

Gage sat on the couch next to him, still looking at his photo. Ulric scrubbed his face. "Give it back, Gage. Stop looking."

But Gage held up the driver's license, comparing Ulric's past to his present self. Ulric winced. He was on the fast track to no more sex with Gage Frost, ever.

"Gage."

"You're just as cute as you were back then." Gage tucked Ulric's driver's license back into its plastic sleeve, the one with a cartoon duck sticker strategically pasted so it would cover up his old photo.

"I'm not cute."

"Yes, you are." Gage returned the license to its original pocket. Then he counted out his $200, pocketed it, and returned the wallet to Ulric. "Why wouldn't I call my best friend the cutest person ever?"

Ulric's heart missed a beat. They were best friends now? "Because that's just weird."

Gage shuffled over, bumping their arms. Ulric tried not to pay attention to the skin contact, he tried not to fill his lungs with Gage's pine scent. But the more their bodies touched, the more he wished he could have this man.

"When will your ribs be ready?" Gage asked.

"Two more hours."

"Want to watch a movie? I'll pick Bloody Hollows."

Ulric stared. "Why would you want to watch that?"

"So I can scream, and you'll get to be all alpha and comfort me." Gage grinned. "No?"

Ulric tried to wrap his mind around that. "You're kidding."

"Nope." Gage stuck out his pinky finger. "Promise me you won't laugh if I scream."

Despite his doubts, Ulric linked their pinkies together. "I promise."

He bought the movie and started it. Like they had the other night, Gage leaned against him, his warmth soaking into Ulric's arm.

The movie began with a lightning strike just above a creaky old house, the surrounding trees rustling ominously. Gage grimaced.

"It's not so bad," Ulric said. "Horror movies like doing this."

"But it's telling me that everyone will end up dying."

Ulric shrugged. "Probably."

Gage sighed. "I hate it when the good guys die, though."

"Same here."

"Then why do you watch it?" Gage seemed confused. "Why not watch something with a happy ending?"

Ulric tried to find the words to explain himself. "Because it feels real enough that I don't have to think about real life for a bit. It's nice when all I have to be scared of is whether the zombies will eat me."

Gage stared at him for a long moment. Then he linked their fingers together and snuggled closer. He kissed Ulric's shoulder. "I'll stop them from eating you."

Ulric's heart skipped. "I'd do the same for you."

Gage smiled, and they settled into the movie. Like Gage had warned, he tensed up through the show. He swore and jerked at the jump scares, he gripped Ulric's hand painfully tight when some of the good guys were killed.

Ulric leaned in to comfort him, kissing the back of Gage's hand. Gage answered by pressing kisses to Ulric's knuckles.

They were being friends. Kisses were just a part of that, right?

When the ending credits began to roll, Gage sagged into the couch, looking exhausted. "That was better than I expected."

"Because not everyone died?"

"Because I wasn't watching it alone." Gage angled a warm smile at Ulric; that warmth went all the way to Ulric's toes.

"Want to watch another?" Ulric teased.

"No." But Gage was still holding Ulric's hand, and they were leaning against each other, relaxed. "Thanks for not laughing at me."

"To be fair, you didn't scream," Ulric pointed out.

"Damn near did a few times."

Ulric laid his head on Gage's shoulder, chuckling. "I've screamed, too, you know. It's okay to scream. That's why they're called horror movies."

Gage huffed, but he leaned in, kissing Ulric's temple. "I'll remember that."

He didn't have to kiss Ulric there. Ulric's heart fluttered. He stroked the back of Gage's hand—it was large and strong, his fingertips calloused. Like the rest of his body, Gage's hands looked better than Ulric's, too.

It felt like all of these moments came from borrowed

time; sooner or later, Gage would get tired of Ulric, and start looking for an omega. Someone better, someone who could give him a family. The things a normal person would want.

"What's wrong?" Gage murmured.

Ulric shook his head. "Nothing."

"That's not nothing. You look sad." Gage turned, at the same time Ulric's phone alarm went off—loud and jarring in the quiet room.

Ulric jumped. But he was also secretly glad for the distraction. "Looks like my ribs are done. The house smells like meat."

Gage narrowed his eyes. Ulric hurried away to the kitchen, forcing a smile onto his face. Gage didn't need to know how he felt.

He pulled his ribs out of the oven, picking the foil carefully open. Steam billowed into the air. When it cooled enough that he could pry off the rest of the foil, Ulric stuck a fork in the meat—it all but fell off the bone.

Gage rumbled his approval. "It looks good."

So Ulric handed him the fork, heading to the fridge for his BBQ sauce. "It's better with this, I think."

Gage was already picking a chunk of meat off the bone. He blew on it, and then popped it into his mouth, his eyelids slipping shut. "Mm. Pretty damn good, O'Neil."

Ulric laughed, the ball of nervous energy in his chest unraveling. *Gage likes it.* "It's ribs. They're pretty easy if you give them some time. But it's nothing like the one you made." Ulric shrugged. "I would've lost, either way."

Gage met his eyes, giving him such a fond look that Ulric had to break their stare, his face burning up. "You made this," Gage murmured. "I'm not comparing it to mine."

"That's like you saying I'm cute," Ulric muttered. "Shit about not comparing to yourself."

Gage reached over and hugged him from behind. Ulric yelped. Gage's solid chest brushed his back; his arms were warm and strong around Ulric's body—all the parts of himself he was ashamed of.

"To be honest," Gage whispered in his ear, "I like all of this." Gage ran his hand down Ulric's side, along all his curves. "More to hold."

Ulric's blush scorched all the way to the back of his head. "That's just bullshit."

"You're not the one holding you, so that's not a valid point." Gage nuzzled Ulric's ear, hugging him tighter. "I'd love to hug you all day, every day."

Ulric's breath stuck in his throat. "If you keep saying things like that, I'm going to hold you to it. Extra rent. Five minutes of hugs a day."

Gage laughed. The sound vibrated through Ulric's back—so very lovely. "What about the days when our schedules clash?"

"Then you'll make up for it another day." Ulric thought maybe Gage might say it was crazy, but Gage just held him tighter.

"Deal."

"I'm going to make a spreadsheet for it," Ulric said. "And I'm going to circle all the days you don't pay up with your hugs."

Gage laughed again. "You know, they say everyone has their bad sides. Is this your bad side? You want hugs on a schedule?"

Ulric snorted. "You think *that's* my bad side?"

"Yup."

"How should I change my bad side, then?"

"Unscheduled hugs!" Gage shrugged. "I don't know.

It doesn't matter to me, actually. Schedule it. Whatever makes you happy."

Ulric stared, unable to believe all the acceptance Gage was showing him. He wouldn't question it—if he looked at everything too closely, it might fall apart. Instead, he pretended that he was living in a world where everything turned out perfect.

A world where Gage liked touching him.

He looked at Gage's arms wrapped around his belly, Gage's fingers lightly stroking his side. Gage didn't know it, but every brush sent an explosion of tingles through Ulric's skin.

It was a lot more than anyone else had given him. His throat tightened.

"Don't fall in love, okay?" Gage murmured against Ulric's hair, his breath warm. "We'll just be best friends."

"I promise," Ulric said, his heart squeezing.

He hoped like crazy he wouldn't break his word.

14

GAGE DOESN'T REALIZE IT, BUT

Gage looked sidelong at the alpha beside him. He'd been watching Ulric for the past half-hour, but little had changed. Despite his smile, Ulric was still tense.

"What's wrong with visiting the neighbors?" Gage asked.

Ulric jerked out of his thoughts. "Nothing."

Gage reached over, rubbing his neck. "Worried that they'll reject your ribs?"

Ulric hugged the casserole dish closer to himself. "Maybe."

They were walking down the street to the house at the end—really, with all the rooms that had been added over the years, it looked more like an eccentric wizard's haphazard mansion.

"Worried that they won't like you?" Gage asked.

"Kind of." Ulric chewed on his lip.

It wasn't normal for an alpha to be this uncertain. Gage had come across plenty of alphas in his life. Alphas tended to be confident, they tended to be straightforward and aggressive, and unafraid of anything. On the surface, anyway.

So Ulric being uneasy like that... It sent red flags up in Gage's mind. "Did you have bad neighbors?"

Had someone hurt Ulric in the past?

A low snarl of anger rose through Gage's chest. Before Ulric could answer, though, they arrived at the tall iron fence, Ulric pressing the doorbell at the gate. Then he straightened his shoulders, putting on a bigger smile.

Gage was forced to let the matter slide. He wanted to get to the bottom of this, though. He wanted to see what Ulric could be like when he wasn't afraid like he was right now.

He touched the small of Ulric's back. When Ulric turned, Gage kissed his cheek. "You'll be fine," Gage whispered. "I won't let anyone hurt you."

Ulric's smile faded a little—he almost looked sad again. Gage wrapped his arm more tightly around Ulric. Screw what everyone else thought. There were married alphas around. The neighbors could assume that Gage and Ulric were dating, or something. Gage didn't mind.

"You shouldn't do that." Ulric nudged Gage's arm off. "It's not appropriate."

"They can think what they want." Gage held him. "Unless you violently disapprove."

Ulric looked torn. So Gage kissed his jaw.

"Hey there," someone said. "You guys are earlier than we expected."

Ulric jerked away from Gage like he'd been burnt. Gage breathed out his disappointment.

When he turned, he found a too-familiar figure striding toward them. Gage blinked. He'd seen that face on TV, and sometimes on the news. *Isn't that...?*

Phil O'Riley. Retired basketball star. He'd played for

the New York Rockets—and he was pretty damn good at what he did. Gage had spent weeks of his childhood watching Phil's basketball games on TV. Was this his house? Why had Ulric not *told* him?

"King," Ulric said, recognition lighting his face. He looked relieved. Not surprised. Did he already know, and he'd meant to surprise Gage?

But Ulric didn't look at Gage with any sort of glee. He looked at Gage like he needed support, and then he showed King the casserole dish, all covered up with plastic wrap.

"I made some ribs," Ulric said nervously. "As thanks for inviting us."

King unlocked the gate, waving them in. "That looks delicious. C'mon in!"

As he stepped in, Gage held his hand out. He hope he wasn't overdoing this. "Great to meet you, Mr. O'Riley."

King shook his hand and winked. "My friends call me King. You must be Gage."

It was pretty damn surreal, a basketball star knowing your name. Gage wanted to text his siblings, maybe show them a picture of Phil O'Riley. It'd be rude to do it right now, though.

Ulric looked oddly at Gage. "You know King?"

Gage frowned. "Don't you?"

King laughed and beckoned them toward the house. "I'm just your friendly neighborhood dog-walker," he said, snapping his fingers at a mutt scampering across the lawn. "Don't mind me."

As King headed for the front door, Gage grabbed Ulric by the arm, leaning so close that his lips brushed Ulric's ear. Ulric flushed. "He's Phil O'Riley," Gage whispered. "You've never heard of him?"

Ulric looked bewildered. "Maybe?"

He was clueless and more than just a bit adorable, and Gage couldn't help chuckling. "It's fine. Let's head in."

Gage rubbed Ulric's back, following him into the house. Before he could, the dog hurried over, sniffing at him and Ulric. It wagged its tail excitedly.

Inside, the place was vast—the foyer led to the sitting area, and the dining room had a chandelier in it, complete with floor-to-ceiling French windows and a fancy-looking patio in the back.

Gage had grown up in a small apartment on the other side of town. He hadn't really thought about the houses here—mansions with beautiful marble floors and wide doorways and... the dining table could seat *twelve*. He felt like a pauper with his eyeballs falling out, but he couldn't help it.

Ulric didn't even bat an eyelid.

"You had to invite them?" another voice drawled when they moved into the sitting room.

The speaker was a thin man—older, omega, but also familiar. This time, Ulric tensed.

When Ulric had told Gage about their visit to "Phinny's place", Gage had thought it an odd name for someone they'd both never met. Now, Gage realized that "Phinny" was King's nickname for *the* Phoenix Blues, a singer who had dropped out of the public's eye a few years back.

Gage hadn't even realized that Phoenix was their neighbor. How was that possible?

Ulric sent Gage a helpless look. Gage felt the exact same way.

"Yup, I invited them," King said, grabbing a cocktail as he sat down. The mutt trotted over and lay contentedly at his feet. "They passed Crumbs' test.

Anyway, we need some fresh blood in this group, or it'll just be Nate and I watching football when you go off on one of your jaunts."

"This is my property, you realize." Phoenix rolled his eyes, but he waved toward the mini bar in the corner of the room. "Drinks are there. Help yourselves."

Ulric straightened. Then he smiled like he was a whole other person, and lifted the wrapping off his casserole dish. "I baked some ribs for today, ah, thinking they were for more ordinary folks. It's probably not what you're used to, though."

King perked up. "Ribs are my favorite. What did you season them with?"

"These are spiced with steak seasoning and BBQ sauce—not elegant, but they're fall-off-the-bone tender. Would you like some?" Ulric looked hopeful, but he was so damn polite that Gage's chest swelled with pride. That? That was a sweet recovery. Better than Gage would've done.

"Yes, please," King said. "I'll get the plates."

Phoenix glanced warily at the ribs. "I'll see if King likes his."

"No worries," Ulric answered. Then he turned to the other person in the room—an alpha in his forties that Gage didn't recognize. He assumed that was Nate.

"I'll have some," Nate said, looking interested.

"You don't happen to be anyone famous, do you?" Gage blurted. "I feel as though we've just crashed a really high-profile party."

Nate laughed. "Nah. I'm just a regular firefighter. That's all."

"Pfft." Phoenix rolled his eyes like there was something important Nate wasn't telling them, but neither of them elaborated.

"Is it okay if I get this heated up a bit more before I serve it?" Ulric wriggled his casserole dish.

Phoenix pointed. "Kitchen's there."

Ulric hurried off. Gage was tempted to follow him just to see if he'd be fine. But Ulric seemed to have things under control now—so Gage poured himself a drink at the bar, taking a seat awkwardly at an unoccupied couch.

"My name's Gage. I'm a personal trainer at Meadowfall Fitness," Gage began. "If you encounter any sports-related injuries, or if you'd like to develop an exercise routine, I might be able to help."

Like hell Phoenix or King would come to him for help. They probably had their own doctors on speed dial. Gage felt silly for even saying it, but he didn't know what else these guys would be interested in.

"I'll keep that in mind." Nate gave him a thumbs-up.

Phoenix looked Gage in the eye, nodding at the kitchen. "Are you and the other kid a thing?"

Well, that was awkward.

"There's a security camera at the gate," Nate explained. "Phinny and I were trying to figure out who you were, until King told us."

So... they'd seen Gage kissing Ulric, then. Ulric would be so embarrassed. Feeling bad for him, Gage said, "He's a really good friend of mine. I moved in with him recently."

"Ah." Phoenix smiled. Then he seemed thoughtful, and Gage knew he was trying to guess which of them bottomed for the other. Like sex was already a given.

Truth be told... Gage had been getting curious, himself. He'd glimpsed a movie folder on Ulric's TV, one that had been named *Misc*. The thumbnails in that folder had been flesh-colored.

He'd never asked to peek inside. Maybe he should.

Then he imagined Ulric jerking off, and his cock thickened. Definitely not the right time for this.

"Ulric's actually the sweetest alpha," Gage said. "He's a data analyst for big pharma, and he's not available for dates."

Gage scowled at Phoenix, just in case Phoenix had ideas. He figured he should protect Ulric from someone famous.

But Phoenix only laughed. "How cute!"

He pulled out a cigarette box; Nate made a face. "Must you?"

"My house," Phoenix said, lighting up. "Sit out in the lawn if it bothers you."

Nate chuckled.

"I like that brand," Gage said.

Both Phoenix and Nate looked at him in surprise; Phoenix offered him a stick. "Really? Gym rat like you?"

Gage declined. "Nah, I don't smoke. But it reminds me of when my dad brought us to the Christmas markets —there would always be a few smokers around, and it was always this scent. Just gives me the warm fuzzy feelings."

Phoenix laughed, blowing a puff of smoke into the air. "I think I like you."

Ulric had been walking back with his casserole dish; he froze when Phoenix spoke, looking quickly between Gage and the singer. Did he think Gage had been flirting with Phoenix while he was gone?

Unwilling to let Ulric believe that, Gage stood, taking the casserole dish from him. Then he kissed Ulric on the cheek. "Only you," Gage whispered.

Ulric flushed so red, Gage thought he might've turned around and fled.

"Wow," King said. "Have you proposed?"

What? Gage leaned back; Ulric scrambled away, wide-eyed.

"Nothing's going on," Ulric said.

"We're best friends," Gage added.

King broke into a laugh. "You know, we might just have to invite you guys over the next time."

"Seconded." Nate raised his glass.

Phoenix just smiled like a sly cat.

"Anyway, the ribs," Gage said. He sliced them up and dished them, and King all but inhaled his share. Nate did, too. Phoenix was finally convinced to try a piece.

The rack of ribs disappeared a lot faster than Gage expected—by the end of it, Ulric looked relieved, almost happy. Gage touched the small of his back. It seemed that Ulric liked these neighbors a lot better than his previous ones. That was good.

An hour later, when Ulric looked ready to leave, Gage linked their fingers together. "I think we should start heading back," Gage said.

Ulric smiled, squeezing his hand.

"Aw," Phoenix said.

"Shh." Nate shook his head. "You know what they say—a watched pot doesn't boil."

Phoenix flipped him off. "Yes, Professor Nate," he muttered in the most sarcastic tone. "I've never heard that in my entire life."

Gage decided that he should get Ulric out of here, before Ulric fainted from blushing so much. He tugged Ulric to the door; King followed them.

For a second, Gage thought about asking King for a selfie—his siblings would be thrilled. But was that out of line? By inviting Gage and Ulric to the get-together, King had already done them a favor.

"King," Ulric said suddenly. "If it isn't too much to ask, could you sign on my shirt? Something really cheesy. I know someone who'd really like it."

King laughed. "Sure."

While Ulric fumbled around for a pen, King disappeared into the house, returning a moment later with a marker. "What sort of message would you like?"

Ulric shrugged. "Something weird? What about 'With lots of crazy love'? Or anything, really. It's up to you."

Gage bit down his smile. *Damn, Ulric. You beat me to it.*

King scribbled on Ulric's shoulder blade. Then he signed off and clapped Ulric on the back. "Done."

"Thanks." Ulric looked immensely grateful. "I can't thank you enough for inviting us over. It was an honor."

King met their gaze. "We're brothers on this street. Happy to find more family."

Gage was only living temporarily with Ulric, and Ulric was just renting the place they were in. But if this somehow became a permanent sort of brotherhood... that would be sweet. It'd feel like a home away from home.

Mostly, Gage wondered how long he'd be living with Ulric here on Meadow Street. How long he had before things inevitably fell apart, like all his friendships and relationships tended to go.

They bade King goodbye, heading back to Ulric's place. On the way, Gage slipped his arm around Ulric, pulling him closer. Ulric was soft against him, warm. And Gage couldn't help eyeing the autograph on Ulric's shoulder. *With loads of love,* King had written.

"You have a damn big pair," Gage said.

"Pair of what?"

"Balls." Gage laughed. Were this any other alpha friend, Gage would've reached down and grabbed those balls to weigh them, right then and there. With Ulric...

things were a bit different. Maybe Gage would do it later.

"They aren't that big." Ulric glanced down. Then he grinned. "Anyway, I didn't get that autograph for myself. It's for you."

"Me?" Gage stared. "He's Phil-fucking-O'Riley. You sure you don't want to keep that?"

Ulric shrugged. "I didn't even know who he was until you said it. And I saw the way you looked at him, Gage. It's worth a lot more to you."

A huge wave of fondness swelled through Gage's chest. He pulled Ulric closer and kissed his shoulder, and Ulric's smile grew.

When they'd both stepped into the house, Ulric shrugged out of his shirt. "There."

Then he scrunched it into a ball, crammed it against Gage's face, and slipped away. Gage breathed in a lungful of honey oak. "Hey! Ulric."

By the time he pulled the shirt off his face, Ulric was already halfway up the stairs. "I'm getting another shirt," Ulric said. "Be right back."

"What other shirt? You don't need one, stud muffin."

Ulric snorted. "Yeah, right. You're the stud, and I'm the muffin."

Well, maybe. But he was an adorable muffin. Gage hurried up the stairs, following Ulric into his bedroom. Then he launched himself at Ulric and took him down, pinning him roughly against the mattress. "You're so fucking adorable," Gage growled, kissing Ulric's shoulder. His hands wandered up Ulric's sides. "The way you were scared earlier, I didn't think you'd ask King for his autograph."

Ulric stiffened beneath him. "I wasn't scared. And I need a shirt. Get off."

Gage hummed, sliding his palms up Ulric's chest, cupping his pecs. They were nice, actually. There was muscle beneath his curves—you just couldn't see it straightaway. "Nah. No need for a shirt." He found Ulric's nipples, pinching them.

Ulric sucked in a sharp breath. "What're you doing?"

"Trying to see if you're different from me. Not really."

Ulric snorted. "Maybe you need to open your eyes, Gage."

"Maybe you need to close yours."

Gage wrapped his arms around Ulric, holding him close. This felt nice. Comfortable. And Gage couldn't help looking at the tiny spots of ink on Ulric's shoulder, left over from King's black marker. When they'd first left to go to Phinny's place, Gage had wondered if Ulric would freak out. He'd come up with all these excuses to get Ulric home.

"What happened with your previous neighbors?" Gage murmured.

"Nothing."

"Ulric." Gage kissed his nape. "Tell me."

Ulric was quiet for a long moment. Then he sighed. "My mom always told me I should dress up real nice whenever I walk down the street, because no one wants to see me like this." He gestured at his belly. "She said she couldn't face her neighbors because I'm so overweight."

"What the fuck?" Anger rippled through Gage. "Your mother said that to you?"

Ulric shrugged, his ears turning pink. "Anyway."

"No. That isn't all of it, is it?" The way Ulric was self-conscious, the way he kept comparing himself to Gage... That wasn't *normal* for an alpha. "What else did she say?"

Ulric pushed his face against the mattress. "Nothing."

"It's not nothing."

His silence said so much.

"I want to know," Gage murmured. "I promise I will never laugh at you."

Ulric sighed, bringing his arms up around his head, as though he was trying to protect himself. "You've never had your friends laugh at you for being out of shape, have you? Every grade, every new school... it's the same. Sometimes they threw trash at me. Sometimes I had awful notes shoved into my locker. Sometimes they stole my lunches as a joke. I didn't get an allowance, so those days, I was hungry all the way until I got home."

Gage's heart ached for him. "Did you tell anyone?"

Ulric shrugged. "My mom said I deserved it."

"What the fuck?"

"She tried everything to get me to lose weight. Like diets and after-school exercise programs. She tried piling my dinner plate with boiled vegetables only, but she and my dad had actual food on their plates. The veggies were so bad, I—I cried. I was pretty young at that point. Then she started telling me that no one would ever love me because I'm—"

He stopped talking, but Gage heard the words Ulric didn't say, he heard Ulric's heartbreak, and the broken, unloved bits of his past.

Then, so quietly that Gage almost didn't hear him, Ulric added, "I mean, it's true."

Gage stopped breathing, his heart squeezing tight. He didn't know which was worse: that Ulric had grown up in such a terrible environment, or that Ulric believed no one could love him because of how he looked. That Ulric hadn't been loved until now.

Gage touched Ulric's throat, his heart pounding so hard he couldn't hear himself think. It wasn't fair that

Ulric thought all that crap about himself. Ulric was gentle and sweet, he was cuddly and so easily flustered.

"Who the fuck wouldn't love you?" Gage growled, angry with everything. He'd grown up poor, but at least he had an awesome family, at least he had parents who had been supportive of the things he did.

And here Ulric was—Gage didn't know if Ulric had any family nearby. Ulric sure didn't sound like he had friends.

"Tell you what," Gage said, his chest burning. "I'm gonna be your best friend forever. I swear."

Ulric turned, looking warily at Gage over his shoulder. "You don't have to."

"I want to." Gage leaned heavily into him, wrapping his arms around Ulric. "I don't care where we go from here, and I don't care if I have to move away or things like that. You can tell me anything, and I'll listen."

Ulric stared, still disbelieving. "Why?"

"Because." Gage hugged him tighter, so tight that their bodies were pressed flush together, his jaw against Ulric's naked back. "Everyone needs a friend."

"You don't need me."

"You need me," Gage whispered. And he dragged the scent gland on his wrist down Ulric's arm, leaving a trail of pine. People usually reserved that scent marking for bondmates. Gage didn't have one. But a best friend was important, too. Enough that he wanted to mark Ulric as his own. "There. That's my promise."

Ulric sucked in a shaky breath, his eyes growing wide. "But that's—"

Gage kissed his back. "See, I don't care what you look like. I mean, I care, but you look fine to me."

"I don't look great," Ulric muttered.

"Then do something about it. But it's not something I

need you to do. I'll be here regardless." Gage snuggled against him, holding him tight, trying to convince him that he was perfect just the way he was.

"Let me—" Ulric swallowed. "Let me think about it."

"Okay." Gage brushed his knuckles along Ulric's jaw, stroking his shoulder. Just small touches to show he cared. "Mind if I poke around on your TV?"

Ulric shrugged, looking down at himself. "Go ahead."

Gage kissed the back of his head. It was a lot for Ulric to absorb—Gage understood. And Ulric would need time. So Gage pulled off his own shirt and tucked it under Ulric's chest, as an exchange for the shirt Ulric had given him.

Then he left Ulric's bedroom quietly, hoping that Ulric would take his words to heart.

15

BURN

When he was properly dressed, his dignity scraped back together, Ulric stepped out of his bedroom. The house was quiet. Night had fallen, cloaking everything in shadow.

Neither of Gage's rooms were lit. The bathroom was dark, and so was the living room. Ulric assumed that Gage had gone out, all the way until he saw light from the TV flashing across the couch.

Gage was sitting alone, his gaze transfixed on the screen. Had he silenced the TV?

Curious, Ulric padded down the stairs. Then came a soft groan—not from Gage. And a quiet, rhythmic slapping began.

Oh.

Ulric froze, his face starting to burn. He hadn't meant to intrude on that. He hurried off the stairs, halfway to the kitchen when Gage said, "Hey."

His voice had turned husky, a sweet rasp that curled down Ulric's spine. Ulric's breath snagged in his throat. "Yeah?"

"Come over here for a sec. Watch this with me."

Ulric wasn't sure he'd heard right. Watching porn with Gage? Was Gage serious? Ulric didn't even like omegas that way.

But if this meant that Gage was going to jerk off... Ulric couldn't resist the urge to peek. He made his way back to the couch, his throat dry. "What're you watching?"

Gage nodded at the screen. "I found this in one of your folders."

Ulric's stomach dropped. "What?"

"You said I could poke around on this." Gage raised his eyebrows. "Should I not have?"

Ulric couldn't move. He had a few lewd movies stored on the TV—some were his favorites, some he'd saved to watch later.

None of them contained any omegas at all. Had Gage noticed that? He had to have, if he was halfway through the current movie.

"You're not..." Ulric tried to gesture with his hands. "You're not watching something else?"

Gage shrugged and grabbed the remote, pausing the video. It froze with one alpha's cock halfway into another alpha's ass, both of them looking like they were on the verge of blowing their loads.

It was one of Ulric's favorites. Did Gage... find it weird?

"Sit down." Gage patted the couch next to him.

Woodenly, Ulric planted himself on the couch. What were the chances of Gage actually jerking off to this? Probably close to zero. Disappointed, Ulric glanced at Gage's pants. Was that his bulge...?

"You like alphas," Gage said quietly, meeting his eyes. "Not omegas?"

Ulric's face scorched. He must've been an idiot, if he thought he could keep that a secret from Gage. "I like omegas as friends. Like—Like Flores. He's married to one of the firefighters."

"You wouldn't marry one, though?" Gage looked thoughtful.

Ulric huffed. "Funny story—I was also engaged to Flores."

Gage's eyebrows crawled up. "You were? What happened?"

"Arranged marriage some years back. His alpha crashed the wedding. I was so jealous."

"Because he had an alpha?"

Ulric's face betrayed him with all that heat. He looked at his hands, folding his fingers together. "Does it matter?"

"Yeah." Gage shuffled closer, bumping their arms together. "Why didn't you just find an alpha?"

"No one wants this face," Ulric hissed, his old wounds reopening. "I had one, and he left me for an omega. He said I'm too—"

Ulric looked down at himself, wishing this wouldn't keep coming up. He needed to shed some weight, he needed to just... look normal.

"Ulric." Gage leaned in, kissing his cheek. "You're perfect."

"Fuck off." Ulric stood, suddenly angry with himself for being so hopeful. He wanted Gage. He would give just about anything to suck Gage off, and it hurt that Gage kept saying shit like that. Because they would be friends, and nothing else.

Gage caught his hand, yanking him back. "Wait."

"Quit asking me to watch porn with you," Ulric snapped. "You don't even like this anyway."

"I don't mind trying it."

Fuck. Ulric closed his eyes, his chest tight. He knew the risks. He knew the reasons why he shouldn't get closer to Gage, and yet... he kept lapping up all the intimacy Gage gave him, desperate for more.

"What do you want?" Ulric asked, his heart sore.

"Sit with me," Gage murmured. "I want to understand."

He squeezed Ulric's hand. Ulric swallowed hard, sinking back onto the couch.

"Let's be bros." Gage leaned into him. "We can jerk off to the same things, right?"

Fuck, fuck. Ulric wasn't ready for this. Especially not for Gage to find out what things made him come. "You do it. I'll just... I'll just watch."

Gage huffed. "It doesn't work that way."

No, it didn't. Ulric squirmed, tempted to say yes. Just to see Gage's cock. He glanced up to find Gage watching him, Gage's eyes warm, his lips full, looking ever so soft. Ulric's throat tightened. He wanted a kiss from Gage, too. He'd been dreaming about it, he'd imagined Gage kissing him just a bit further to the left, he'd imagined turning his head so their lips met.

There was another way to get a kiss from him. It wouldn't be a real kiss, but...

Ulric wet his lips. "Help me practice."

Gage raised his eyebrows. "Practice what?"

Ulric squirmed. "For—For when I get a boyfriend. I suck at kissing."

Gage froze, surprised. For a second, Ulric thought he saw unhappiness flicker through Gage's expression. Then it was gone, and Gage made himself smile. "Okay."

"You don't have to."

Gage shook his head. "No, it's really fine."

Ulric thought Gage might just lean in and give him a quick peck on the lips. But Gage took off Ulric's glasses, setting them on the side table. Then he swung his leg up and straddled Ulric's lap, filling Ulric's vision.

Ulric stopped breathing.

"Is this how alphas do it?" Gage asked, cracking a smile. "Or should I not sit on you?"

"This is fine," Ulric blurted.

Gage was heavy on him, all strong and muscled. Just having him this close, his legs open around Ulric—this was like a wet dream come true.

"Okay." Gage smiled. He cupped Ulric's neck and pressed their foreheads together, and his eyes blurred into a sea of green. Ulric froze. In the shadows of the living room, it felt like anything could happen between them.

"This is how you kiss," Gage whispered, his breath hot on Ulric's lips.

Then he slanted his mouth across Ulric's in a slow, exquisite brush. Tingles exploded down Ulric's nerves; he gasped. Gage kissed him more firmly, and his lips felt glorious, his teeth grazing Ulric's skin.

Ulric forgot to breathe. This was supposed to be a practice kiss. Every slide of their mouths felt decadent, surreal, and Ulric wanted more, he wanted to touch Gage in return. He didn't know if he should.

"Kiss back," Gage whispered.

Ulric tried. His thoughts spun. His cock was growing thick, and he wasn't sure if Gage could feel it through their clothes. Scarcely had he set his hands on Gage's strong thighs, when Gage flicked his tongue against Ulric's lips. Then he thrust in without warning, a hot, hungry presence that swept into Ulric, tasting him everywhere inside.

Ulric's instincts *roared*. Gage was inside him. Blood surged between his legs. He groaned, and Gage answered with a snarl, yanking on Ulric's hair to tip his head back. Gage sealed their lips together, his tongue damp inside Ulric's mouth, devouring him.

Ulric grew so hard, he couldn't think. He bit Gage's lip, grasping his shirt. Then he yanked Gage closer and thrust his own tongue into Gage's mouth.

Gage tasted like apple cider and crackers. He slid their tongues together, sending a burst of electricity up Ulric's spine. Then he rocked his hips against Ulric's, a rough, deliberate grind, and their cocks shoved together, Gage's length thick against his. Ulric grew achingly hard in seconds, he plunged into Gage's mouth, in and out, the exact same way he wanted to fuck into this alpha.

"Damn, Ulric," Gage hissed.

And he reached down, grabbing Ulric between the legs. His hand was hot, his grip tight. Ulric pulsed so hard, he almost came right there.

He knocked Gage's arm away, panting, his precome smearing wet around his tip. He should've known that kissing Gage would make him hard. And now Gage had discovered that about him, too.

"You're so fucking hard," Gage whispered, his gaze too shrewd. He reached for Ulric again, his palm a heavy pressure stroking down Ulric's length, base to tip.

Ulric almost speared through his clothes. "Stop that."

"Or else what?" Gage's expression had turned hungry, dangerous. And it riled the animal that had awakened within Ulric, the beast he became when he lost control.

"Or else I'll fucking come," Ulric snapped.

"Then come," Gage whispered. And he pushed his hand into Ulric's pants, his hot grip sending sheer *need* through Ulric's veins.

Ulric shoved Gage off his lap, he slammed Gage down onto the floor, pinning him with his entire body. Then he crammed his bulge between Gage's open legs, letting Gage feel every inch of his cock. Everything that would go into that spread ass.

Gods, that ass. Ulric had dreamed of opening Gage's cheeks, he'd wanted to plunge his cock inside and hear Gage scream. All he needed was to tear Gage's pants off, stretch his hole, and slam his cock in.

Ulric curled his fingers into Gage's waistband, yanking it halfway down his ass. Gage shoved Ulric's hands off. "Not so fast."

At the back of his mind, it occurred to Ulric that maybe… Gage didn't want this.

This was supposed to be a kiss. A practice one.

And he'd gone and let Gage feel his cock. Gage now knew how hard Ulric had gotten for him.

Ulric froze, his heart sinking. His body wilted a little. He tried to get his thoughts under control; his instincts didn't want him to pull away, or apologize. He wanted to *take*.

"I—I'll stop," he said, his tongue too thick. Gage didn't want to fuck him.

Gage grabbed his hand. "Not what I meant."

Gage shuffled into a sitting position, their foreheads bumping, his legs draped over Ulric's thighs. Then he curled his fingers into the front of Ulric's pants, he popped the button, and unzipped Ulric's fly. Ulric stopped breathing. What was Gage doing?

He thought maybe Gage just wanted to look at his cock. Maybe Gage wanted to compare sizes. Except Gage pushed his fingers into Ulric's boxers, his fingertips brushing Ulric's sensitive skin. Pleasure whispered into

Ulric's body. And Gage wrapped his hand around Ulric's tip, easing it out.

Ulric's breath punched out of his lungs. Gage was touching him *there*. And his precome smeared wetly against Gage's hand—there was no way Gage didn't know how desperate Ulric was for him. "Gage—"

Gage pushed Ulric's waistband down, he pulled Ulric's cock out into the open, so it jutted up between them, flushed and thick.

Ulric shoved it down, his face burning.

"Don't." Gage caught his hand. He made Ulric release himself so his cock jerked back up, musky and incriminating.

Instead of just looking, Gage touched his knuckles to Ulric's underside. He followed the ridge up, a barely-there pressure that Ulric felt in the deepest parts of his body. "Why the hell are you—"

Ulric bit his words off, unwilling to say it. Not right now.

"Why am I touching your cock?" Gage's eyes darkened. And he wrapped his fingers around Ulric, dragging his fist all the way to Ulric's tip. Pleasure sizzled through his veins; Ulric panted. It felt so much better when Gage touched him, than when he touched himself. It was as though Gage had lit up all his nerves.

"You're so fucking hard for *me*," Gage rasped.

He brushed the pad of his thumb all the way around Ulric's head. Then he squeezed Ulric's tip, and a droplet leaked onto Gage's finger. Ulric thought Gage might ignore it.

But Gage brought his hand to his lips, licking off Ulric's precome. And he rolled it through his mouth, rumbling low in his throat. "Salty."

Gage had *tasted* him. Ulric's head burned, his pulse

beat like a drum between his thighs. Gage smiled, looking hungrier than Ulric had ever seen him.

Again without warning, Gage closed his fist around Ulric's base, dragging it all the way up to his tip. Pleasure pulsed through his body; Ulric's eyes rolled back in his head. "Fuck, Gage."

Gage pumped him harder, then harder again, until his calluses scraped against Ulric's skin and it felt as though he wouldn't stop. Ulric writhed, yanking Gage's hand away so he wouldn't come right there.

"You're so fucking close," Gage whispered.

He pulled his legs off Ulric's thighs, he shuffled back a little. Then he leaned in and took Ulric's tip into his mouth.

16

BURN PART 2

ULRIC COULDN'T BREATHE. Gage was hot inside. Damp. And he sucked down Ulric's cock, all snug and sinful, his tongue stroking Ulric where he was sensitive.

Ulric's spine arched, his senses overloading. On instinct, he grabbed Gage's head and shoved him down, so his cock hit the back of Gage's throat. That sensation hauled him over the edge; Ulric cried out in surprise, pleasure ripping through his body as he spurted over and over down Gage's throat, filling him with come.

For a while, he drifted, his thoughts hazy, the aftershocks of his climax echoing through his body. He thought he felt something rumbling against him.

It wasn't until he could think again, that he realized his cock was still buried deep in Gage's mouth. Gage had tasted him. Hell, he'd *come down Gage's throat*. And Gage was growling around him, his tongue sliding against Ulric's cock.

Ulric shoved Gage off, his heart tumbling. He hadn't meant for any of this to happen. What would Gage think of him?

When Gage glanced up, his eyes were dark. He didn't once look away from Ulric as he licked his lips. Then his throat worked, and Ulric realized that... Gage had swallowed every drop of his come. Ulric froze.

"I don't think you realize how fucking hot you are," Gage rasped.

Then he leaned in, he grabbed Ulric by the nape and crashed their lips together, and he thrust his tongue into Ulric's mouth, tasting like bitter come.

The retreating beast came snarling back. Ulric groaned, tangling his tongue with Gage's. He tasted himself on this alpha, he smelled musk. When he reached down, he found Gage hard behind his pants. Because of Ulric.

Gage shoved down his own clothes. His cock jerked up, pushing hungrily against Ulric's palm. It was hot, thick, longer than Ulric's. Ulric groaned, sliding his palm down Gage's silky length. He wanted it everywhere on him. On his face, in his ass, he wanted it covering him with come. It'd feel so good. "I—"

Gage thrust his tongue into Ulric's mouth. He tasted Ulric everywhere inside, he stole all of Ulric's breath. And he caught Ulric's sac in his hand, squeezing it so pleasure jolted up Ulric's spine.

"Damn big balls," Gage murmured. Then he shoved Ulric backward so Ulric's back hit the floor. And Gage pinned Ulric down with his own body, he shoved Ulric's legs apart, grinding his bare cock against Ulric's ass.

Ulric's breath rushed out of him. "You can't be serious."

"What part of this isn't serious?" Gage growled. He grasped Ulric's pants, he ripped them down Ulric's ass like Ulric had done to him. And he fitted his cock between Ulric's cheeks, a thick, heavy slide that spread Ulric open, grinding damp and hungry against his hole.

Ulric's throat went dry. Gage's tip was right where he was the most vulnerable. He could push harder, and Ulric would open for him. Ulric shoved Gage away, kicking off his own pants for greater mobility. "I won't submit that easily."

Gage's eyes gleamed. "Yeah? But you'll submit?"

"No." Ulric lunged, pinning Gage hard against the floor. Then he shoved his still-hard cock between Gage's thighs, he angled it under Gage's sac, and then up, thrusting enough to spread Gage's tight cheeks.

And now Ulric's tip was lodged against Gage's hole, and it didn't matter that he couldn't see it—he could feel where they touched. He rolled his hips, grinding against Gage's entrance. He wanted to stretch it, he wanted to fit every inch of his cock inside.

Gage swore, his own length jerking. But he heaved Ulric off, a feral smile curving his lips. "This is how we're playing it?"

"Yeah." And Ulric lunged at Gage, at the same time Gage knocked him down onto the floor, grabbing Ulric's knot. Ulric groaned; Gage shoved Ulric's legs apart, catching his knee to haul it up, exposing his hole.

Ulric yanked his leg out of Gage's grasp, but not before Gage crammed his fingers between Ulric's cheeks, right against his entrance. Ulric stopped breathing. Cocks felt amazing, but fingers went in a lot easier, a lot faster. What would Gage's feel like?

"Say 'no', Muffin," Gage whispered. "That one word. Any others, and it'll mean you want this."

"Damn you," Ulric hissed.

Gage pushed his fingers hard against Ulric, forcing him to stretch open. Then he plunged inside, all dry friction, thick and demanding. Ulric wheezed, his body yielding, his cock pulsing.

Gage was inside.

"Fuck, you're tight." Gage shoved his fingers all the way in. It burned. Then he found Ulric's prostate, grinding his fingers against it. Pleasure throbbed through Ulric's body, stealing his thoughts away. He might've made a sound.

"Yeah? You like that?" Gage murmured. He crammed his fingers hard against that spot, rough and insistent in a way no one had done before. Ulric groaned, his body winding up tight, his cock aching.

"Perfect," Gage whispered. Then he began a relentless massage, back and forth, stroking that sensitive spot, every touch crackling with bliss. Ulric tried to breathe, his eyes rolling back in his head.

But he didn't want Gage to think he was weak. He knocked Gage's fingers out of himself. Then he rolled over to get his feet beneath him.

Gage crashed into him from behind, he slammed Ulric face-down against the floor, shoving his cock between Ulric's cheeks. Precome smeared between them; Gage rolled his hips, his tip raking up Ulric's crack, staking its claim.

Ulric's breath punched out of him; his hole squeezed in anticipation.

"Gonna take this, Muffin," Gage growled. He set his hand between Ulric's shoulder blades, pinning Ulric down with his weight. Then he grabbed Ulric's asscheek and spread it wide, cool air brushing Ulric's hole. "Fuck, you look perfect."

Heat crept up Ulric's neck. Gage was looking at his hole.

Gage spat. Wet fingers touched Ulric's entrance,

rubbing firm and reverently. Then Gage sank a finger in, swearing.

It felt so good whenever Gage touched him inside. Ulric bit down his moan. "Need lube. Drawer."

He waited until Gage had found the lube, Gage smearing some over his cock. Ulric heaved Gage off, making to escape. Because like hell he'd wait for Gage to push into him.

Ulric got to his feet; this put his ass right in front of Gage's face. Gage grabbed him around the thighs and crammed his fingers between Ulric's cheeks, and he found Ulric's hole in a hot second, plunging inside like he had every right to be there. Ulric's breath left his throat. "Fuck, Gage."

"You keep fighting me," Gage growled, doing wonderful, magical things with his fingers. Ulric shuddered. "But all you really want is for me to pin you down and fuck you 'til you cream."

That sounded amazing. Ulric's hole squeezed; Gage swore.

"I felt you clench, Muffin," Gage rasped. "Gonna be tight like that around my cock?"

Ulric bit down his groan. "Keep thinking that."

"I will." And Gage spread his fingers inside Ulric, forcing Ulric's hole to open wide. Then he grabbed Ulric's knot and squeezed. Pleasure shot up Ulric's spine; Ulric pulsed, needing more.

Gage shoved hard against the back of Ulric's knee, bringing Ulric crashing down. Ulric threw his arms out to catch himself; he landed on all fours. And Gage slammed him back against the floor, shoving his cock between Ulric's cheeks. "Say 'no,'" Gage growled. "And I'll stop."

"Fuck off," Ulric snarled, his body singing, his hole squeezing tight. He made to escape again.

Gage laughed. He anchored Ulric down and slid his blunt tip between Ulric's cheeks, cramming it against his hole. Ulric's breath punched out of him.

Gage didn't ask again—he snapped his hips and *pushed*, forcing Ulric to open for him. Ulric took all of Gage's length as it plunged inside, stretching him with its blissful thickness. He tried to breathe. Gage was big. Delicious. With every inch he thrust in, he stretched Ulric further, until Ulric was sure he could take no more cock.

Then Gage began to move, in and out, each stroke turning more savage. Pleasure throbbed through Ulric's body. He spread his legs wider, accepting every inch as Gage fucked into him, claiming him inside. It had been so long since he'd had anyone there. And Ulric loved that Gage was his first in a while.

"Fuck," Gage panted. He snapped his hips again, plowing his whole length inside.

Ulric thought maybe a noise slipped from his own throat. "That's hardly anything," he growled.

Gage's laugh was deep, hungry. "Yeah? What about this?"

And he began a hard rhythm, one that sent his cock slamming right into Ulric's prostate, over and over until Ulric trembled against him, gasping for breath, his entire body throbbing with pleasure.

He didn't think he could come again. He'd emptied out his balls. But Gage's strokes grew deeper, more feral. Then he grasped Ulric's knot and squeezed hard, ramming his cock into Ulric's body like a beast. Ulric's pleasure spiraled, his need pounding between his legs.

"Come for me, babe," Gage murmured in his ear.

Then he bit into Ulric's shoulder, and Ulric came, his body squeezing tight, his spine arching, waves of pleasure rocking through him like an earthquake.

Vaguely, he heard Gage's breathing hitch. Gage's thrusts turned feverish, his body hot as he crammed every inch of himself inside. With a snarl, Gage thrust in a last time, his warmth filling Ulric, his pleasure tangible between them.

Ulric basked in the afterglow for as long as he could. He didn't think something this perfect would happen again, Gage holding him as they caught their breaths together, Gage warm and ever so comfortable against Ulric's back.

So he pretended that this would go on forever, that Gage would continue to hold him like this, pressing soft kisses along his shoulder. It was such a glorious daydream.

"Want my knot?" Gage murmured.

Ulric's heart missed a beat. "Yeah," he said, just to prolong this moment. If Gage had somehow seen Ulric as an omega, or if he'd somehow seen Ulric as *less* for bottoming, then Ulric may as well be hung for a sheep.

Gage growled, tightening his arms around Ulric, fitting his length deeper inside. His knot swelled, thick and heavy, stretching Ulric as it locked them together.

Ulric loved being knotted. He loved that momentary closeness, he loved the feeling of belonging to someone. And it was better when he couldn't see Gage's expression, so he could continue pretending that everything was perfect.

"Hey," Gage murmured, stroking Ulric's arm. "C'mon, get on the couch. It'll be more comfy that way. I don't wanna kneel this whole time."

Ulric wasn't keen on spending the next half-hour on

the floor, either. Slowly, he shuffled to his feet, Gage holding them snug together, their thighs bumping as they eased sideways onto the couch. With every movement, Gage's knot tugged inside him, a warm, intimate pressure. Ulric flushed.

"Lie on me," Gage said, tugging gently on Ulric.

"I don't want to crush you."

Gage huffed. "You won't."

He pulled Ulric back, so Ulric all but lay against his chest, Gage's breath warm on his shoulder. In the dim glow of the TV, Ulric stared at Gage's muscular arms around his belly, and his bare legs—he should've gotten a blanket to cover up. At least Gage couldn't see much of Ulric's skin.

"You're squeezing around me," Gage murmured. "What's wrong?"

"Nothing." Ulric wet his lips, beyond glad that Gage couldn't see his face. Bad enough that Gage could feel what went on inside his body.

But Gage stroked Ulric's jaw with his fingers. "You're upset about something."

"I'm not."

"Tell me." Gage kissed his shoulder.

Ulric's face heated at that intimacy. "We're still friends, right?"

Gage was silent for a moment. "You want to be friends?"

Ulric's stomach dropped. Did Gage *not* want to be friends? "I—Yeah."

Gage trailed his fingers up Ulric's side. Then he brushed his wrist along Ulric's arm again, marking him with pine. Ulric's face burned. He wished they were bondmates. He looked down at himself, and he didn't feel proud of anything he saw.

"I—I want to lose weight," he blurted. In case there was a chance he could look better.

Gage kissed his nape. "It's not because of me, right? You're perfect as you are."

Ulric prickled all over with embarrassment. "How can you say that? You see me, Gage—"

"I see who you are inside." Gage slid his palm over Ulric's heart.

"I'm not right," Ulric blurted. "I'm not an omega. I'm not special or anything. All I am is just f—"

Gage clapped his hand over Ulric's mouth. "All you are, is adorable."

Ulric's heart tumbled. "Why?"

"Because." Gage kissed his shoulder. "We could be more."

Ulric's entire body froze up. "M-more?"

Gage leaned to the side, trying to meet his eyes. "You don't want to?"

"You—You're talking about being boyfriends. Us."

"Yeah."

Ulric tried to wrap his mind around that. He badly wanted to. But he was also afraid of Gage finding someone better, he was afraid of Gage breaking up with him. Gage's "Notify me when this alpha becomes available" email waiting list had probably grown twice as long this past month.

Even though his instincts told him to say *yes*, Ulric shook his head.

"Okay," Gage murmured. He held Ulric more tightly, kissing his spine. "But we'll still do this? Is that okay with you?"

"'This'?"

Gage reached down, running his fingertips lightly over Ulric's cock. Pleasure whispered through his body.

Ulric gulped, his face burning. Gage was touching him there again. "Yeah. Sure," he choked. Like it hadn't just made his entire week.

"You don't sound so excited about it," Gage said dryly.

"What, you thought I'd blow my load the moment you asked?"

Gage laughed. "I thought you might."

Ulric squirmed, hating that he was so predictable. The moment Gage's knot receded, he eased himself off, trying not to moan. Then he grabbed his pants and pulled it on so Gage wouldn't have to see his bare ass. "I'm going to go work out."

Gage hummed. But his gaze slid over Ulric's body, warm and... appreciative? Ulric wasn't sure what had changed between them. "Need help with spotting?"

Ulric wanted to prove that he could do this himself. So he shook his head, heading upstairs.

If he exercised enough, if he lost enough weight... maybe he'd be good enough for Gage. Maybe he'd be alpha enough.

Hope blossoming in his chest, he went to change into his exercise clothes.

17

NEW ARRANGEMENTS

A WEEK LATER, Gage received a text from his brother: *I lost my job.*

He stared at the message, his heart sinking. Wilkie had been struggling lately—they all were. Because of Debbie's illness, Wilkie had taken up a part-time job to pay the bills, even though Gage had told him to focus on his studies. Now that Wilkes didn't have a job, he would concentrate on school, right?

Trying not to worry, Gage called him.

"Gage?" Wilkie sounded miserable.

Gage wanted to reach through the phone and hug him. "Hey. How're you doing?"

Wilkie sighed. "I'm okay."

"Do you still have a roof over your head?"

No answer. Then, hesitantly, Wilkie replied, "Not for long. I might have to move out of the dorm if I can't find another job."

"Drop the job hunt," Gage said. "Focus on your schoolwork. You could move back in with Mom and Dad and Debbie, or... maybe you could come live with me."

He'd said it because he couldn't bear the thought of Wilkie wandering around on the streets. But the moment it left his lips, Gage realized it wasn't the best solution. When Ulric had made Gage the offer, he hadn't said Gage could invite someone else to room with him. Not only that—the parts of Debbie's bills that Wilkie couldn't help with, Gage would have to cover.

So much for paying double rent next month.

"Really?" Wilkie sounded hopeful. "You found a new place?"

Crap. Gage sighed, flopping onto his bed. He stared at the ceiling. "Kinda. I don't know if I'll be here long, though."

From the corner of his eye, Gage saw Ulric walk out of his office, freezing mid-step. Ulric glanced over; their gazes met. He'd heard Gage, then.

"When can I move in?" Wilkie asked.

Gage pinched the bridge of his nose. "Hang on. I'll check." He turned to Ulric, feeling sheepish. "My brother's looking for a place to stay. Would you mind if...?" He gestured around himself.

Ulric's throat worked. "Yeah, sure. I mean, go ahead. I don't mind."

"He'll share my room and everything. I swear he won't be a bother."

Ulric nodded. "You said you wouldn't be staying long, though?" He sounded disappointed.

Gage didn't want to discuss this with Wilkie still on the phone. He patted his mattress, inviting Ulric over. As soon as Ulric sat on Gage's bed, Gage leaned close, burying his nose against Ulric's soft side. Ulric always smelled so good.

"Who's that?" Wilkie asked. "Your roommate?"

Gage rolled over, laying his head on Ulric's lap. It was

firm, warm, and he found that he liked looking at Ulric from this close. "Ulric's a really good friend. I want him to be my best friend."

Ulric blushed. Was he still not convinced?

Wilkie laughed. "You know, people usually say that about bondmates, not best friends."

Gage was damn glad that Ulric couldn't hear him. "Yeah, well. He's special."

"Stop that." Ulric scowled.

Gage only smiled.

"So when can I move in?" Wilkie asked again.

"Next week? Give me some time to make space. We'll have to fit two beds in here." Gage watched Ulric for a reaction. But Ulric didn't seem to mind the short notice, either. That was really generous of him. With a smile, Gage tugged up a corner of Ulric's shirt, kissing his abdomen.

Ulric froze, sucking in his belly.

"Don't do that." Gage kissed him again, more firmly this time.

"Ew, Gage. What're you doing?" Wilkie sounded horrified. "Are those—sex sounds?"

Gage snorted. "No. It's kiss sounds."

"*Ew.*" Wilkie gagged. "Not in my ear."

Ulric turned red. "I'm leaving."

"Is he... an alpha?" Wilkie asked. "You're kissing him?"

Gage wrapped his arm around Ulric, shuffling further onto his lap to weigh him down. "No, you aren't leaving." To Wilkie, he said, "Yeah, Ulric's an alpha."

"And you're... kissing him?" Wilkie sounded confused. Hell, Gage would've been, too.

"It's complicated," Gage said. "You'll understand when you meet him."

"Huh," Wilkie said.

"Anyway, I have to go." Gage nuzzled Ulric's belly. "Quit looking for a job for now, all right? I'd rather you focus on your studies. Get that done, and then you can help again when you've gotten back on your feet."

Were it anyone else, Gage would've told them to get another job. But because Wilkie had been worrying about Debbie and the family's finances, he was having trouble with his grades. The added burden of a job would sink him into a deeper mess.

Wilkie sighed grudgingly. "Fine."

They ended the call, Gage dropping his phone onto the bed. Then he tackled Ulric in a bear hug, pinning him down against the mattress. Ulric yelped. "Hey!"

Gage leaned over him, grinning. "Thanks for helping. I wasn't expecting you to."

Ulric shrugged self-consciously. "Is your brother in trouble?"

"He needs a place to stay for a while."

"Kind of like you?" Ulric studied Gage; Gage's cheeks prickled with embarrassment.

He wasn't rich like Ulric was. Come to think of it, Gage still had to negotiate a new rental agreement, now that Wilkie was coming to live with them. "I'll pay the full sixteen hundred for rent," he said. And after this conversation, he was going to look for a second job. "For me and Wilkes."

Ulric frowned. "No, you won't."

Gage scowled. "My responsibility, Muffin. I'll handle it."

Ulric flushed. "I told you, you can live here for free."

"My brother, too?"

That, Ulric didn't answer.

"Either way, it's wrong," Gage said. "I'll pay you back."

"But you need the money."

Gage tried to ignore the burn of his humiliation. He was an alpha. He wanted to provide for everyone he cared about, but he wasn't earning as much as he needed. And Debbie's bills never seemed to end.

"You can pay with other things." Ulric's ears turned pink. "Like—Like the hugs. Twenty minutes a day, instead of five."

Gage considered it. He'd been hugging Ulric way past the five-minute mark lately. It didn't even feel like a payment. "You don't have to, you know. I'll look for another job."

Ulric flushed. "The hugs are worth more to me."

"They're just hugs." Then another idea struck him. "Say we extend the hugs to twenty minutes. How about I throw in a blowjob every day? More on my days off."

Ulric grew so red, he looked like he might burst. "N-no."

But he'd loved that one time in the living room. Gage had sucked on him, and Ulric had come so hard, he'd made *Gage* throb. Hell, the thought of having sex with Ulric every day—that was sending blood between Gage's legs.

"Why wouldn't you want that?" Gage kissed his jaw. "You can ask for anything. You can fuck me, you can knot me, you can tie me up. I'd do it."

Ulric bit his lip, looking so tempted that Gage knew it wouldn't take much more to convince him. "But it'll change things, won't it?" Ulric asked. "We wouldn't be friends anymore."

"We will." Gage linked their fingers, kissing Ulric's knuckles. "I promise."

It was a long moment before Ulric finally said, "Twenty minutes of daily hugs. And—And sex. Once a month."

"Just once?" That was disappointing.

Ulric twitched his shirt down over his belly, unable to meet Gage's eyes. Gage's chest burned with anger at the people from Ulric's past, the kids who'd bullied him, the parents who had never shown him any love.

It took a lot to break an alpha. And somehow, they'd done it.

Gage cupped Ulric's face, turning Ulric to face him. Then he kissed Ulric on the lips, a slow, sweet touch.

Ulric's breath hitched; his eyes grew wide. Gage slid his fingers down to Ulric's throat, and Ulric's pulse thudded against his fingertips.

"You're beautiful," Gage whispered. He almost felt embarrassed for saying it—he'd been thinking it to himself, keeping it a secret.

Ulric looked disbelieving. Then, hurt. "I'm not paying you to say shit like that," he growled.

"Yeah, precisely." Gage shoved him against the bed, pinning him down. Then he kissed Ulric again, harder. "I'm doing this because I like you. I'm touching you because I want it. Not because I owe you."

Ulric stared, his disbelief growing. "What the hell do you see in me?"

"I told you. You're kind. You're generous. You're amazing." And so much more. Gage slid his fingers into Ulric's hair, pressing their bodies flush together. "You're fucking sexy."

Ulric punched him lightly in the jaw. Pain burst through Gage's bones, but it didn't last so long. "You need to get your head checked," Ulric muttered. "Get off me."

"No." Gage leaned in, trailing kisses down Ulric's throat. "I jerked off to you last night, you know," he murmured. "And the night before. The entire week, I've been thinking about you. On top of me, under me. You've been making me come so hard, babe."

That admission made Gage's ears burn. They were housemates. He'd promised not to push Ulric into a relationship. But he needed Ulric to understand that he was desirable.

Ulric froze. He blinked hard, looking between their bodies. "Why would you?"

"Because you're hot." Gage reached under Ulric's shirt, squeezing his pecs. "Mm." Before Ulric could protest, Gage let his legs fall open around Ulric's thigh, so his growing length pressed against Ulric's hip. "There. Feel it?"

Ulric's breath hitched. Gage knew he could feel that bulge—it was thickening, eager to push inside Ulric's pants. Maybe he could slide it into Ulric's hot tightness again. And *now* he was hard.

"Is this some weird kink?" Ulric blurted, his neck red. "Where you like people like—like me?"

Gage scowled. "Not people like you. I like *you*."

He'd been serious when he'd asked if Ulric wanted to be boyfriends. Hell, Gage had no confidence in relationships, and he was ready to risk this falling apart.

Ulric stared, speechless. Gage waited for him to understand.

This wasn't something he could judge—Ulric was all twisted up inside, and Gage had the feeling it would take a while to make him confident again. Just like salvaging a snarl of crumpled wires—you couldn't pull them apart with a flick of your wrist. You had to pluck out every single strand, and hammer them flat so you could work them into a thing of beauty.

Gage had sat with his sister on many afternoons, helping her straighten out the jewelry wires she'd picked out from somewhere. It was slow work, and it was tough. But the final artwork made it all worth it in the end.

"What else do I have to say to convince you?" Gage murmured, nuzzling Ulric's jaw. "You don't believe that I get hot for you?"

Ulric hesitated, looking between their bodies. So Gage lifted his hips, he took Ulric's hand and pressed it flush against his covered cock. Ulric's palm was warm, a firm pressure. Gage couldn't help rolling his hips, letting Ulric feel how hard he'd gotten. "All for you."

Ulric's breath rushed out. He tightened his fingers around Gage, sliding them down to Gage's base, then back up. "Fuck."

"Believe me now?" Gage whispered. "No one here but us, babe. I'm not jerking off to porn or pretending I'm with someone else. It's just me and you."

Ulric swallowed audibly, staring at Gage's hips. So Gage undid his pants, he pulled out his cock, and wrapped Ulric's hot fingers around it. They both groaned.

Gage dragged a pillow over, turning Ulric so they both lay on their sides, facing each other. "Do what you want," Gage said. "If I come, it's because of you."

Ulric's pupils dilated. He looked at where they touched, Gage's cock stiff against his fist. Then, slowly, he pumped Gage, back and forth, sending jolts of pleasure up Gage's spine. Gage swore. Ulric stroked him harder, his own chest heaving, the line behind his pants growing thick.

Gage thrust into Ulric's fist, his breath rushing out.

"Yeah, like that. Been thinking about you touching me there. You feel good, Ulric. You're perfect."

Ulric growled. But he kept on stroking Gage, he cupped Gage's tip and flicked his wrist, the friction a blissful surprise. Gage tensed with his impending climax, watching the pleasure on Ulric's face.

Then Ulric ducked down, he closed his mouth around Gage and moaned, sucking so hungrily that his desire went right to Gage's balls. Gage swore, fucking up. Ulric was hot inside, eager for his come. Gage wanted to claim him, he wanted Ulric to be his.

He came in a rush of pleasure, emptying himself into Ulric, his spine arching, his legs trembling. The whole time, Ulric sucked on him, swallowing every drop.

Gage flopped onto his back, trying to catch his breath. "Fuck, babe. That was amazing."

Ulric wiped his mouth, sitting back. And there was a damp, dark spot on his pants, at the very tip of his bulge. Gage reached for it.

Ulric pulled his hips backward. "You don't have to."

Gage caught his hand and linked their fingers together. "Which part of this says I don't want to?"

He pointed at his still-hard cock. Ulric shrugged uncomfortably. "I don't... need it."

"C'mon, it's fair play. You made me come, now I get to return the favor."

"I can deal with it myself." He covered up with his hand—kind of pointless when his cock was bigger than that.

Gage leaned in, kissing Ulric's damp tip through his pants. Then he closed his mouth around it, and sucked lightly.

"Fuck, Gage." Ulric shoved his fingers into Gage's hair, pushing him away. But his eyes had darkened, his hand still fisted in Gage's hair. He was *especially* hot when his alpha instincts surfaced.

Why was he so resistant to Gage helping him, though? When he'd moaned so loudly the other day?

"You've had sex before, right?" Gage asked. "Before me."

Ulric shrugged. "Yeah, so?"

"What happens when they come before you? You let them jerk you off?"

Ulric blinked. Then he looked at his hands. "I finish off."

The way he said it, though... He couldn't possibly mean... "Alone?"

Ulric shrugged. Gage stared in horror. "Which bastard fucked you and then left before you came?"

"My ex." Ulric sighed. "It doesn't matter."

"Did he even... stay behind to get you off? At least once?"

Ulric shook his head.

Gage snarled, not even trying to suppress his anger. "No. They don't fucking get to do that to you."

He bowled Ulric over onto the mattress, kissing him hard on the lips. Gage straddled Ulric, dragging his wrists all over him, marking Ulric with pine. So Ulric belonged to *him*, so Ulric wouldn't let anyone else neglect him again.

"Mine," Gage growled, kissing Ulric so sweetly that Ulric groaned, his legs parting, his hands coming up to grasp Gage's shirt. "I'm gonna give you the best damn orgasm, babe."

"You already did," Ulric blurted.

Gage rumbled, sliding his tongue into Ulric's mouth. "Then I'll give you another. I'll give you so many, you won't remember the fuckers you dated before."

He pushed his hand into Ulric's pants, waiting until

their eyes met. Ulric bit his lip. But he spread his legs wider—an invitation. And Gage took Ulric's hard cock, he pumped it roughly, so Ulric tipped his head back, his mouth falling open.

That first time he'd gotten Ulric off—Gage hadn't been focusing on Ulric's pleasure so much. All he'd wanted was to claim Ulric, he'd wanted to get Ulric off at the same time he did.

Gage undid Ulric's pants, he pulled Ulric's cock out, letting that thick length jut up between them. It was musky, hot, and Gage pressed kisses along it, all the way to its tip. Then he licked it, rolling Ulric's salty precome through his mouth. Ulric was wet for him.

Gage had slept around with a bunch of people in the past. He wasn't particularly proud of it, but right now, he was glad for that experience. Because he now knew ways to make Ulric come, he knew ways to keep Ulric on the edge, to hold him until he thrashed and throbbed and swore.

By the end of tonight, Ulric would be so blissed-out, he wouldn't even want to leave Gage's bed.

And *that* was a wonderful thought.

Gage pushed his tongue into Ulric's mouth, thrusting in, stroking Ulric's cock in time with every thrust. When Ulric began to pant, Gage broke the kiss, trailing kisses down Ulric's jaw, down his throat, to his collarbones and his chest.

He kissed Ulric through his shirt—Gage knew Ulric wasn't ready to be naked in front of him. So he made his way down, all the way to Ulric's hips. There, Gage kissed Ulric's cock, up and down its length. Then he kissed Ulric's sac and squeezed it, and took Ulric's tip into his mouth.

Ulric wheezed, his spine arching. Gage pulled away before he could come.

"Damn it," Ulric hissed, his eyes flashing, his hands yanking on Gage's hair.

Gage grinned. "It'll be a long ride. Sit back and enjoy the show."

"I want to come," Ulric muttered.

Gage hummed, pulling Ulric's pants and boxers off. Then he spread Ulric's knees, and *fuck* Ulric's hole was small and pink. Gage throbbed at the sight of it.

He remembered how Ulric had felt inside. Tight, hot, slippery with lube. It had been mind-blowing. Because Ulric had let Gage enter him.

"I love the view," Gage told him.

Ulric flipped him off.

Gage leaned in, kissing down to Ulric's hole. Then he rubbed it slow and teasingly, he spread it open until he could see the dark shadows inside. He pushed two fingers in, dry. Ulric swore. But he bit his lip and took Gage, his throat turning pink.

Gage added some lube and stroked him there. Over and over, he teased Ulric's prostate, at the same time he sucked Ulric off. He worked Ulric until Ulric thrashed and gasped, rearing up, reaching for his own cock to bring himself off.

Gage pinned him down; Ulric snarled, and Gage held him until the moment passed, until Ulric wasn't on the verge of blowing his load anymore. Then, when Ulric's gaze lost that feral edge, Gage did it all again.

He lost track of how long he spent edging Ulric. He might've done it five times, maybe ten. By the time Gage began thinking he needed restraints for Ulric, Ulric's cock was flushed a dark red, his balls pulled tight, a sheen of sweat covering his skin.

"Damn you," Ulric hissed, his stare dangerous, his lips bitten red.

"Fuck, babe," Gage rasped, his cock aching. "I want a picture of you like that. You're so scorching hot, I'm gonna cream myself."

Ulric glanced at Gage's cock. And he lunged—Gage threw himself forward, slamming Ulric back against the bed. Ulric reared up anyway, snarling, trying to bite Gage's nose, his lips, his chest. Gage needed to restrain this alpha, he needed to claim him, and sink his cock inside.

"Down," Gage whispered, knocking Ulric's knees open, pinning his arms up above his head. "Be good, and I'll let you come."

"I'm done being good," Ulric snapped.

Gage's insides grew molten-hot. "Fuck, yeah." He leaned in, he shoved his cock up against Ulric's ass, and spread his cheeks with it. So Ulric could feel Gage's hunger, and how much Gage needed to plow inside him.

"Not gonna—" Ulric reared up; Gage threw himself against Ulric, weighing him down with his body. Then he grabbed the lube, he squirted some onto his hand and pushed it between them, slicking himself up.

"Damn you," Ulric hissed. But his eyes turned coal-dark, his pupils a thin ring of hazel.

"I'm gonna put this inside you," Gage rasped, sliding his tip down the crease of Ulric's thigh, letting him feel it. "And I'm gonna fill you up with my come."

Ulric thrashed against him, all alpha strength, at the same time musk billowed off his skin.

"Say 'no'," Gage whispered. "Just one word, and I'll stop. Nothing else is gonna end this."

"Fuck you," Ulric snarled.

And that was all the permission in the world.

Gage pushed his cock down, fitting it against Ulric's entrance. Ulric wheezed and bucked, trying to shove him off. And Gage plunged into his stretched-open hole, slamming his entire cock inside.

Ulric roared, taking him. Gage held him down, he locked their gazes together. Then he pulled back and snapped his hips, and his cock ground deep, the friction proving to both of them that Gage was inside, stretching Ulric open where he was vulnerable.

Ulric panted, adjusting to Gage's presence. And Gage began a vicious rhythm, he fucked Ulric the way he wanted to—rough and hard, so Ulric slid backward on the bed with every thrust, their hips meeting with loud, forceful slaps, Ulric's hole trying to suck him in deeper. Gage dragged him back and crammed his cock back inside, watching as Ulric's hole opened around him.

"Like my cock, babe?" Gage growled.

Ulric's only answer was a pleasured groan. It made the animal in Gage's chest roar.

He thrust in harder. And harder again. Until Ulric's groans filled his ears, until Ulric's cock flushed dark and ravenous between them, leaking so fervently that Gage grasped it, pumping it in time with his thrusts.

Ulric's spine arched. He dug his fingers into the sheets, his chest rising and falling in great, heaving pants. Gage almost left him hanging again, except Ulric looked so needy that Gage didn't have the heart to deny him further.

"Mine," Gage rasped, aiming for Ulric's prostate over and over. Ulric writhed and bucked beneath him. He ground hard against that one spot, all the way until Ulric choked on his moan.

Then he stroked Ulric's cock, firm and forceful, hitting every nerve until Ulric's eyes rolled back and he came and came and *came*, great spurts of white that streaked all over his chest, onto his neck and his face, his body clenching so hard around Gage that Gage came inside him, violent and unexpected.

Right after, Gage withdrew, flopping next to Ulric on the bed. Then he gathered Ulric against himself, just catching his breath.

Ulric pulled off his come-streaked glasses, slinging his arm across his face. "Fuuuck."

Gage smiled and kissed him. "You can still talk? Means I didn't do a good job."

"That was..." Ulric tipped his head back, a low growl rumbling from his throat. "Damn."

"Never had anything like that?" Gage kissed him again.

Ulric shook his head. Gage felt a surge of pride. He'd been Ulric's first for something. And that meant a lot.

"That's how you should be treated," Gage murmured.

"I swear I was gonna murder you." Ulric narrowed his eyes. "I wanted to fucking come already."

"Yeah, and you were so damn hot when you did that." Gage snuggled against him. "I love when you get all fierce-alpha on me."

Ulric stiffened.

"What did I say?" Gage frowned, thinking back. "You don't like being told you're hot?"

Ulric looked uncomfortable. "You said the L-word. I hope you didn't mean it."

Oh. Gage rubbed his mouth. Had he meant it? "I don't know."

"I'm going to have a shower," Ulric muttered, rolling away.

Gage caught him around the middle, pulling him back. "Stay for a bit," he murmured. "I like having you in my bed."

Ulric snuffled, looking down as though he hadn't realized where he was. And Gage marked him again, trailing his pine scent down Ulric's body. "I like when you wear my scent, too," he added.

Ulric swallowed. "This isn't a payment, is it? Tonight."

"No." Gage smiled, wrapping himself around Ulric. "That was freely given, babe. I don't expect anything in return. All I wanted was your company."

Ulric flushed pink; Gage's heart missed a beat. "I'm not a babe."

"You're one to me."

"But isn't that what you call omegas?"

"Nah." Gage kissed his nape. "It's what I call someone I really like."

Then he kissed Ulric again, just breathing in that honey oak scent. Ulric sighed, finally relaxing, burying his face against the mattress. They stayed like that for a while, Gage stroking Ulric's side, holding him in a loose hug. That wasn't a payment, either.

"I can't give you a family," Ulric mumbled into the mattress. "I'm just..."

"You're perfect," Gage whispered.

He looked at Ulric's flushed cheek, and his pink ear. Something in his chest *tugged*. It felt as though he was falling and falling, and he didn't know when he would hit the ground, or if he ever would.

Being with Ulric made him feel that way. Gage tried not to think about why, or the possible consequences this had.

So he buried the feeling, pretending that everything

was the same as before. He didn't know how to deal with relationships. His life was still surrounded by bills he couldn't pay off.

He tucked his face against Ulric, and imagined that Ulric was the only thing that mattered.

18

YOU'RE DATING AN ALPHA?

Ulric should've known that Gage's brother would be just as beautiful as he was.

Wilkie Frost was an omega in his early twenties, a slender young thing that Ulric's parents would've wanted him to marry in a heartbeat. That was all Ulric could think about as Gage helped Wilkie move first a mattress, then a bed frame upstairs.

When they were almost done with the moving, Gage joined Ulric in the kitchen, pulling a chair over to the island counter. "Did something happen?" Gage asked, stroking Ulric's back. "You look sad."

Ulric shrugged. "Sometimes I wish I was normal. Like everyone else."

Gage huffed. "Yeah, same here."

"*You?*" Ulric tried not to roll his eyes. "You'd win like, ten beauty pageants in a row."

Gage smiled wryly. "And then what?"

"And then you'd get everything in the world."

"Doesn't always work that way."

That, Ulric found hard to believe. "It doesn't?"

Gage leaned into him, all pine and fresh sweat scent. "I'm living in your fancy house because I'm broke, Ulric."

There were two ways to look at that. One, Gage wouldn't be here if he wasn't broke. Two, Ulric had invited Gage to live here precisely because he'd been a sucker for Gage's looks. He was still a sucker for Gage's face, and now, his hands, too. Along with everything else about Gage.

Either way, both trains of thought were pretty depressing.

"I think I've just upset you more." Gage winced. "What did I say wrong?"

"Nothing." Ulric left his seat, heading to the fridge.

"Hey."

"I told you, it's nothing."

"Don't lie to me, babe." Gage caught Ulric's arm, turning him around. And he pressed Ulric lightly against the fridge, leaning in so his lips brushed Ulric's cheek.

Ulric stopped breathing. He still couldn't believe it, every time Gage kissed him. "Is this a—"

"Not a payment." Gage leaned in, pressing their mouths together. Pleasure hummed through Ulric's nerves. "Mm. You always taste good."

Ulric's face heated up. "We're just—just friends."

"Yeah." Gage kissed him deeper, and Ulric's knees grew weak.

Sometimes, he wondered if Gage minded his fumbling kisses. *Gage* kissed like a pro. But when they kissed, instead of mentioning Ulric's lack of experience, Gage only cupped Ulric's face and fitted their mouths more snugly together. Ulric hadn't the confidence to initiate this with him.

Gage found him hot, though. As crazy as it was, Ulric believed that now. Gage liked hugging him.

Actually, maybe Gage liked kissing him, too.

Ulric broke the kiss, his heart pattering. "Why?"

Warmth filled Gage's smile. "Because. You need a reason?"

"Everything has a reason." That was the basis in Ulric's data analysis. Hell, it was his job to find out why the numbers worked the way they did.

Gage pressed their foreheads together, bumping into Ulric's glasses. "Do you not want me living here because I'm broke?"

Ulric's thoughts tilted sideways. "How'd you even come to that conclusion?"

"Because you weren't happy when I said it."

"That's not what I was unhappy about."

"Then what is it?" Gage cupped his jaw, brushing his thumb across Ulric's lower lip. Tingles raced through Ulric's skin. "Tell me, Muffin."

Ulric sighed. "Am I really a muffin?"

Gage grinned. "Well, you said I'm the stud."

"That's true."

In a whisper, Gage added, "I like your curves. A lot."

Ulric thought about protesting, but Gage took his hand, rubbing it against his bulge. *That* was inappropriate. And lovely.

"Gage, where is—" Wilkie stopped abruptly in the kitchen doorway, his eyes almost falling out of his head. Then he spun around, heading straight out. "I did not just see that."

Ulric's heart sank. He hadn't realized that he'd wanted Gage's family to accept him, too.

It's not like Gage wants you to be part of his family.

"Hey, Wilkes. Come back." Gage leaned away, grasping Ulric's hand. "We'll need to get this straight now that you're living here."

Ulric flushed. Wilkie turned back, looking awkward.

"Time for proper introductions," Gage said.

"We already went over that," Ulric muttered.

Gage gave him a pointed look. "Ulric, this is Wilkie, my little brat brother. He's working on a college degree right now."

"I'm not a brat," Wilkie said. He smiled at Ulric, though. "Thanks again for letting me come live with you. If you want to win any favors with Gage, he's a sucker for lemon popsicles."

"I didn't know that," Ulric admitted, tucking the information away.

"And he also likes lace panties." Wilkie rolled his eyes. "Ask me how I know."

"How?" Ulric asked, glancing at Gage. Lace panties, huh?

Gage's ears turned pink. "Wilkes, you traitor!"

Wilkie puffed up, all indignant. "Well, if you didn't bring some random person home and they threw their panties on my teddy—which is pretty gross, just so you know—"

"I threw it in the trash," Gage protested. Then he met Ulric's eyes, looking apologetic. "I don't remember who it was, actually. Couldn't have been all that interested in them. And I scrubbed down your teddy, Wilkes."

"Teddy turned all splotchy after that," Wilkie said. To Ulric, he added, "You probably don't want Gage scrubbing you down, or you'll end up with missing patches—"

"Wilkes. I'm sorry about your teddy, but *hush*." Gage flipped him off. "Anyway, this is Ulric. We're really close friends."

Wilkie looked from Gage, to Ulric, and back to Gage. "Friends, huh?"

Ulric's neck heated. The things he did with Gage... those weren't what regular friends engaged in. Not the kisses, not the cock-sucking, and definitely not any intimate touching in front of family.

Gage met his eyes, looking as though there was more he wanted to say. In a regular movie, this was where Gage would introduce them as boyfriends.

Except they weren't.

"So... you're not boyfriends yet?" Wilkie asked. "Just alpha friends-with-benefits?"

Ulric cringed. That sounded a lot worse than 'friends'.

"We're still considering it," Gage said, sliding his arm around Ulric's waist. He looked wistful. "I don't think we're ready yet."

They'd probably never be, really.

They waited until Wilkie left the kitchen. Gage pulled Ulric close, kissing him on the lips. "So... you still don't wanna be more?" Gage murmured.

Ulric's heart skipped. "You still want to?"

Gage gave him a lopsided smile. "Yeah. I told you, I like all of you."

That sounded too good to be true. "It's not... some kind of payment? For you living here?"

Gage's smile fell. "You think I'd do that to you?"

Ulric bit his lip. He wanted to know what it was like to be Gage's boyfriend. He wanted to be Gage's, so much that his heart hurt. Every time Gage smiled at him, every time Gage told him he was perfect, Ulric's defenses crumbled a little. And the wall around himself right now —it was almost paper-thin.

"I'm still trying to look good enough for you," Ulric mumbled.

Gage pressed him against the counter. "You're doing great with your diet. You've been getting really good with your cardio, too. But honestly? I just want you to be healthy so I can have you for a long time, babe. That's all. I like your curves."

"But you're a gym rat," Ulric protested.

Gage laughed. "Did I ever tell you why I got into this fitness thing?" Ulric shook his head. "I wasn't gonna lose in a fight again. Going to the gym, getting stronger—all that became a habit. I enjoy it. But I don't need you to do the same."

Ulric turned Gage's words over in his mind, trying to look for a nugget of judgment that would prove that Ulric wasn't good enough. But he couldn't find it. Gage just smiled at him, looking fond.

Ulric gulped. What if... Gage really thought he was perfect, and they could be more? "We'll see," he said.

Gage squeezed his ass. "No rush." He kissed Ulric on the lips. That sent tingles all the way to Ulric's toes. "Anyway, I stink from all that moving. I'm gonna take a shower, and then we'll watch a movie, all right?"

Ulric nodded, smiling when Gage pressed a kiss to his temple.

He leaned back against the kitchen counter, half-thinking that maybe all of this was a dream. Then he went to the fridge, craving a sweet snack.

There were no sweets in the fridge—there hadn't been for weeks. Ulric wanted a slice of cake, or maybe a fizzy drink. Or ice cream. Donuts. Muffins. Cookies. He checked every corner, and even the freezer. But he'd been thorough in purging all of those.

He sighed and looked down at himself, wishing this diet would show some results more quickly. They never did. Eventually, he settled on an apple that Gage had bought, crunching through its crisp flesh.

Ulric's phone buzzed. He pulled it out—there was a

new message from his mom. His heart sank. Was this the part where she told him she didn't mind who he fell in love with?

He held his breath and opened the message. Against the gray background, her text read, *I'll be in southern California this week for a business meeting. I'll expect you to show me around the city while I'm there.*

Ulric sighed. He shouldn't even have tried to hope. He had known how it would turn out.

Sometimes, he wished that maybe she could just... love him. He'd tried asking her to. She never listened. And then Ulric wished he had one of those loving parents like the ones on TV. The sort who loved you regardless of anything.

If Mom ever met Gage... would she convince Gage to see Ulric the way she did?

Ulric's stomach dropped. He closed the message and shoved the phone into his pocket. He wasn't going to think about it.

19

THE SURPRISE

On his lunch break, Gage drove to the bakery downtown, where the best cakes in town were. He'd just received his paycheck. He wanted to do something nice for Ulric.

The selection at Ben's Buns was one of his favorites—whenever his mom or sister felt disheartened, Gage came here to get a treat for them. Ulric wasn't unhappy, but over the past week, Gage had caught him staring listlessly into the fridge. He'd been eating healthily lately—Gage wanted to reward him with something nice.

He stepped into the store, heading over to the refrigerated cakes. Individually-wrapped slices lined the top shelf—fruit cakes, chocolate cakes, strawberry cakes... His sister loved the Blackforest cake, and his mom, the tiramisu.

"Hello," Ben said cheerily behind the counter. "What would you like today?"

"A slice of the coffee cake, please," Gage said. After some consideration, he added, "And the tres leches."

Ulric loved coffee, Gage knew. So the coffee-cream

cake was a good bet. The tres leches was Gage's favorite —it was cake soaked through with three different kinds of milk: whole milk, evaporated milk, and condensed milk, and it was topped with a layer of whipped cream. To Gage, it was pretty damn decadent. Would Ulric enjoy it, too?

He paid at the register, about to leave when the door chimed behind him.

"Gage?" Jesse asked. "Didn't think I'd meet you here."

Gage turned to see his cousin at the store entrance, Jesse's three-year-old toddling off to peek at the buns in the display cases. Jesse's husband wasn't with them— Dom was probably on duty at the fire station.

But what caught his eye was the bulge of Jesse's abdomen—instead of the gentle curve of a beer belly, the bump was a lot more pronounced. It looked... like an omega's belly, a heavily pregnant one.

Jesse was an alpha.

"Uh," Gage said, alarmed. "What the hell happened to you? Do you need to see a doctor?"

A few patrons glanced over; Jesse turned so they weren't facing the rest of the bakery. "What does it look like to you?"

Gage stopped next to him, unable to help staring. This really did not look right.

"Wanna touch it?" Jesse grinned, waving toward his belly.

So Gage put his palm on it, half-expecting this to be some medical condition he'd never heard of.

Somewhere in Jesse's abdomen, something kicked against his palm. A child? Gage's mouth fell open. "Fuck. How?"

Jesse smiled wryly. "Long story. But the short version

is that I had an organ implant." He tugged his shirt up to reveal a long silver scar going down his abdomen, stark against the stretch marks and various other scars covering his skin.

"So—so you're pregnant," Gage said, his mind going several different directions at once. Alphas could get pregnant. He was looking at a pregnant alpha right now. Could *he* get pregnant?

"Yup, twins. After this, I'm gonna have the uterus removed," Jesse said, looking pretty damn calm despite what he was telling Gage.

Gage tried to digest all of this. "So, Owen..."

"He came from me, too." Jesse grinned. "He looks like me and Dom, huh?"

Gage stared at the kid running around the store, darting between patrons to return to his dad. Yeah, Owen was pretty cute. But he'd come from an alpha dad. Two alpha dads.

"So you can just... walk into a hospital and ask for a uterus?" Gage asked.

Jesse's expression closed off. "No. But if you're interested, I can dig up some contacts. It's a long process."

Something wasn't right there. Carefully, Gage asked, "You weren't on board with the—the uterus? But you kept it anyway?"

Jesse cracked a smile. "Some things are worth fighting for, Gage."

Gage thought on those words, watching as Jesse picked out a pile of chocolate donuts. Then Jesse called Owen over, and got a cheesy bun for him.

What would Ulric say if he discovered that alphas could get pregnant, too? Not that they were even boyfriends, but... this was news that Gage couldn't keep to himself.

When Jesse was done paying for his donuts, Gage asked, "Can I take a pic of your belly? To, uh. To show a friend."

Jesse grinned. "That boyfriend of yours?"

Gage's face heated. "He's not my boyfriend."

Jesse snorted. "You smell like another alpha, Cuz."

That was because Gage had pulled Ulric close last night, and he'd dragged Ulric's wrists all over himself. He sniffed at the honey oak scent on his skin, mixed in with his own pine. "We're just really good friends."

"Don't forget to invite us to the wedding."

"Fuck off," Gage muttered under his breath. He might be willing to give a relationship a try, but marriage was so far off the table, Gage couldn't even smell it.

Jesse pulled his shirt back up, looking proud. And now Gage realized why Jesse had been defending his belly that time they'd play-wrestled—Jesse had been protecting his unborn babies back then.

What did it feel like to be a dad?

Gage snapped a quick picture with his phone, intending to show Ulric later tonight. "See you around," Gage said. "Congrats. Sorry for trying to hit your belly that other time."

"It's fine. You didn't know." Jesse waved. "And text me if you want to babysit. You've seen how many kids the team has."

Gage remembered the children running around during the barbecue party, the pair of snake-aficionados with their snake streamers fluttering in the breeze. "Can Ulric and I crash the next station party, too?"

Jesse shrugged. "I don't see why not. I'll text you."

They parted ways at the street, Gage returning to the

gym, tucking his precious cakes into the staff pantry fridge.

Then came the long wait—despite loving his job, time dragged all the way until he could clock off.

In the middle of waiting, Gage got a text from his mom: *Looks like we got an extra bill this month. I don't want to tell Debbie. She'll feel even more guilty.*

Mom had included a picture of the extra money owed—mid-four figures. Gage thought about the cakes he'd stashed in the fridge, and sighed. Maybe he needed that second job anyway.

And he wasn't going to tell Ulric about his financial troubles; he didn't want Ulric feeling obliged to pay for anything.

At 5PM, Gage checked out with his supervisor, grabbed his cakes, and set off.

Ulric was typing at his computer when Gage got home. Gage hid the cakes in the fridge and went back upstairs, his heart skipping. "Hey, babe."

"Give me a minute." Ulric finished with his reports—all the math and charts and graphs that Gage didn't understand, and probably never would. Gage was content to pull up a chair next to him, and breathe in his scent.

After some minutes, Ulric shut down his computer, sagging back into his seat. "That's done. I'm off work now."

Gage grinned and pounced on him. "What do you want to do tonight?"

Ulric smiled, not protesting when Gage tipped his face up and kissed him full on the lips. "I guess I should go work out before we eat."

Gage ran his hands down Ulric's front, then his sides and his back, just touching him all over. It had been hours since he'd felt Ulric against him. "I'll spot for you."

Ulric sighed, his eyelids fluttering shut. "I can manage it."

"Why don't we try some back squats today?" Gage asked. "Builds your core."

"I don't even know what back squats are."

"That's okay. I'll teach you."

Mostly, he just wanted to spot for Ulric. Back squats had a reputation for having one of the most awkward spotting positions—you had to spoon someone, all but cup their chest in case they needed help with the barbell.

Gage was a professional at the gym, and he had no inclination to touch any of his clients more than he needed to. But Ulric was different. Gage wanted every excuse to touch him. And it just so happened that they had the privacy of their own little gym. "Go get dressed," Gage murmured, kissing Ulric's ear. "I'll meet you in the exercise room."

Ulric shivered, his lips curving into a smile. Gage had the feeling it wasn't a workout that Ulric was excited about.

20

SO YOU WANT A BABY?

Gage suppressed the urge to 'accidentally' step into Ulric's bedroom while he was changing. He had seen every part of Ulric now, but in stages—his back, his belly, his exquisite ass. He wanted to see all of Ulric at once, though.

He was content to wait. Ulric knew that Gage would touch him all over, even with all his clothes on. And he enjoyed Gage's touch. That was the best part.

Some minutes later, Ulric stepped into the exercise room, clad in his usual T-shirt and pants. Gage set down the barbell he'd been doing reps with, pulling off some weights so it'd be more manageable for Ulric. "Get over here."

"I'm not some dog," Ulric said, but he was smiling.

They went through some stretches together, before Gage had Ulric pick up the barbell, resting it across his shoulder blades. "Comfortable?"

Ulric nodded. So Gage stood behind him, holding his hands inches away from Ulric's pecs. He followed Ulric through a squat, then another, barely any space between their bodies.

Ulric's ass bumped into Gage's hips, his back slid against Gage's pecs. Ulric huffed. "I see why you wanted to do this," he rumbled.

Gage grinned. "Just wanted to teach you a new exercise, was all."

"Yeah, right."

"C'mon, do another five reps."

Ulric acquiesced, squatting with the barbell, breathing deeply with each rep. Gage gave up all pretenses and just held his chest, squatting with him, sometimes brushing his hips against Ulric's curvy ass.

"Best way to exercise," Gage murmured.

"Do you do this with everyone at the gym?" Ulric scowled over his shoulder.

"Nope. Just you. Been waiting all day." Gage kissed his nape. Then, while Ulric continued with the squats, Gage kept one hand against his chest, sliding his other palm down Ulric's front, all the way to the bulge between his legs.

It was *so* nice when Ulric squatted, his legs wide open, his cock hanging down for Gage to play with.

"Gage Frost," Ulric muttered, sounding amused.

"Fucking sexy stud muffin," Gage whispered, squeezing his cock. "'Specially when your pants wedge between your asscheeks. Leaves nothing to the imagination, babe."

Ulric turned pink. "You're checking out my ass?"

"Amongst other things. All good." Gage growled, trailing his wrist down Ulric's body, marking him all over.

"You didn't do this while I was back at the gym," Ulric said.

Gage snorted. "More privacy here. It lets me do this."

He stroked down Ulric's entire length, squeezing his tip. Ulric's breath rushed out; he lost his balance and tipped forward. Gage hauled him back so their bodies pressed flush together, his own bulge nestled between Ulric's asscheeks. Then he continued stroking Ulric, until Ulric grew thick against his palm.

"What kind of exercise is this?" Ulric hissed, his breaths coming sharper now.

Gage laughed. "We're pumping. Keep doing your squats."

He pulled Ulric's cock out, angling it downward. When Ulric squatted again, his tip brushed the exercise mat—he swore at the friction.

"It's kissing the floor," Gage murmured. "You're forging a whole new relationship with the gym, Muffin."

"Fuck off," Ulric muttered, but his cock jerked against Gage's fingers. Gage rocked his own length against his alpha, just enjoying this intimacy, Ulric letting Gage play with his body. Then, on Ulric's next squat, when Ulric's ass was nice and spread, Gage fitted his cock flush against Ulric's crack, Ulric's cheeks squeezing around him when he stood back up.

"Mm, fuck," Gage growled.

"You're having way too much fun with this," Ulric said, breathless.

"I'm having way too much fun with *you*." Gage grinned, kissing his shoulder. "Has working out ever been this much fun? For you, I mean."

"Well, no." Ulric huffed. "Save for the time you spotted for me on the bench press—you damn near straddled my face. I could almost see your cock."

"I'll let you see it the next time," Gage promised. "I'll even let it drag all over your face."

"Damn it," Ulric groaned.

"Consider it a reward." Gage scooped Ulric's balls out of his pants, squeezing them. He angled Ulric's length so it pointed straight ahead, pumping it nice and slow, in time with Ulric's squats.

"You'll drive me insane," Ulric panted.

"Are you close?"

"No."

"Guess I'll have to try harder. I want your come spraying everywhere, babe. Have you seen that one video? Where some guy sits on an exercise machine handle, and he fucks himself on it? He came so many times. I want to do that to you."

Someone shut a door loudly—Gage's bedroom? A moment later, Wilkie stalked past the exercise room doorway, his face scrunched up, his gaze locked straight in front of him.

Had he heard their conversation? Gage bit down his grin. "Sorry, Wilkes."

"Go away," Wilkie said, halfway down the stairs.

Ulric winced. "Your poor brother."

Gage just laughed. "Pros and cons of having siblings. You hate them and love them at the same time. But more love than hate."

Then he thought about the twins Jesse was expecting, and he remembered the picture on his phone. And the surprise he still had for Ulric in the fridge.

"Here, set the barbell back," Gage said.

Ulric replaced it on the rack; Gage pulled Ulric flush against himself, pumping his cock good and hard. Ulric's breath rushed out. "But the workout—"

"I have something better. C'mon."

Gage worked him over, slipping his fingers between Ulric's cheeks, teasing his hole. He pushed harder on it, he flicked his fist around Ulric's tip, and Ulric tensed, riding the path to no return.

With a groan, he spilled hot into Gage's palm, so fucking sexy that Gage wanted to pin him down, and ride him for a good long while. Instead, Gage licked Ulric's bitter come off his hand. "Let's get some dinner."

"What about you?" Ulric tipped his head back against Gage's shoulder, his eyes glazed over.

"Later. I've got some important stuff to show you." Gage straightened Ulric's clothing, tugging him out of the exercise room. They made their way down to the kitchen, where Wilkie was perched at the island counter, eating out of a can.

Ulric frowned. "Is that enough for you?"

Wilkie glanced up. "Yeah, I've been getting by on this. It's pretty good."

It was canned soup. Not a surprise to Gage, but Ulric frowned harder. "Are you sure?"

"I'll make burgers," Gage said, his heart swelling for Ulric. "Want one, Wilkes?"

Wilkie glanced at his phone, hesitating. "Nah."

Had Mom sent him the news about the other bill? Gage should've told her not to. Damn it. "I'll make you half a burger," Gage said. "Eat that so you won't get hungry tonight."

He tucked the cake box deeper into the fridge so Ulric wouldn't catch sight of it. Then, while he waited for the burgers to sizzle, Gage pulled out his phone.

He thought about showing Ulric the picture first, before reconsidering—would Ulric think Gage wanted him to have a baby? Gage decided it was safest to start the conversation with Wilkie, and see how Ulric responded.

"I bumped into my cousin today. Remember Jesse, Wilkes? He's pregnant. Like, about-to-pop pregnant."

Wilkie's eyes nearly fell out of his head. "But he's an alpha. How can he get pregnant?"

Ulric had been scrolling through something on his phone. He looked up, his attention snared. Gage showed Wilkie the picture of Jesse; Ulric padded closer, looking over Gage's shoulder.

Ulric sucked in a sharp breath. "That's... an alpha."

"Yeah. Remember seeing him at the barbecue party?" Gage asked.

Ulric nodded. "He had his husband with him."

For a second, his expression turned wistful. Then he looked down at his own belly. "How did he get pregnant?"

"He said he had an implanted uterus. Didn't want to tell me how he'd gotten it, though." Gage zoomed in on the biggest scar on Jesse's abdomen. "But damn, look at that."

He imagined being cut open, having an organ put inside his body. How did that even work? You'd probably have to slice apart the abs to fit the uterus in there, and then let the abs heal so they could support the weight of a baby. Not to mention all the physical therapy.

And this was Jesse's *second* pregnancy. How did he even get a uterus to stick around for that long?

"So... so you want a baby?" Ulric asked, his voice slightly off.

Gage froze. Had he offended Ulric? "Do you want one?"

"No, I was just—Hypothetically speaking."

Gage hadn't thought that far yet. But maybe... "You didn't answer my question. Is that something *you* want?"

Ulric squirmed, looking away. "I don't know."

To the side, Wilkie snorted, covering up his smile. "Yeah, you guys are just friends. You don't need a baby. Yet."

There was that, too. Gage went back to flip his burgers, wondering about Ulric's blush. Did he, or did he not want a family? Or should Gage even be asking those questions?

"Oops," Wilkie said. When Gage turned, Wilkie was behind him, handing his phone back. "Don't leave your phone lying around."

Gage glanced at his screen—the image had somehow changed to his mom's photo of the new bill. Gage's heart sank.

Even if he wanted a baby, he couldn't afford it right now. He shoved the phone into his pocket, sighing.

"What's wrong?" Ulric came up to him, touching Gage gingerly on the back.

"Nothing," Gage said.

Ulric frowned. "Something upset you."

Gage shook his head. "Nah. Just life."

"I should just get a job," Wilkie muttered.

"No," Gage growled, turning. "Get your life back together first."

But Wilkie scowled. "What, and let you shoulder all the bills?"

Gage froze. He glanced at Ulric, who had gone still. "No, we'll talk about that later, Wilkes."

"Why can't we talk about it now?" Wilkie straightened his shoulders, pissed. "Debbie—"

Gage dropped the spatula and dragged him out of the kitchen, clapping his hand over Wilkie's mouth. "Don't mention it in front of Ulric," he hissed, afraid that Ulric could hear any of this.

Wilkie glared. "Why not?"

"Because." Gage didn't want Ulric to see him differently. He didn't want Ulric to feel obliged to pay, he didn't want to turn their relationship into a money thing. He didn't want to be an alpha who had to rely on someone else to fix his problems. "It'll mess up what I have with Ulric," he said. "Please don't."

Wilkie stared at him for a moment. Then his shoulders sagged. "But I don't want you to be sad, either."

"I'll manage." Gage smiled crookedly. "I'm an alpha. We fix things."

Wilkie rolled his eyes; Gage kissed him on the forehead. Then he ushered Wilkie back into the kitchen, sitting him down. "Don't fill your stomach with that soup," Gage told him. "You're eating a burger tonight."

"You said half a burger!" Wilkie protested.

"I changed my mind." Gage ruffled his hair. "You need to eat better, Wilkes."

Wilkie scowled. When Gage turned back to the stove, someone came up behind him, sliding warm arms around his waist. Gage's heart missed a beat. Ulric rarely initiated hugs with him, so this—it was special.

Ulric leaned into his back. "You're a good brother."

"I'm just looking out for Wilkes because he won't look out for himself," Gage muttered.

"Hey!" Wilkie scowled.

"Just the truth," Gage retorted.

"But who's going to look out for you, Gage?" Ulric asked.

Wilkie laughed. "I think I like you, Ulric."

Ulric snuffled awkwardly, his face turning pink. Gage's instincts rumbled. "Hey. Don't you go flirting with him, Wilkes. He's mine."

"He's your *friend*," Wilkie said. "I can flirt with him all I want."

Would Ulric... respond to that flirting? He'd said he only liked alphas, but... Gage turned, wondering if he needed to stake his claim in front of Wilkie. Ulric laughed softly. "Jealous, Gage?"

"I'm not," Gage growled.

"I like omegas enough to dance with them," Ulric said, holding his hand out toward Wilkie.

Wilkie frowned. "I don't know how to dance."

Ulric wriggled his fingers, beckoning him over. "Just don't step on my feet."

He pulled Wilkie into an awkward dance—was that a waltz? Who even danced waltzes these days? Ulric talked Wilkie through a short segment of a dance, showing Wilkie where to put his feet, and where to move next. Wilkie fumbled some, but Ulric corrected him patiently each time.

He felt... a bit like a teacher. And maybe also a dad. Gage had the distinct impression that Ulric would make a great father.

Ulric began counting out the beats, pulling Wilkie closer as they did a series of fumbling steps through the kitchen. Gage knew it was just a dance, and he knew Ulric wasn't interested in Wilkie, but *damn*, he should be the one in Ulric's arms.

"Sounds like there's a growling dog in the kitchen," Wilkie said, sending Gage a shit-eating grin. "Maybe I should stand closer—"

Wilkie tripped and face-planted across Ulric's chest.

In a heartbeat, Gage was on the other side of the kitchen, crowding up against Ulric's back, sliding his arm between Wilkie and Ulric. "Fuck off, Wilkes," Gage muttered. "Mine."

"Not yours until you mark him," Wilkie said, lifting his eyebrows.

Ulric sucked in a sharp breath.

Gage growled. And he sank his teeth into Ulric's skin—not his scent gland, but close. Then he bit harder, sucking on Ulric's neck so hard that he'd leave a hickey there. A big damn one. "Mine."

Ulric grunted. "Fuck."

Wilkie released Ulric so fast, Gage's instincts rumbled with delight. "Gross," Wilkie said. "Don't do that with me around."

Gage shoved Ulric against the wall and sucked on his neck, hard enough that Ulric's breath hitched and he curled his fingers into Gage's hair. "What the hell, Gage?"

But his pulse raced beneath Gage's tongue. Gage bit harder, tasting Ulric's sweat from the workout earlier. "Mm. Mine."

By the time he released Ulric, there was a prominent pink spot on Ulric's neck, that would turn into a bruise tomorrow. And Ulric was flushed a dark red. He looked wonderful.

"You free this Saturday?" Gage growled. He wanted a whole day in bed with Ulric, he wanted to mark the rest of this alpha. Until every inch of his body was all Gage's.

Ulric winced. "I, uh. I have to go to Highton."

He hadn't mentioned that earlier. "I'll come with you," Gage said.

"No! I mean, I have an appointment. It'll be inconvenient." Ulric eased himself away, suddenly unable to meet Gage's eyes.

"I'll wait until it's over. There's a couple of good restaurants there."

Ulric winced. "No, it's fine. I'll go with you another

time."

Why was he so uneasy about Gage going to Highton with him? Gage frowned. "What's wrong? What're you going there for?"

"Nothing." Ulric squirmed. "I mean, it's something. Nothing important."

Gage stared, trying to figure this out. At the back of his mind, little alarms rang. "At least tell me what's going on."

"I have to go meet someone."

"Who?"

Ulric shrugged. "Just—someone. No one you need to see."

He couldn't be meeting some secret lover that Gage didn't know about. Ulric wasn't that sort of person. But why didn't he trust Gage with his concerns? "It's a long drive to Highton. I'll drop you off," Gage said.

"No. I'll be fine." Ulric pursed his lips tightly.

"Is someone going to Highton?" Wilkie poked his head back into the kitchen. "I need to hitch a ride there."

Ulric stared at him for a long moment. Then he sighed. "I can take you."

"But not me?" That just wasn't fair. Gage narrowed his eyes. "Ulric."

He would trust Ulric with his life. Wouldn't Ulric trust Gage with the same?

"The burgers are burning." Ulric pointed at the stove. Gage thought he was trying to fake his way out at first, except he smelled the faint smoke.

Gage swore, whirling around to save the burgers. It wasn't like him to burn those things. But it wasn't like Ulric to keep secrets, either.

By the time he turned back, Ulric had disappeared from the kitchen.

21

THE BOX AT THE BACK OF THE FRIDGE

Ulric crept down the stairs, his heart thumping. His stomach felt like it was about to digest itself.

All night, he'd cooped himself up in his bedroom, unwilling to go out and face Gage. Gage had knocked on the door. He'd sent a text, too, telling Ulric he'd left a couple of burgers in the fridge. Ulric wished that Gage wouldn't keep being so nice.

He'd looked in his mirror at the hickey. It was redder now—a marking that Gage had left on him. Just the thought of it—it made Ulric tingle all over.

This was what it felt like to belong.

And it was dangerous. Ulric wanted more of those marks, he wanted Gage's lips all over him.

He shoved those thoughts aside, turning on the kitchen lights. On the fridge, Gage had stuck a piece of paper with an arrow pointing toward the door handle. *This shelf,* he'd written.

Ulric's heart fluttered. How many omegas had Gage done this for? He didn't want to know.

He heated up the lettuce-wrap burgers in the microwave, before pulling up a stool to the island counter, tucking into the burgers. Savory meat juices leaked onto his tongue; he groaned. Even when it was slightly burned, Gage's food was amazing.

Ulric polished off the burgers, licking his fingers. Then, because his mom wasn't here to judge him, he licked his plate, too.

He could still hear her voice, though. *Don't laugh like that, Ulric. It's embarrassing. Why are you looking at that alpha? You shouldn't. Respectable alphas don't fawn over their peers.*

He imagined introducing her to Gage. He imagined telling her, *This is who I really like.* And she would scoff and tell him there was no point to that relationship. It wouldn't benefit their family.

Even if Gage made his heart sing, even if Ulric wore Gage's scent on his skin.

Ulric's heart tightened. He tried not to think about Saturday, but the thoughts and anxiety crept up on him, making it difficult to breathe. He didn't want to spend hours with his mom. But he couldn't abandon her when he'd agreed to show her around, either. He just... had to ignore whatever hurtful things she would say to him. She'd probably say he'd put on weight. Even with the twenty pounds he'd lost.

He needed to distract himself.

He opened the fridge, looking for something sweet. He didn't want the tomatoes, or the celery or carrots or anything healthy. He just wanted... something good. Something comforting.

He was about to reach for an apple when he glimpsed a cake box at the back of the fridge. It hadn't been there this morning.

It wasn't his. But it was the only delicious thing in

the fridge, Ulric knew, and... was it Gage's? Could he eat its contents, and perhaps replace it tomorrow before Gage found out?

Ulric held his breath, straining his ears for any sound. The house was silent. His fingers trembled as he reached into the fridge, picking up the box. He listened again. Then he pulled open the plastic bag, he carefully pried open the box.

His heart leaped. There were two slices of cake inside. A coffee cake, and something Ulric wasn't sure about—it looked kind of plain. But good, nonetheless, because it was cake.

Even though he wasn't hungry, his mouth watered. Ulric grabbed a new fork, he tucked himself behind the island counter, out of sight from the kitchen doorway. Then he scooped a corner of the coffee cake into his mouth—it was soft as a cloud and sweet, the coffee cream rich on his tongue. He groaned, scooping another mouthful, all but inhaling it.

He tried the other cake. It was also sweet, soaked through with milk. Also really good. He shoveled another bite into his mouth, then another, wishing there was an entire cake instead of just one slice.

The more cake he ate, the lighter that twisted, awful anxiety became.

He was almost down to the last few bites of cake, thinking about heading out to look for a 24-hour store with cookies, when someone rounded the side of the island counter.

Ulric's heart clenched; he jumped and hunched around his cake box, the fork clattering onto the floor.

Gage looked down at him, dressed in his sleeping clothes. But because Ulric was huddled into a ball on the floor, Gage looked tall, and kind of intimidating.

Ulric wiped his mouth hurriedly, his throat squeezing tight. Gage had discovered him stealing cake. Was he going to think badly of Ulric for breaking his diet? Was he... not going to kiss Ulric anymore? Ulric tried to breathe. "Is this yours? I promise I'll get a new box tomorrow. When they open. I just saw it in the fridge and I—"

"Ulric." Gage knelt in front of him, his gaze never leaving Ulric's face. Ulric's heart felt like it might burst. "It's fine. That's for you."

Ulric panted, the words swimming around him, not sinking in. "But—"

Gage took the box out of his hands, setting it to the side. Then he hauled Ulric against his chest, pulling him into a tight hug. "It's okay," Gage murmured in his ear. "I bought it for you."

For... me? "Why?"

"Because you've been doing great with everything." Gage pressed a kiss to his cheek, then another beneath his ear. "I thought you might like some cake."

Ulric gulped down some breaths, his heart still pounding. "I'm not supposed to eat cake."

"It's okay if you eat it once in a while."

"But I stole it."

Gage huffed. "You can't steal it if it's already yours."

Ulric looked at the box, and the half-eaten cake inside. On any other day, he would've shared it with Gage. It just hadn't occurred to him when he'd been trying to shovel away the anxiety.

He felt so terrible about that. "I'll get you some in return. I wanted to share it. I just—"

Gage tipped his face up, pressing a soft kiss to his lips. "Shh. It's okay."

Ulric tried to calm down. "It's not okay."

"Yes, it is."

"But—" Ulric looked at the few bites left in the box. "You should try that before it's all gone. It's good."

"Yeah?" Gage smiled. "You liked it?"

Ulric nodded.

"Even the tres leches? That's my favorite."

Ulric winced. "I should've left that for you—"

Gage leaned in, pushing his tongue into Ulric's mouth. "Mm."

He tasted Ulric deep inside, tangling their tongues, licking every part of Ulric he could reach. Ulric stopped breathing. "Gage—"

Gage pressed him against the counter and kissed him, and Ulric's world spun, leaving him and Gage in the middle of it all, Gage holding him, never once blaming him for the cake. Gage had bought the cake for Ulric, and...

"You shouldn't," Ulric whispered.

Gage kissed him harder, insistently. Something in Ulric's chest just... broke.

It felt like he'd lost something to Gage, but he didn't know what it was. All he knew was that it was dangerous, letting Gage have so much of him.

Gage could leave him, Gage could break him, and he could shatter Ulric so badly, Ulric wouldn't know how to put himself back together again.

And yet Ulric held on to him, reluctant to let go.

22

ULRIC HAS A NEW SECRET

"So... you and Gage," Wilkie said that Saturday, while they were driving to Highton. "Are you and him... serious?"

Ulric hesitated, unsure if he wanted this conversation. "Does it matter?"

Wilkie seemed curious. "He's never had a steady boyfriend or girlfriend. You knew that, right?"

Ulric's heart sank. "No. I didn't."

"Oh." Wilkie cringed. "Sorry. I didn't mean to be a downer."

It shouldn't matter. Gage and Ulric were just friends. With... an intimate side to their friendship. Where Gage touched Ulric between the legs, where Gage gave him things and kissed him, and none of this was supposed to matter in the long run.

"We're just friends," Ulric said.

"I've seen the way he looks at you. That's not a look he gives his friends. Hell, it's not even a look he gives his boyfriends."

Ulric's heart stuttered. "You mean, it's a look he gives fat people?"

Wilkie stared incredulously at him. "No. I'm saying that Gage might be in love. With you."

Ulric almost swerved into another car. "You can't be serious."

"Hell yes, I am." Wilkie puffed out his chest. "And I don't even know what love looks like. Well, technically, I do. I've seen it with my mom and dad. They're your textbook definition of a couple in love. Like, sometimes it rots my teeth. I'm surprised I have any left." Wilkie looked at his teeth in the side view mirror.

Ulric's heart yearned, at the same time his mind said it wasn't possible. "I'm an alpha. And so's Gage."

Wilkie shrugged. "Our cousin married an alpha. You saw Jesse with Dom, right? I guess they love each other so much, they want even more babies."

Ulric remembered the kisses between those two alphas, he remembered feeling so damn envious that they'd found each other. Ulric wanted his own alpha to spend his life with, he wanted... well, he wanted to do that with Gage. "Jesse and Dom are an anomaly. And people break up all the time."

"What's to say that you and Gage aren't an anomaly, too?"

Ulric sighed. He didn't want to explain this. "Because Gage is—I don't know if you're aware. But your brother is the perfect alpha specimen. He has gorgeous muscles and teeth and that face—"

Wilkie gave him a mischievous look. "So are *you* in love with him?"

Ulric spluttered. He *wasn't*. "I'm just saying that he probably has a line of people waiting to be his."

"And you're first in line?" Wilkie winked. "Like, you'd be there camping a week before the queue starts."

Well, Ulric would be there a whole year early if it meant he could have Gage. He scrubbed his face, embarrassed. "Let's talk about something else."

"Yup." Wilkie nodded sagely. "Because you and Gage are just friends."

"Exactly." Besides, there was something else he'd wanted to talk to Wilkie about. Without Gage listening in. "So... you mentioned bills the other day."

Wilkie froze, suddenly wary. "What about them?"

"What kind of bills do you have?" Ulric tried to sound innocent. "It must be pretty bad if it made both of you homeless."

Wilkie pursed his lips, looking uneasy. "It's just bills."

From that argument the other night, those weren't ordinary bills. "I want to help with them," Ulric said.

Wilkie squirmed. Then he fiddled with his phone, unlocking it, locking it back up. "It'll... It'll pass. I've been looking for work on the side. Don't tell Gage."

Aha. "Nope. I'm going to tell him. He might make you move back in with your parents."

Wilkie groaned. "That's not fair!"

"Or you could tell me." Ulric gave him an inviting look. "And I could take some of the pressure off Gage."

Wilkie bit his lip, torn. "He doesn't want me to tell you," he finally admitted.

"Why not?"

Wilkie shrugged; his face said he knew, though.

"Tell me about your family, then," Ulric said to get an idea much help Gage needed. "What do your mom and dad work as?"

"Mom's a seamstress. Dad works at the car repair

place. Debbie—" Wilkie clammed up.

"Debbie?" Ulric frowned. "Who is she?"

"Our sister." Wilkie fidgeted.

"You have a sister?" Gage hadn't mentioned her.

"That's because no one wants to talk about it outside of family." And then Wilkie looked angry with himself. But it only made Ulric's curiosity grow.

"Is there something wrong with her?" At Wilkie's expression, Ulric's heart sank. "Is she sick?"

Wilkie deflated, closing his eyes. "Yeah."

Crap. No wonder Gage had been struggling with money. Ulric's chest squeezed. "Is she... going to get better?"

Wilkie nodded. "We just have to get through this treatment. The doctors are pretty optimistic."

That was good. So Ulric could chip in, maybe, and then everything would be okay. "Gage never told me."

"He doesn't want you to know." Wilkie sighed. "He said it might fuck with your rela—your friendship."

Ulric's thoughts raced. If he could help Gage in secret... would that make things better? If Gage didn't know, then he wouldn't feel as though he owed Ulric.

His heart thumped as he kept his breathing even, trying not to give away his plans. "I hope things will get better for you guys."

Wilkie sagged despondently. "Same here."

They didn't speak again until they arrived in Highton. Ulric made sure Wilkie had some lunch and dinner money before dropping him off at a fabric store. Wilkie would have to entertain himself for the next several hours—Ulric was due to meet his mom at the airport in ten minutes.

At least he was early. He sighed.

He pulled up five minutes later at the airport's pick-up area, his heart thumping when he glimpsed her familiar face. Would she be excited to see him? He hadn't lived this far away from home before. Would she... notice that he'd lost weight? Would she be happy about it?

Ulric parked, hurrying out to help with her suitcase.

"You're late," she said, glancing disapprovingly over his body.

That shot his hopes down. "I'm five minutes early."

"I had to wait here for a long time," she snapped. "That means you're late."

Ulric bit down his protest; there wasn't any point trying to argue—she would always be right in her eyes. So much for her noticing he'd lost weight.

They got into his car, Mom sniffing at the air. "You found an omega?"

"No." Ulric blinked. Or had she smelled Wilkie's buttercup scent?

Unlike the woodsy scents of alphas and the grassy scents of betas, omegas had a distinctive floral scent. They smelled nice, too, but Ulric's attraction to omegas ended there.

"No?" Mom's eyebrows drew low. "Don't lie to me, Ulric. You had an omega in here."

"Yeah, we're friends. But that's all."

"Which family is he from?" Mom's expression grew calculating; Ulric's dread began to rise.

"The Frosts."

"I haven't heard of them." She sniffed disdainfully. "Haven't I told you to mingle with people of our stature? You're wasting your time with anyone less."

Gage isn't a waste of time, Ulric wanted to retort. Gage had made Ulric the happiest he'd been in a while. It sucked that his own mother only thought of wealthy people as important. He suppressed the whisper of dejection in his chest. He just had to get through today and go home. And do this again tomorrow. And the day after. All the way until Mom was done with her business here, and she left.

"Where's your chauffeur?" she asked a moment later.

"I don't have one."

Mom grimaced. "It's not a good look, driving your car yourself."

"I like being in control." It had been one of the few luxuries he'd had, back when he'd been living with his parents. Mom had every last say in the house. Their meals were prepared by a chef. The only times Ulric got to choose what he did, was when he'd gone to college, or when he'd taken his car out for a spin.

"You can be in control from the back. That's what money is for," she answered.

Probably the same reason why Gage didn't want Ulric's help with his problems. Except if Gage took on a second job like he'd been talking about, Ulric would hardly get to see him at all. And Gage brightened his day so much.

"I like driving," Ulric said.

Mom scoffed, turning back to her phone.

In between her business calls, Ulric took his mom to the various attractions in Highton—the city hall, the famous theaters, the scenic piers at the beach. It was only after dinner, when they were on their way to Mom's hotel, that Ulric's phone buzzed.

Could you pick me up? Wilkie had texted. *I'm in a bad part of town. I should've left earlier.*

Ulric wasn't so familiar with Highton's dangerous areas, but it was dark out, shadows spilling onto the streets. The thought of Wilkie somewhere out there—

that made his stomach squeeze. He did a U-turn. "I have to pick my friend up. He's in a bad place."

Mom frowned. "Is this so urgent?"

"Yes." She could wait a few moments. Ulric wouldn't be able to live with himself if Wilkie got hurt because of him.

The drive took twenty minutes; Mom tapped on the door handle, sighing impatiently. Ulric tried not to let her disgruntlement seep into his heart.

They ended up driving along streets with metal grilles over the shop front windows, iron gates that closed over the regular shop entrances. Ulric had the feeling that if Gage knew where Wilkie had been, *he* would blow an artery.

He found Wilkie huddled up at a well-lit bus stop. Ulric heaved a sigh as he pulled over; Wilkie hurried to the car, slipping into the backseat. The moment the door shut, Ulric hit the gas pedal so they could get out of there. He wasn't used to being in places like this. "You okay?"

Wilkie nodded. "Yeah. Thanks for picking me up."

Mom had turned to survey the new arrival. Instead of the frown she'd been wearing, she now looked... shrewd. "You're Ulric's 'friend'?"

"Uh. Yeah?" Wilkie seemed confused.

Ulric sighed. She was trying to play matchmaker, wasn't she? "To be specific, he's a brother of a friend."

Wilkie snorted—at least he didn't let Ulric's mom in on the joke.

"I suppose you could settle," Mom said. "He doesn't look half-bad. Fertile, at least."

Wilkie's amusement evaporated. *What?* he mouthed at Ulric through the rearview mirror.

"No, he's off-limits," Ulric said.

Mom waved dismissively. "There are no limits—only the right amount of money."

Were they really talking about this now? "I'm not interested," Ulric said.

"You need an omega," Mom answered.

"No, I don't."

Ulric tried not to feel Wilkie's stare on him. At least Gage wasn't here. Ulric wouldn't know what to do if Gage met his mom.

"Anyway, we're heading to your hotel now," Ulric told her. Time for some damage control.

Mom gestured toward Wilkie. "What's your name? We'll arrange for a lunch next week. We'll fly Ulric's father down."

"Mom, no." Ulric blew out his exasperation. "You're not arranging another marriage for me. I'm not interested in omegas."

Wilkie's disbelief had been slowly growing in the backseat. "Yeah, actually. Ulric already has someone else he's seeing."

Ulric's stomach dropped in slow motion. His mother turned, her eyes lighting up. "Really?" she asked. "And you didn't tell me?"

He focused on driving so he didn't have to answer her. At least, until they approached the hotel. "No. You wouldn't approve," Ulric said. Mom's smile fell. "He's an alpha."

She snapped then. "Honestly, that's a phase, Ulric. Stop being childish."

What part of their friendship was childish? "He likes me."

Mom scowled. "You can fool yourself into thinking he likes you, but all he's after is your money. With that kind of fat on you, no one in their right mind would think you attractive."

Ulric tensed, his ears burning. "He says I'm fine."

"Didn't you have a boyfriend before you left?" Mom scoffed. "*He* thought you were fine, all the way until he dumped you like a bag of trash."

Could that happen with him and Gage? Ulric didn't want to think about it, but he remembered Wilkie saying, *Gage's never had a long-term boyfriend before.* How long would it be until someone pretty came along? Someone who was an omega, and a better fit for Gage?

"I told you to go on a diet," Mom said.

"I've lost twenty pounds," Ulric answered quietly. "I've been exercising. And I'm on a diet."

"You just look fatter than you were before. I don't want to be seen with you in public."

Ulric's body felt too heavy, all over again. He glanced down and only saw all the terrible curves. Did Gage mind his weight in secret? Was it one of the things he would never tell Ulric, like how he'd been hiding his sister's illness from Ulric?

The entire car was silent. Ulric pulled up at the hotel's warmly-lit drop-off zone, a slender bellboy coming up to open the door.

"You should meet Gage sometime," Ulric said. "You'd like him."

Mom scoffed. "Is he a blind man? Is that why he can't see all that excess fat?"

Ulric's chest tightened. All his life, he'd only wanted to be accepted by her. But she never had.

"Gage loves him," Wilkie growled, his voice low with anger. "He can see better than you ever will."

Mom's face twisted into a scowl. "On second thought, maybe you won't be a good match for Ulric at all."

"Thank goodness," Wilkie retorted.

The bellboy opened the car door; Mom stalked out. Ulric sighed and forced himself to follow her out of the car. By the time he reached the trunk, Mom already had her suitcase—the bellboy had retrieved it for her.

"Well, I'll see you tomorrow," Ulric said, his heart heavy.

Mom grimaced as he stepped closer; she didn't like being seen this close to him in public. But she would throw a fit if he didn't kiss her goodnight.

She turned her cheek toward him; Ulric kissed it. Then she stalked up the elegant stairs to the hotel lobby, never once looking back.

When Ulric ducked back into the car, he found Wilkie in the front passenger seat. "You're perfectly fine," Wilkie muttered. "And Gage thinks so. Don't listen to a word she said."

It was so difficult to breathe. "Don't mention this to Gage."

Wilkie frowned. "Are you sure?"

"Yeah." Ulric put the car into drive, taking them away from the hotel. He didn't want Wilkie to remember what his mom had said, he didn't want Wilkie telling Gage.

His body prickled all over. When Gage saw Ulric... what did he really see? Ulric couldn't imagine that he saw anything but Ulric's excess weight. At some point, when Gage really opened his eyes, he would leave, wouldn't he?

Ulric's heart hurt. He shoved those thoughts out of his mind, heading for home.

It'd be best to savor what he had, while it lasted.

23

GAGE IS SUSPICIOUS

When Ulric got home with Wilkie, he looked... a lot worse than Gage had expected. Even Wilkie looked troubled.

"What happened?" Gage's heart sank. "Babe?"

Wilkie gave him an uneasy look before slipping upstairs. Which only mystified Gage more. "Did something happen to my brother?"

Ulric shook his head. "I picked him up from Crock Street, though. That was pretty bad. You might've thrown a fit."

Gage frowned. Crock Street wasn't the best part of Highton, but Wilkie seemed to be okay. "It's something else."

Ulric skirted around Gage; Gage snagged him by his middle, pulling him close. Ulric stiffened. That felt wrong. Ulric leaned into his hugs these days.

"Hey." Gage turned Ulric around, kissing him on the lips. Ulric hardly returned the kiss. "Ulric."

"I need to grab a shower," Ulric muttered. "I stink."

He smelled... okay. There was a slight whiff of

perfume on his skin that made Gage's instincts growl. Who had he gone to meet? "I'll come with you."

Ulric shook his head forcefully. "No."

"Someone did something to you." Gage slipped his hand up Ulric's shirt, touching his skin. "Babe."

"I'm not a babe," Ulric said, growing agitated. "Just—Leave me alone right now. Please." He pulled Gage's hand out of his shirt, hunching into himself.

"What happened in Highton?"

"Nothing."

"It's not nothing." Gage turned Ulric back around; Ulric shrugged him off and headed up the stairs. The last time Gage had seen him that worked up, Ulric had huddled into a ball in the kitchen, stuffing his face with cake. And the look in his eyes that night—he'd been nervous somehow.

Was that related to this?

Gage stopped by his bedroom, where Wilkie lay sprawled on his bed, typing into his phone. "Hey, Wilkes. Tell me about today."

Wilkie looked over warily. "What's there to tell?"

"Who did Ulric meet in Highton?"

Wilkie cringed. "You'll have to ask him."

That wasn't fair, either. "You can't tell me?"

"Nope." Wilkie mimicked zipping his lips. "I promised Ulric."

Damnit. Gage growled, needing to solve this. What was Ulric hiding? More than that, he didn't want Ulric going to bed looking like someone had kicked him in the gut.

So he slipped into Ulric's bedroom, filling his lungs with that honey oak scent. Ulric had a nice king-sized bed, with a few cartoon duck plushies along one wall, some posters on the other walls, and another of Gage's shirts tucked halfway under his sheets. When Gage picked it up, he found it crusted over with dried come. A lot of it.

Gage's instincts rumbled, satisfied. Although, to be honest, he would much rather get Ulric off himself. So he could hear Ulric gasp, so he could feel Ulric shudder in his arms.

He perched on the edge of Ulric's bed, facing the closed bathroom door. Just waiting. He listened to the sounds of Ulric showering, imagining rivulets of water on Ulric's skin. The shower spray stopped. There was a bit of silence—probably Ulric drying himself. Gage's cock thickened at that image.

Then, finally, the door swung open, Ulric with a bath towel wrapped around his waist. He took one look at Gage, sucked in his belly, and slammed the door shut.

Gage's heart sank. "Hey. Babe." He hurried over. "You look perfect."

"Why're you here?" Ulric's voice was muffled.

"'Cuz I want to see if you're okay."

"I'm fine."

"Need me to hand you some clothes?" Gage asked.

There was a pause. Eventually, Ulric muttered, "Yeah."

Gage riffled through his closet and found a comfortable shirt and pants. He knocked on the door; Ulric opened it by a crack, took the clothes Gage offered, and shut the door tight.

"You're beautiful with nothing on," Gage told him. "Been wanting to see it."

"No, you don't."

"I'll show you how hard I'm getting for you."

"You shouldn't," Ulric grumbled.

"Well, I am. All for you, babe. Want a few inches inside?"

Ulric swore. So Gage pulled down his waistband and let his cock jut up, just waiting.

When Ulric opened the door, shower water dripping off his hair, he froze. His gaze raked heavily down Gage's front, pausing at his hard length.

Gage pumped it. "See?"

Ulric swallowed, looking uncertain. His lips had pulled into a pout, and he looked like he needed a good kiss. "You could've been jerking off to someone else."

Gage rolled his eyes, taking Ulric's hand. Then he wrapped that hot fist snug around himself, thrusting hard into Ulric's fist. "For *you*, babe. No one else."

Ulric groaned; the sound went right between Gage's legs. Gage leaked, his tip dragging wetly against Ulric's shirt.

For a moment, Ulric looked torn. Then, haltingly, he said, "We could—with the lights off."

"Yeah?" Gage's cock grew heavier. "Will you let me take your clothes off?"

Ulric paled.

"In the dark. You can blindfold me if you want."

"No. Clothes on."

That was disappointing, but Gage wasn't going to push it. "Get on the bed. I'll make you come real hard."

"Damn it, Gage." Hunger flickered through Ulric's gaze; Gage reached down, squeezing Ulric through his pants. *He* was getting hard, too.

"Look how perfect this is," Gage murmured, wrapping his hand around Ulric's tip. "Want to put it inside me?"

Something flashed in Ulric's gaze, something feral. And Ulric grew rock-hard against his palm. In seconds.

"I shouldn't," Ulric breathed, but beneath his words lay a thread of hunger. "I'll ruin your hole, Gage. I want it so bad."

Fuck, Gage couldn't say no to him. "You'll have to fight me for it."

Ulric's pupils dilated; musk billowed off his skin. "You shouldn't stay," Ulric rasped. "I—"

"You...?" Gage stroked his entire length, encouraging him.

"I—" A flush crept up Ulric's throat. "I'll need your safeword."

That sounded dangerous. It thrilled Gage. "Yeah?" He murmured, crowding closer, his instincts growling just beneath his skin. "Why?"

"I—" Ulric tensed. "I like it when you hold me down," he breathed. "When I—When I fight you off and you fuck me anyway."

Gage's hole squeezed. "And you want to do that to me?"

Ulric couldn't meet his eyes. "Yeah. Actually, you should just leave. Please. Right now."

He looked embarrassed but hungry, and in his eyes, that feral part of him lurked. Gage's instincts roared. "If you want a fight, I'll give you a fight."

"Fuck." Ulric's pupils blew wide.

Gage's throat went dry. He rarely saw this side of Ulric. And he wanted to. He wanted to know everything about Ulric there was to know. And if it helped Ulric forget his discomfort from earlier... "It starts now," Gage said, shoving his pants off.

Ulric swore, his chest heaving. "Gage, no."

Gage clambered onto Ulric's bed, spreading his legs open. And Ulric *lunged*, he snarled and shoved Gage down against the mattress, grinding his covered bulge against Gage's ass, his cock pushing an indent into Gage's cheeks. Gage's instincts demanded to pin *him*, to claim Ulric as his own.

"Tell me your safeword," Ulric panted, pressing Gage's chest against the bed. "Or you need to fucking leave."

But Ulric's desperation kindled Gage's own need. Ulric wanted a fight—Gage would give him the best one he'd ever had.

"'Popcorn'," Gage said. He'd never had a safeword before. "That okay?"

"Popcorn," Ulric repeated, his breath rushing hot into Gage's hair. "Say that if you want me to stop."

He reached down, grasping Gage's cock roughly, yanking on it. Pleasure burst through Gage's body; he swore, fucking into Ulric's fist. And Ulric kicked off his own pants, he slid his tip between Gage's cheeks, hot and thick. Gage stopped breathing.

He'd felt Ulric's cock there before, Ulric shoving against his entrance, needing to push inside. Gage hadn't thought he actually would—until now. He'd never been on this end, he'd never had an alpha inside his body. Ulric's touch sent heat coursing through his veins.

Gage groaned, muscling Ulric off himself, rolling them over so he pinned Ulric with his own weight. Ulric growled and reached down; Gage shoved his hands away, rubbing their bare cocks together. His skin tingled wherever they touched.

"Try harder, babe," Gage whispered against his lips. "You want this hole, you'd better fucking work for it."

Ulric struggled, eyes flashing. Gage smiled and rocked their hips together. Then he straddled Ulric properly and rubbed his balls against Ulric's cock, before sitting down on it, letting Ulric feel his entrance.

"It's right here," Gage murmured.

Ulric lunged; Gage rolled off to give him some leverage. Ulric slammed him back down against the mattress, working his fingers between Gage's cheeks. Gage's hole squeezed in anticipation.

Having Ulric hold him down like this—his instincts growled for the upper hand. Briefly, Gage remembered another time, when he'd been held down and beaten up by people he couldn't trust. But that was a long time ago, and he was here with Ulric.

And he trusted this man.

Gage knocked Ulric's hands away. Ulric grabbed his arms and pinned them above his head, and then he sank a finger into Gage's hole, dry.

It burned a little. Mostly, what caught Gage's attention was the feeling of Ulric inside him, Ulric wanting to own him, claim him. With his leg, Gage shoved Ulric's hand away so his touch slipped out. Ulric's eyes gleamed; he pushed his finger back inside, swirling it around.

It felt a lot better than Gage expected it to.

"Fuck, you're so hot inside," Ulric whispered. Then he pushed another finger in, his musk growing heavy, his cock a thick, damp weight on Gage's thigh.

Gage throbbed, just having him this close. And he planted his feet on Ulric's chest, shoving him backward. "That was just a taste, babe."

He flew at Ulric, pinning him down again. Ulric reached around and grasped Gage's ass, spreading him open so his hole was completely exposed. Gage leaked onto him. "Not there."

Ulric reached down; Gage knocked his hand away. But Ulric slipped his other hand back there, and all the warning

Gage received was a caress between his cheeks. Then Ulric shoved his fingers in, a rough, demanding burn all the way to his knuckles. Stretched open, Gage swore and clenched.

Ulric found a spot inside. Then he pushed down hard on it, and bliss shot down Gage's nerves, sending sparks through his vision. Ulric rumbled, pleased. He worked Gage's prostate, over and over, until pleasure coursed through Gage's limbs and his precome squirted between them, his balls pulling tight.

"I'm gonna—" Gage lifted himself off Ulric.

Ulric shoved him to the side and pounced, slamming Gage down against the mattress. He grasped Gage's ass, spreading him, shoving his blunt tip between Gage's cheeks.

Gage's instincts snarled. Just as Ulric was about to push inside, Gage heaved him off. "Nope."

"Gods, Gage." Ulric growled, prowling back. Gage shoved him off with his feet; Ulric struggled, knocking Gage's feet to his sides. Then he grasped Gage's legs and spread them wide, he slammed Gage back down onto the mattress, cramming his tip into Gage's crack, right against his hole.

"Fuck off," Gage hissed—just because Ulric liked it.

"Mine," Ulric growled, snapping his hips, spreading Gage's cheeks with his sheer width. Gage wasn't sure how it'd fit inside. His balls pulled tight.

He shoved Ulric off and pinned him, pushing *his* cock against Ulric's hole. Ulric thrashed and heaved him off, and *now* they were fighting for real, Ulric struggling against Gage, his entire body rubbing up against Gage's front.

"Feel my cock," Gage whispered, grinding it against Ulric's thigh. "This is gonna go into *you*."

Ulric hissed, heaving him off. And his cock strained between them, heavy and ravenous.

Ulric shouldered Gage into the mattress, ripping Gage's pants off his legs. Then he shoved Gage's knees apart, he pushed them so far up, forcing Gage's spine to arch and his ass to tilt up toward Ulric, his hole exposed.

Ulric groaned, reaching down to pump his cock. This gave Gage an advantage; he rolled out of Ulric's grip, snatching the lube off the nightstand. Just as he was about to squirt some onto his fingers, Ulric grabbed the tube, squeezing a huge dollop onto *his* cock. And he smoothed the gel down the length of it, cramming two fingers into Gage's hole, forcing Gage to open for him.

Ulric found that one spot again—a shower of sparks sizzled through Gage's body. Gage swore and arched. Ulric jammed his fingers against it, over and over, until Gage's hole squeezed tight and his cock fucking hurt, and he knew he was about to blow.

Ulric pulled his fingers out, leaving him on the edge. Then he mounted Gage; Gage squirmed out from beneath him, refusing to give this to him easy.

Except Ulric snarled and threw himself bodily on Gage, he pushed his cock between Gage's thighs and crammed his tip against Gage's entrance. And Gage knew that Ulric would push in this time.

"'Popcorn'," Ulric rasped, his cock leaking onto Gage's hole. "Say it and get out now, Gage."

But this was the alpha side of Ulric, the part of Ulric that he kept buried until times like this. Gage flipped him off, shoving Ulric off his back. "Not in a million years."

He was about to clamber off the mattress when Ulric slammed into him from behind, bringing them both crashing down. And Ulric's cock pushed thick between Gage's cheeks, he crammed his blunt tip against Gage's hole and *shoved*, and it opened Gage wider than he'd ever been, inches upon thick inches pushing inside, stretching Gage so much that Gage couldn't breathe.

Fuck, Ulric was big. And he felt even bigger inside.

"Take it," Ulric snarled, slamming every inch into Gage. Gage roared and arched, his body opening, all his nerves lighting up as his alpha claimed him then and there, Ulric's cock filling him up so full that he knew no other alpha would ever be enough. Just Ulric.

"Fuck, babe," Gage rasped, clenching around him.

Ulric panted, his strokes growing uneven, his cock keeping Gage spread as he began to pound in, harder and harder. "'P-popcorn'," Ulric hissed, his grip tight on Gage's hips, his cock growing thicker. "Now."

"No," Gage spat. And Ulric cursed, slamming in so hard that he shoved Gage forward on the bed. And he yanked Gage back, plunging every single inch in.

Gage struggled. Ulric weighed him down, his cock pistoning inside Gage, over and over, a demanding thickness that told Gage he belonged to Ulric. And that Ulric wouldn't let Gage go until he'd been properly fucked.

The longer he plowed into Gage, the closer he urged Gage toward the edge. Gage couldn't believe he was still hard, he couldn't believe he had Ulric inside him. And it felt so damn fucking good, Ulric coaxing every single one of Gage's nerves to sing, so much that his balls pulled tight and he thought he would explode all over Ulric's bed.

Ulric bit hard into Gage's shoulder, his strokes turning uneven, desperate. He was close. Then he snarled, thrusting in a final time, slamming Gage against the mattress. Warmth flooded Gage inside—that was

Ulric's pleasure, Ulric's marking. Gage couldn't hold back. Pleasure crashed through him in a bright-white wave, arching his spine, ripping his come out of him.

They breathed together for a long moment, Gage holding onto Ulric, pulling Ulric's arms around himself. That had been the first time he'd let an alpha claim him. It had been Ulric. And Ulric had felt phenomenal.

Gage would feel Ulric's fucking well into next week, but that only made him happy. He liked wearing Ulric's marking. They should've done this so much sooner.

When the fog in his mind cleared a little and Ulric began to pull away, Gage tugged him back. "I want your knot."

Ulric sucked in a sharp breath. "But I—" Over his shoulder, Gage found Ulric with his face red, unable to meet Gage's eyes.

"Knot inside me," Gage whispered. "Tonight."

Ulric pushed back inside. Gage groaned, Ulric's knot stretching him open, growing round and heavy in his body. Gage had never been on this end of a knot, either. But with Ulric, it felt right. Ulric's knot locked them together, Ulric a solid presence inside him.

Gage sighed in pleasure, burying his face in Ulric's pillow.

Ulric pressed his forehead against Gage's shoulder, his voice barely audible as he mumbled, "This shouldn't have happened."

"Why not?"

"Because I—You saw me do that." Ulric dug his fingers into Gage's waist. "I'm not right in the head."

Gage brought Ulric's hand up to his lips, kissing him there. "It's not the first time we've done that."

"It's the first time it's been—" Ulric swallowed "—this violent."

Gage pushed their hips together, so Ulric's knot sank deeper inside him. "And we both enjoyed it."

He hadn't met another person who wanted what Ulric had asked for. If it had happened with anyone else, with no safeword, Gage would've been alarmed.

Ulric had been honest with his request, though. And Gage had played along willingly, trusting him. Because he trusted that Ulric would not hurt him, because he trusted that Ulric would've stopped if Gage had asked him to.

Ulric eased his hand away from Gage, looking embarrassed. Gage caught his fingers and kissed them again. "You're fine."

"I'm—"

"If that's your kink, then I'll explore it with you," Gage murmured. "Here, where it's safe to. We can talk about it."

Ulric blushed redder, shoving his face against Gage's back. "You shouldn't."

"I want to."

"Why are you this nice?" Ulric muttered, looking uneasy. "You don't have to be."

"Because." Gage couldn't say it. *Because you mean more to me than anyone else I've dated.*

"That isn't a reason."

Gage pulled Ulric's arms snug around him, before tugging the sheets over both of them. "Mind if I sleep here tonight?"

Ulric tensed, his breath rushing out of him. "Why would you want to?"

"Because you're cozy." Gage smiled, ignoring all the little voices telling him that this couldn't possibly last. "Because I've been dreaming about sharing your bed for a long while, Muffin."

Ulric cracked a shaky smile, tightening his arms around Gage. "Fine."

He didn't sound convinced, but he was letting Gage stay. And that was a step in the right direction.

24

GAGE FINDS OUT

A FEW DAYS LATER, Gage set down some food at the grocery store checkout stand. It wasn't a lot—the cheapest pork roast he could find, some broccoli, and a bulk container of oats for Wilkie. He'd made sure to total them up twice; he knew he had just enough on his bank balance left for this.

But there was always the possibility that other charges had come up, and that the remaining amount wasn't what he'd remembered. He bit the inside of his cheek, opening his wallet. Did he want to risk an overdraft fee...?

He counted the loose bills he had, pausing when he found a $20 mixed in with them. Gage frowned. He could've sworn he'd used his last twenty yesterday. He couldn't have remembered wrong, could he? Or had Wilkie returned him money without telling him?

He paid for his groceries with the bill, dropping his coin change into the donation box at the register. Then he set off for home, wishing it were the end of the week

—that was when the wages from his new job would get deposited into his account.

A couple days ago, despite Ulric's protests, Gage had found a job at a bar downtown. He'd be there only for a few hours every night, but every bit of cash helped. And his shift began in half an hour. There wasn't time for his hugs with Ulric.

Feeling guilty, Gage returned home to drop off the groceries. He found Ulric in front of the TV, looking miserable.

"Hey." Gage planted a quick kiss on Ulric's forehead, his guilt intensifying. "Had a good day?"

Ulric shrugged. "Fine, I guess."

He had that odd perfume scent on him again. "Did you go to Highton?"

Ulric tensed. "How—"

Gage tipped his face up, kissing him full on the lips. "Sometime soon, you'll have to stop going there, babe. It's killing you."

"I wish." Ulric looked... upset. Bitter.

Gage set down the groceries, joining him on the couch. "I have to leave in five," Gage told him, pulling him into a tight hug. "But I'll do the hugs when I get home later."

"I told you, you didn't have to get a second job," Ulric muttered.

"I'm not going to leech off you, Muffin. And I don't want to be your kept alpha." Gage ran his fingers through Ulric's hair, stroking his back, touching him all over. "Mm. I missed you."

Ulric sighed, looking doubtful.

"Ready to tell me what you've been doing out of town?" Gage asked.

Ulric shook his head. So Gage sat with him, holding

his hand, just pretending that this was all he had on his schedule for the rest of the night. Five minutes flew by way too quickly.

"I wish you'd stay," Ulric said.

"I'll spend the rest of tonight with you in bed," Gage promised. "That's six hours of hugs."

"But I wouldn't be awake to enjoy it."

Gage laughed and nuzzled him. "You might be just a bit greedy." Ulric flushed. "But so am I," Gage whispered in his ear.

He gave Ulric's ass a squeeze, kissed him a last time, and then went to get ready for his next shift.

Hours later, when he got home smelling like booze and sweat, Ulric had fallen asleep. Gage grabbed a quick shower, dried off, and slipped under the covers naked, spooning Ulric from behind. Ulric felt perfect in his arms. Gage wanted to feel Ulric on every inch of his skin.

Ulric stirred. "Gage?" he mumbled.

"Here," Gage whispered, kissing his cheek. "Go back to sleep."

Ulric reached behind, splaying his hand on Gage's bare thigh. Then, half-awake, he stroked Gage up and down, making a soft sound when he found Gage's bare abs, and then his cock.

"Sleep," Gage said.

Ulric shuffled around and buried his face against Gage's chest, working Gage over until he'd gotten Gage pulsing-hard. Except his movements grew slower, his breathing deeper.

Ulric fell back asleep.

Figures. Gage sighed exasperatedly, getting himself off the rest of the way. Ulric had found another of Gage's used shirts—Gage cleaned up with that, tossing on the floor so he'd remember to put it in the laundry hamper tomorrow.

He turned off the lights and fell asleep.

Sometime in the middle of the night, he woke to the sound of a muffled crash. It was brief, quiet. Gage drifted in and out of the fog between sleep and reality, unsure if he'd dreamed the sound, or if he'd really heard it.

Through his eyelids, he sensed a light somewhere in the room—not bright enough that it was painful. Just enough that he knew he wasn't alone.

He opened his eyes to find himself in an unfamiliar bed—too big, but it smelled like honey oak. Ulric's bed. Ulric wasn't with him, though. And the ensuite bathroom door was ajar, light spilling out around it.

Ulric was probably taking a piss. Gage closed his eyes, waiting for his alpha to return.

But there came no sounds of pissing. Or the toilet flushing. "Babe?"

There was a quiet shuffling noise. Ulric didn't answer. Was he in trouble?

Blearily, Gage crawled out of bed. He crossed the room, pushing the door open.

Ulric jumped and dropped something onto the bathroom counter, papery things fluttering around him. "G-Gage?"

Was that... money? And Gage's wallet? "What're you doing?"

Ulric swept the notes into a pile, shoving Gage's wallet into his pocket. "Nothing."

That was enough to wake Gage right up. "Ulric. That was mine, wasn't it?"

Ulric froze, meeting Gage's eyes in the mirror. "It's..."

Gage stepped behind him; he reached into the pocket of Ulric's sleep shorts. Ulric shoved the wallet further down into it. Gage caught his hand, lifting it out. At least his workouts came in useful for something.

Then he took the wallet out of Ulric's grasp—it was Gage's. Gage couldn't help the betrayal coiling through his chest.

He opened the wallet, flipping through the bills in there. Instead of missing notes, there were now two twenties tucked in with the rest of his money. More fives and ones than Gage remembered, too.

Ulric's neck flushed red. "I was just—trying to help."

Humiliation prickled down Gage's skin. "I don't need an allowance, Ulric."

Never mind that he'd spent that twenty earlier—that had been from Ulric, too, hadn't it?

"I'll take it back." Ulric reached for the wallet; Gage placed it in his hand. He didn't know how he was going to get by with the few dollars he had left, but *damn* he had his pride. And he wasn't stooping so low as to receive handouts from Ulric.

"Don't do that again," Gage muttered.

Ulric thinned his lips. "Then how am I supposed to help you?"

"Don't."

Ulric scowled, pulling out some notes from Gage's wallet. He left an extra five in there; Gage took it out and added it to Ulric's pile of cash.

Yeah, Ulric was loaded and Gage wasn't, and maybe if they were in an actual relationship, maybe they would pool their finances together. But right now, it just felt like a donation. Besides, Gage's wages were going to Debbie's hospital bills. He couldn't possibly ask Ulric to help with those.

Ulric set Gage's much-thinner wallet down on the

counter. Then he eased out of the bathroom, not touching Gage at all.

When Gage returned to the bed, he found Ulric curled up on his side, facing away. "Are you mad at me?" Gage asked.

"No." Ulric fidgeted.

Gage wasn't sure what to think of all this. Ulric sneaking around at night to give him handouts, Ulric keeping secrets from him. It wasn't right. He was starting to care too much for Ulric, and it scared him, knowing that he was now vulnerable to this man.

He couldn't help remembering Ramsey, the best friend he'd trusted. And who'd ended up betraying him in front of the entire school. He didn't think Ulric would do the same, but tonight... it had changed something between them.

Gage hoped this wouldn't shatter like all his other relationships had.

25

THE WRONG GAMBLE

ULRIC BREATHED out his relief when his mom disappeared into the airport, her suitcase in tow. She was finally taking a flight back to New York. And he would finally stop being a disappointment.

At least, he would finally stop hearing about being a disappointment.

He knew he'd fucked up the other night with Gage. He didn't regret trying to give Gage money—what he'd regretted was tripping over some shirt on the floor, and waking Gage up.

Either way, there was a distinct rift between them now: Gage didn't hold him for so long these days, and Ulric didn't want to look at Gage for longer than he had to.

Maybe his mom had been right. Maybe Gage would now see how ugly Ulric was, and he'd leave. His chest squeezed tight.

Ulric set off, making the hour-long drive back to Meadowfall. When he got back to the house, only Wilkie was there. And Wilkie was pacing in the kitchen, biting his thumbnail.

"What's wrong?" Ulric asked.

Wilkie looked at his phone before shrugging. "Nothing."

"More bills?"

Wilkie cringed. "We'll be fine."

"Because Gage's working two jobs now?" Ulric couldn't help the resentment seeping into his voice; Wilkie looked up.

"Things aren't okay with you guys, are they?" Wilkie asked.

Ulric pinched the bridge of his nose. "We're just friends. How much is the bill this time?"

Wilkie studied Ulric for a long while. "You don't have to help."

"I don't, and I hardly see Gage around anymore." Was Gage's pride more important than spending time with Ulric? Clearly he wanted to work more than he wanted Ulric's help.

Ulric stalked up the stairs to his study, grabbing his checkbook. He tore out a check, went back to the kitchen, and asked, "How much is the bill?"

Wilkie stared. "You can't be serious. It's a ton of money, Ulric."

"I didn't ask for an opinion. How much?" Ulric must've growled that; Wilkie stiffened, looking wary. "Sorry. I didn't mean to scare you. Just show me the bill amount, please."

Wilkie clutched his phone to himself. "It's four-figures. You can't possibly..."

Ulric made the check out for ten grand. Then he signed it and shoved it at Wilkie. "Take this to your mom. Cash it, pay the bills. Whatever."

Wilkie glanced at the check and did a double-take. "This is too much."

"You'll have bills coming next month too, right? And the month after that? Just take it." Ulric shoved his pen back into the pen jar, stalking out of the kitchen. What was the point of having money if it only made his heart hurt?

Wilkie hurried after him. "Don't you need this money?" he asked, incredulous.

"No." When Wilkie didn't move from the living room, Ulric turned. "Aren't you going to cash it?"

Wilkie hesitated. "I don't know if my mom and dad will accept it, honestly. It's way too much."

Ulric sighed. Was Gage's entire family like this? "Just make sure your sister gets better. That's all I ask."

Wilkie's face pinched; he looked tearfully at the check. "I've never held this much money in my life."

Ulric cracked a smile. He went over and ruffled Wilkie's hair. "Get going. Before your brother comes home and throws a fit."

Because that would happen. The moment Ulric handed the check over, he'd known that Gage would find out. And that Gage would be pissed. His stomach turned.

How long did he still have left with Gage?

He returned to his computer, trying to focus on his work. The whole time, his stomach kept tying itself into knots. In the end, he dug out a bottle of vodka from the kitchen cabinet and poured himself a few shots, just to get his nerves to calm the fuck down.

Ulric was buzzed, typing up a report for some new drugs being used in a clinical trial, when the front door slammed shut.

He wasn't expecting it. But his instincts reared up, a growling animal under his skin that thirsted for a fight.

To solve things, to get him out of this state of being nervous all the time.

He turned his office chair around, his heart pounding in his ears, waiting as the stairs creaked and Gage's footfalls sounded through the hallway.

Then Gage stopped in the office doorway, his gaze blazing. A surge of recklessness rushed through Ulric's veins. "Something wrong?" Ulric asked.

"Yeah." Gage narrowed his eyes. "I told you not to help me. Why the fuck can't you listen?"

"Why the fuck can't *you* listen?" Ulric snapped, rising to his feet. He wanted a fight. This time, it wasn't with sex in mind. "I told you I can help—"

"I don't need your help." Gage stalked in; Ulric saw the anger on his face. And he had the ominous feeling that this was the beginning of the end. "You keep going behind my back—"

"Because you keep refusing everything," Ulric hissed. *Because you keep rejecting me. When all I want is for you to spend time here instead of elsewhere.*

"Yeah?" Gage's eyes flashed. "Did it occur to you that you're fucking betraying me every time you do shit without my permission?"

Maybe. But it wasn't like Ulric was trying to buy Gage's affections. He just wanted to get the pressure off this man so he could have some intimacy. Which Gage had been terribly stingy with lately.

"Why should I care when you've gone and gotten another job, anyway?" Ulric snapped. "I hardly see you anymore. It's not like you're around—"

"We're just friends," Gage retorted. "Or have you forgotten that, Ulric? I don't owe you anything."

That hurt like a punch to his gut. Was that all he was to Gage? Ulric tried to breathe. He couldn't help remembering his mother's words, that Gage would never love him for who he was. Gage had just been intimate with him because it was convenient. And Gage would leave, sooner or later. He'd find someone else prettier, better.

Ulric stalked up to him, shoving his front against Gage's, trying to get the upper hand. Gage shoved back, his eyes narrowed, his mouth a thin line.

There wasn't any fondness in his eyes now. Just anger.

Just like that, Ulric realized that the last few weeks had been a lie. They'd been intimate, but Gage's promises—those had been empty. Gage had used Ulric just like he'd used all his other boyfriends, and maybe they'd lasted longer with him because they didn't look like Ulric did.

Ulric was just a warm body that Gage had grown tired of. He felt so awfully heavy and round and ugly.

"You know what? Just leave," Ulric said, the sick feeling in his stomach intensifying. If Gage really cared, he would come back.

Gage narrowed his eyes, turning away. "Yeah, maybe I should."

He said it like he didn't care anymore what happened to Ulric. Ulric watched with slow-growing dread as Gage stalked toward the door, ready to cast Ulric aside like he did with everyone else.

Ulric almost wanted to go up to him, he almost wanted to punch Gage and ask what the hell they'd been doing all these weeks.

Except it didn't matter anymore, did it? No one in Ulric's life ever stuck around. Mick had told Ulric he should lose some weight. Ulric's mom never hugged him once this trip.

What was the point of trying so hard, when everyone ended up leaving him anyway?

Gage's footsteps drifted down the hallway. Then the front door shut, and his car engine rumbled. He drove off.

Ulric sank into his chair, his chest so tight that he couldn't breathe.

At least with Mick, Ulric had had an inkling that things weren't going so well. Mick had never given him any promises. And with Mom, Ulric had grown used to her abandonment over the years.

Gage had promised to be his best friend. He'd held Ulric and told Ulric he was beautiful. He'd promised acceptance.

And now he was gone because Ulric had pushed too hard. There was only the hollowness left in the house, where he'd once been.

Ulric hurt all over. It wasn't until much later, when he scrubbed the wet tracks off his face, that he realized his heart had broken.

26

GAGE GETS GRILLED

The atmosphere at the dinner table was a lot more solemn than Gage expected it to be. He helped his mom bring the dishes over, frowning. "What's with all the long faces?"

Wilkie looked accusingly at him. "You don't know?"

How should Gage know? Had something happened that his family hadn't told him about? He glanced at Debbie.

But Debbie only wrinkled her forehead—she would've raised her eyebrows if she had any hair left. "We were going to invite Ulric over," she said. "You know, get to know him and everything."

Gage's stomach squeezed. So this had to be about Ulric, huh? "You can invite him over when I'm not around. I'm leaving for my shift soon, anyway."

Bad enough that they'd accepted Ulric's money without asking Gage. Bad enough that they all liked him without even meeting him. It was a week after the breakup, the first meal Gage was having with his family, and they all had to shove Ulric's donation in his face.

Mom clucked. "That's not how you're supposed to treat him, Gage."

Gage's anger kindled in his chest. "He's just a friend."

And now everyone at the table stared at him, mixed looks of disapproval and disbelief.

"You don't give a 'friend' your scent marking, son." Dad shook his head. "And you most certainly don't break that promise when you've given it to them."

How much had Wilkie told the rest of their family?

"That's not the same as a bonding mark," Gage muttered. Scent markings were... one step below a permanent bite mark. "Scents aren't promises."

"It's a marking you give someone you're serious about," Dad said.

Like Gage didn't know that. His face burned. "I can give a friend-with-benefits scent markings, too."

"Ew," Wilkie said—that traitor. "I didn't need to know that."

Dad gave Gage a severe look. "Is that what he really is to you?"

No, Ulric wasn't. Gage swallowed, his chest tight. He didn't want to think about it. They weren't seeing each other anymore. He couldn't even say they'd broken up, because they were never together in the first place. "He's an alpha."

"That's no reason to treat him as anything less than a bondmate," Mom said.

That hurt. Being bondmates was something that *Ulric* didn't want. Looking back, maybe that had been a blessing in disguise. "He lied to me," Gage growled. "He fucking did things behind my back. I don't want him as my boyfriend, much less, my bondmate."

All of Ulric's secrets and lies—the middle-of-the-night sneaking around, him hiding his whereabouts, him paying Gage's bills even though Gage had told him not to help... All those things left a bad taste in Gage's mouth. He didn't need to be betrayed again. He didn't need someone else he couldn't trust.

Wilkie's mouth thinned. "Are you still upset over him going to Highton?"

"So what if I am?" Gage retorted.

And Wilkie straightened, the angriest Gage had ever seen him. "Ulric was showing his mom around the city," Wilkie said. "And she treated him worse than a bag of chickenshit. *That's* why he didn't want to tell you what he was doing. *That's* why he kept going back every day, even though it fucked with him. You would've flipped out."

Gage stopped breathing. "What?"

Mom frowned. "That poor dear."

Wilkie's eyes flashed. "She told him that no one would want him because he's fat. She said people only cared about his money. He didn't give us that check thinking you were going to fall for him, Gage. He knew you were going to be pissed. He just wanted to help. Did you know? He kissed his mom goodnight and she just walked away like he was dirt under her shoe."

Gage stared, trying to process all of that. He'd known about Ulric's mom. But he didn't know she was still treating him this badly, he didn't know all this had just happened in the last month. And Ulric had just taken that crap from her, he hadn't even told Gage about it.

Why the hell had Ulric let her do that to him?

Despite his anger at Ulric, Gage's protective instincts rose up, the side of him that wanted to return to Ulric and make sure he was okay. But Ulric would be okay. He hardly ever went anywhere outside his home.

Gage shoveled food into his mouth, trying not to think about that alpha. He had his reasons for leaving.

And Ulric should've told Gage about his mom. So Gage could... what, console him?

"I told you," Wilkie said, looking pointedly at Gage. "He loves y—"

"Don't." Gage swallowed the rest of his dinner, his heart pounding.

He couldn't help remembering the times Ulric had hidden away his body, pulling his shirts down over his belly. He couldn't help remembering the brittle, jaded looks Ulric had given him, whenever he'd talked about his weight. And yet Ulric had returned to the exercise room, over and over, he'd looked so hopeful when he'd stepped on the weighing scale. Those times, he would peek at Gage, quick and surreptitious, as though... he wanted Gage to accept him.

Gage's heart squeezed. *No. I shouldn't.*

He rinsed his plate at the sink, hugged his family, and then set off for work. He wasn't going to think about Ulric again. He'd had enough of that alpha.

Except his bed was so empty now, and he didn't want anyone else filling it. He'd been wishing for another whiff of that honey oak scent. He wanted to see Ulric's flustered, adorable smile, he wanted to feel Ulric's warm, soft body against his own.

"Stop it," Gage told himself, starting up his car.

His heart latched onto the trace of honey oak in his memory, and refused to let go.

27

TROUBLE BEFALLS ULRIC

ULRIC REACHED into the bag of treats, pulling out a sugar donut. It wasn't his first, or even his second. Hell, it was probably his tenth this week, not counting the cakes and cookies he'd been stuffing his face with.

Ever since Gage had left, Ulric hadn't seen the point in losing weight anymore. He'd gone to the nearest store and bought some ice cream. Then he'd visited Ben's Buns toward closing, and bought Ben out of all his remaining donuts and buns. Every single day.

At least he'd done someone a good deed.

Ulric watched as cars rumbled along the street, absently polishing off his donut. Then he reached for the next thing a butt-shaped pizza bun dotted with pepperoni slices, covered in melted cheese. He ate that, too.

He stayed on the roadside bench as the traffic ebbed and flowed, pedestrians drifting past him, absorbed in their own lives. No one noticed him; that was fine. He'd spent years being forgotten. It wasn't so difficult to return to that.

What he didn't want to return to, though, was home. It was too empty in that house right now, too quiet. Wilkie came and went, and he was okay to be around. But what grated on Ulric's nerves was his too-large bed, the kitchen that held all his memories of Gage, the living room couch where they'd snuggled together and watched movies.

He couldn't help remembering the times Gage had teased him, the times Gage had hugged him and held his hand. Some nights, he pretended that Gage was in bed with him, and that Gage desired every inch of his body.

Gods, he was pathetic. Maybe he should just move away and get a fresh start. All over again.

Ulric crammed another bun into his mouth, wishing the ache in his chest would fade. Night had fallen; the streetlamps had come on. Most of the shops on this street had closed. Ulric still wasn't keen on going home, though. Maybe when he'd finished all his buns.

He was in the middle of a fruit tart when a family strolled down the sidewalk—Ulric recognized that scarred face. It was Gage's alpha cousin, Jesse. And Jesse no longer had that swollen belly.

Instead, he had a support band wrapped around his flat abdomen. His husband, Dom, wore a child harness with two infants—Ulric had heard they were both boys—and a toddler bounced along the sidewalk between them, looking delighted.

Ulric tried to glance away before they saw him. Nothing like being *this* out-of-shape in front of two firefighters. Except Jesse caught his eye and waved. "Hey! You're Gage's friend, aren't you?"

Ulric's heart sank. He pasted on a smile, hurriedly wiping his hands on his pants. "Yeah. Congrats on the birth."

"Thanks." Jesse shook his hand. "How are things with you and Gage?"

Ulric tried not to wince. That still hurt. And it was so embarrassing. "We, uh. I think we're still friends."

Concern darted through Jesse's expression. "I'm sorry to hear that."

"I'm fine." Ulric shrugged. It wasn't like he could fix any of this. He didn't need anyone else knowing he couldn't keep an alpha, either—especially not two other alphas who were happily married. "Things will get better."

"Ooh! Can I have one?" Jesse's son asked, peering curiously into Ulric's bag of treats.

Happy that he wasn't the only one who loved those buns, he nudged the bag toward the boy. "Sure. Pick however many you'd like."

"Just one," Jesse told his son. "We shouldn't be greedy, Owen."

Even though Ulric knew that wasn't directed at himself, he felt the weight of every single treat he'd eaten, he felt all the pounds he'd gained over the last week. He had shoved the scale under the bathroom counter, not wanting to break it with how he was now.

Owen fished out a cheesy bun from the bag, looking delighted. Jesse nudged him. "What do we say when we get a present, hon?"

Owen beamed at Ulric. "Thank you!"

Ulric cracked a smile. The boy was kind of cute. And he didn't think badly of Ulric for his weight. If Ulric ever had a child, would they be like that too...?

Jesse followed Ulric's gaze. "Gage was asking about surgical implants. If you're still interested in it..." He pulled out a card from his wallet, handing it to Ulric. "Rutherford's the doctor who pioneered the technology, but he's based on the east coast. If you'd like to chat with someone closer to home, there's Nate, who's a firefighter in Meadowfall. He has some experience with the process."

Ulric looked at the names Jesse had scribbled on the card. "I think my neighbor Nate is a firefighter. Is he the same guy?"

"Probably." Jesse grinned. "It's a pretty small world."

Ulric tucked the card into his pocket, his heart sore. What he would do with all this information? He didn't have anyone who wanted to raise a family with him. "Thanks."

"Things will get better," Jesse said, patting Ulric's shoulder. "I'll have a chat with Gage."

At that, Ulric's stomach tightened. "No, you don't have to."

Jesse looked doubtful. Had life always been easy for him and Dom? Ulric didn't know.

"I'm glad things are going well for you," Ulric blurted. At least Jesse had an alpha who loved him. And a family, too.

"Thanks. I'll check back on you sometime," Jesse said, still concerned.

Ulric shook his head. "It's okay, really. I'm thinking of leaving Meadowfall."

"Huh. Does Gage know?"

Ulric thought about Gage finding out, and being nonchalant about it. That hurt. "I don't think he cares."

Jesse frowned. "I see. Take care, okay?"

"Will do." Ulric watched as Jesse and his family strolled down the street, Dom wrapping his arm around Jesse's waist, Jesse ruffling Owen's hair. They all looked so happy together. Ulric wished he could have something like that.

WEIGHT OF EVERYTHING

Should he have withheld the money? Should he have just... let Gage struggle? That wasn't the right way to treat someone he loved.

He loved Gage—he knew that now. And that helped no one at all.

Ulric looked down at his bag of treats, feeling lonelier than before. Would having a uterus make him more attractive to anyone? Would it have changed Gage's mind? He touched his belly, his chest too tight.

He thought about all the what-ifs, he wondered if Gage was happier now that he'd left. He wondered if other people had already begun hitting on Gage at the gym. Or if Gage was already going on dates, Ulric long-forgotten.

Ulric huddled into himself on the bench, his eyes burning. *Forget Gage,* he told himself.

He lost track of time, all the way until the passing cars grew few and far between. Then footsteps sounded behind him, too quiet and purposeful to have come from a pedestrian.

A knife gleamed suddenly next to his throat. Someone shoved a large gloved hand over his mouth. "Hand over your wallet."

Ulric sighed. "Did you have to do this right now?"

"What?" The robber lifted his hand off Ulric's mouth.

Ulric shoved it away and crammed his bag of buns against the robber's knife, springing to his feet. He didn't have the advantage of speed, but he had some strength.

Except another person stepped out of the nearby shadows—also with a sharp knife. That was bad. Ulric froze, his heart thudding. He could possibly handle one assailant, but not two. There weren't any witnesses; it was useless for him to shout. No time to call the police.

He backed away slowly, one step at a time. But one of

the robbers lunged, knife outstretched. "Hand over your damn wallet!"

Ulric ducked sideways but he wasn't fast enough. The knife stabbed into his arm. Pain lanced through his body. Then the other robber leaped, grabbing Ulric's neck from behind.

"Grab his wallet," the other robber muttered.

Ulric struggled. He knew he should let this go, he knew the wallet wasn't worth his life. But his instincts surged beneath his skin, eager for a fight. He couldn't submit.

He twisted around and slammed his elbow into his captor, shoving the knife away. Then he smashed the back of his head into the man's face, breaking his nose with a crunch.

The robber swore. His accomplice heaved Ulric toward the shadows of an alley, shoving his hand into Ulric's pocket. Ulric spun around and punched him hard in the face.

But a weight crashed into him from the side, ramming him into the rough brick wall. His breath punched out of his throat; two knives pushed up against his neck, nicking his skin. Blood trickled warm and ticklish down his throat.

"Hand it over, and we'll let you live," the robber said.

"Fuck off," Ulric snarled.

He wanted to lunge forward and punch them, he wanted to break free. But the sharp tip of a blade dug under his chin, slicing into his flesh.

If he moved, he ran the risk of them slicing his throat open.

What were the chances of them taking his wallet, and stabbing him anyway? What were the chances of him leaving this place alive? Ulric did the calculations in his head. They weren't so great.

In the moments when the robbers snatched the wallet out of his hands, their knives ruthless against his neck, Ulric's mind drifted. He thought about Gage, he wondered what Gage would think, if he were here. He wondered if Gage would help him. If Gage would be concerned.

He wondered if he could've fixed their relationship, if he'd just straight-up told Gage that he wanted to be boyfriends. That he wanted Gage's marking permanently on him.

He wondered if Gage would've acted differently, if Ulric had said *I love you.*

He wondered about a life where he believed Gage, where he thought he could be beautiful.

He wondered about a future where he and Gage had a family together.

And that broke Ulric.

He roared and shoved at the robbers, not caring that their knives dug into his skin, slicing him open. He needed to get free. To see Gage again. Just to find out if there was a way he could salvage things.

Maybe he wanted to steal a kiss. Just a last one.

Then a knife flashed, and metal stabbed into his side, a searing jab of fire that winded him. And the robbers shoved him onto the grungy alley floor, kicking at his face, his stomach, every blow thudding painfully through his body.

"Maybe we should kill you," one of the men growled. "Remove the evidence."

Ulric tried to stand. They punched him so hard, he almost threw up. He staggered, his vision hazy.

Maybe... he might not make it out alive, after all.

28

GAGE MAKES AMENDS

The text came in just as Gage was clocking off work. *You broke up with your friend?* Jesse asked. *He told me he's moving away.*

Gage stared at those words, growing still. Ulric was leaving Meadowfall?

Why did that sound so wrong?

He shoved the phone into his pocket, pulling on a clean shirt. They'd broken up. He shouldn't care anymore where Ulric was. But he couldn't help remembering Ulric again, Ulric when he was vulnerable, cramming cake into his mouth. Ulric when he sought comfort, burying his face against Gage's shoulder.

You need to protect him, his instincts whispered.

Ulric didn't need protection. He was an alpha. Frustrated with himself, Gage grabbed his things from the locker, heading out to his car. It was dark, the parking lot lit up by orange streetlamps. His phone buzzed again.

Despite his resolve not to look, Gage opened up Jesse's next message. *He was sitting out by Ben's Buns when we passed him earlier. He looked pretty upset.*

Gage's heart squeezed. He didn't want to feel bad for Ulric, but... he didn't like the thought of Ulric sitting alone, unhappy. Ulric had spent a lot of his life being miserable. He didn't need more of that.

Gage got into his car, thinking maybe he'd drive by the bakery. Just to make sure that Ulric had gone home. There had been reports of robberies around here lately—Ulric knew that, right?

Probably not. He didn't follow the news so closely.

Gage held his breath, pulling his car out onto the road. The bakery was a couple streets away—he'd just pass by and...

There was a bag of stuff that had rolled off the sidewalk, onto the asphalt. In front of a bench. Gage would've thought it was trash, except he recognized the bakery logo, and the shapes of some uneaten buns spilling out of the bag.

That wasn't right.

His chest tight, he turned down that street, did a U-turn, and pulled up behind the abandoned bag of buns. A distinct honey oak scent lingered around them. Then there came the sounds of some muffled swearing, someone groaning.

Where was Ulric?

His heart pounding, Gage followed the sounds to an alley, where two figures were kicking at someone on the ground—they were all alphas, from their broad shoulders. Except the one on the ground was heavier, all curled-up like he was hurting, and—Gage recognized him. Only too well.

They were beating up his alpha.

Gage's stomach clenched. Then rage exploded in his gut, blazing and ferocious. He roared, charging them down, punching the closest one in the face. The other guy had blood dripping from his nose and a knife in his hand. Before he could slash at Gage, Gage grabbed his wrist, yanking his knife away. Then he punched the man in the gut, he slammed him against the wall, cracking his skull against the brick.

He wasn't about to stop, but the man's accomplice swung another knife at him. Gage barely dodged; the knife whistled inches away from his face. And Gage grabbed him, he punched that guy hard, vicious strikes that would hurt for days to come.

He would've beaten the crap out of them both, except Ulric groaned. And he was far more important than the bastards who had attacked him.

Gage shoved them toward the street. "Get out of here," he snarled, placing himself between them and Ulric. "Or I'll fucking kill you."

They bristled, sizing him up. But they must've realized he was serious, because they ran, hurling something at him.

It hit him in the chest—a wallet? They'd stabbed Ulric over that?

Gage took the wallet and hurried back. Ulric had wrapped one arm over his head, the other pressed against his side. Ulric flinched when Gage touched him; Gage swallowed his anger, gathering Ulric into his arms. "Hey. Where're you hurt?"

Ulric groaned. "Everywhere."

Then he looked up and met Gage's eyes. Ulric tensed, sucking in a sharp breath.

There were scuff marks all over him. He looked like he'd put on weight. Ulric moved his hand back over a dark spot on his side, pressing down on it—and Gage realized that the dark patch on his shirt was blood. It wasn't just a small stain, either. There was a lot of it. It was still leaking out.

Gage's blood grew cold. "You're hurt."

"It's just a small wound," Ulric muttered, but his breathing was pained and shallow, and he'd clenched his jaw.

How deep was that wound? That knife hadn't been clean at all, had it? Gage froze, his thoughts spiraling. "We need to get you to the hospital."

"I'm fine," Ulric hissed.

"No, you're fucking not." Gage hauled Ulric to his feet. Ulric staggered a little. The bundles of anxiety in Gage's body grew into a larger mess. What if Ulric had hit his head? What if that stab wound infected him inside, and it slowly killed him?

Gage pulled his phone out and dialed 911, his heart clenching so tight, it almost burst.

"Hang in there," Gage muttered. "Don't die on me."

"I won't die," Ulric said, but he looked uneasy. At least the bleeding seemed to be slowing down. At least he was still conscious.

Gage heaved him back to the sidewalk, sitting him on the bench. He told the emergency call operator about Ulric, and where they were. The whole time, he couldn't tear his gaze away from Ulric. The way Ulric held himself tight, the way he stole glances at Gage, time and again, before looking at the fallen buns on the road.

Gage glanced at the side alley, at the bench, and he imagined not stopping by to check on Ulric at all. Ulric would've been in that alley, alone with his robbers, and... they might've killed him. Stabbed him, taken his phone, and left him to die.

That single thought seared away everything else, until it consumed him with the horror of it.

He imagined a world without Ulric. Without Ulric smiling at him, without Ulric all flustered. He imagined never joking with Ulric anymore, never kissing or hugging him again. He imagined not being needed by this man. Not hearing his laugh. Not holding his hand.

He'd been taking Ulric for granted, he realized. And maybe he shouldn't have minded so much that Ulric had tried to give him money. Maybe he shouldn't have cared that Ulric had been keeping secrets—those were Ulric's decisions to make. None of which had harmed Gage at all.

If he'd lost Ulric today... Gage knew he would've regretted leaving Ulric behind. He would've lost the most important part of his soul, and it would've been the result of such a petty argument.

I should learn to trust him, Gage thought. *Because he's worth fighting for.*

Was there time to fix this?

His heart pounding, Gage sat heavily next to Ulric, tangling their fingers together. Ulric stiffened, glancing down.

"Bad time to be having this conversation," Gage blurted. "They said the ambulance will be here in a few minutes. Think you'll survive until then?"

Ulric nodded. "Yeah."

Relief seeped into Gage's chest. "Thank the gods." He leaned in, at the same time Ulric moved—Ulric's nose bumped his cheek awkwardly. Then he pulled away, his eyes wide with surprise.

"What was that?" Gage asked. He didn't dare hope.

"I just—" Ulric's neck turned pink. Then he leaned closer and slanted his mouth over Gage's, a warm, gentle touch that felt like uncertainty and longing. It felt like desire and affection. Gage's pulse stumbled.

It was the first time Ulric had kissed him, without Gage initiating it.

The next moment, Ulric shoved himself back against the bench, looking away, his flush deepening. Gage's throat grew tight. "You're gonna pretend that you didn't just kiss me?" Gage murmured.

"That—That was thanks." Ulric wet his lips, looking nervous and awkward. Ever so adorable.

Gage's heart swelled. "That's it? Just thanks?" He leaned in, needing so much more. Needing to show Ulric how important he was. Needing to just—claim him again. "That's not enough, babe."

Ulric's gaze flew up, locking onto him in surprise.

"I'm sorry," Gage whispered, pressing their foreheads together. "I shouldn't have left."

"But I—I did things." Ulric squirmed. "I should've just talked to you first, maybe."

Gage huffed. "And me being a knucklehead, I would've just turned you down." He pulled Ulric closer, cradling him. "I appreciate what you did for my family."

Ulric snuffled, his eyes growing wide. "You're not... pissed anymore?"

Gage shook his head. "Nope. I was being an idiot. I'm sorry."

Ulric still looked disbelieving. In a smaller voice, he said, "I didn't want you to work so many hours. I just—wanted you to stay home. With me. You weren't hugging me much anymore."

Gage's chest squeezed tight. "You were always asleep when I got home. I didn't realize that the hugs were so important to you."

"That's why I gave your mom the money," Ulric said. "I don't want you to think I'm buying you, or anything. 'Cause I'm not. I just..." He gulped.

"You just...?" Gage nuzzled him, just savoring the weight of Ulric in his arms, Ulric recovering a little from that altercation.

"I don't want you to stress out over money all the time," Ulric blurted, looking embarrassed. "I love you."

The warmth in Gage's chest built, like a steady flame growing in a hearth. "Love you, babe. I'm sorry it's taken me this long to realize it. I'm sorry for all the crap I said."

Ulric's mouth fell open. "You... what?"

"Love you," Gage said again. "And I'm sorry. You heard that, right?"

"But I..." Ulric looked at the buns on the ground. "I've been eating so much, Gage. All the weight I lost, I think I've put it back."

"Doesn't matter. It's never mattered to me, Muffin." Gage cupped his nape, pulling him close. Ulric made a soft sound of surprise; Gage kissed him, slow and sweet, a proper kiss that sent tingles exploding through his skin. Ulric groaned. "Gods, I've missed you," Gage whispered. "Will you—"

And now his heart thumped, his stomach squeezing. Ulric had turned him down before. He could do it again. Gage swallowed. "Will you be my boyfriend? I know I've fucked up. I might fuck up again. But you have every right to tell me I'm being an idiot."

Ulric's mouth fell open; Gage wasn't sure if Ulric was breathing.

"Please say yes," Gage whispered, his pulse thudding in his ears. "I want you in my life, babe. For a very long time."

Ulric was still in pain, but there was hope in his gaze now, disbelief and warmth. "I... Yes." He ducked his head, leaning into Gage. "I'm sorry I kept putting it off. I just..."

The tightness in Gage's chest eased. "When we get home, I'm going to kiss every inch of you," Gage whispered. "Will you let me?"

Ulric sucked in a quick breath. "You—You promise?"

"Yeah. I promise."

Gage held him tighter, stroking his scent all over Ulric's skin. In the distance, the siren of an ambulance wailed.

This was a new beginning. And Gage wasn't going to mess up again. "I'll prove it to you, babe. However many times you need."

Ulric looked down, smiling to himself. Gage didn't want to let him go.

29

GAGE CONVINCES ULRIC THAT HE'S BEAUTIFUL

GAGE PRESSED Ulric up against the front door, slanting their lips together. "Mm, babe."

Ulric's heart skipped. This still felt surreal. Gage had been with him this whole time—he'd followed Ulric to the hospital, he'd stuck around anxiously while Ulric received his stitches. Then Ulric had been held under observation for some hours, and Gage had squeezed onto his hospital bed, unwilling to let him go.

"You haven't hugged me enough yet?" Ulric asked, holding his breath. Was this a dream?

Gage smiled and kissed him. "Nope."

He slipped his hands under Ulric's shirt, caressing his back, his side, being careful to avoid the stitches. He pressed kisses all over Ulric's face, his lips pulled into a warm smile. Then he reached down, grabbing Ulric by the ass. "Fuck, babe. I love your ass so much."

Ulric's face grew hot. That was the first time he'd heard Gage say that. "Because you like being inside?"

"Because I like holding you there. Mm." Gage pushed his hands into Ulric's pants, down his underwear, grabbing one cheek in each hand. Privately, Ulric thought his own ass was a bit much. But the way Gage kneaded his cheeks, squeezing them, cupping them, his eyelids half-shuttered in enjoyment... His bulge hadn't been this big when they'd left the car.

Ulric had been watching Gage this whole time; Gage seemed to honestly like spending time with him. He'd been smiling and nuzzling Ulric, and Ulric felt like he'd been forgiven. It was such a weight off his chest.

"C'mon, let's get upstairs," Gage murmured, thrusting his tongue into Ulric's mouth, tasting him again. "Wanna show you how hard you make me."

Ulric groaned, reaching down to caress his alpha. There was no mistaking the line in Gage's pants, the thick length he wanted to slide into Ulric. Gage smelled like musk, pine and, faintly, the liquor from his job last night.

Gage had called in to the gym today—so he could care for his sick boyfriend, he'd told his boss. He'd given his notice at the bar, too.

"I'm gonna drink from your spout," Gage whispered, grinding roughly into Ulric's palm. Ulric's blood surged between his legs. And Gage slipped his fingers between Ulric's cheeks, searching out his entrance.

"You just want that hole," Ulric muttered.

"I want to kiss it." Gage smiled. "Make love to it like how I'm gonna make love to you."

Ulric flushed. "That's too cheesy."

"Only too cheesy if I sprinkle some parmesan on you."

"Please don't."

Gage's eyes gleamed. "Why? Afraid I'd love licking you all over? Every tiny crack? Or... here?"

He slid his fingertip over Ulric's hole, a feather-light

touch, too faint to do anything but tease. Ulric's nerves tingled all over. "Gage."

"Yeah?" Gage licked his lips. "What do you want?"

Ulric squeezed Gage's covered cock, a demanding pressure that made Gage's eyes darken and his cock shove against Ulric's palm. It would stretch Ulric open so nicely.

"Fuck," Ulric groaned. They weren't even undressed yet, and his pants were growing tight. "I always thought you were perfect. But it figures that your cock's perfect, too."

"For gods' sakes," Wilkie said somewhere behind Gage. "If you're making up like that, I think I have to move out."

"Use the back door." Gage didn't even turn to look at him. "But the house's back door, not Ulric's. That's *mine*."

Ulric spluttered. Wilkie swore and stormed out, slamming the door behind him. Gage's smile turned hungry; he ground a fingertip against Ulric's hole, circling it, tapping on it, never once dipping inside. In fact, he spread Ulric's cheeks apart, exposing Ulric's hole. And he teased it again, soft strokes that *promised*.

Ulric growled, yanking on Gage's shirt. "You gonna go in, or what?"

Gage laughed. Then he surged forward, crashing their lips together, sweeping into Ulric's mouth with all the force of a ravenous beast. "I'm gonna go slow because you're hurt," Gage whispered. "When you get better, I'm gonna ruin that pretty hole of yours, babe. Just like what you did to mine. All it'll know is my cock claiming it inside."

Ulric's hole squeezed. Gage would leave his entrance gaping by the time he was done with it. And Ulric could already imagine his alpha's come leaking down his thighs. "Gods."

Gage released him, yanking open Ulric's pants. Ulric's cock shoved out. "Look how hungry this is," Gage whispered, stroking it lightly. Pleasure sizzled down Ulric's nerves. "This is how I want to kiss you."

And he sank to his knees, leaning in so his breath feathered across Ulric's sensitive skin. Ulric swallowed. He'd never imagined Gage kneeling in front of him. An alpha like that, looking up at Ulric with adoration in his eyes. Being at Ulric's mercy.

It felt as though Gage had given him all the power in the world.

He wet his lips, cradling his alpha's face. "Gage—"

"Love you," Gage murmured. And he pressed a damp, gentle kiss to Ulric's underside. He trailed kisses up Ulric's desperate length, rubbing his lips against the bundle of nerves beneath Ulric's tip. Sparks burst through his skin. Needing more, Ulric hissed and thrust at him, trying to push his tip into Gage's mouth.

"Not so fast, babe." Gage planted his hands on Ulric's hips, shoving him back against the door. But the smirk Gage wore—Ulric wanted to wipe it off, he wanted to claim Gage inside.

As though he could read Ulric's mind, Gage kissed down Ulric's cock, all the way to his aching balls. Gage cupped those and kneaded them; electricity jolted up Ulric's spine. He jerked, swearing. And Gage kissed back up to his tip, every touch slow and purposeful.

It wasn't enough, not in the slightest.

"Damn it, Gage," Ulric growled, grasping Gage's hair. "Don't tease."

"All right," Gage said. "Just a little suck."

He licked Ulric's head, his tongue a flat, soft pressure.

Then he closed his lips around the bead of precome at Ulric's tip—he was just *right there*. Ulric's control fractured. He hauled Gage closer and *pushed,* and his cock parted Gage's lips, sliding into the snugness of his alpha's mouth.

Gage looked so good like that, his lips wrapped around Ulric's sensitive flesh.

Gage groaned, hollowing his cheeks. The pressure around Ulric's cock spiked—it went straight to his balls and pulled them tight. Ulric cursed; his hips snapped up. His cock hit the back of Gage's throat.

"Fuck," Gage growled around his cock. And the fabric at his tip began to grow dark. Ulric bit off his moan, plowing again into his alpha, over and over. Just savoring the friction between them, the exquisite slide of Gage's tongue against his sensitive head.

The harder he fucked his alpha, the larger that wet spot grew.

Ulric's instincts snarled to the surface. They wanted him to pin his alpha, they wanted him to search out Gage's hole with his cock, and claim him inside.

"Gage," Ulric hissed.

Something must've changed in his voice, because Gage pulled away, his lips glistening. "Break time," Gage murmured, blowing cool air all over Ulric's desperate length. "I haven't kissed the rest of you yet."

Ulric's cock ached. "I want to fuck, not kiss."

Gage smiled. "Nope. Too late, babe."

Then he grasped the hem of Ulric's shirt, lifted it, and kissed Ulric's hip. Before Ulric could move, Gage lifted the shirt higher, kissing the curve of Ulric's belly. And he lifted it further, until Ulric could see his own navel.

Ulric froze. If there was anything he was self-conscious about, it was his belly. Or rather, his entire body. But his belly was where it was most obvious—he didn't have sculpted abs like Gage did. And it was right in front of Gage's face.

Gage met his eyes. "Relax, Muffin."

"I'm exactly that. A muffin." Even though they'd talked about this, having Gage kiss him all over... This was scary. It was real. And Ulric couldn't help the way Gage felt. For all he knew, Gage might regret his decision.

"But you're *my* Muffin." Gage kissed around the stitches, where they still hurt. "And you're damn fucking adorable, Ulric."

Ulric bit his lip, watching as Gage pulled his shirt higher, exposing his chest. That, too, wasn't anything like Gage's.

Gage buried his face in Ulric's chest, groaning. "Been dreaming of you naked, babe."

Ulric winced. "Naked?"

Gage took Ulric's hand, pressing it against his bulge. "Not convinced by this, huh?"

Ulric shook his head.

"Looks like we'll need a better way to do it." Gage linked their fingers. Then he tugged Ulric up the stairs with him, to Ulric's bedroom. That smelled too much of honey oak and musk, and not enough pine.

Gage shut the door and lowered the blinds until shadows filled the room. "Get on the bed."

Ulric sat gingerly on the edge of the mattress, looking down at his curves. He'd never been fully naked in front of Gage before. Or anyone else.

This terrified him, just a little.

"Here. What if we use this?" Gage found a dark pillowcase, folding it up. Then he pressed it gently over Ulric's eyes. The room went black. "Just for today, stop judging yourself. Let me show you how I feel about you."

Uncertainty slithered through Ulric's chest. But Gage had said he loved Ulric, and... maybe Ulric should learn to trust him. He bit his lip. "Okay."

Gage secured the blindfold around Ulric's head. Then he helped Ulric scoot further up the bed. He plucked off Ulric's socks and stroked Ulric's calves and thighs. "Remember me touching you here?"

He'd done that, sometimes. When they'd snuggled together on the couch and Ulric pulled his legs up. Gage would reach over and touch Ulric's knee, or his lap. "Yeah."

"Here, slide your pants off," Gage said.

Ulric didn't mind removing his pants—Gage had seen him a few times without. Hell, Gage knew what his hole looked like. And... maybe Ulric didn't mind giving Gage an eyeful of his cock. He squirmed out of his pants, the cool air of the bedroom skimming his thighs.

"Mm." Slowly, Gage pressed Ulric backward, until his back thumped against the mattress. Ulric's stitches twinged. "Lie back for me, babe."

The sheets rustled. Gage caught Ulric's knees, spreading them open. Ulric's face grew hot. "But this is fucking," Ulric said.

Gage chuckled. "Nope. Still kissing."

He lifted one of Ulric's legs, kissing from his ankle up the side of his calf, to his knee. Ulric held his breath. He'd never been kissed there before. And Gage's lips trailed over his skin, a light, damp touch. Ulric bit back his groan.

"Feels good?" Gage's voice slid down his spine.

"Yeah."

Warm breath raced down the inside of Ulric's thigh.

Not long after, Gage's mouth followed—soft kisses, the sharp points of teeth on Ulric's sensitive skin. Gage bit him lightly, just enough to let Ulric know he was there. Then he kissed higher and higher, until he reached the crease of Ulric's thigh. Ulric thought Gage might kiss his cock. He held his breath.

Instead, Gage switched to his other leg, doing the same. Ulric's instincts grumbled. "You missed something."

Gage laughed. "Yeah? What'd I miss?"

Ulric spread his legs wider, showing him. But rather than touching Ulric's cock, Gage slipped a finger between Ulric's cheeks, stroking around his hole. "I'll kiss this at the end," Gage said. "There's still the rest of you."

"Fuck." Ulric growled, wanting more. Wanting to hide in the desperate need of sex, instead of letting Gage see the rest of him. But he'd agreed.

Gage reached the top of Ulric's thigh. Then he began unbuttoning Ulric's shirt. Ulric's stomach flipped.

"You're beautiful," Gage murmured. "See, everywhere I kiss, I think that's beautiful. Give me a chance to show you, babe."

He kissed all the way along the underside of Ulric's belly, from one side to the other. More and more of that fabric fell away, until Ulric's belly was entirely exposed, and then his chest. Every inch Gage uncovered, he kissed.

He reached the last button on Ulric's shirt, popping that open. Gage kissed Ulric's collarbones, then his shoulders. Then he kissed up Ulric's neck, and Ulric knew Gage could see his whole body now. He felt far too naked.

Gage lay down next to him, still clothed, and pressed

kisses all over Ulric's face. "This is beautiful, too," Gage whispered. "This right here. What I'm kissing."

Ulric's throat grew tight.

Maybe he couldn't see himself in the same light yet, but he felt Gage's complete acceptance of him. He felt as though he could be utterly naked with Gage, and... it would be all right.

Through the blindfold, Gage kissed his eyelids. Then Gage kissed his nose, and his mouth. "Turn over," Gage whispered. "I'll get your back, too."

His whole front covered in kisses, Ulric eased out of his shirt. He rolled onto his unhurt side; Gage kissed his hair, then his nape. Then he dropped kisses all across Ulric's back, down his spine, and to his ass.

"Told you this is a fucking beautiful ass," Gage growled, squeezing it. "Loved it the moment I spanked you."

Ulric flushed. He remembered that popcorn incident. "It's just my ass."

Gage smacked his cheek lightly; Ulric felt it bounce. "Mm, fuck," Gage whispered. Then he grasped Ulric's ass, spread it open, and kissed between his cheeks, all the way to his hole. Blood surged between Ulric's legs. Gage's face was pressed intimately against his cheeks, his stubble scraping Ulric's skin. He couldn't possibly...

Gage kissed him right where he was vulnerable, a slow, deliberate touch. And he flicked his tongue against Ulric's entrance. "Relax for me, babe."

"But—" Ulric swallowed.

Something stroked him there, soft and wet. Then it nudged at him like it was seeking entrance.

It wasn't a spot where anyone had ever kissed, either. Ulric's face scorched.

"Feel good?" Gage's voice vibrated through Ulric's most sensitive parts.

"Fuck."

"Relax." Gage kissed his hole again.

So Ulric relaxed. And Gage pushed his tongue inside, a hungry presence spreading him open. Ulric forgot to breathe. Gage was tasting him *there*. "What—What're you..."

Gage's breath rushed against his skin. Was he amused? "Have you never been kissed here?"

"No."

Gage's rumble of delight went all the way through Ulric's insides. "I didn't realize you were a kiss virgin, babe."

"What's a 'kiss virgin'?" Ulric was glad he couldn't see Gage's expression. He wasn't anywhere as experienced as his alpha was.

"It's what I call someone who hasn't been kissed in places." Gage licked Ulric's hole, firm and slow. Then he groaned, pushing his tongue back in, sliding out, pushing in again. As though he was fucking Ulric there, but with his tongue. Pleasure scattered down Ulric's veins.

Ulric bit off his groan. He hadn't expected this to feel so good.

"Getting you all ready for me," Gage murmured. He slid a finger into Ulric, and then another. Ulric's nerves sang as his body stretched around Gage, clinging to his fingers, begging for more.

"Gods, you're so damn ready," Gage rasped, pulling his fingers out. He patted Ulric's hole lightly, before leaning away. The nightstand drawer rumbled open.

Then fabric rustled, and the next time Gage pressed up against him, he was completely naked against Ulric, his thick cock wedging between Ulric's cheeks.

Ulric's instincts came roaring back; he growled, turning to try and seek leverage.

Except Gage pinned him down from behind, a delicious slide of skin on skin. And he slid his entire length against Ulric's hole, showing him what would go inside. Ulric's breath shuddered out of him.

"This is what you do to me," Gage murmured, snapping his hips, his cock grinding against Ulric's entrance. "Don't move so much, babe. You just got stitched up."

Ulric wanted to move, he wanted to pin Gage down and dominate him. "You'll have to make me."

"Gladly." Before Ulric could start struggling, Gage anchored him against the mattress. Slick sounds came from further down. Then something touched Ulric between his cheeks—Gage's fingers, covered in lube. And they shoved roughly inside, stretching Ulric, lubing him up. Getting him ready to receive his alpha's cock.

Ulric throbbed, growing so hard, he hurt. He wanted Gage. He wanted Gage's desire. And Gage was touching him all over, despite all his nakedness.

"I'm not making this easy for you," Ulric growled, struggling.

Gage shoved him down with a snarl, his cock plunging between Ulric's cheeks, smearing lube over his hole. "Mine," Gage rasped.

He lodged his blunt tip against Ulric's entrance, a girthy promise. Then he snapped his hips, pressing hard against Ulric's hole, forcing it to stretch open around him. And Gage plunged inside, inches at once, so big that Ulric forgot to breathe.

"Fuck, those sounds you make," Gage whispered in his ear. "When you take my cock." He gave a deep thrust;

Ulric swore, an animal sound ripping out of him. "Yeah, like that. Fuck."

Gage buried his cock to the hilt, so savagely that Ulric rocked forward. Ulric groaned as his hole opened for his alpha, eagerly taking all that Gage gave him. And Gage began to build a rhythm, slower than he had before.

"I can take it," Ulric growled. "Harder, Gage."

"Don't wanna hurt you." Gage tightened his grip, his breaths coming more sharply, his groans bliss to Ulric's ears.

"My ass isn't hurt," Ulric retorted. "You don't have to be fucking gentle with it."

Gage snarled, plowing so deep that pleasure jolted through Ulric's veins and his spine bowed. It almost erased the pain of his wounds. Ulric struggled harder—just to provoke his alpha.

"Stop moving, damn it," Gage hissed. He shoved Ulric against the bed and fucked in hard—a punishment? But pleasure burst through Ulric, more intense than before.

"Not gonna stop." Ulric thrashed again. His stitches pulled; Gage swore and held him down, thrusting harder, his cock plunging into Ulric like an unyielding length of steel, filling him up over and over, staking his claim.

Ulric shoved at him. Gage gripped his hips and crammed his cock all the way in, swearing. Ulric almost came right there. He reached back to grab Gage; Gage caught his hand, bringing it to his lips.

And he sank his teeth into Ulric's wrist, a spot that was far too sensitive to be just another part of his body. Ulric's nerves lit up; his cock swelled so thick, it fucking hurt.

Then he realized that Gage had bitten the scent gland on his wrist—a bonding mark. His heart leaped.

"Wait," Gage said, his thrusts slowing down a little. "I—I marked you."

"Not yours unless you claim me properly," Ulric growled. He bucked at Gage, ignoring the pull on his stitches. "My neck."

He tilted his head, offering the scent gland there. Gage swore and leaned in, biting hard into the crook of Ulric's shoulder, right where that sensitive spot was. Pain and pleasure tore through Ulric's spine, pulling his balls tight. He tried to catch his breath but he couldn't, his entire body pulsing with need.

Gage had bitten him. He was Gage's.

"Mine," Gage snarled. "So fucking beautiful." And his strokes deepened, his cock slamming into Ulric, a desperate sort of rhythm that showed just how much he wanted Ulric to be his. "Gonna fill you up with my come, babe. Gonna make you all mine."

Ulric's entire body sang. "Please."

"Fuck." Gage roared, his fingers digging bruisingly-hard into Ulric's hips. He leaned in and slammed a final time into Ulric, a flood of warmth filling Ulric inside.

Ulric imagined his alpha's pleasure—his control shattered. Pleasure ripped through his body in a deluge, arching his spine, rolling his eyes back into his head.

For a long while afterward, all he felt was Gage's bare skin against his own, Gage pressing slow, muzzy kisses across his shoulder. Gage pulled Ulric's blindfold off.

He was completely naked. And Gage was still kissing him. In fact, Gage was stroking the scent glands on his wrists down Ulric's sides, marking him with pine. He brushed his scent over Ulric's chest, over Ulric's belly, over all the curves of Ulric's body that weren't as perfect as his own.

"I think you might be insane," Ulric mumbled.

Gage huffed. "Nah. I'm just lucky. Because I found the best gift in the world."

Then he kissed Ulric's nape, a slow, lingering touch. Ulric's heart stuttered.

"I love you," Gage said again. "All of you. Every single bit. Do you believe me now?"

Ulric looked down at Gage's arm wrapped around his belly, caressing him fondly. Gage's body pressed against his own, skin on skin. Gage's mouth on his ear, nipping at him.

Gage had seen all of Ulric, and he was still here.

Ulric's throat grew tight. "Yeah," he croaked. He'd never had anyone love him this way before. "I just... It seems too good to be true."

Gage kissed his shoulder. "Beauty isn't always visible. A lot of things are invisible and beautiful. Like love. Like kindness. Like your soul." He pressed his palm over Ulric's heart.

"You can see kindness, sort of," Ulric protested.

Gage smiled. "You can see the results of kindness. But it comes from here." He rubbed Ulric's chest. "That's not all, though. The visible parts of you are all beautiful, too." He stroked Ulric's arm and kissed his nape. He dragged his wrist over Ulric's belly, covering Ulric with his scent. "All of this here—regardless of whether you get heavier or lighter, regardless of whether you get old and wrinkly, all of this is beautiful, because it's part of you. And that's important, too. All of you is important.

"At some point, I want you to see yourself the way I see you, babe. I think you're perfect. Every inch of you." Gage nestled his legs against Ulric's, and cuddled him close. "Everything I see here, I'm proud that it's mine."

Ulric swallowed hard, glancing at his belly, and his

arms, and the rest of himself.

Maybe... he could be beautiful. Maybe he already was. He just had to see himself differently.

"Here, I'll prove that I didn't mark you only because you made me crazy horny," Gage said. He took Ulric's hand, bringing it closer. Then he sniffed at Ulric's unmarked wrist, found a spot, and kissed it. Ulric's heart fluttered.

"You're okay with this, right?" Gage asked.

Ulric swallowed hard, nodding. "Yeah."

Gage sank his teeth lightly into Ulric's skin. "This is how much I want you to be mine," Gage whispered.

And he bit down hard, breaking skin, sending pain and pleasure twisting through Ulric's body. Ulric gasped. When Gage released him, droplets of blood beaded on his skin. Gage kissed them away. "Mine," he growled. "Never leaving you again."

Ulric's chest squeezed tight. "Will you—let me do the same?"

Over his shoulder, Gage smiled. "Thought you wouldn't ask." He gave Ulric his hand; his knot had begun swelling in Ulric's body, a heavy presence inside that locked them together. "Later, when we aren't knotted together anymore, I want you to mark my neck, too."

A smile threatened to burst across Ulric's face. Gage really wanted him. He turned Gage's hand over, sniffing carefully at his wrist. One spot in particular smelled most strongly of pine—Gage's scent gland.

Ulric licked it. Behind, Gage sucked in a deep breath. But he didn't pull away.

Ulric bit down hard, enough that Gage jerked and swore against him. When Ulric released his alpha, he found a set of teethmarks on Gage's wrist—the broken skin would heal into a bonding mark.

Gage was his.

Gage growled, pressing himself flush against Ulric's back. "Yours," he whispered. "It feels kinda strange."

"Strange?" Ulric frowned. "How so?"

"Never belonged to anyone before." Gage smiled against Ulric's shoulder. "You're my first. And last."

Ulric's heart tumbled. He wanted to hold Gage close, he wanted to show the world his alpha. But he didn't know who else would be happy about his news, though. He didn't have much of a family to return to.

"What's wrong?" Gage whispered.

Ulric twitched his shoulders. "I don't think my family wants this. You and me."

A growl began in Gage's chest. "You're coming to visit my folks with me," Gage told him, anger edging his voice. "You're welcome there, babe. All of them want to meet you."

"Even if..." Ulric looked down at their linked fingers.

"You're my bondmate," Gage told him. "That's all that matters. You'll get a whole new family where no one will say shit about you."

That also sounded too good to be true. Ulric settled back against Gage, imagining it. Then he looked down at his belly, wondering if Gage would ever want a family in the future. If either of them could get pregnant, what would Gage say?

It was too soon to think about it.

30

A FAMILY...?

The children giggled as they chased each other around the pavilion, sunlight glinting off their hair, their snake-skirts fluttering in the breeze.

They looked so happy that Ulric couldn't help smiling.

"Something you haven't told me?" Gage murmured, slipping his arm around Ulric's waist.

Ulric leaned into him. It had been months since they'd become bondmates. Wilkie had moved back into their parents' place, and from Gage's conversations with him, Wilkie had been up to some questionable things that Gage wasn't too happy about.

That aside, everything was good. Ulric had met Gage's family on a few occasions—Gage's mom fawned over him like one of her own, and Gage's dad had taken them out on some bike rides. Ulric had discovered that he enjoyed going cycling outside the gym, too. It was more fun when he had company, when he wasn't thinking of exercise as work.

This past Sunday, Debbie had joined them—she'd

finished the last rounds of her chemotherapy, and she was slowly recovering. Gage no longer minded that Ulric had contributed to a significant portion of her bills.

"Papa! Papa!" A child ran under the pavilion. He seemed about nine, one of the boys who had waved around some snake streamers months back. Going by the snake skirt he now wore, the child seemed just a little obsessed.

"What is it, Caleb?" one of the off-duty firefighters asked.

"Can Izzy and I go treasure-hunting?" Caleb bounced on his heels, looking so enthusiastic that Ulric would've caved and let them go play. Another boy hurried up next to him, also his age. "There's a magic house in the woods," Caleb said. "I think that's where all the snakes come from!"

"We'll hide some eggs in there," Izzy whispered. "It's pretend-eggs. One day, there'll be a whole family of snakes all tangled together!"

A few of the firefighters laughed. By this point, Ulric was familiar with the trouser snake joke drifting amongst the team.

Caleb's dad exchanged a look with his omega, before grinning. "All right. Let's race to the forest. You all right with that, Izzy?"

Izzy nodded, linking his fingers with Caleb's. "I think so. I can't run so fast, but I'll try."

"I'll wait for you." Caleb gave his friend a fond smile. Hand-in-hand, the three of them set off for the nearby woods.

Ulric watched them go. What would it be like to have a family? To have excitable children who were so happy when you joined them on an adventure?

"What're you thinking about?" Gage murmured in his ear.

"Those kids." Ulric's heart thumped. "They seemed nice."

"Yeah?" Gage's smile widened. "You want a couple?"

Ulric's neck heated up. They hadn't been officially dating for so long. But the more time he spent with Gage, the deeper in love he fell. And Ulric... kind of wanted to have Gage's babies.

But he was an alpha. He couldn't really *give* Gage a child. Worse, he hadn't even mentioned children to Gage. Did Gage want a family? With Ulric?

"Your—your cousin mentioned something about implants," Ulric mumbled.

Gage slid his hand down Ulric's belly, his eyes darkening. "Yeah? What about them?"

"You... ever thought about a uterus implant?"

"For me, or you?"

Ulric blinked. He hadn't thought Gage would consider it for himself, too. "You'd want one?"

Gage cracked a smile. "Let's just say I've been thinking about you knocking me up."

Ulric turned to gape at him. Gage? Having a kink like that? "So... so we're really serious about this," Ulric said. "Me and you."

Gage laughed. Then he rubbed his thumb over the scent gland on Ulric's wrist, where his marking was. "I made a promise, didn't I?

Ulric's heart skipped. "Yeah. You did."

Over the past few months, Ulric had thought maybe Gage might get tired of him. He'd thought maybe Gage might want him to lose weight. But Gage hadn't mentioned his extra chub at all—he'd only encouraged Ulric to eat his vegetables, and exercise more. *Remember, I just want you to be healthy,* Gage had murmured in bed one night. *So I can have you for a long time to come.*

"You're okay with having kids?" Ulric blurted.

"I want a family with you, babe." Gage kissed his neck. "I want us with little ones running around. Is it okay if we have more than one?"

Ulric's heart tumbled. "Yeah. Of course."

Gage smiled, drawing circles on Ulric's belly. "What if we do this together? Both of us."

"You mean us... getting pregnant? At the same time?" Ulric's thoughts went sideways. He hadn't considered *that*. "Is it possible?"

"I don't know." Gage grabbed his cousin as he walked past. "Hey, Jes. We have questions."

Jesse stopped next to them, eyebrows raised. Over the past months, his scent had changed from cinnamon to birch.

"That doctor friend of yours," Gage said. "Is he accepting new patients?"

Jesse glanced at Gage's hand on Ulric's belly, his eyebrows crawling up. "It'll be a long process. You know that, right? Might take a few years. He'd have to get your stem cells, modify them, and then cultivate new organs from those so your body won't reject them. And *then* he'd have to put those in you, stitch you up, and you'd have to heal before you can even begin the pregnancy."

It sounded a little daunting. Maybe it'd be more expensive than Ulric could afford.

When he glanced at Gage, though, he found his alpha looking thoughtful. "We'll think about it," Gage told Jesse. "Thanks."

Later that day, as they were driving home, Ulric asked, "Still want to go through that process?"

"I think it'll be pretty pricey," Gage said, biting his lip. "I'd have to—"

"Not another job." Ulric frowned.

Gage smiled. "I was just gonna say that I could stop ogling all those fancy gym upgrades. And... maybe we might have to move into a cheaper place."

Ulric had grown fond of their neighbors. If they didn't have a better choice, though... "We could."

King jogged by with his dog just as they'd parked in the driveway. "Hey." King waved. "We're having another get-together in a couple weeks. You guys in?"

Gage and Ulric exchanged a look. "We might be moving out," Ulric said.

"That's a bummer." King seemed disappointed. "What happened?"

"We're saving up for a family," Ulric answered. "Although it's a bit more complicated than that."

"Tell me," King said.

So Ulric told him about the experimental process, the organ implants, and the eventual pregnancy, feeling like maybe he was overloading King with too much information. Just because he and Gage wanted to knock each other up.

"You know, I think there might be other folks in your situation," King mused. "You said Nate might know this doctor?"

They were getting more and more people involved in this, which wasn't what Ulric wanted. He winced. "It's fine, really. We'll manage."

"I'll have a chat with Nate," King said. "Don't worry about it."

He disappeared down the street, leaving Ulric and Gage staring after him in bewilderment.

"What did I do?" Ulric mumbled.

"Possibly a very good thing." Gage tugged him closer, kissing his ear. "Do you think we'll have two boys, or two girls?"

"At the same time?" Ulric gulped, thinking about both of them with swollen bellies. "You know we're going to attract stares. Maybe not so much me, because I'm already fat—"

"You're perfect."

"—but you have a job at the gym, Gage." Ulric grimaced. "Are they going to be okay with you getting pregnant?"

Gage shrugged, kissing Ulric again. "It'll be a while yet. We'll deal with it when that happens, babe."

Ulric still wasn't convinced.

"Here, let me show you how I'll knock you up," Gage whispered. He pulled their bodies flush, a sweet friction that distracted Ulric from his thoughts. "Lots of time to practice."

Ulric gave in. Maybe it was because of his job, but Gage demonstrated things very well. Especially in the bedroom.

He followed Gage into the house, setting his worries aside.

31

MAKING BABIES

"Are you able to do a few sit-ups for me?" Dr. Rutherford asked, waving them over to an exam bed

Gage nodded for Ulric to go first; Ulric frowned. "You first," Ulric said. "You've been doing way more than you should."

Rutherford fixed Gage with a chiding stare. "You should have let your body heal."

"I felt fine. Was starting to hurt when I stopped working out after the surgery." Gage got on the bed, doing a set of ten easily—just to prove he could. He liked working out; it loosened his muscles and helped him sleep better. And, now that he'd had an open-body surgery, it felt good to know he was back in shape.

Rutherford listened to Gage's heart, before checking his abdomen. "You do seem to have healed well. How are you coping with the hormones?"

"Not bad."

Some time before the implantation surgery, Rutherford had given them increasing doses of omega hormones, to let them adjust to the hormonal cocktail that came with having omega parts.

It felt... strange. Gage had been noticing different things—he'd been thinking maybe they needed some prettier curtains in the house, and he'd been wanting to put on some flowing lacy clothes. Jesse had let Gage borrow his bottles of nail polish. Coloring his nails felt really weird, but also good.

Now that they each had an ovary and uterus implanted, Rutherford had given them a hormone suppressant to prevent unexpected heats from happening.

"Your turn, Ulric," Rutherford said. "A few sit-ups, please."

Ulric took his spot on the bed; Gage caught his ankles, leaning close. Just like they did at home. Ulric's mouth twitched. With some effort, he heaved himself up, enough that he could now meet Gage's lips over his knees. Gage kissed him lightly, his mouth tingling.

This was the best part about exercising with Ulric—all the rewards Gage dangled in front of his alpha, he enjoyed, too. And Ulric was motivated by the rewards a lot more than he was by the exercise.

With the doctor watching, Ulric did a total of five sit-ups, before sagging back against the bench. "Haven't done that many in a while," he puffed.

"You did great," Gage told him.

"Does any part of your abdomen hurt?" Rutherford asked, carefully prodding at Ulric's belly.

Ulric shook his head. "Just tired from the strain. That's all."

The doctor went over their progress from the last few weeks, and they discussed the details of an alpha pregnancy.

Then, armed with some alcohol swabs and a scalpel, Rutherford removed the hormone suppressant implants from their arms, stitching them back up with some surgical thread.

"All done," Rutherford said. "You should experience your heat in a couple hours. You'd best start looking for a room."

He smiled crookedly as they stood to leave. It had to be weird, an omega like him helping alphas get pregnant. Gage glanced at the wall of pictures to Rutherford's side, with happy families and smiling parents. No pictures of Rutherford himself.

Did he not have a family? Rutherford was in his forties, Gage figured. Surely he had to have found someone.

"You've done this surgery several times, huh?" Gage asked, gesturing at his abdomen.

The doctor froze, as though surprised. Then he recovered. "Ah, just a couple times in the last few years." He smiled, tight-lipped. "Most of my patients request mammary implants for breastfeeding—that's what this clinic specializes in, after all."

"Did something go wrong?" Ulric asked, worried.

Rutherford shook his head. "Just the circumstances surrounding some surgeries, that's all."

He looked honest, but beneath his smile was a dark, bottomless regret that Gage wasn't going to touch. He hoped someone would help the doctor with it, though. It seemed that even doctors couldn't heal everyone. Or maybe they just couldn't heal themselves.

"Come visit Meadowfall sometime," Gage said. "The sunshine might be good for you."

"That's where Nate is, isn't it?" Rutherford smiled wanly. "I'll keep that in mind."

Gage tugged Ulric along as they left the clinic. "He seemed sad, don't you think?"

Ulric winced. "Yeah, he did. I wish I could help."

"Like being his alpha?" Gage wriggled his eyebrows.

"Pfft." The next moment, Ulric looked sorry. "You know I can't get hard for an omega, Gage. Like, I've tried. It just doesn't work."

Gage patted between Ulric's legs. "Works for me, though."

Ulric flushed a bright red, looking around. "We're not alone," he hissed.

Gage just laughed. "You're fucking adorable when you're flustered."

Ulric flipped him off.

They found a hotel—a decent one, not the best. Even with the discounts Nate and King had worked out with Rutherford, this was still a costly endeavor. It was kind of crazy, every time Gage thought about it. And yet they were here, they both had uteruses grown from their own DNA implanted in their bodies.

As they waited for the hotel's computer system to check them in, warmth began to pool in Gage's veins, a hungry, incessant whisper that raked down his spine. He wanted his alpha closer, he wanted to breathe the scent off Ulric's skin. And he wanted to hear Ulric groan in his ear.

He squeezed Ulric's hand. "Is it just me, or are you feeling it, too?"

Ulric's pupils had dilated. "Not just you."

His voice had deepened into a delicious rasp, musk coiling off his skin. The implants weren't the only thing that was different about them, though. Instead of Gage's pine, his scent had sweetened into clove. Ulric's honey oak had turned into an enticing anise scent.

Gage all but grabbed the key card when the receptionist handed it over. The moment the elevator door shut, he shoved Ulric roughly against the wall, dragging him into a scorching kiss.

Ulric growled, his pupils blowing wide. "Fuck, Gage."

"I hope you're as wet as the doctor said you'll be," Gage whispered, reaching behind to stroke Ulric's ass. Something about the omega hormones.

Neither of them identified as omegas, but Gage sure wouldn't say no to some extra lube. Especially when it'd make Ulric feel good. "Ready to take my cock, babe?"

Ulric groaned and hauled Gage closer, pushing his tongue into Gage's mouth. "I'm gonna fuck you first," Ulric hissed. He shoved his hand down the front of Gage's pants. "Cream inside you."

"Mm." Gage's blood surged south. "I thought you were blazing hot before, babe. But if this is you in heat, maybe I want you in heat all the fucking time."

Ulric's smile turned hungry; his eyes lit up. He bit hard on Gage's lip, sucking it into his hot, wet mouth. Gage fucked Ulric's mouth with his tongue, he rocked their bulges together until Ulric groaned.

Then Ulric wheezed, his breath punching out of him. He panted, looking down as though he was... surprised?

And a wall of musk slammed into Gage like a sledgehammer.

"Think I'm in a rut," Ulric whispered, the aching need on his face going straight between Gage's legs.

"Yeah?" Gage had never been with an alpha in a rut before. He grasped Ulric's bulge, squeezing it. It had grown thicker, harder. The touch yanked a snarl from his alpha.

Ulric slammed him into the elevator wall, dragging

him into a savage kiss. Fuck, he was hot. Gage panted, pulling him closer, trying to get enough of his alpha. Trying to just breathe.

Someone cleared their throat loudly. Gage glanced over to find people outside the elevator, waiting to get in. *Crap.* He shoved Ulric off and dragged him out, fumbling with his bearings.

Then he realized they were on the first floor.

Ulric followed his stare. "Did we even... go upstairs? Did you hit the button for our floor?"

"I thought I did." Gage tried not to adjust his too-tight pants. "Did we make out for so long that the elevator went back down?"

"We must've." Ulric huffed, his cheeks faintly pink. "Oops?"

Except the desire in his eyes far outweighed his amusement. He stared at Gage, as though he might pounce on Gage the next moment, and tear his pants right off. Here. In the lobby.

"Keep this clean," Gage murmured, hitting the elevator call button. "At least, until we get to our room."

"What part of this is clean?" Ulric's stare dropped to Gage's hips. "You're a second from ripping your pants."

Gage shoved down his bulge. They were both indecent right now, their cocks straining, musk wafting off them like they were in some sort of soft porn movie.

It was forever until the elevator door opened again. This time, Gage kept his hands off Ulric. "I'm not touching you until we get to our room, babe. Or we'll be riding the elevator all day."

Ulric laughed and followed Gage in. "Yeah, we'll be riding each other while riding the elevator."

"As much as I'd love to ride your ass here, I'm giving

it a pass," Gage muttered. "I want to fill you up properly. Get a full load of come inside you. Give you a baby."

Ulric swore. Despite his resolve, Gage skimmed his fingertips against the curve of Ulric's ass, just next to his hole. "Felt it there, didn't you? Your hole got all tight imagining me."

Ulric's eyes flashed; he whirled around on Gage, his entire body tense with need.

The elevator doors opened. Gage grabbed him and shoved him out, barreling him into the wall. "Three seconds, babe. Wait until we get to our room."

"Don't know where it is," Ulric muttered. He grabbed Gage's bulge and squeezed it.

Gage dropped the key card. He bent over to pick it up. Ulric grabbed his hips and ground his cock between Gage's cheeks, a good, hard thrust. Just like how he'd push inside. Gage throbbed, his instincts roaring for him to pin Ulric down and claim his hole.

He growled, shoving Ulric off. "Get to the room first."

"Want to strip you here," Ulric whispered, his gaze dark. "Let you take my cock."

Fuck. Gage's throat went dry. Now that Ulric was comfortable around him, Gage had begun to see much more of Ulric's other side, the side of him that was feral. The side of him that was *alpha*.

He shoved Ulric off and found their room somehow, pushing the key into its slot. Ulric slammed him against the door, grinding hard against Gage's ass. "Mine," Ulric growled. "Gonna give you a baby, Gage."

Gage's hole squeezed. The door unlocked; he pushed it open, and Ulric shoved him into the room, tearing at Gage's pants, cramming his fingers between Gage's bare cheeks.

Then he worked his finger up against Gage's hole, pushing inside.

Gage clenched around him, hissing. There was a little less burn now, a little more wetness. "Still need some lube." He shoved some packets of lube into Ulric's hand. "Get this in there."

Ulric's only answer was a hungry growl. He tore open a packet; Gage yanked at Ulric's belt, undoing it. Then he yanked down Ulric's pants and grabbed his cock, and Ulric snarled, thrusting thick and heavy against Gage's palm. It was beyond ready to impale Gage.

So Gage grabbed Ulric's shirt. He tugged it off his alpha's head, leaving him mostly bare—all broad shoulders and pink nipples, some muscle beneath the curves on his chest. And a silvery scar down his middle.

Instead of shying away, Ulric let him look. Gage leaned in and bit his nipple; Ulric hissed. But these days, he didn't mind Gage admiring him. "Beautiful," Gage murmured, sucking on that pink disc.

And he brushed his palm down along Ulric's cock, under his tight balls, all the way to the lush cheeks hiding his hole. Gage eased his fingers between them, stroking Ulric's entrance. It was very slightly damp. Far less than an omega's slick, but still appreciated nonetheless.

Ulric knocked his hand away, his gaze flashing. "Me first."

Gage's mouth tugged into a savage smile. "That's how we're playing it?"

He grabbed Ulric by the hips and shoved him hard against the wall, stepping down on his pants to get it completely off his legs. And now Ulric was bare, not a stitch on his body—just the way Gage loved him.

Ulric snarled and barreled Gage backward; Gage's shoulders hit the opposite wall. And Ulric yanked open Gage's pants, he hauled Gage around to face the wall, shoving his waistband down just enough to expose his ass.

Before Gage could push him off, Ulric shoved his blunt tip between Gage's cheeks, grinding it hard against his hole. No lube. Precome smeared over his entrance. Gage's cock throbbed.

"Fuck, babe," Gage hissed, shouldering his alpha off. "Not so easy."

Ulric grabbed Gage's shirt and ripped it open, buttons popping, bouncing off the dresser. Then he smoothed his palm up Gage's abs, groaning in appreciation. "Always so beautiful, Gage."

"So are you."

Just like Ulric, there was a silver scar on Gage's front now, going right down his abs. The addition of the uterus wasn't really obvious; Rutherford had said it would only become apparent when they developed a baby bump.

Ulric dragged him over to the bed and flung him down. Gage twisted around onto all-fours, scrambling further up the mattress. "Fuck, Gage." Ulric grabbed Gage's waistband and hauled him back. He ripped Gage's pants off his ass. Then he shoved his fingers between Gage's cheeks, plunging one straight into Gage's hole, deeper than before. "I love claiming you."

Ulric drove his finger hard against Gage's prostate; pleasure seared through Gage's body, pulling his balls tight. "Damn, babe."

Gage threw himself forward to escape Ulric; Ulric bore down on him, grasping his knees, shoving his legs open. Gage was about to struggle, except Ulric grabbed his cock and balls, a tight grip that shot up his spine. And now he was at his alpha's mercy, Ulric leaning in to lick Gage's balls, then his cock, a damp soft touch that had Gage gasping.

Ulric pushed two fingers into Gage's hole, parting them to stretch him further. A low groan slipped from his throat. He withdrew his touch for a second; Gage turned to find Ulric tearing open a lube sachet.

Ulric pushed his fingers back into Gage, spreading him again. And the crinkled edge of the foil packet pushed into his ass, a second before cool wetness trickled into his body.

"You fucking me with that lube packet, babe?" Gage growled.

Ulric glanced up. Then he smiled and pushed the packet deeper into Gage, in and out, so Gage felt the brush of its smooth foil edges against his sensitive parts. His cock jerked. Ulric moaned, and Gage squeezed around him, at the same time Ulric withdrew the lube packet and his fingers.

While he tore open the next packet, Gage kicked off the rest of his clothes. Then he grabbed the lube packet out of Ulric's hands and reached between his alpha's cheeks, finding his tight pink hole.

"Mine," Ulric growled, snatching at the lube.

Gage lifted it away from his reach; Ulric scowled and clambered forward, about to make a grab for it.

Gage wrapped his legs around his alpha and shoved him down onto the bed, Ulric's back thumping against the mattress. Gage straddled him properly. Then, he shoved his cock against Ulric's belly, reaching behind himself for Ulric's legs, searching out his hole.

Ulric grasped his own cock and pushed its wet tip

between Gage's cheeks, a thick, blunt presence that robbed Gage of his breath. He *wanted*.

"Not so easy," Gage growled, clambering away.

Ulric grabbed him and rolled them over, his eyes coal-dark with need, his chest heaving. "Mine, Gage," he whispered, his cock straining between them. He leaned in to slant a hot kiss against Gage's lips, his breath warm on Gage's skin, his body a welcome friction all along Gage's front.

Something *yanked* behind Gage's stomach right then, something hot that went down to his cock and made it so hard, it fucking hurt. Gage wheezed, trying to breathe. All he smelled was musk and more musk. And all he wanted was his cock deep inside Ulric, pumping him full of come.

"You, too," Ulric whispered, licking his lips. He reached between them, grasping Gage's cock, pumping it.

Gage's instincts blew through every last bit of his restraint. He shoved Ulric off himself and grasped his legs, spreading them wide. Exposing Ulric's hole to his cock.

Ulric snarled, yanking his legs away. He reared up and barreled Gage back onto the bed; they shoved their chests together, skin on bare skin, wrestling for dominance.

"Not gonna win, babe," Gage hissed, shoving his cock against his alpha's.

Ulric muscled him against the mattress and slid their cocks together in a slow, sweet slide, friction bursting through Gage's body in a shower of bliss. "Fuck."

Gage shoved the lube packet between Ulric's cheeks, squeezing some there, getting Ulric all slippery for him. He pushed his fingers into Ulric's hole—gods, it was so damn tight.

Ulric hissed and clenched around him; Gage needed to be inside him, right now. Except Ulric grabbed another packet off the bed and tore it open. Then he emptied it onto his hand and shoved it between them, lubing up his own cock.

Gage's hole squeezed. When Ulric leaned back, Gage grabbed Ulric's slippery hand, shoving it onto his cock. So he got some of that lube, too.

Ulric smiled. "Not gonna be first, Gage."

And Ulric shoved apart Gage's knees, spreading them to expose Gage's hole. Gage groaned, relaxing for him. Ulric swore. He rammed his cock between Gage's cheeks in the next second, pushing hard against Gage's entrance, his chest heaving. "Gonna be mine, Gage."

"I'm already yours." Gage fought down his instinct to struggle. Then he remembered that Ulric would love it, and he reared up, growling, trying to shove his alpha off.

Ulric roared and slammed him down against the bed, and he snapped his hips, his tip cramming its way into Gage's body, blazing its way inside. Until he had every single inch stretching Gage open. So desperate to fill him with come.

Gage snarled at its presence—thick and heavy and demanding. He shoved at Ulric, but Ulric had a look of bliss, hungry and animalistic. And he rutted in hard, his cock brushing right against Gage's most sensitive spot. Gage arched, his own cock aching; he had to reach down to pump it.

Ulric knocked his hand away and grasped Gage's cock, jerking it in time to his thrusts, every stroke winding tension through his body. Gage couldn't breathe, he could only take his alpha's cock, his own aching, dripping onto his abdomen. "Babe—"

Ulric's strokes grew harder, rougher, so savage that

Gage knew he'd feel this for days to come. Ulric pounded deep into his body, sending him sliding backward. Then he dragged Gage back and slammed into him. Gage roared, his cock throbbing, needing to unload inside his alpha. "Can't hold back much longer," he rasped.

"Gonna give," Ulric hissed, his hips pumping, his cock massaging Gage inside, every stroke so blissful that Gage's eyes rolled back. He grasped his cock, trying to hold off.

Then Ulric roared and plunged his entire cock in deep, and Gage felt him pulse, big spurts that filled Gage up inside. Gage would get pregnant from that. Ulric was giving him a baby, right now.

He throbbed, sweat beading across his skin. Fuck, he needed to come.

Ulric waited a couple moments for every drop to land inside Gage. Then he pulled out, and Gage lunged, shoving him down against the bed, hauling his legs open. "Gonna take it, babe," Gage hissed, his tongue so thick that he couldn't say anything else, he could only squeeze an open pack of lube onto himself, slicking his cock up in two quick strokes.

He found Ulric's hole, pushing a couple fingers inside. But his alpha didn't need so much stretching; Gage had been there earlier today. Ulric sucked in a quick breath.

Gage fitted his tip inside and slammed his cock home, so hard that Ulric arched and panted, taking him, his body hot like a furnace.

"Perfect," Gage panted. Then he gave in to his instincts, thrusting into his alpha faster and harder, watching Ulric's pleasure as he tipped his head back in bliss. And Gage crammed his entire length inside, holding it there, just letting Ulric adjust to his size.

When Ulric could breathe again, Gage picked up his rhythm. He watched the bliss on Ulric's face as he rode him, until each thrust rocked his alpha and his cock swelled, about to blow.

"Gonna give you a baby," Gage whispered.

"Please," Ulric begged.

That word ripped pleasure through Gage's body; he pushed himself deep inside as he emptied spurt after spurt of his seed into his bondmate, the thought of giving Ulric a child delighting his instincts.

Then he collapsed next to Ulric, pulling Ulric close, nuzzling his face.

"I've never had a rut before," Ulric said hazily. "That was amazing."

"Because it was with me?" Gage rubbed the back of Ulric's hand, smiling goofily.

Ulric nodded.

Ruts only happened when you were with an omega you had an emotional attachment to. But with these new hormones, and these new scents... it was a very special thing that Gage had just experienced with his alpha. He didn't know if many others could say they'd been in a rut and in heat at the same time.

Already, the desperate need of his heat had begun to fade. Gage wasn't sure if it was because he'd just come, or because he'd already conceived. But he had Ulric's seed inside him. And possibly, Ulric's baby.

He touched his abdomen gently, imagining a new life there. Then he touched Ulric's belly, too.

Ulric curled up next to him, comfortable with Gage. He wasn't quite as confident about himself as Gage wanted him to be, but he was miles better than he had been.

Gage trailed his fingertips down Ulric's front, just

admiring him. Just appreciating the warmth of his body, and his presence.

"I never expected anyone to like this," Ulric mumbled, gesturing at himself. "I spent a long time just hiding. Sometimes I look back at myself, and I feel like a coward."

Come to think of it, Gage wasn't sure if that was such a bad thing. "Maybe you've just been saving yourself for me." Gage kissed his forehead. "I'm so damn lucky to have found you, babe. I'm glad you moved to Meadowfall. And came to visit the gym."

"Yeah, I fell on my face and had my clothes ripped off," Ulric muttered.

"Love your ass," Gage whispered, remembering that day. "Maybe that was your mating dance, and you got me right there."

"*That* was no dance."

"Yeah, it was just you flaunting your sexy curves."

Ulric rolled his eyes. Gage kissed him on the lips, his heart full.

"If we get pregnant... *When* we get pregnant—what do you think our children would look like?" Gage asked.

"I hope they look like you," Ulric said.

"But I want them to look like *you*," Gage said.

Ulric's forehead crinkled. "But you're the handsome one."

"Sometimes, I wish people wouldn't judge me by my looks."

"You sure get advantages, though," Ulric said.

Well, Gage couldn't deny that. "One thing I know, is these looks sure snared you."

Ulric flushed. "I was not," he spluttered.

"You so were." Gage grinned and pinned him, tickling his alpha. Ulric thrashed. Gage kissed him sweetly on the lips, just savoring the way their bodies brushed. Then he released his alpha, just snuggling with him.

"I'll love our kids no matter what they look like," Ulric said.

"Same here." With a laugh, Gage pressed their foreheads together. "I think we're a good match, you know. You get me."

Ulric cracked a smile. He looked so good that Gage cradled his face, kissing him again.

"You'll get weird stares, you know. With this." Ulric stroked the scar on Gage's belly. "When it swells up like your cousin's did."

Gage shrugged. "They can stare all they want. But they won't have what I do, babe. And that's you. And your babies."

Ulric brightened, kissing Gage softly. "You're the best thing that ever happened to me."

"Now you're getting sappy," Gage told him.

"Oh, hush." Ulric kissed him harder. "We need to make sure that I've really gotten you pregnant."

That sent tingles racing down Gage's body. "Yeah? Are you going to strut your stuff? I brought some lace panties."

Ulric's eyebrows crawled up. "You did?"

Gage leaned away, grabbing his pants. He rooted around the back pockets and found a few lacy scraps—he'd had them custom-made. There wasn't much room in omega underwear for alpha cocks, after all. "I got a few. Not sure which would fit you perfectly. But I was gonna let you wear them *before* we went into heat."

"A little late for that." Ulric took the lace from Gage, fingering the delicate material. "They feel nice, though."

"I thought you might like them. You've been looking at pretty things lately."

"Like you haven't." Ulric glanced up from the panties. "Would you rather have been born an omega?"

Gage looked down at himself. "I don't know, to be honest. I like being an alpha. I'm comfortable in my skin." Then he met Ulric's eyes. "And someday soon, I hope you will be, too."

Ulric gave a lopsided smile. Despite Gage's insistence that his original weight was fine, Ulric had lost a few pounds. Gage had been convincing him to eat more veggies, and the occasional cake rewards worked really well for him.

Two days a week, Ulric had his choice of mashed potatoes and ice cream and pizza, and various other decadent things—the only criteria being that he didn't eat too much of it. But he'd taken a liking to Gage's pan-fried zucchinis, and every so often, Gage surprised him with a mouthful of ice cream. Little treats. Things that made him smile.

Some days—a rare thing now—Ulric caved and binged on things in the fridge. That was okay, though. They wrote off those days as cheat days, and Gage made sure Ulric didn't blame himself for it. Instead, they went on long walks together, just enjoying each other's company.

He made sure to remind Ulric that it didn't matter what he looked like. The most important part was that Gage wanted him to be healthy, because Gage was selfish. Because Gage wanted his alpha with him for decades to come.

He snuggled sleepily against Ulric. "Nap first? After that, we'll try this impregnating thing again. Just because."

Ulric laughed. "With the lace panties? I'll wear them for you."

He felt good enough about himself to do that. And that made all the difference in the world. "Fuck yeah, babe. You'll look gorgeous in them."

Ulric flushed, and Gage thought... maybe he should propose, too. Just because.

32

PREGNANCY

Ulric stepped into the kitchen and immediately wished he hadn't. Somehow, the smell of mushroom soup made him need to throw up. "Why are you making that?"

"Craving it," Gage answered. "You want some?"

"I'm going to puke."

Ulric hurried into the bathroom and crouched, emptying his stomach—some crackers he'd eaten earlier today. That had been all he could swallow; Gage's mushroom soup had undone all his efforts. How did omegas deal with this?

Granted, most omegas probably weren't living with another pregnant person, who also had very specific foods that they could keep down.

"Sorry." Gage followed him into the bathroom. "You okay?"

"Not a fan of mushroom soup right now." Ulric heaved again.

Gage crowded close, rubbing Ulric's back. Then he grabbed a mug and filled it with water—it had since been dubbed the Vomit Washer. Ulric took it with a murmur of thanks, rinsing out his mouth.

"I'll air out the kitchen as soon as I can," Gage said.

"It's fine." Ulric sniffed at him—Gage smelled like the honey of his pregnancy, and also faintly like his soup, but at least that was tolerable now. "Remember last week, when I made leek stir-fry and *you* threw up?"

Gage snorted. "Yeah. Definitely do. But the one we'll tell our kids about is the time both of us had to share the toilet."

Ulric snorted. That... had been a memorable experience. One he wasn't so keen on repeating. "I'll use a different bathroom the next time."

"Yeah? You don't like the thought of my puking making you puke more?" Gage wriggled his eyebrows.

Ulric elbowed him in the stomach. "Shut up."

Gage grinned and hugged him around the waist. Ulric leaned in to nuzzle him, except he caught a whiff of mushroom soup on Gage's breath.

On any other month, that would've been fine. Ulric barely got his puke in the toilet instead of on his alpha's face. "Can't kiss you right now. You need to wash your mouth with soap."

Gage covered his mouth, his words coming out muffled. "Got it."

He stuck around, though, rubbing Ulric's back until Ulric's nausea faded. Then he brushed Ulric's hair out of his face, even though Ulric's hair wasn't all that long. Ulric's heart pattered.

Gage loved him. And every day, he showed it with all the little gestures that said Ulric was important, that it didn't matter what Ulric looked like. Gage made Ulric feel as though he was a good person. Worthy of love.

"I love you," Ulric blurted.

Gage smiled and nuzzled Ulric's shoulder. "Love you. This may be the new way of kissing, though. At least, until this morning sickness thing goes away."

Ulric laughed.

Three months into their pregnancy, Gage's baby bump had become obvious. His abs had lost a bit of definition on the surface; he'd said that he could feel the uterus pressing lightly against his insides. Ulric felt the same in his own body.

"It won't be long until we can't hug each other this way," Gage said, pulling Ulric against his chest.

Ulric looked down at his own abdomen—his curves made it hard to tell that he was even pregnant at all. At least the morning sickness had faded. "Has anyone at the gym noticed?"

Gage shrugged. "Kinda. They've been starting to joke about my beer belly."

Ulric winced. "What did you tell them?"

"That it was gonna be a surprise. My boss knows, though."

Ulric could only imagine Gage telling his boss, and the increasing disbelief on Gage's boss's face. But Gage had gotten permission to take a couple months off work after the birth, so Ulric wasn't too worried about that.

"You didn't show off your belly?" Ulric asked.

"Babe, the only person I show off to is you." Gage pressed his baby bump against Ulric's belly. "Think they can hear each other? I mean, if we hug like that, they're practically side-by-side."

"That's a really weird way to say hi."

"You know what, we haven't tried something. I can't

believe it." Gage dragged Ulric into the bedroom, nudging him onto the mattress. Then he lay down in the opposite direction—a little too high for a proper 69.

He was in the perfect position to kiss Ulric's belly, though. Gage peeled Ulric's shirt up, pressing his face against Ulric's skin. "Hey," Gage murmured. "I think both of you can hear me at the same time."

Ulric's heart swelled. "That's brilliant."

Gage pulled up his own shirt in invitation; Ulric leaned in and blew a raspberry against Gage's baby bump. "Hey! Damn you, babe."

Ulric laughed. "Don't set a bad example for the children, Gage."

Gage flipped him off, but he was grinning. "I'll show you bad example," he growled.

Ulric tingled all over. "Let me say hi first." He kissed Gage's abdomen, breathing in Gage's clove scent—he was finally getting used to it. "Hey there," Ulric said, letting his voice rumble into Gage's body. "It's your other dad and me. I don't think you know it yet; there isn't just one of you, but two. Right now, one of you is with me, and the other is with your other dad. You'll meet when you're born. I think you'll have lots of fun growing up together."

Gage found Ulric's hand, entwining their fingers. "Looking forward to bringing you both into our family."

Ulric couldn't wait for that day. He pulled Gage's knee up and rested his head on Gage's thigh, kissing Gage's baby bump. "I love that we can talk to both of them at the same time."

"Pretty soon, we might feel them kick at the same time."

"I hope that doesn't turn into a kicking contest." Ulric winced.

"Come to think of it, maybe they'll kick hard enough that they can feel each other." Gage laughed.

He pulled Ulric closer and gave Ulric's belly a loud kiss. Then he sat up, kissing Ulric on the lips. The look in Gage's eyes—it made Ulric melt inside.

"Lazy afternoons are the best with you," Gage said fondly. "Best enjoy them while we can."

Ulric grinned. "Wise words. I hope you won't regret this."

This time, Gage cradled Ulric's belly, and his kiss was slow and lingering. "Nah, I won't. You can hold me to it."

By the time the twenty-week ultrasound rolled around, Gage had felt their baby kick, but the one in Ulric's belly hadn't budged yet.

"I hope it'll be okay," Ulric said, his stomach twisting. Had something gone wrong with the pregnancy? This wasn't quite a natural process, after all—not for alphas who'd artificially placed a uterus in themselves.

Except Gage's baby had moved. Not Ulric's. Did Ulric's weight have something to do with it?

He worried at his lip, his heart thumping when they stepped into Rutherford's office.

"It'll be okay," Gage whispered. But even he was nervous.

Rutherford looked a little harried. "Hello there. It's been a while. How are the two of you doing?"

They went over Gage's progress first, then Ulric's. "I haven't felt our baby move," Ulric said, wincing when Rutherford turned his solemn gaze on his belly.

It wasn't so often that Ulric felt out-of-place these days. But now that he was nervous, he felt far too heavy next to Gage, and Rutherford's slim frame. What if he was too unhealthy to carry a baby?

"Here, lie back on the exam bed," Rutherford said. "We'll do your ultrasound first."

Ulric held his breath, his heart thumping. Gage crowded next to him and held his hand.

The ultrasound gel was warm on his belly; Ulric barely felt that. Instead, he felt his curves, he felt as though he needed to hide his body again.

The doctor examined the inside of Ulric's belly this way and that, the monitor's black-and-white speckles changing with his movements. Then a small, curled-up figure came into view—their baby. Gage sucked in a sharp breath. Ulric stopped breathing.

Aside from the morning sickness and the fatigue, aside from his honey scent and the stiff shape of the uterus in his belly, Ulric didn't feel quite so pregnant. Whereas Gage's baby bump looked like a baby bump, Ulric's belly looked like he'd just put on more weight.

But the ultrasound image—that made his pregnancy very real. There really was a baby inside him.

After he'd examined the fetus from all angles, Rutherford looked up with a smile. "Your baby seems to be developing well. Some pregnant folk may feel the flutters as late as the twenty-fourth week, so there's no cause for concern yet."

Ulric could finally breathe again. So maybe this wasn't as bad as he'd thought.

Gage leaned in and kissed his lips. "See, you're both fine."

Ulric was too weak with relief to answer.

He clambered off the exam bed and cradled his belly, waiting while Gage had his turn with the ultrasound. Gage's baby looked just as beautiful as Ulric's—these were both their flesh and blood. And it never ceased to amaze him that they were carrying their babies at the same time.

Later, they left Rutherford's clinic, walking hand-in-hand through the outskirts of New York City.

"He looked pretty stressed-out," Ulric said.

"Who? Rutherford?" Gage frowned. "I think he might really move to Meadowfall. He sure could use a break."

"Imagine if he became our neighbor." Ulric laughed. Wilkie had been talking about moving in with his friends on the next street; Ulric wasn't sure how Wilkie had gotten to know them, but Wilkie hadn't stopped with his questionable side gig thus far. Gage had been arguing with his brother a lot more lately.

"Maybe Wilkie and Rutherford should both be our neighbors." Gage scowled. "I'd rather Wilkie move closer so I can keep an eye on him."

"He's an adult, you know."

"If he keeps up the way he is, he's going to get into trouble one of these days. And not any sort of good trouble."

Ulric smiled at Gage's protectiveness. "Maybe things will turn out fine. Like it did for us."

"Maybe," Gage grumbled.

"He could hook up with an alpha, and they'd protect him."

Gage's scowl deepened. "No. What if they manipulate him? He's—He has issues."

"What if he finds someone he loves?" Ulric pointed out.

"What if they use him, and he thinks he's in love?"

Ulric could understand Gage's protectiveness, though. Wilkie was a dear; Ulric didn't want anyone to break his heart.

He tugged Gage onto a less-crowded street so they wouldn't get as many looks their way. Then he brought Gage's hand to his lips, kissing it. "Give him a chance," Ulric said. "You can always be the good older brother and swoop in to save him."

"I hope," Gage said darkly.

Ulric was about to kiss Gage's wrist to distract him, when a car pulled up next to them. It was familiar. Ulric didn't think much of it, until the door opened and his mother stepped out.

His stomach sank. He'd known they shouldn't have stayed out so long, but he'd wanted to show Gage some of his favorite places from his childhood. Somehow, it had slipped his mind that his mom frequented these particular streets, too.

She stalked toward him and Gage, her expression filled with contempt. Gage glanced over. "You know her?"

"My mom."

Gage stiffened, his mouth pressing into a thin line. He moved to step in front of Ulric; Ulric shook his head. He couldn't hide behind his alpha for anything. Especially not this.

So he held still and waited until she stopped in front of him with a disgusted stare. "Nothing has changed with you, has it?" Mom asked, flicking a glance at Gage. "Or have you started paying for an escort?"

Gage's eyes flashed. "I'm no escort."

"He's my bondmate." Ulric held his breath. He remembered being afraid of his mom turning Gage against him. He remembered being afraid that Gage would leave. "Gage, this is my mom. Mom, this is Gage."

Mom's scowl twisted further. "*Bondmate?* Who in their right mind would bond with you? You're ugly, you're grossly overweight, and I don't know what you did to your stomach, but—"

Ulric's chest squeezed. He glanced at Gage, half-thinking that maybe with enough of those words, Gage might possibly be convinced.

"Me," Gage snarled, taking a step forward. Ulric had to restrain him. "Just because you can't see the good in him, doesn't mean no one else can."

Mom flicked an incredulous look at him. "That's a waste of your looks."

"I don't care what you think of my looks," Gage retorted. "But I care that you've never done your part as a mother at all."

"I've provided for him," Mom snapped. "He should be grateful. What other lies has he told you?"

"None." Gage looked like he was about to snap further at her, except Ulric knew he would never change her mind. Gods knew he'd spent years trying to. Every time he'd failed, it had broken him just a little more.

"I'm carrying Gage's child," he said, straightening to his full height. He hadn't stood up to her in a long time. And now that he was, now that he risked her disowning him, his heart felt like it might explode. "We're preparing for a family."

She looked at his belly in horror. "Alphas can't get pregnant. That's disgusting."

"It's not." Ulric met her eyes. *Gage loves me,* he told himself. *Everything will be okay.* "I'm sorry you feel that way, but I'm happy now. I think that's all that matters."

"You're not my son," Mom snapped. "I'm sick of wasting my time on you." Those words rang in Ulric's ears; he couldn't breathe.

She looked like she was about to hurl more insults at him, except Gage took Ulric's hand. "We've got somewhere better to be, ma'am," Gage said in his polite personal trainer tone. "Ulric has a family who accepts him for who he is. We're returning to them. Have a great day."

Then he turned Ulric away and tugged him down the sidewalk. Some of the pedestrians clapped for them. A couple of people came up, asking how Ulric had gotten pregnant. Gage gave them the details of Rutherford's clinic.

They ducked down a quiet alley, and it was only then that Ulric realized his hands were shaking, his heart pounding in his ears.

He'd never walked away from his mom before. It had always been her leaving him behind.

"How're you feeling?" Gage asked, cradling his face.

Ulric took several deep breaths, blowing out the anxiety in his chest. "I'm okay. I think."

It hurt that his mom no longer wanted him. But maybe... she'd never wanted him in the first place. It had taken him until now to realize it. And that still hurt, no matter how far behind he'd left his past.

"I love you," Gage murmured, kissing him. "You'll remember that, right?"

Ulric bit his lip, his eyes burning. "Yeah. I just wish... I was strong enough to deal with this."

Gage pulled him into a tight hug. Their bellies bumped, and the embrace was a little awkward. But Gage ran his fingers through Ulric's hair, pressing kisses all over Ulric's face. "It's okay if you cry," Gage whispered. "You've always wanted her love, and you've never received it. Hell, if it happened to me, I think I'd break, too."

Ulric buried his face in Gage's shoulder, feeling as though he might crack. Alphas shouldn't cry.

Gage kissed his neck. "You'll feel better if you let it out, babe. It's perfectly fine."

"I'm already not enough of an alpha," Ulric muttered.

Gage pressed him up against a wall. "You're *enough*. More than enough. The only person who should mind is me, and I love you, babe. You're perfect as you are."

That struck deeper than Ulric would like to admit. He bit his lip, blinking hard. And the memory of his mother disowning him welled up in his chest, until it overwhelmed him.

In his arms, Ulric broke down. Gage held him tight, stroking his back, never once letting go.

When he finally pulled away, scrubbing at his wet cheeks, Gage caught his hands. And he kissed off the dampness on Ulric's face. "I'm going to ask Mom to bake a cake," Gage said. "The most special coffee cake for you."

Ulric snuffled. "But I'm not supposed to have—"

Gage kissed away his protests. "She'll be delighted if you want her as your mom. We'll have cake to celebrate."

Ulric gulped, his throat tight. "Really? I couldn't possibly…"

"Yeah." Gage pressed their foreheads together. "She's just been waiting for you to ask. You're already part of the family, Muffin."

Ulric stared, trying to believe all of this. Losing one family but gaining another. Gage holding him, Gage never judging him at all, even now.

"I love you," he croaked.

Gage smiled and nuzzled his ear. "You're the very best thing that happened to me."

Ulric held his alpha, grateful for this man. In his belly, something fluttered. He looked down in surprise.

"Felt something?"

"I... don't know." Ulric touched his belly. Then came a stronger flutter, that was most definitely *not* his stomach gurgling. "I felt it." He held his breath, meeting his alpha's eyes. "I felt our baby!"

Gage's entire face lit up. "Damn, babe." He pressed Ulric back against the wall, kissing him thoroughly. Then he plastered his hands over Ulric's belly, trying to feel it, too. "Might be too early for me."

"You'll feel it soon," Ulric breathed, pulling Gage into a kiss. He couldn't wait to feel the kicks from Gage's belly, too. And a bubbly excitement began in his chest, that pushed away his misery from earlier.

Their babies were fine and healthy, and growing every day. Back home, there was a family who accepted him, waiting for them to return.

And in his arms, Ulric held the best alpha in the world.

33

CHILDBIRTH

Gage's mom was assembling a meat pie in her kitchen. Ulric sighed longingly. He hadn't eaten in hours—not that there was much space in his stomach right now, with the baby pressing against his insides.

"This is going into the freezer for you." She clucked. "It'll be just a while longer."

"Seems like that's forever away." Ulric's heart crashed against his ribs. The surgery would take place in a couple more hours; he was part-excited and part-nervous about it.

Over the last few months, he and Gage had been getting the house ready for their babies. They'd installed cribs and changing stations, they'd painted the nursery room walls and picked out baby clothes, and they'd gone over so many lists of names that Ulric had gone cross-eyed.

Ulric was glad they'd gotten all of those done weeks ago, because they could only waddle like a pair of ducks now. At least he'd been staying home—he preferred not being stared at.

Gage, on the other hand, had kept working at the gym for as long as he could. He'd told his supervisors, he'd told the gym regulars, and after the initial jokes and stares, he'd gone back to being a regular gym employee—it was rare that the gym regulars batted an eyelid at him anymore.

At thirty-seven weeks, Ulric felt as though he might pop soon; he was glad they'd scheduled the c-section sooner than later. They'd been massaging each other's crampy feet, speaking against each other's bellies in that 69-position, and the kicks felt like a gut-punch, more often than not.

But he was happy. They were carrying each other's babies. And he loved seeing the excitement on Gage's face every time Gage rubbed his own belly, or Ulric's.

"Since you're giving birth on the same day, are those twins?" Gage's mom asked, pressing down the edges of the pie crust with a fork.

"We're thinking of them as twins," Gage said. "When they get older, they'll get their cots pushed together in the middle of the nursery, but for now, they'll just be sharing a single cot."

His mom grinned. "That's just adorable."

"Sure is," Ulric said. "We're excited."

Gage rubbed Ulric's belly, grinning when his baby kicked. Then he brushed his swollen belly against Ulric's —they couldn't hug face-to-face anymore. For a while now, all their hugs had been from the side, or from the back. Not that Ulric minded, when Gage always gazed at him so warmly.

"I think we should get going," Ulric said.

Gage fingered a small bump in his pocket that Ulric hadn't noticed before. "Yeah, we should."

Ulric made to reach for it. Gage swatted his hand

away, his ears turning pink. Which only made Ulric more curious. "What's that?"

"Just, ah. Just a bit of pocket lint."

Gage's mom laughed. "You sure are convincing, hon."

Did she know what it was? Ulric frowned. Because it sure wasn't some random lint.

"C'mon, time to meet our babies," Gage said, turning Ulric toward the kitchen doorway. "Where's Dad?"

Gage's dad drove them to the hospital, overnight bags and all. Ulric thought it awkward that both he and Gage were sitting in the backseat, but Gage only snuggled up with him. "Unless we get to share a bed when we recover, this will be all the snuggles you'll get for a while," Gage said.

That was disappointing. "At least we'll be able to spoon again when we get home."

"Oh, yeah." Gage grinned. "Can't wait for that, too."

They checked into the hospital, changing into gowns soon after. Gage sidled over to Ulric and lifted both their gowns, rubbing their bellies together.

"Gage," Ulric hissed. They were naked from the waist down.

"Nothing they haven't seen before, probably." Gage pulled Ulric closer, their abdomens bumping awkwardly. Ulric shook his head.

"Here, before we head into the operating room," Gage said. He hauled over his overnight bag and reached inside. "I have an important question."

"We already decided on names." Ulric scrunched up his forehead. Or was this a silly question like what ice cream they would have in bed when they got home?

But the look in Gage's eyes—he really was serious about this. And he looked nervous, too. Ulric's instincts rumbled. Why was Gage nervous? "Gage?"

"Probably the most important question I'll ever ask you," Gage whispered, his breath hitching. He took Ulric's hand, folding their fingers together. Then he pressed something cool and circular against Ulric's palm. Two somethings? "Love of my life, alpha of my heart, father of my children—"

"That's way too cheesy, even for you," Ulric blurted but he was getting an inkling where this was headed. His heart skipped.

Gage huffed. "Yeah, I brought cheese, too." He reached into his overnight bag and pulled out a bottle of powdered parmesan. "Because this is going to be the cheesiest moment of our lives."

Ulric groaned. "I can't believe you. Gage, we're here for a c-section and you brought a bottle of cheese."

"At least I'm not sprinkling it on you." Gage kissed Ulric's knuckles. "But maybe we can do that at the wedding?"

Then he froze.

Ulric bit down his smile, but his heart was racing now. "What wedding?"

"The, uh." Gage scowled. "Damn it."

"Were you... going to propose?" Ulric couldn't help smiling. He peeked between their hands—there were rings there. Gage had gotten them both rings. Simple steel bands with words engraved across their curved surface.

Ulric's throat grew so tight, he couldn't speak.

"Let's just start from the beginning," Gage muttered, mad at himself. "Ulric. Father of my children, love of my life, alpha of my heart, the most perfect person in the entire world—"

Ulric scooted close and kissed his cheek. He couldn't

let Gage do all of this himself. "Will you marry me?" Ulric asked.

Gage cracked a smile. "I'm never going to have the most perfect proposal, am I?"

But he folded their hands tightly together, leaning his forehead against Ulric's.

"It doesn't matter if it's not perfect," Ulric whispered. "You're perfect to me."

"Damn, babe," Gage growled. "I love you."

He kissed Ulric fiercely, so possessive that delight raced all the way to Ulric's toes. So Ulric kissed him back, biting his lip, claiming his alpha's mouth. Because he liked being possessive, too.

"Yes," Ulric whispered. "I'll marry you. It'll be an honor, Gage."

Gage's eyes lit up; he growled and brushed his fingers through Ulric's hair, cradling him close. Relief flickered through his eyes. "Thank fuck. Wouldn't have known what to do if you'd said no."

"You could ask me again." Ulric grinned, kissing his lips.

Gage laughed. And now his entire body relaxed; he dropped kisses all over Ulric's face. "I can't wait for us to be husbands, babe. Such an honor."

Ulric's heart swelled so much, it felt like his chest might burst. Gage traced his scent all over Ulric's skin.

When Ulric looked back at the rings, Gage took one of them, sliding it onto Ulric's finger. "It says, 'To the most beautiful alpha'," Gage whispered. "'Cuz I want you to remember that."

Ulric's heart fluttered. "You're too good to me, Gage."

"You're my favorite person in the world." Then Gage picked up the ring he'd gotten for himself, smiling wryly.

"I'd wanted to have them carve 'The Muffin's Stud' on here, but I figured it was kind of silly."

"Aw, that would've been perfect." Ulric laughed. "What do you have on yours?"

Gage showed him. In small lettering, Gage's ring held the words, *Remember where home is: Ulric*. Ulric's throat tightened. Gage kissed him again, and Ulric felt every ounce of Gage's love in his touch.

A knock came on the door. Then the midwife stepped in, clucking at them. "Lie down on the beds, both of you. We'll need to prep you for surgery."

Ulric's pulse tumbled. Gage squeezed his hand and helped him onto the bed. Then he shuffled onto his own, more nurses coming in to clean them up.

After what felt like an eternity, they were rolled into the operating theater—they'd made a special request for both of them to be in there at the same time.

The spread of scalpels was pretty fucking intimidating. The doctor set up a curtain around Ulric's abdomen so he couldn't see the grisly details. The nurse gave him some local anesthetic.

Ulric reached out; so did Gage. They linked their fingers across the space between their beds, oxygen masks on their faces.

That skin contact with his alpha made all the difference in the world.

He felt the faint pressure of the scalpel; Gage's grip tightened around his own. Ulric squeezed his hand. "I'll be fine," he said.

But Gage looked more worried than ever. Ulric suspected that he'd feel the same when it was time for Gage to have the surgery. So he touched Gage's wrist, the part where he'd left his bonding mark. That was a promise.

Gage's lips thinned. Ulric wanted to go over and hug him, and tell him that everything would turn out all right.

The doctor sliced deeper and deeper. Ulric caught a glimpse of blood; Gage's grip tightened so much, Ulric thought Gage might yank his fingers off. "I'm okay," Ulric said.

"Fucking tell me when it's over," Gage muttered, his eyes narrowed. "Hate that I can't do anything to help."

"You're helping." Ulric squeezed his hand. "This helps."

Gage huffed into his mask; Ulric focused on him instead of the disconcerting pressure of the scalpel—he didn't know how omegas did this, either. But he now had a newfound respect for them.

As the c-section progressed, Gage held Ulric so tightly that his fingers went numb. He felt Gage's worry thumping through his own heart, he felt Gage's sheer hope that things would turn out okay.

Just when he thought the doctor could slice no deeper, the doctor lifted out a small, bloody shape—their baby. Ulric stopped breathing.

The nurse cleaned their baby's airways. And Florin began to wail, tiny jerky movements of his limbs. Ulric reached out for him; the nurse set his baby gently on his chest. Florin was tiny against him, his little face and his delicate hands, his eyes shut tight.

This was his and Gage's baby. Ulric didn't know how, but he felt a connection to this child immediately—Florin was the most beautiful little bundle in the world. "Hey," he murmured. "It's me. Your other dad's there, I'm gonna hand you over to him real soon."

Florin fell quiet, listening to Ulric's voice. He was adorable. And everything they'd done—the implants and the hormones and the doctor visits—that had all been worth it to have him.

When Ulric looked up, he found Gage staring at them with an intensity that made his heart tighten.

"Love you both," Gage murmured.

Ulric brushed his wrists over Florin. A nurse brought their baby over to Gage, and Gage cradled him, blinking hard. Then he murmured at Florin and marked him, too.

Gage looked so good, holding their child.

The doctor cleaned Ulric up and stitched him back together. Soon after, the nurses gave Gage some local anesthetic, and brought over a fresh set of tools for Gage's c-section. Ulric's heart thumped.

"I'll be fine," Gage said, squeezing Ulric's hand.

But now that he could only sit by and watch while the doctor sliced open Gage's belly, Ulric couldn't help feeling nervous, too. Gage's face twitched with each incision; Ulric remembered what that had felt like. And he didn't like the thought of Gage being cut open, even if it was necessary for the birth.

"We'll be watching a ton of movies together after this," Gage said. "Relax, babe."

"I've already given birth," Ulric said. "You can't tell me to relax."

Gage's smile widened. "*Relax.*"

"If I relax enough, I'm going to piss myself." Truthfully, Ulric wouldn't be able to relax until they had both their babies with them, and Gage recovered from the surgery safe and sound.

"Hush," the doctor said.

Ulric bit down his words, holding Gage's hand. Gage squeezed his fingers.

As the c-section progressed, the doctor's scalpel went deeper, disappearing from sight. Inside Gage. Ulric struggled to breathe, his heart thumping, his stomach twisting. Then, finally, the doctor lifted out their second child, just as bloody as Florin had been. Ulric sucked in a quick breath; Gage stroked his fingers.

The doctor suctioned Sage's mouth and nose. Sage began to wail—such a wonderful sound. And the nurse brought him over to Gage, gently setting their second son on Gage's chest, next to Florin. Ulric's heart missed a beat.

"Hey, Sage," Gage murmured. "This is Florin, your brother. I'm your dad, and your other dad's waiting to come say hi."

Ulric wanted to hold them, too. "You did it," he told Gage, his voice rough.

"*You* did it, too." Gage grinned, his arms full with their babies. Ulric would've reached out for him otherwise.

It wasn't until Gage had gotten stitched up and they'd all been wheeled into the neonatal ward, that Ulric had a chance to cuddle with his family. Gage got permission to push their hospital beds together. He and Ulric shuffled sideways until they lay next to each other, their arms brushing, one son on each of their chests.

Then Gage rested his head against Ulric's, bringing Ulric's hand up to kiss his fingers. "This is what it'll look like when we get home, too."

Gods, Ulric looked forward to that. Gage helped ease Sage onto Ulric's chest, next to his brother. And now there were two children on Ulric—the babies that he and Gage had been carrying for so long. Two lives that he and Gage had created together. They smelled sweet, along with Gage's clove and Ulric's anise scent. They smelled like family.

"They're so beautiful, babe." Gage smile warmed

Ulric's entire body. "Can't wait 'til we can snuggle together with these guys."

Ulric had a sudden vision of all of them together, the boys growing up happy in their home, Gage with him every step of the way. Ulric would make sure that his children both knew they were loved.

It hadn't been an easy journey, facing his fears, his poor regard of himself. But then he'd met Gage. And Gage had showed him that he was worthy of love; Gage had proved over and over that he would be there for Ulric no matter what.

Ulric could look at himself without cringing now. He could appreciate the sight of Gage kissing his bare body —he could almost see what his alpha saw in him.

His heart full of gratitude and love, Ulric held his children close, bringing Gage's wrist to his lips. He kissed the silver scar on Gage's scent gland. "Thank you for being mine," Ulric murmured, so happy he could cry.

Gage's smile in return was full of joy. "Forever yours, babe."

EPILOGUE

"Dino roar!" Sage stuck his fingers out in an imitation of a T-rex's claws, chasing Gage through the living room. "Eat Papa!"

Gage laughed and ran away in slow-motion, giving Sage a chance to catch up. Before Sage could, Florin cornered Gage from the other side of the couch, flapping his arms like one of the flying dinosaurs.

"I eat, I eat!" Florin tried to bite at Gage; Gage had the good sense to stay away from those teeth. Except Florin latched onto him anyway, tiny teeth gnawing at his pant leg.

"Nooo," Gage groaned. "I'm being eaten! Daddy, save me!"

"Technically, I'm not old enough to be your daddy," Ulric said, biting down a laugh.

Gage rolled his eyes. "Not *that* sort of daddy."

Ulric grinned. "I think that new dino cartoon was a fantastic idea. Keeps them occupied, lets their imagination run wild."

"Yeah? Are you going to turn into a dinosaur and eat

me, too?" Gage grasped Sage and swung him up into the air; Sage shrieked in delight. At his feet, Florin reached up, wanting a Sky High Fly too.

In a way, Gage was glad Sage and Florin weren't identical twins—it would've been so difficult to tell them apart. Unlike his brother's green eyes, Florin's were hazel like Ulric's, except they both had Gage's dark hair.

Ulric strode over, swinging Florin into the air. Florin squealed. "Maybe I'll eat you later," Ulric said. "After these dino terrors have gone to bed."

"Terrors!" Florin said, smiling toothily.

"Yeah, definitely terrors." Gage hugged Sage close, flopping down onto the couch. Moments later, Ulric followed suit, Florin squirming on his lap.

The boys had turned two a couple months back. They'd gone to the park to celebrate, Florin and Sage sharing a birthday cake. Ulric had picked it out; after the initial cake-eating, Gage had fed Ulric some of the leftovers in bed.

After spending entire days with their boys, sometimes it was nice just to have some quiet time with his alpha, too.

Sage squirmed off Gage's lap, squeezing with Florin onto Ulric. "Me, me, me!"

"What do you want, hon?" Ulric asked.

"Hug!" Sage beamed.

Ulric laughed and pulled both boys into a hug.

Having Sage and Florin didn't just bring Gage and Ulric closer—the children had loved Ulric from the very first day. Gage had witnessed Ulric's delight when he played with them, he'd seen Ulric looking at himself in a mirror, only for any wistfulness to fade away when one of the children tottered up to him, wanting kisses.

Slowly, over these years, Gage had convinced Ulric

that he was beautiful all the way around. Ulric still had curves, and Gage especially loved his ample ass. Sometimes he thought maybe Ulric might get tired of how much Gage grabbed his butt, except Ulric always smiled whenever Gage did that. These days, Ulric walked more confidently, he held his head higher.

Ulric thrived when he was loved; Gage was only too happy to give it all to him.

"You're beautiful," Gage whispered in his alpha's ear. "My stud muffin babe."

Ulric snorted, elbowing Gage lightly. But the compliment turned the tips of his ears pink.

"Damn, Ulric." Gage caught Ulric's chin and kissed him full on the lips. Every time Ulric got flustered, Gage wanted to pin him down and kiss him senseless. "So glad I married you."

He stroked the ring on Ulric's finger, remembering Ulric walking down the aisle with him, hand in hand, Gage's family surrounding them. Their neighbors had been there, too. So had Gage's cousin, Jesse, and *his* family. They'd all shaken powdered cheese onto the aisle.

Ulric had been breathtakingly beautiful in his suit, promising to be Gage's. Then Gage had kissed him, and like a lot of the times he kissed Ulric, everything else faded away, leaving just them and their little family, Ulric the most perfect person in Gage's life.

Ulric's parents hadn't been at the wedding. His mom had said something about her failing business. Gage was kind of glad they were absent—they'd ended up sharing that day with people who were happy to see them married. And that was important.

"You know, I don't think we've danced since the wedding." Gage nudged his husband. "Dance with me, babe."

Ulric cracked a smile. "Right now?"

"Why not? We could show Florin and Sage, too."

The only other time Gage had seen Ulric dance was when he'd done it with Wilkie, back in the kitchen so long ago. Gage pulled Ulric to his feet; the boys scampered off, and Ulric put on the waltz music they'd played after the wedding. The dulcet notes of a saxophone purred through the room; Gage's heart skipped.

"Still remember how to dance?" Ulric grinned mischievously.

"You might have to show me." Gage held Ulric close, squeezing his love handles. "Gorgeous."

Ulric let Gage lead the dance—really because it was easier for him to match Gage's footwork, than for Gage to try and keep up.

Joy bloomed through Ulric's face as the music filled their chests. Fifteen seconds in, the boys came running up, reaching for Gage and Ulric, wanting to join in. Ulric laughed.

"Is there such a thing as a family waltz?" Gage asked. "Four of us in a circle?"

"I don't know, but I've seen two-year-olds dance before." Ulric looked excited. "I think we'll be able to teach them."

They had Sage and Florin join in, one boy on each side. Ulric started the music over, showing their children the basic steps of a waltz. Five minutes in, the boys were mimicking him, fumbling a little, but they were all having fun.

Then the boys got distracted, Florin wandering off to cuddle with his stuffed dino, Sage following him. Gage pulled Ulric back into a slow waltz, pressing their bodies together.

None of Gage's internet mailing list had this kind of fortune.

"What's so funny?" Gage frowned.

"Nothing." Ulric bit down his smile. "It's just... I used to imagine you had this mailing list. You know how some online stores have a button? 'Notify me when this item becomes available again.' Except it was a mailing list for when *you* became available."

Gage furrowed his brow. "Why?"

"Because everyone would want a piece of you!" Ulric laughed. "I figured there'd be a long line of people waiting for your attention—five hundred? Two thousand? And I'd never get a chance."

Gage shook his head, smiling, too. "I suppose that's possible. None of those mailing list people got me, though."

"Nope." Ulric looked at Gage's arms around him, so happy that Gage's heart skipped.

As the next song began, Gage pulled Ulric into yet another dance.

"How about we do this for the rest of our lives?" Gage murmured, kissing his alpha. "You and me and our children, and all the love in the world."

Ulric turned his hand toward Gage, his ring sitting snug on his finger. The warmth in his gaze melted Gage's heart. "I already promised it, Gage. You'd better be in for the long haul."

Gage laughed and kissed him harder, grateful for everything. "Definitely, babe."

34

BONUS CHAPTER

[THIS TAKES PLACE BEFORE THE EPILOGUE]

Ulric woke blearily, feeling like he'd been run over by several heavy cheese wheels. *Cheese... wheels?* Where had that thought come from, anyway?

He turned and found Gage watching him—*that* was where it had come from. A couple hours ago, Gage had woken him up by sleep-talking about cheese wheels. On his barbell or something. It wasn't Ulric's preferred use of cheese, but he smiled at the thought of Gage lifting parmesan weights in the exercise room.

"What're you smiling about?" Gage snuggled closer, kissing Ulric's knuckles.

"You. And your cheese. Do you remember what you dreamed about?"

Gage shook his head, giving Ulric a warm smile that went all the way to his toes. "Aside from you?"

Ulric huffed, and then winced when his stitches pulled. "Ow. Don't make me laugh, it hurts."

"Sorry." Gage rolled closer, wincing himself.

Since they'd gotten home, they'd taken to wearing loose shorts—the incisions from the c-sections were still new, and Ulric hurt whenever he did anything. The pain was absolutely worth the bundles of joy in the cot next to their bed, though.

For the past few nights, Sage and Florin had taken turns to wake up, demanding to be fed. Gage and Ulric had alternated their feeding duties, gingerly rolling out of bed to prepare formula for their babies.

Looking at the sprawling nest of things around their temporary bed—baby formula, milk bottles, diapers, along with an electric kettle and some drinking water—Ulric was glad that Gage's mom had suggested they bring everything within reach. With his abdomen hurting like it was, and with all the interrupted sleep he'd been getting, he couldn't imagine rooting around the house, or climbing the stairs to look for fresh clothes.

So what if their temporary bed was right in the middle of the living room? It meant that they were closer to the kitchen, and that Gage's mom didn't have to go far whenever she visited to check on them.

Sage began to make soft little noises—it sounded like he was hungry, or maybe he needed a diaper change.

"I'll do it," Gage said, preparing to get off the bed. He looked tired, too.

Ulric grabbed his arm. "It's my turn. You're supposed to be resting."

Gage grinned. "I can do it, babe."

Ulric glowered. "No. Stay down and rest."

Gage laughed. Then he shoved his hand against his stitches. "Damnit, ow. Stop being sexy."

Ulric rolled his eyes. In the years they'd been together, he'd come to discover that Gage appreciated whenever Ulric was assertive. But this was just Ulric insisting that Gage rest, because he wanted Gage to heal.

"Fine, I'll rest." Gage flopped back against the

mattress. "But I'll recover faster than you, and then I'll make you rest all the time."

Ulric scowled. "No, you won't."

Gage smiled like he had secret plans. Ulric elbowed him gently in the side.

Truthfully, this wasn't their first downtime. They'd each had an open-body surgery to implant the uteruses—that had been the first time Ulric had experienced this pain.

They'd managed to get uninterrupted sleep the first time, though.

He rolled onto his side; Gage helped to support him from behind. Then Ulric slid his legs off the bed and got slowly to his feet, making sure not to pull too hard on his stitches.

He hurried to the cot. Florin was sound asleep. Sage looked at him with those huge, beautiful eyes, and made those sounds again. Both of them were so adorable; Ulric couldn't help smiling. He checked on Sage—no diaper change yet. Going by Gage's notes on the chart next to the crib, Sage had been fed four hours ago. He was probably hungry now.

Ulric lifted Sage out of the cot and cuddled with him for a while, before handing him over to Gage. Gage's entire face lit up; he swaddled Sage back up and lifted him high, then brought him back down—like some sort of a kiddy ride.

"Are you doing a bench press with him?" Ulric asked.

Gage paused. "You know, that didn't occur to me. But I think I might be, yeah."

"You and your exercise." Ulric grinned. "I can just imagine you tying tiny baby hammocks to your barbell and then doing bench presses with them both."

"Depending on how sturdy I can make those, that

might not be a bad idea." Gage looked like he was seriously considering it.

Ulric wasn't sure if he found that funnier, or if the image of Gage with a cheese wheels-barbell was. He grabbed the electric kettle, made sure the water was the right temperature, and then shook up a bottle of milk for their son.

When it was ready, Ulric returned to the bed, sitting upright this time. Sage was suckling on Gage's finger. Ulric wondered if Sage felt a little betrayed that fingers didn't give him milk like bottles did. He took Sage and the bottle from his alpha, holding their son close.

While Ulric fed Sage, Gage shuffled up onto the pillows with them, wincing a little. Ulric scowled. "Get back down."

Gage grinned. "You're not making it any easier, babe. *You* are the reward for me misbehaving."

Ulric wasn't sure how else he was supposed to get Gage to rest. "What if you lie down, and I give you a handjob?"

"Hm. Nah." Gage slid his arm around Ulric's shoulders, leaning in. "Ow, it hurts no matter where I try to kiss you."

"That's because you're supposed to rest."

"Giving me cheek, Muffin?" Gage thought back on his words. "Or both cheeks?"

Ulric snorted, and then *his* abdomen hurt. "Stop it."

Gage stroked Ulric's belly. "Hard to. I love seeing you smile."

Ulric didn't know how to answer. So he watched Sage drink from the bottle, tiny bubbles rising through the milk. Sage smelled like sweet baby scent, he smelled like Gage and Ulric, and Ulric felt the greatest sense of peace, with his family all around him.

Gage crowded close, hugging them both. "I can't wait for this to heal," he murmured. "And I also can't wait to get some proper sleep. Then I'll mark you everywhere."

"You can already mark me everywhere right now." Ulric grinned.

"Not the same." Gage matched his smile, stroking Sage's cheek. "They're both so beautiful. We did great, babe."

Ulric's heart swelled. Gage kissed him again. When Sage was done with his milk, Ulric burped him. Gage cuddled them—all the way until Sage needed a diaper change. Ulric cleaned him up; they waited until Sage had fallen back asleep, before Ulric set him back in the cot with Florin.

Finally, Ulric returned to the bed, his belly hurting from the exertion.

"Feel okay?" Gage asked, snuggling close.

Ulric blew out his discomfort. "I'll be fine."

Except Gage frowned. "That's it, you're off-duty."

Ulric scowled. "I'm really fine, Gage. We're supposed to walk around a little so we can heal faster, right?"

"You can walk around when you've stopped hurting so much." Gage looked pointedly at him. "Give it an hour or two."

"But—"

Gage leaned in and kissed him on the mouth, and Ulric's thoughts fluttered away. "You'll have to remember to take care of you, too," Gage whispered. "It's not good enough that you're okay with all this." He stroked Ulric's heavy thighs. "When your body needs rest, you let it rest."

Ulric bit his lip. Gage had noticed. Ulric was *okay* with the way he looked, but being okay with it, and going out of his way to treat his body nicely—there was a difference. It was a leap that he hadn't made yet.

"Think about it," Gage murmured. He tugged on Ulric's milk-damp shirt. "Here, let me get this off."

"It won't stay clean for long," Ulric mumbled. "I may as well keep wearing it."

"You're off-duty. I want you to feel comfortable." Gage reached for a clean shirt to the side, dropping it in Ulric's lap. Then he unbuttoned Ulric's sleep shirt, peeling it off his shoulders. Gage rumbled. "Oh, yeah. There's another reason I want your shirt off."

Gage's gaze coasted down Ulric's chest; Ulric's breath left his lungs. He wasn't exactly in the mood for sex, but the way Gage looked at him—it made him feel... desired. Worthy. Despite all his curves, despite how his belly was still round.

"I still look pregnant," Ulric said. Over the last few months, he'd grown the heaviest he'd ever been.

"You look like you're my alpha," Gage growled. Gage didn't have much definition on his abs, either, but Ulric knew Gage would get his sculpted body back sooner than later. Gage didn't look at himself, though. He pressed Ulric back against the pillows and kissed him deeper, sliding into his mouth.

Pleasure whispered through Ulric's veins; Gage stroked his sides, leaving tingles wherever he touched. Then he cupped Ulric through his shorts and squeezed, and Ulric felt his alpha's touch right between his legs.

"We aren't supposed to," Ulric said.

"I didn't say I'm going in." Gage huffed, his breath warm on Ulric's cheek. "Just wanted to help you let off some steam."

"Aren't you hurting, too?"

"A little." Gage grimaced. "But it's worth it to touch you."

Ulric frowned. That wasn't right. "Lie back and rest, Gage Frost."

"Damn, babe."

Gage was about to kiss Ulric again, when another sound came from the bedside cot. This time, it was Florin. Both of them looked over. Florin had woken up, squirming in his swaddle.

Gage shook his head wistfully. "We're going to need some luck if we ever want to fool around again, huh?"

"Or even sleep properly again." Ulric laughed. And then his belly hurt. "Shoo, Gage. Seriously. Stop making me laugh."

Gage smiled and trailed his wrist over Ulric's belly. Then, with a groan, he shuffled off the bed, getting gingerly to his feet.

It was just the first week of their recovery, but Ulric couldn't wait to share the rest of his life with his alpha. And the next few weeks seemed like a wonderful start.

SIX WEEKS IN, Ulric felt like a zombie dragging himself around.

They trudged into the grocery store, cool air sweeping over them. Next to him, with Florin strapped into a child harness against his chest, Gage looked just as worn out.

"Regretting this yet?" Gage joked, his lips pulling into a wry smile.

"Nah." Ulric brushed his wrist against Sage. Aside from the doctor's office, this was the only other place they'd visited since the birth. At least his c-section wound didn't hurt so much anymore.

Despite his fatigue, though, Ulric still felt a little self-conscious. His pregnancy belly hadn't receded by much. He'd seen post-partum pictures on the internet. Hell, Gage had already been working out to lose some of his pregnancy weight. Next to all these people at the store...

Gage leaned in. "You're perfect. All of us think so."

That brought a smile to Ulric's lips. Over the past weeks, Sage and Florin had learned to recognize Gage and Ulric's faces. Sage cooed whenever Ulric stepped into a room, and Florin's eyes lit up.

In their own ways, they were telling Ulric that he mattered. With the boys' acceptance, Ulric was starting to believe what Gage saw in him, a little more.

He straightened his shoulders, feeling a bit more confident in himself.

They were almost at the fruit section when a neon SALE banner caught Gage's eye. It hung above the deli section, right over a display table—empty save for one large wheel of cheese and a sign.

Gage's eyes lit up, his entire body tensing. This was the most awake Ulric had seen him in a while. "You want that?" Ulric asked.

Gage all but dragged him over. "A whole wheel? Is that even for sale?"

It was. The deli staff had stuck a price tag on it, and next to the cheese was a sign: *This is all our remaining stock, sorry!*

Closer to the table, Gage paused, looking hesitant. A trio of men had stopped on the other side of the table, also staring at the cheese wheel.

Ulric recognized them. The alphas, Harris and Valen, were firefighters who attended Dom and Jesse's team barbecues. Their omega, Sam, was the chef at a drive-in ramen place. The three of them stared at the cheese wheel, and then at Gage and Ulric.

It seemed that they all came to the same conclusion at the same time.

Tense seconds ticked by.

"I can go without," Sam said, turning away. "It took us long enough to finish that last one."

Valen, his younger alpha, caught his hand. "But that's your favorite."

"We're not buying it," Gage blurted. "You guys go ahead."

After he'd gotten so excited over the cheese wheel... that didn't seem right. "Are you sure?" Ulric frowned. "You really like parmesan." Gage had been talking about having guests sprinkle cheese on them as they walked down the wedding aisle.

"I've never had this huge a thing of parm before," Gage muttered. He glanced at the price tag again.

At nine hundred dollars, Ulric knew the only time Gage spent that much willingly, was when he'd deliberated for a whole year over which gym upgrade he needed the most. And Gage had refused to let Ulric buy them all for him—Gage didn't want to be spoiled.

Ulric really wanted to spoil him, though. "You've finished the wedges I got you last month. This wouldn't take you long, right?"

"It's—" Gage glanced at the price tag "—seventy-two pounds, babe. That's half the weight of a small adult."

And it was imported from Italy—actual Parmigiano-Reggiano, instead of regular parmesan cheese. Last year, before they'd gotten pregnant, Ulric had bought some of that expensive coffee that Gage liked. Gage had been over the moon.

Harris, the older of Sam's alphas, cleared his throat.

"How about we split the cheese?" he suggested. "Fifty-fifty. I'm sure the deli wouldn't mind dividing it for us."

"Deal," Ulric said.

Sam squawked. Gage scowled and smacked Ulric's ass, even though his mouth had curved into a tiny smile. "You bastard, Ulric."

"I love you," Ulric said, his heart skipping. "I just wanted you to be happy."

Gage rolled his eyes. "I'm already happy."

Then he leaned in and kissed Ulric on the mouth, right there in the store. Ulric tingled all over. No matter how many times Gage had kissed him in public, Ulric still wasn't used to it. Gage fingered the ring on Ulric's hand, smiling against his lips.

"So glad you're mine," Gage whispered.

Ulric's heart tumbled. "Not right here."

"Especially right here," Gage growled. "*Mine*, babe."

He was about to kiss Ulric again, except Valen coughed lightly and stepped over, grabbing the cheese wheel. "I'll get this to the deli counter," Valen said. "You guys just had surgery not too long ago, right?"

Gage kissed Ulric and looked over. "Yeah, thanks. It's Ulric's second time to the grocery store, actually."

"Congrats!" Sam approached them to fawn over Sage and Florin. "They're so beautiful!"

Ulric couldn't help the pride surging through his chest. "They really are."

It didn't take long for the deli to divide the cheese wheel. Gage wandered around the grocery store with Ulric, clicking his tongue at the boys. Then he grinned when they smiled.

"I love their little smiles," Gage rumbled. "So adorable. Do you remember when they'll start laughing?"

"Four months, I think." Ulric brushed his wrist over Sage's back. "I can't wait."

"Me, neither."

They got the groceries they needed, and then a little extra just in case. Gage grunted as he heaved the half-wheel of cheese into the car trunk. "Wow, I'm out of shape."

"Does that mean you'll be doing bench presses with these guys?" Ulric teased, handing him the rest of the bags.

"I've been looking into it, babe." Gage grinned. "I found some steel barbell attachments. They seem sturdy enough to hold a couple of small hammocks. I'll have to test them."

"What about actual cheese wheels? Will you attach those, too?"

Gage raised his eyebrows. "You're really serious about that, huh?"

Ulric nudged him. "*You* started it!"

Since that first night, Gage had mentioned cheese wheels on his barbells a couple more times. "You know how they say dreams stem from your subconscious?" Ulric added. "I think maybe you secretly want to live in a giant cheese wheel."

"Might not be a bad idea." Gage grinned. "We'll have the cheesiest happily-ever-after, babe."

Maybe Ulric could be convinced of that.

Especially if Gage did his bench presses naked.

It was when they'd gotten home, both boys tucked into their cot, that Gage pulled Ulric toward the bed. Then he shoved Ulric onto the mattress and climbed on top of him, and his weight was glorious on Ulric, all warm and solid.

Ulric sighed, leaning back against the pillows. He

wanted to fall asleep like this.

"Thanks for getting me that parm," Gage murmured. "You know you didn't have to."

Ulric laughed—he was glad it didn't make his belly hurt anymore. "I figured you'd appreciate it."

"I appreciate *you*." Gage nuzzled him and meshed their lips together, kissing him thoroughly. Ulric groaned into the kiss.

Despite the late nights and spotty sleep, any time he spent with Gage was good. Ulric loved when Gage touched him, when Gage kissed him and marked him all over. They'd had a couple of handjobs so far, but most days, they ended up falling asleep before either of them could find release.

Right now, he wasn't sure he could stay awake, either. The bed was just so comfortable. "Come nap with me," Ulric said, wrapping his arms around Gage. Their bellies bumped.

Gage's attempts at losing weight were a lot more successful than Ulric's had ever been. Granted, Gage needed to get back into his 'personal trainer shape', now that he'd started working part time at the gym.

"Still worried about your belly?" Gage murmured, trailing his wrists down Ulric's abdomen. Most mornings, he kissed the scar and nuzzled Ulric there. "You're amazing, babe. And I kind of want a bath with you."

From the look in his eyes, it wouldn't be an ordinary bath, either. Ulric laughed. "Maybe after a nap."

He did want to feel desired, though. And he wanted Gage to mark him properly, like he'd promised to weeks ago.

Gage slid off his body, pressing himself snug against Ulric's back. Ulric hesitated. Then he hooked his thumb into his waistband, hitching it down a little. Just enough to show Gage his ass. "There, both cheeks."

Gage laughed and growled, pushing his hand down Ulric's pants. "Fuck, babe. Don't show me that if you don't want me all over you."

He squeezed Ulric's cheeks and massaged them, spreading them apart. His touch sent tingles through Ulric's body; Ulric bit down his groan. He was exhausted. But he wouldn't say no to pleasure, either.

Gage slipped his fingers between Ulric's cheeks, stroking him there, back and forth, not venturing deeper. In fact, he teased Ulric for so long that Ulric growled, glancing over his shoulder. "Are you gonna, or not?"

His alpha smiled wider. "I was just waiting for you to ask."

Gage grabbed the long-forgotten bottle of lube off the nightstand, popping its lid open. When he next touched Ulric, his fingertips were cool and slippery, and they went straight to Ulric's hole. Ulric's breath snagged in his throat.

"I haven't been here in weeks." Gage massaged him there, slow, purposeful strokes that brushed all the nerve endings at Ulric's hole. "Think it remembers me?"

Ulric's throat went dry. He leaned forward a little, giving Gage better access. "No."

Gage's growl turned dangerous. "Yeah? Does it need a good reminder?"

And he grabbed Ulric's pants, yanking them down his thighs. A thrill shot up Ulric's spine. "Are you sure it'll be a good enough reminder?" Ulric hissed, his cock growing hard. "You might be too tired to."

Gage's eyes darkened; he pushed his fingers back between Ulric's cheeks, grinding against his hole. "I'm all awake now, babe. Looks like someone needs a good, hard claiming to remember."

Oh. Ulric couldn't fathom where Gage was getting his energy from. Maybe he just needed to be challenged. And Ulric had gotten pretty damn good at challenging him. "Prove it, Gage. It's not yours until you claim—"

Gage pushed two fingers in without warning, a smooth, deep slide that stole the breath from Ulric's lungs. Then he pulled them out and pushed them back in, spearing Ulric open again. "This is just the start, babe," Gage growled, leaning in, sniffing at Ulric's neck. And his fingers swirled around inside, an intimate pressure that made Ulric's cock thicken.

Gage reached between Ulric's legs, grasping his cock. His hot grip went down to Ulric's balls; pleasure whispered through his veins. And Gage stroked him base to tip, grinding his thumb against the sensitive spot beneath his head. Ulric jerked; Gage angled his cock down, trapping it with his pants so it strained, its tip dripping.

"Thought you were gonna fall asleep," Ulric breathed, need chasing away his fatigue. Right now, he wanted Gage more than he wanted to sleep—he didn't think he could doze off, not with Gage's cock pushing hard against his thigh.

"I want to claim you properly." Gage's voice had turned husky; he scissored his fingers, stretching Ulric further. Cool air slipped into Ulric's hole. "This right here, it's all gonna be mine, babe. You'll take my knot."

Ulric's hole squeezed. Gage swore, and Ulric suddenly wanted more from his alpha. He turned, shoving Gage's fingers out of him. Gage's eyes flashed. And he crammed his fingers back between Ulric's cheeks, plunging them back into Ulric's hole.

"This is how I'll fuck you, babe," Gage murmured, thrusting his fingers deeper. "Open you up for me. All the way."

Ulric grew hot inside. He knocked Gage's hand away and turned, and he found Gage's lips pulled into a savage smile, his eyes all lit up. So Ulric pummeled his alpha into the bed, shoving his bare cock against Gage's bulge, grinding them together. "Maybe I'll win this time."

"No, you won't," Gage whispered. And he heaved Ulric off, he slammed Ulric hard against the mattress, and he grabbed Ulric's knees, pulling them up, exposing Ulric's hole to his cock.

There wasn't any warning this time; Gage yanked his own cock out, pushing his blunt tip between Ulric's cheeks—it had been so long. And that thick, slippery pressure was so welcome against his hole. Ulric groaned.

"Yeah, make that sound again," Gage whispered, rolling his hips, his cock kissing Ulric's hole.

Ulric grabbed the bottle of lube and threw it at him; Gage caught it. Then he leaned back, he crammed the bottle's tip against Ulric's hole. Cool liquid filled him up inside.

That had been a lot of lube. Looking at Gage's face, Gage knew it, too. He wasn't going easy this first time. Ulric throbbed.

He yanked off his own pants so he could move around the bed if he wanted to. Except Gage grasped Ulric's knees and pinned them open wide, and he snapped his hips, his cock sliding sweetly all along Ulric's crack. "Babe," Gage growled. "You're so damn hot, I don't think I can hold it in for long."

"Try it," Ulric growled. Then he struggled, trying to get Gage off himself. He wanted to see Gage fight back.

Gage snarled and pummeled Ulric back into the bed,

and he thrust hard, his tip pushing against Ulric's entrance, forcing him open.

He sank into Ulric, half his cock at once, so thick that Ulric forgot to breathe. "That's not enough of a claim," Ulric spat.

Gage's eyes darkened; he tightened his grip on Ulric's knees. "Yeah? How about this?"

Then he pulled out almost all the way, leaving his tip inside. And he slammed his cock back in, every single inch. Pleasure jolted through Ulric. He arched clean off the bed, panting for breath, trying to deal with his alpha inside him all at once.

Gage didn't give him time to breathe. He began a hard rhythm, deep and forceful, his cock sliding so sweetly that sounds escaped Ulric's throat and he couldn't think. Ulric writhed; he shoved at Gage.

Gage bore down harder on him, cramming every inch of that cock inside. Ulric pumped his own cock, panting, his balls pulling tight. He hadn't been claimed in such a long time—every nerve had come alive, and all he could see was Gage above him, pleasure scrawled through his face, all he could feel was Gage inside him, his cock surging hungrily, touching Ulric in the most intimate places.

"I'm gonna come inside you, and I'm gonna mark you with it," Gage snarled, pounding into Ulric, so violently that Ulric's body sang and his cock pulsed, and he couldn't breathe.

Then he hit that one sensitive spot, and Ulric shuddered, his entire body tensing, right at the edge. "Gage—"

"Mine," Gage growled. "Come for me."

And he plowed deep into Ulric, ripping pleasure through Ulric's body in a bright-white wave. Gage clapped his hand over Ulric's mouth; Ulric snarled and came, his body wringing tight with pleasure, his eyes rolling back in his head.

"Fuck," Gage hissed. He leaned in, his strokes growing feverish, his entire body trembling as he snapped his hips, trying to bury himself deeper. Then he bit hard into Ulric's shoulder and thrust in a final time, and his warmth flooded Ulric inside, marking him everywhere.

Before he collapsed, Gage was already dragging his wrists down Ulric's sides, pulling them closer, dropping sloppy kisses all over Ulric's face. "Always so amazing, babe," Gage murmured, kissing him softly on the lips.

Ulric sighed as Gage's knot began to swell inside him, Gage's scent all over his body. All of this felt good—the tension and need, the pleasure, and then the release that shook him, leaving him a boneless mess.

He was now twice as exhausted as he'd been before, but it was a good sort of exhaustion. Especially when Gage rearranged himself so he spooned Ulric once more, sliding back in, making sure his knot locked their bodies together.

"You're so much more than I—" Ulric paused, thinking about it. Gage wouldn't want him to say it.

"More than you...?" Gage's pointed stare tickled his back.

Ulric looked down at Gage's arms wrapped snugly around him. "I was going to say 'deserve'."

"You deserve all the good things in the world," Gage growled.

Ulric cracked a smile. "Yeah, I knew you were going to say that." And maybe... it was okay to deserve all the good things. Maybe it was okay to take some time off and do something he liked. To let his body heal. This intimacy with Gage—it was self-care, too, right?

"So I should change it," Ulric continued. "You're so much more than I expected."

Gage huffed, kissing his shoulder. "So are you." He hugged Ulric tighter, tracing his wrist down Ulric's front, lingering at Ulric's belly. "Best Muffin in the world."

"Imagine if you had that carved on my ring." Ulric laughed.

Gage laughed along with him. "I'd thought about it, babe. Then I thought maybe I could write it on you. You know, with my cock."

Ulric grinned. "I'll hold you to that."

Gage leaned up, meeting his eyes. "You really wanna?"

"Sure." Ulric kissed him, his heart fluttering when Gage growled and kissed back. "Write it all over me. And whatever else you want."

Gage looked contemplative. Then, excited. "Yeah, I can think of a million things to write on you."

"There wouldn't be space." What would Gage write? From the look on his face, it would range from something sweet, to something hot, to something adorably silly. Maybe even a line with all three.

"I can always write over everything," Gage answered, snuggling closer. Then he yawned, which made Ulric yawn. "But maybe after a nap."

With the urgency of the past minutes fading away, Ulric was quickly drifting off, too. The exhaustion sank back into his bones. "Maybe," he mumbled, snuggling into his alpha.

The boys slumbered in their crib, tired out from their trip outdoors. In his alpha's arms, Ulric fell asleep, at peace with the world.

ALSO BY ANNA

Meadow Street Brothers

Non-shifters - Close-knit "brothers" find the bondmates of their dreams. MPreg!

Meadowfall Firefighters

Non-shifters - steamy/funny! - hunky alphas and the broken men they heal. MPreg!

Men of Meadowfall

Non-shifters - accidental pregnancies + hurt/comfort! - broken omegas who find their happily-ever-afters with some really protective alphas. MPreg!

Shifters of Cartwell

Dragon and wolf shifters! MPreg!

Taboo books (Not available on Amazon)

Resistance is Fertile (non-con, breeding kink)

Ironwrought

Vampire novellas, NOT Mpreg!

ABOUT THE AUTHOR

A huge fan of angst and bittersweet tension, Anna has been scribbling since she was fourteen. She believes that everyone needs a safe place, and so her dorky guys fall in love, make mistakes, and slowly find their way back into each other's arms.

Anna loves fine lines on her notebook paper, and is especially fond of her tiny glass globe. She is currently living on the west coast of the US with her husband and a menagerie of stuffed animals.

For more book information:
https://www.amazon.com/Anna-Wineheart/e/B01KIFJ9S0
Or email Anna at
anna@annawineheart.com

Printed in Great Britain
by Amazon